For Mom-Mom, Captain Julia T. Fossler,
who taught me how to be strong, and to all the other strong women out there
including my own mother, Patty Valenti, my grandmother, Mary Valenti, and
Mother Mary and Lisa Scottoline; who encouraged me to pursue my
dreams of writing.

ACKNOWLEDGEMENTS

Thank you to my Editor, Caitlyn Averett, for dealing with my constant messages and questions, and for helping me with my first novel.

Thank you to my family, friends, and my boyfriend, for you constant support and your patience.

Thank you to Gabrielle Prendergast, for designing my beautiful cover.

Thank you to Soot, my beloved German Shepherd, even though you can't read, for all the kisses and late night cuddles when I was down with writers block.

Thank you to Major Bill Ramsey, 1SG Christopher Brownawell, CPT Richard Cruz, CPT Stephen Kuhl, SFC Jeromee Brown and CPT Louis Rettenburg, who shaped me into the Soldier that I am today.

Anomic

Julia Valenti

Copyright (c) 2015 Julia Valenti

For information, please contact Julia Valenti at HYPERLINK "mailto:k9soot@gmail.com" k9soot@gmail.com

Cover Design: Gabrielle Prendergast

Edited by: Caitlyn Averett

First Edition: September 2015

ISBN: 9780692525654

Public notice 24   Order no. # 7743169000354

All Anomics are hereby eighty-sixed from their current sectors, and are forbidden from associating with any resident still residing in the sectors. Any personnel seen associating with a known Anomic, will be eighty-sixed immediately. Any Anomics who chose to disobey this order, and remain in the sector, will be immediately executed.

This order has been published by the Sector Commander.

1.

A cool breeze blew the sheer curtains over my face, and I flickered open my eyes. The dim-lit room began to gradually come into view, and my vision cleared up to see the wooden ceiling fan slowly spinning.

I sat up abruptly, ignoring the first wake dizzy spell, placing my hand on my pistol. It was very unlike me to fall asleep on my watch. I looked in the bed to see my partner on the cot next to me. I made a mental note that next time we were assigned to protect the Sector Commander, the mere idea of even sitting on a bed while running on only three hours of sleep over the past three days was a horrible idea.

I leaned further to my right to see that my partner had fallen asleep as well. "Jax," I said, scanning the room for any other signs of life. I swung my feet out of the bed, and took my hand off my pistol belt. "Jax," I said, shaking him slightly.

He leapt to his feet, his hand immediately reaching inside the folds of his gray jacket. His gray eyes stared at me fiercely. When his vision cleared up and he saw that it was me, he relaxed slightly. He shook his head in frustration. "You know not to do that to me," he said with a moan, looking around the room.

"Sorry, but I had to wake you up somehow. If there was one thing that I learned from our deployment to Afghanistan, it taught me that you can sleep through any sound," I stated.

"Right...what are we doing here again?" he spoke up again, making eye contact with me.

"We came here last night to watch the Sector Commander," I said, looking over at the his door. The room we were in was quite small. Two cots were placed on either side of the narrow entryway, the Commander's door just five feet behind us.

"Well I doubt anyone came in here, we would have heard them come through here..." Jax said, moving back towards the door.

I smirked to myself. "Your ass wouldn't have heard anything anyway," I commented, remembering how heavy of a sleeper Jax was.

"Last I checked it was not a crime to get a little bit of shut eye," Jax said, pointing a finger at me.

"Will you just knock on the freaking door already and make sure he's still alive?" I questioned, rolling my eyes.

I watched as he knocked three times, before turning to face me. Jax was my partner even before the war broke out. We toured Afghanistan and Iraq together. Even though the military is a brother and sisterhood, Jax was the only one I could truly trust as far as the word went. He knew everything about me, and I did mean everything.

The door flew open and the Sector Commander stood there, his blue eyes blood shot. The smell of whiskey instantly washed over my face, and I curled my lip up slightly. This was the fourth time this week. The smell of whiskey never used to bother me, favoring the crisp burn of Jack Daniels myself in my younger years. It wasn't until our Sector Commander regularly began to have the stench on him that I lost any and all cravings for alcohol in general.

"Sir," I said, nodding my head slightly. Although given his current condition, I was not fond of calling him 'sir'. He looked both me and Jax over, before clearing his throat.

"Any news for me?" he asked, his voice breaking slightly.

"No incidents, sir. None from inside the Sector, nor from the..." I paused, and bit my lip. "From the *eighty-sixers*...sir..." I finished. Jax looked to the ground. He knew that I hated the word, he knew that I hated most of the laws here. The Sector Commander began to laugh for a second, before stepping closer to me.

"You know we can't have them in here for a reason, Ms. Waters...." he said, gritting his teeth. I made eye contact with him, desperate to hide all emotion.

"Yes sir," I said, reluctantly. He nodded stiffly, before heading back to his room.

"I will be in conference with the other Sector One Commander for the next few hours... you are dismissed," he said, without even turning around. The door slammed shut, and Jax continued to stare at the door.

"You know, the worst part about this is... I'm tired of following people who have absolutely no military experience whatsoever," Jax said, motioning for us to walk out. I couldn't help but smile slightly. I did agree with him.

"You just don't like anyone who outranks you period," I stated, biting the side of my cheek. Jax tossed an amused look at me over his shoulder.

3

"That's not true, we've served under plenty of leaders that I've liked...or at least I was told I had to like," Jax muttered, kicking the wooden door open.

"You know you just proved my point, right?" I joked.

We stepped outside into the cool, misty morning fog. The Sector Commander's quarters laid just on the eastern end of the sector, backing up against the electrocuted, 30 foot high fence. I heard footsteps in the distance, and I saw a man pushing a wheelbarrow carrying bags of food.

"There aren't very many of us.. military originated.. soldiers left anyway...at least not in this sector," I said, pushing my M9 down in its holster for comfort.

"Yeah, well I still think one of us should have been appointed Commander," Jax grunted.

For the past seven years, we had all lived in this state of fear. It all began with a single bullet. A member of a group called the *Relinquished* fired a single bullet into the heart of the President of the United States of America. That single bullet, followed by thousands of others.   America was instantly broken into chaos. Multiple government installations and military installations were compromised. It was a modern day civil-war. Soldier turned on soldier that day. It wasn't until a certain group of people, possessing a very particular supernatural power showed up and put an end to the murders by instilling fear into the murderers.

Without a President, our nations remaining leaders gathered together to break the country down into sectors. Eight sectors. Those eight sectors were to be divided throughout the country, to minimize the movement of freedom that people had. They figured by dividing America up, more people could be scrutinized. Eight people were chosen to rule these sectors. We were the Northeast sector, stretching from Maryland up to Southern Connecticut. We had daily patrols that traveled in vehicles to check on the further areas that were too far to travel by foot.

Then there were the *eighty-sixers*, also known as the outcasts. They were told they could not live in any of the sectors, for a variety of reasons. Some were criminals, some took a stand and refused to live by anyone's dictations and others...were thrown out of the sectors and placed in isolation.

4

I always had a fear of becoming one of the eighty-sixers. Not because I was a criminal or had intentions to commit a crime, but because of a particular gift that I possessed. I come from a very unordinary family. We all possess a very particular gift.

Following the war, Sector Commanders had two options. Either eliminate my kind entirely, or isolate us. Despite how many lives we saved, it didn't matter. They saw how powerful we were and knew we were capable of overthrowing anyone whom we wished to overthrow.

In other words, if the Sector Commander's find any reason to be afraid of someone...
that person would become one of the *eighty-sixers*. The only reason I was never discovered was because my partner made sure I was never discovered. He was the only person inside of the sectors who knew what I really was.

"Yeah, you go ahead and do that... let me know how that works out for you," I said, somewhat distant.
"Which way first?" Jax asked, turning to face me. I shrugged for a second, my eyes scanning the ground.
"I guess we could try the city," I said, nodding to our left. An eerie fog rolled over the train tracks that lead directly to the city of Philadelphia. Jax turned to face me.
"Are you sure?" Jax questioned, tilting his head slightly. "We can always patrol somewhere else..."
"Yeah, it's got to get patrolled. I'm willing to bet Amanda and Matt are still in Baltimore again today. I know there was some insane shit going on down there yesterday," I said, beginning to walk on the train tracks. We hardly used trains. Normally they only ran Tuesdays, and that was only for purposes of trade.

"What happened in Baltimore yesterday?" Jax questioned, jogging to catch up with me.
"People are getting angry beyond belief. They hate that they are forbidden to visit relatives in other sectors," I said, looking over at Jax. He nodded, turning away from me to scan the distance to his right.
Jax knew how it must have felt. His wife was in Florida at the time of the break-out of the war, so she was kept there. He had not seen her in seven years. I knew the only reason he was still in the service was because by being in the service, you had better pay than the majority of the people in any of the sectors. He would send money to her, so that she could afford to live decently in her sector.

5

In the sectors, everyone had some form of a job. But they were not a Sports Journalist, a CEO, or a Baseball player. There were four options. Medical, Produce, Construction, or Military. If you chose the military, they would test you to the point of where you almost broke.

A sudden rustling caught my attention, and I quickly drew up on my flashlight. My other hand rested comfortably on my pistol.

"MacKenzie?" Jax questioned, sounding slightly confused.

"I thought I heard something..." I said, narrowing my eyes so that I could see farther.

"I think you just get a thrill out of doing that, I swear it happens almost every-time we go out on patrol..." Jax said, laughing slightly.

I pocketed the flashlight, and turned to face him with a small smile. "Yeah, you caught me..." I said, sarcastically.

As we walked down the train tracks, we saw multiple figures appear. At 0600, the work day had begun. Various people were carrying hammers, bricks and the like, trying to rebuild the city. The city had been torn apart by the war, as did many of the major cities, and it was per order of the Commanders that all cities be rebuilt. I guess it was their way of finding something for us to do. After all, the sight of hundreds of charred buildings amidst an eerie fog was not so appealing.

I saw a small girl with curly, red hair jumping in puddles of water. Her nose scrunched up as she giggled with each puddle she jumped in. I couldn't help but smile. It was nice to see pleasant, little things like this. As we got closer, she turned to look at Jax and myself. Her blue, polka dotted dress blew in the wind slightly as she raised her hand up to wave at us. She ran towards us, her red curls bouncing on her shoulders as she did so.

"Powice!" she said, excited. I could hear Jax chuckle to my right. He loved kids. Had he and his wife not been separated for seven years, I'm sure he would of had several by now.

"What's your name, princess?" Jax asked, squatting down so that he was on her level.

"Georgia," she said, bashfully beginning to sway from side to side.

"Well, Georgia, you are as pretty as a peach! What are you doing outside today?" Jax asked. I could hear his South Carolina accent coming out.

God, I always did love those southern accents. Being from a northern state, I very rarely heard anyone with a southern accent. That was until I met Jax, of course.

"I like the puddles," she said, pointing at them. Jax and I both chuckled slightly. She looked up at me and tilted her head slightly, folding her arms behind her back.

"You're pretty, are you a princess?" she asked me, her blue eyes lighting up with hope. I felt Jax's gaze land on me and I couldn't help but blush slightly. It had been awhile since anyone had called me pretty, or anything of the like. If Jax had not been with me, I probably would not be so embarrassed.

Mostly, because Jax was a very attractive man himself. His 6'2 frame and extremely well-toned and tan body on-top of his occasional southern drawl made him incredibly attractive. Not to mention that he had served as an Army Ranger for four years. Despite this, I still respected the fact that he was married even though his wife was thousands of miles away.

"No, I'm a soldier. I protect all the princess's and princes out here!" I said, still feeling Jax's gaze on my face. If you were to consider the Section Commanders royalty, then this statement would be true.

"That's cool! Can I be like you one day?" Georgia asked, jumping up and down. "I want to meet a princess!"

I smiled, before reaching into my black leather jacket chest pocket. I pulled out one of my old 'US ARMY' name-tapes and handed it to her.

"Of course you can, just keep this with you and one day, you can wear it too," I said, handing the nametape to her. She began to clap her hands in excitement.

"Thank you! Thank you!" she said, taking it and then sprinting off into the fog towards her friends.

I stared after her for a second, before turning to look at Jax. Jax nodded in respect, before turning away with a smirk on his face.

"Let's go, princess.." he said, as he took a few steps forward.

I smirked in amusement, before following after him.

"Although I have to be honest, you're probably one of the only princess's I know who wears such attire," he added, crossing over the tracks.

As we passed under the old, rusty sign that once read *30th Street Station*, I paused to steal a glance at myself in the window. My dirty blonde hair still reached my mid-back, despite my efforts to secure it by putting it up in a tight pony tail. The black, tight leather pants were snug, slightly torn around the ankles. My black tank top that I wore underneath the matching leather jacket revealed a sliver of cleavage, causing me to laugh.

"I can't believe you're letting me out here and I'm not even dressed yet..." I said, zipping up the black leather jacket to hide the cleavage.

"I mean, hey, I wasn't going to complain! Give me a break, I'm still a guy," Jax joked, his chuckle carrying back to me. I rolled my eyes and scoffed slightly.

Jax turned to face me, a devilish smirk on his face. "In fact, I shouldn't have bothered to comment on it at all. You would have never even noticed,"

I shook my head, before quickening my pace so that I could catch up to him. I felt extremely safe and secure when I was with Jax. We both had seen our fair share of ugly combat, and we knew what set each other off. People always asked me what it was like to look someone in the face, and pull the trigger. To be honest, I couldn't tell you exactly what it was like. When the time came that I needed to kill someone, I had to look at their chest or just to their left or right limits. I wasn't a fan of seeing the light leave someone's eyes. I had seen it before, and to this day it still gave me nightmares.

"So, when was the last time you went running?" Jax asked, pausing to pull out a can of chew.

"Well, we went for a run last night, remember?" I questioned, watching as he packed his lip full of the winter-green flavored dip. I was so used to the smell that it didn't even bother me anymore. I remembered when Jax first started dipping, during our second deployment. Let's just say it wasn't too pretty. Eight years later, he had proudly mastered it.

Jax looked over at me as he tucked the can back in his chest pocket. "You know that's not what I was talking about," he said, his strong features concerned. I did know what he meant. Before the war, myself and my family would use our powers freely during the week and run through the night. This way we would be undetected. No, we weren't vampires or werewolves. We were a very particular kind of shape-shifter. We shape-shifted into the most graceful, and dignified predator to walk the earth; Siberian Tigers.

We were never told how this particular power entered my family, just rumors of our Native American descendants praying to the gods for strength. In return, the gods bestowed us with an amazing gift. A gift to shape-shift into the gorgeous animal to chase invaders and threats off of our lands. It was then said that our allies prayed for the same gift, and were granted it as well. Our numbers grew, and before we knew it, seven big named families possessed the gift.

8

I don't know how true this legend is, but all I know is that the power somehow wound up running through my blood. I was special, like my father, I was the White Siberian Tiger. We were rare, supposedly we were to recognize leadership. However, it was very hard to lead ghosts. As far as I knew, I was the last one who remained...at least in the sectors. I never dared to venture past the fence to see if any of the others were alive. My parents and siblings were killed during the war. As far as I knew, I was alone.

I don't believe that bull about the gods bestowing some power on us. There has only ever been one God to me, and as far as I know, He doesn't believe on turning people into monsters. That's what I feel like my tiger is to me, a monster. A demon.

If I didn't possess this gift, I had no doubts that my whole family would still be alive today. Judging by their deaths, it looked as though they were hunted down and murdered in cold blood. My parents were the sweetest, which lead me to believe that they were murdered because of the gift they possessed.

Jax discovering my power was completely accidental. I was returning from one of my 'runs' while we were out on deployment. Jax came to my tent to share updates on the enemy. Instead, he found a White Siberian Tiger in my tent.

Siberian Tigers are not exactly native to Afghanistan. So when I transformed back to myself, Jax had to sit down. He never reported the incident to anyone.

Even when the sectors were seeking out those with powers like me, Jax remained silent. I saw people like me being pulled out of the sectors all over the news. I remember wanting to turn myself in, but Jax refused to allow me to do so. He told me that the leaders were foolish, that one day we would be needed again.

As we made our way down Broad Street, I turned to look at what remained of the Wells Fargo Center. There were no professional sports anymore, so the building was simply vacant. There was much ivy growth starting to crawl up the side of the building, and several of the lights spelling out the stadiums name had been punched out. I looked to the other side of the street to see Citizens Bank Park, the old *Philadelphia Phillies* stadium. Half of the stadium had been blown away, showing the now overgrown baseball field. I tilted my head slightly, remembering the scene of a Phillies game.

It really was unlike any other sports experience I had been to. Phillies fans really bonded together at the games, whether they knew each other or not. I remembered the delicious scent and savoring taste of the stadium hot dogs, especially on dollar dog night.

"Since we are in the area, how do you feel about visiting the Major?" Jax asked, taking a sip out of his camelback. At the sound of his voice, I snapped out of my fantasy daydream and back to reality.

"We can do that," I responded. We continued to move in silence for the next twelve blocks, before we came upon the various row homes. Jax scanned the area, before placing his hand on the small of my back and pushing me towards Major Chase's house.

I approached the door, knocking in a distinct pattern. I looked up at Jax, who continued to watch the area. If we had been caught disappearing into Major Chase's house, the consequences would be severe. We weren't supposed to go seek out our old commander, for fear of us re-grouping and coming up with a tactical plan on our own to overthrow the sectors. I heard the sound of several locks being unlatched and then I saw a brown eye peeking at me through a crack in the door.

"Well, well... if it isn't the good old 82nd," I heard a voice say, opening the door fully. Major Chase stood there, dressed in track pants and a loose fitting, very old *Coca-Cola* t-shirt. He was barefooted, seemingly how we always seemed to find him these days when we went to visit him. It was as if he either had given up on life or he just did not give a crap as to what anyone thought about his appearance. If I had to guess, I would go with the second option.

"Pick up your boots and follow me," Jax said, mocking the cadence. We had both served under Major Chase when we were Soldiers in the 82nd Airborne. He had seen us both through jump school and through our different branch choices.
Jax, the Army Airborne Infantry Ranger. Myself, the Army Airborne Military Police Officer. When I first met Major Chase, I was in the worst shape of my life. I could barely do 11 sit-ups on our fitness test. He had trained me hard, working me every day to increase my physical fitness to compete with the guys. To this day, I still shuddered when I remembered the five mile 55 pound sandbag run he made us do.

Major Chase motioned for us to come inside, and we obeyed. "I'm surprised to see the two of you here, to be honest. I don't get many visitors anymore,"
Jax and I exchanged looks, before Jax spoke up. "That's probably because we are being kept on a tighter leash, sir. Which is why we can't stay too long,"

Major Chase nodded in response, running his hand over his fresh buzz cut. His hair looked almost silver in the rising sun. "Oh yeah, our fearless leader. Seems like he wouldn't know a bullet if it hit him in the ass,"
I smiled in response. Major Chase was a leader who consistently cared about the well-being of each of his soldiers that fell under his command. I was willing to bet if you were to quiz him on any of the soldiers that had previously followed under his command, he could still tell you five random facts about them.

10

"All the more reason why you should take over command, sir." I stated. Major Chase laughed slightly.

"They don't want people like us in command, Lieutenant Waters. .." he paused to point to his head. "We're too smart," he said, with a wink.

I allowed the smile to spread across my face at this, before allowing a small laugh to escape my lips.

"Besides, I wouldn't want to be in command now anyway. There are rumors of a big change coming to the sectors. Personally, I've been considering fleeing to the woods...had there not be people I still care about in this sector," he said, referring to his daughter and son. Both his children were currently working on the farms, out in the Western part of the state. They came home every two weeks for four days, and then they were back out into the field again. The twins were not more than seventeen years of age.

"Change, sir?" Jax questioned. Major Chase looked as though he wanted to respond, but something outside caught his attention. His neighbor, Phyllis, was outside in her front lawn again. She had previously reported soldiers coming up to his house to talk, and he had the feeling she was pretending to prune her flowers just so she could see if he had visitors again today.

Phyllis, a woman who was barely getting by on working as the Sector Commanders maid three days a week, was always known for being a snitch. Prior to the war, she would constantly report on her neighbors to the township for the most petty issues. Fence lines being half an inch over the property line, trash cans still being out an hour after it was collected, or Major Chases personal favorite, the time when she stood outside with a pocket watch to see if the neighbors dog barked a second longer than 15 minutes so she could report them to the police.

Now, Phyllis took pure joy out of kissing the Sector Commander's ass just to attempt to get herself back on top of the social pyramid. A skinny, middle-aged widow, Phyllis did not have a lot going for her. Major Chase also suspected that she had it out for him ever since he rejected her invitation to dinner at her house following the death of her husband. Major Chase loved his wife, in life and following her death. Even though breast cancer claimed her life a mere five months before the war, he still loved her all these years later. He loved Marian, and only Marian.

Major Chase turned to face Jax and I again, his expression stern.

"We can discuss this at another time. Come quickly, we will use the back exit..." he said, nodding towards the back of the house.

11

We followed him through the narrow hallways, before lifting up the latch to open the wooden windows. Jax put his hand on my shoulder, as he moved to sit on the ledge. He jumped down, and I could make out the top of his head.

I turned to face Major Chase one last time. "I hope that the change you speak of is a good change, sir..." I said, prying slightly. I watched as his lips formed a tight line, before he shook his head slightly.

"I wish I could tell you it was, MacKenzie...." he muttered. Major Chase patted my shoulder, ushering me to hurry.

I swung my legs over the ledge, hopping off with the guidance of Jax. He froze for a second, and then was quick to take his hands off of my hips. "Sorry," he muttered, turning away rather quickly.

We looked up at the good Major one last time, who nodded us farewell, and then we hurried around the back of the buildings.

For about thirty minutes, we walked in silence. The only sounds that we heard were the factory workers calling to each other, and the hissing of all the machines coming to life in the city.

"I wonder what change the Major was talking about," I spoke up, looking over at Jax.

Jax's face remained stern, but he nodded in agreement as well. "I was wondering the same thing. It is very unlike him to be so concerned about such matters,"

I nodded, continuing to stare at the ground as we continued our patrol. As we approached the edge of the border, I stared at the fence. What used to be the gorgeous Fairmount Park, in Philadelphia. I had many fond memories here as a child. Philadelphia had been my home for as long as I could remember. Sure, I spent my time being stationed in various parts of the country for my Military Career. Fort Leonard Wood, Fort Lewis, and Fort Bragg just to name a few.

Nothing ever beat being home in Philadelphia. I remember what the city was like before the creation of the sectors. The smell of fresh pretzels from the Philly Pretzel Factory, along with the mouth-watering smell of a true Philly Cheesesteak came to my mind. I allowed the smile to cross my face.

Any tourist who came to Philadelphia could not resist going to Pat's or Geno's, to try the famous Philadelphia Cheesesteak. I recall the one time when my friend Kevin and I watched a tourist attempt to order. He had ordered the cheesesteak the incorrect way, and was told to go to the back of the line until he figured out the correct way to order it.

I missed the taste of the Philly Cheesesteak. I missed a lot of things about the city. It was very painful for me to patrol this sector, for multiple reasons. The first being that it was the last place where I saw my family alive, and it was the place where I found their dead bodies.

As I recalled the scene of their bodies on the ground, I could feel my tiger stir inside me as the anger began to rise. I squeezed my eyes shut, focusing on calming myself. Even though I had mastered the art of changing at my own will, along with controlling my rage, there were still times when I almost lost my grip and let the tiger inside of me out.

Jax placed his hand on my shoulder. "MacKenzie, did you hear me?"

I snapped out of my stare spell, before turning to face him.

"What was that?" I questioned. Jax narrowed his eyes at me in slight suspicion.

"Are you sure you're alright?" he questioned, folding his arms across his chest. Jax knew that even all these years later, patrolling the Philadelphia route was still painful for me.

"Yeah, I'm good. Let's get to the briefing room. Our patrol time is just about up," I said, walking back down the train tracks again.

"Funny how fast these days just fly by," Jax commented, following me as we made our way back towards the security headquarters, or rather, *Sanctum* as it was called. We had walked for a good hour when the steel, rectangular building had finally came into view. Every Sunday night we would meet up and have a meeting to discuss what we had seen while we were out on patrol during the week, and if we should be aware of any dangers.

Jax opened the door for me, and I looked to see about ten people already sitting around the table. They all nodded politely to me and Jax, as we took our seats.

Shortly after we had taken our seats, the rear door flew open and a man wearing a bikers helmet stormed in the door. He unclipped it, allowing his blonde bangs to fall into his eyes. He tossed his head to the side, his gray eyes scanning the room.

"Sorry I'm late," he said, a snake-like grin on his face. He set down the helmet on the table, and then pulled off his black leather gloves. I took note of his outfit as he ran a hand over his stringy blonde hair.

His blood-red leather jacket was obviously new, probably gifted to him from the Sector Commander. No one in the sectors could afford anything like that on their own, even with the Chief of Security's pay.

His tight blue jeans were stained with oil, or some other funky substance that I did not care to know of. His name was Damian Meyer, and he was the 'chief' of our security detail for the sector. He had been appointed by the Sector Commander, and had been for the past few years following the suspicious and sudden death of the past chief.

His gaze landed on me and Jax and I could see Jax tense up beside me out of my peripheral vision. Jax was not very fond of Damian, in fact, he hated him. He always said that he didn't trust him and quite frankly, neither did I. There was just something about him that I didn't like. I inhaled deeply, trying to use my feline senses to detect any odd scents on him. Nothing.

Damian took his seat, slowly sitting down. "Though I have no doubts that the two of you just stumbled in, as usual..." he said, glaring at Jax. Jax opened his mouth to say something, but I quickly elbowed him in the side. I flinched in pain, forgetting how muscular he was.

"We're sorry," I stated, not wanting to give Damian the satisfaction of a rebuttal. I knew him too well. He was just throwing bait out there to see if we would bite.

Damian eyed me, before showing his creepy smile once more.

"That's quite alright my dear MacKenzie," he stated. I bit my lip and narrowed my eyes. If he used a pet name with me one more time, I would make sure to wipe that nasty grin off of his face. I looked over at Jax, who continued to stare at Damian with an angered expression.

I reached over and patted his leg, and he turned to face me. I showed him a small smile and he relaxed slightly. Damian folded his hands, before placing them on the table.

"As you all may be aware... the eighty-sixers have been spotted coming close to our borders. The Sector Commander has specifically stated that he does not want them coming within eye-sight of our borders...if you seem them while you are out on patrol, you are to execute them immediately," he stated, putting his feet up on the table and leaning back in his chair. I saw faint bits of mud falling off of his boots as he did so.

"You want us just to kill innocent people?" I heard Matt ask, from the other side of the table. Damian looked over at him, a smirk on his face.

"That's correct. They aren't so innocent, after all. They obviously were *eighty-sixed* for a reason... so they should consider that their first warning," Damian said.

I narrowed my eyes at him slightly. "That seems unjust," I said, before I could stop myself. All eyes turned on me. No one ever really agreed with the laws that Damian laid out, but I was the only one who actually had the courage to say something about it.

"I'll be the one who decides what is justified and not justified, Ms. Waters..." Damian said, his smirk fading.

I leaned back in my chair, refusing to turn away from him. I would not accept defeat by looking away in shame from my standpoint.

Damian sighed, looking at everyone once again.

"Now then, the other thing on the agenda is the matter of security. I will be interviewing each and every soldier we have patrolling to see... well... if you are still wanted on the force. If not, well none of you are quite educated to fulfill another position so I think our only option would be to..." he paused to lean forward, his gaze turning to me and Jax.

"*Eighty-Six* you," he whispered. I heard multiple people stir nervously in their seats, but I kept my gaze on Damian. He was hiding something, and I had every intention on finding out what it was.

He then stood up, clapping his hands together. "Now then, this concludes my meeting... now scurry off you bugs," he said, turning away before anyone could say anything. He disappeared through the back door, leaving us all standing in silence.

2.

"This is just great," Amanda said, pushing her chair in angrily.

"No one is getting eighty-sixed. We all just need to stick together and he can't touch us," Jax said, looking around at everyone. A few people muttered in agreement, before we all started to head out to our respective quarters.

I heard Jax jog to catch up with me. "Dinner tonight?" he questioned.

"Yeah, sounds good... what time do you want to meet?" I asked, looking over at him. He opened the door to our barracks, ushering me to move in front of him.

"An hour? I was thinking about going to the gym real fast... with Matt," Jax said, looking over at me nervously. I began to laugh, earning a confused look from Jax.

"You say it like I would have a problem with it," I said, shaking my head.

Jax shrugged, uneasy. "Well, we're partners... normally we do everything together,"

"So you want permission to have a guys night?" I teased. Jax began to shift uncomfortably and then I began to laugh.

"Please, go ahead. You know how many girls nights we've had that I snuck away to without telling you?" I questioned, slapping him playfully on the arm.

"Really? What do these *girls nights* consist of?" Jax asked, raising an eyebrow. I shrugged, as I pulled out my room key.

"Nothing much, just a lot of talking, drinking and watching movies.." I said.

"Talking huh? Talking about what?" Jax asked, beginning to sound extremely curious. I couldn't help but smile somewhat mischievously.

"Everything," I stated, truthfully.

Jax raised an eyebrow in challenge. "Well, we talk about *everything* at guys nights to..." Jax said, walking backwards to his room. I was somewhat curious, wondering if I was ever a topic of discussion but I did not want him to give the satisfaction of me asking.

"Good!" I said, sticking out my tongue. Jax showed me a small smile.

"I'll see you in an hour," he said, before he disappeared into his room.

I rolled my eyes, before walking into my own room. I tossed my keys on the bed and immediately began to get undressed from my work uniform.

16

My favorite part of the day had to be when I got to take off my uniform and dress into normal clothes. I slid on a simple black tank top and faded jean shorts. I wasn't really trying to impress anyone so I didn't really put a crazy amount of effort into how I dressed.

Shortly after I finished changing there was a knock on my door and I raised an eyebrow in challenge. If it was Jax standing there with a water balloon again I was going to kill him. He pulled that trick on me twice and that meant game off for if he tried to do it a third time.

I threw open the door and to my surprise, Damian stood there. His hands were folded, placed in front of him as if he were in prayer. I could see his eyes dancing with glee when he saw the look of disappointment and confusion on my face.

"Good evening, Ms. Waters...you don't appear to be too happy to see me. Were you expecting someone else?" he questioned. I narrowed my eyes at him slightly.

"No," I lied.

"Oh, good. Random room inspection," he said, a wicked smirk on his face. I folded my arms and bit my lip in frustration. This was the third time in two months that he came to my room for a 'random room inspection', and I was beginning to grow extremely suspicious. As far as I knew, I was the only person that he was doing this to on a consistent basis. I was drawing the conclusion that either he really wanted me off the force, or he was desperately trying to court me like many female officers before myself. Either way, it wasn't going to happen.

I sighed, stepping aside and allowing him to walk in my room. He passed by extremely close to me, inhaling my scent as he did so.

"You smell good, darling.." he said, as he began to wander around the room. I had to bite my lip and resist the urge to punch him in the jugular for calling me yet *another* pet name.

"It's called sweat, but thanks..." I hissed, slamming the door shut. He turned around to face me, holding up his hands in mock surrender.

"No need to get so feisty, I was just paying you a compliment...." Damian stated.

I rolled my eyes, watching him as he began to pick random stuff up. He wandered over to my shelf of books and began to look through them.

"*Lord of the Rings, Darkness Descends: A Skye Faden Novel, Blackhearts, The Underhill Series: Restitution, Lone Survivor*....not exactly the girliest lady on the block, are you MacKenzie?" Damian inquired, winking at me before continuing on.

"Actually the *My Little Pony* coloring books are hiding under the mattress," I sneered, watching as he moved to examine the pictures on my wall. He walked up to the photo of me and my parents and then shifted over to the photo of me and Jax on our first deployment together.

"Ah, the lovely Jaxsy boy... you two sure are close aren't you?" he asked, sounding bored as he picked up one of my pillows.

"Well, Damian, if you were actually in the military you would understand the concept of how close you grow to your battle buddies," I said.
I leaned my back against the door, my eyes following his every mood and attempting to memorize the pattern in which he was moving. After about five minutes, he turned to face me again. "I think I've seen all that I needed to see," Damian said, clapping his hands together.
"Good," I said, pausing to pull the door open. "Have a nice day!" I said, faking enthusiasm.

Damian stepped forward, pushing the door shut. He kept his hand on the door, as he leaned in closer, trapping me between himself and the door. He brought his face inches from mine, and I had to resist the urge to not spit in his face. I was a Philadelphia girl, I never backed down from a challenge. Even if that included a snake like Damian who had breath of a sick crocodile. I knew he was half expecting me to cringe in my spot, or shift uncomfortably. If there was one thing I learned from my deployments, it was that some people had no concept of personal space. Within one week of any soldier deploying, that personal bubble popped.

"You know, MacKenzie... we really don't have to keep playing this game. You consistently playing that you hate me... me coming to your room just to pretend to inspect your belongings... we could just take care of this right here, right now..." he said, moving a finger along my bare arm.

I reached up and grabbed his hand, before pushing it to the side. "My hating you is not a game, and you're out of your mind..."
Damian laughed, before leaning in even closer. "Oh please, tell me that your tight little body doesn't dream of becoming one with mine..."

"It doesn't...now, explain to me why you had red clay on your boots today.." I said, folding my arms.
Damian raised his eyebrows in surprise, before smirking mischievously.

"I don't have any idea what you are talking about, MacKenzie..." he said, taking his hand off of the door and standing up straight.

"When you put your boots on the table, I saw red clay fall off of your boots... there is no red clay in the sector. Which means you got it from somewhere else...I'd like to know where," I said, narrowing my eyes slightly.

Damian let out a heavy sigh, before shrugging. "I have no idea what you are talking about, Ms. Waters. I can tell you, that if this behavior continues, I will have no choice but to select you as the first one to be investigated..."

"Fine, go ahead and investigate me. I guarantee you though, you won't find anything..now, if you'll excuse me.." I said, before opening the door and motioning for him to leave.

Damian smirked, before walking out of the door. "Oh MacKenzie..." he paused, before turning to face me again. "If you're interested, we can always just skip the investigation if you would like to come visit my humble abode one night. It would be my genuine pleasure," he said, mocking a curtsey.

"Leave," I hissed, pointing for the hallway.

He showed me a snake-like smile, before leaning to whisper in my ear as he passed me.

"See you soon, deary..." he whispered, and I cringed slightly as I felt his hot breath roll over my ear. He headed down the hallway, the thunderous sound of his boots echoed through the empty halls. I shuddered, before slamming the door shut. I began to rub my hands over my arms, trying to rid myself of the goose bumps.

I was very rarely afraid of people, but there were certain people who made me feel uncomfortable as hell. Damian, was one of those people. My tiger senses could feel that something was off about him from the day I met him and they never left me. There was something very odd, very wrong about Damian and I had every intention on figuring out exactly what it was.

Had Damian touched me one more time, my hand may have been forced to show him the beast within me. He was the only person I could really say that I still hated in this world, or what was left of it I guess you could say. Everything about him was extremely sketchy, from every blonde hair on his head to his bullshit story on how he came to be in charge of Soldiering operations in the sector. I remember when I caught him in a lie about him ever being in the military service.

He lied about being a Marine before the war broke out, and Jax completely called him out on it. Ever since that day, Jax and Damian especially had not been on good terms. I would fight for Jax to the death, so naturally I agreed with him on the viewpoint that Damian was a piece of crap.

I heard a rapid knocking on my door, interrupting my thoughts. I paused to look down at my watch to see that only a half hour had passed since I had spoken to Jax. There was no way that he would be at my door this soon. I cracked my knuckles. If Damian was attempting to get back into my room then I was not going to hold back anything.

I threw the door open slightly, trying to convince myself to remain under control if it was Damian at the door. The mousey-brown hair that was tied up in a messy bun instantly caught my attention, surprising me. I cocked an eyebrow at her as she struck a drastic pose with her hands on her hips.

"Good evening ma'am!" Katie stated, with an overly dramatic wink. She was in loose fitting track pants and a tank top with the characters Sam and Dean from *Supernatural* on it. Judging by her overly, unnecessary, happy mood she intended to stay for awhile.

"Oh god, what do you want?" I teased, doing a slight eye-roll.

"Just wanted to come talk to you...there's no one here to talk to right now, its really boring. I'm coming in now," she said, pushing past me and into my room.

I couldn't help but smile slightly. Katie was the only other female soldier that was in the same living quarters as me. We had met four years ago, when she was transferred from Sector 3. We were short on female soldiers, and we desperately needed some more. Not only for looks, but also because when it came to personnel searches women in the sectors were either offended by having any other man touch her besides her significant other, or some women liked the touch of a male soldier a little too much. Especially since the soldiers in our sector were on the younger side, the oldest being 42.

She had been deployed to Cuba before the fall of the country and the creation of the sectors. She did Detainee Operations, being assigned there for a year as their platoon leader. She was about to get promoted to First Lieutenant before the breakout of the war.

"So what are you doing tonight?" Katie asked, plopping down on my couch and grabbing a pillow and hugging it against her lap.

"I don't know, probably just hanging out here and then going to the chow hall. You should come with me and Jax, I actually thought you were him at the door...him or Damian" I said, eyeing up the stack of dirty plates that were in the sink. I grimaced slightly. I might as well do something while we waited.

Katie tilted her head, a questioning look on her face. "Why would Damian be coming to your door?" she asked, concerned.

"He was claiming to do a random room inspection," I replied. Katie let out a small scoff. "Again? The guy has it out for you or something..."

I decided it would be in her best interest to not share Damian's invitation to me to go and join him in his quarters later that night. It would result in someone getting their ass kicked, most likely his. The last thing I needed was for one of my friends to get eighty-sixed because of me.

Katie allowed the small smirk to spread across her face. "You also said Jax, huh?" she asked, turning her head to follow me as I made my way across the room.
"Yeah, Jax, my partner...what about him?" I asked, raising an eyebrow at her. I took off my watch as I began to run the luke-warm water over the dirty plates.

Katie let out a mischievous giggle, before laying on her stomach and resting her chin on the couch's arm-rest. "Oh, nothing... you two just spend a lot of time together, that's all..." she stated. I turned back to look at her, giving her a look.

"That's because he's my partner....you would know that if you didn't....play with yours all the time," I teased.
"Oh come on, I only *played* with one of them!" Katie protested. I bit my lip, before casting her a glance over my shoulder. I watch her hesitate slightly.
"Okay, maybe three of them. My point is, I'm a woman... We work with a lot of sexy men, and I want to have my fun...before I completely forget what fun actually is living in a world like this," Katie argued, grimacing slightly.

"Whatever works for you," I said, beginning to scrub the first dish. I paused in thought. "Although, Jax does look just like Jordy Nelson, the former Green Bay Packers player..." I said with a smirk, remembering my old crush on the athlete.
"So if you're not going to play with el Cap-ee-tan Jax, can I play with him?" Katie asked, rolling over so that she was on her back. "I'd love to have that toned body on-top of mine," she purred.

21

I scoffed slightly, placing the dish in the drying rack.

"Stop that, he's married!" I stated. Katie swung her legs around so that she was sitting up.

"His wife is in another sector, and I'm willing to bet she married someone else too. Plus, *Little Miss Philly-Born*, you're a badass... and you're hot. It's just physics. He's hot, you're hot...why not have some fun?" Katie teased.

I let out a laugh as I continued to wash the dishes. "Oh you know it's true. Tell me you haven't thought about those sexy, strong arms of his...I bet he's got an amazing abs and pecs too..." Katie pried.

I hung my head slightly, making sure my back was to her as I suppressed a smile.

"He's married," I muttered. Katie either didn't hear me or she pretended not to.

"Seriously though, I've seen him in a t-shirt, it is clear that man has got an amazing chest. By the way, that was through the shirt can you imagine how amazing it looks without the shirt?" Katie questioned, staring off into space as if she were daydreaming.

"I can imagine you stop drooling over my partner," I said, setting the final dish down. I paused to turn around and smile at her. "*Butter-bar*," I mocked, making fun of her rank just like all new Second Lieutenants get. Her head immediately snapped in my direction, and she pointed a finger at me.

"Listen, you, you're still a Lieutenant too!" she protested.

"Yeah, but I'm a *First* Lieutenant..." I teased, putting quotes around the word.

"Ooooh, the big bad first," Katie mocked, throwing her pillow at me.

I caught the pillow, before laughing and sticking out my tongue. It was at that moment that there was a knock on the door. Katie and I exchanged looks, before I strode over to the door. I peeked through the eyehole to see Jax standing there. I suddenly felt extremely underdressed standing there in my black tank top and faded jean shorts, especially given the conversation we just had.

"Well this is awkward," I said, before looking back at her. "Thanks to you," I said, sticking out my tongue.

"He's here!?" Katie asked, excited. She stood up and happily skipped over to my position.

"Yes, now just...don't talk or say anything stupid," I said, before opening the door.

Jax stood there, and his eyes widened slightly in surprise. Normally when he showed up in a black t-shirt and gray gym shorts, I thought nothing of it. Now thanks to my discussion with Katie, all I could focus on was his body build. She had a point, now that I looked at him, he was extremely toned. I cleared my throat, bringing my eyes to his face.

"Jax, what's up?" I questioned, leaning against the door. Katie stuck her head over my shoulder.

"Hi Jax!" she said, with an exaggerated wave. I closed my eyes in slight embarrassment.

"I didn't realize it was ladies night here, I hope I'm not bugging you two or anything..." Jax said, raising an eyebrow slightly. Before I could answer, Katie spoke up.

"Nope, not at all! We were actually just talking about you," Katie said, before resting her arm on my shoulder.

I shot her a glare with my peripheral vision. Jax raised both his eyebrows this time, before allowing a mysterious smirk appear on his face. "Oh? What was this conversation about?" he asked, folding his arms.

Focus, MacKenzie...you've worked with the man for ten years, stop staring at his arms dammit! You've seen them before!

"Just that we were wondering where you were, we've been waiting to go to chow," I stated. It was partially true. "Ah," Jax said, his face showing a sliver of disappointment for a split second. I couldn't help but tilt my head slightly at his response.

"So are we going? All of us?" he asked, his eyes moving back and forth between me and Katie. "I would love to join," Katie said, walking out of my room and into the hallway. I scoffed slightly, shutting my door and locking it behind me.

I heard her go off on a tangent to Jax about how if the chef didn't give her two full scoops of mashed potatoes this time, she was going to bash his face in with a stapler.

I could hear Jax laughing, somewhat uncomfortably. Which gave me the impression that he was too tired to deal with how overly happy she was at that moment.

Once we arrived at the cafeteria, I was surprised to find it oddly empty. The majority of the silver tables were empty, and looked as though they had either very recently been wiped down, or were completely untouched. There was half a table full of the night patrol soldiers in the far corner, the majority of which were resting their heads on the table, as if to get in one final nap before their shift began.

The chefs were standing behind their serving stations, several of them looking down at their watches, as if they were trying to figure out how they could possibly survive another hour of work. After signing in, I grabbed my tray and began to move down the line.

The lady handed me back my plate of BBQ chicken, string beans and mashed potatoes. After grabbing a bottle of water, I planted myself at the closest table. I never really interacted with the night patrol soldiers, so I always found it awkward whenever I saw them in the cafeteria.

Shortly after I sat down, I caught a movement out of my peripheral vision. I turned my head to see two other soldiers approaching me with trays full of food. "Mac!" the younger of the two exclaimed.

His olive green eyes were dancing with joy at the sight of a familiar face, and his fiery red hair was falling into his eyes slightly. "How's it going Adam?" I asked, watching as he took a seat across from me.

"Great! We patrolled the old NYC part of the sector today, nothing really exciting.. just more people claiming that they are seeing alligators in the sewers," Adam stated, with a smile.

"Are you really still pitching that joke?" Andrew asked, taking his seat next to Adam. He looked over at me with a friendly smile. "Hey MacKenzie," he said, happily.

"Greetings," I responded, returning the smile. Katie plopped down next to me, humming a tune to herself. As she looked up and made eye contact with Adam, I saw her cheeks turn a shade of pink. This was not a typical reaction for Katie. Normally she would get all giggly and overly happy when we were with a group of guys, which lead me to believe that she had stronger feelings for Adam then she was willing to admit to.

Jax sat at my other side, nodding over to Adam and Andrew. I felt Katie elbow me in the ribs, before winking at me. I rolled my eyes in response. I don't know why she felt the need to keep insisting that Jax and I 'hook up' or whatever it was called these days.

Jax had a wife and to be honest, I was not very interested in a relationship anyway. It probably sounded horrible to say, but if he didn't randomly tell me something about her, I didn't really want to inquire about it. I felt as though people's relationships were their own business, as I would want mine kept secret as well.

"So Mac, did you tell them about how Damian came to your room again?" Katie asked, digging into her potatoes. I closed my eyes and let out a silent, frustrated exhale. I knew that she had just opened a can of worms, it was only a matter of time before Jax went off on his rant.

As if on cue, Jax turned to face me. "Damian was in your room?" he questioned, anger clearly in his voice. I opened my eyes, before I began digging into my food.

"Yeah, he came by for a random room inspection... its nothing to worry about, it didn't last more than ten minutes..." I said, shooting Katie a glare. She raised an eyebrow in confusion. I understood that she only wanted to look out for my best interest, but I couldn't help but feel slightly annoyed. She had known Jax and I for years, it should have been implied that anything with Damian intruding in on one of us would fire him up.

When Jax didn't respond, I turned to meet his hard stare. "What?" I asked, slightly annoyed.

"Mac, this is the third time in two months he's come to your room, there is something wrong with that... why didn't you tell me?" Jax questioned.

I watched as Adam and Andrew stood up, awkwardly. "We should go grab some bread for the table...come on, Katie..." Adam said, tapping her shoulder. Katie mouthed a quick 'sorry' to me, before standing up and leaving with the two guys.

Although I shouldn't have been surprised by their sudden decision to flee. For those who did not know Jax, he could be pretty intimidating when he was angry.

I sighed, before looking back at Jax. "Jax, I didn't think it was that big of a deal. If he comes back again I swear to you, I will tell you this time... I can handle Damian on my own, he's nothing but a snake..."

Jax turned away from me for a second, before letting out an angry exhale. "I'm not angered with you, MacKenzie. I just hate the guy, and I have this feeling that there is something about you that he wants..."

I let out a small chuckle. "More than you think...considering he invited me to his quarters..." I muttered. With that, Jax stood up.

"He did what?" he said, his voice booming through the cafeteria. A few people looked over our way, with curious glances. I was even startled to the point that I jumped in my seat.

I grabbed Jax's arm, pulling him to sit back down. "You know I'm not the first female he has said that to, and I made it very clear that he should never bring that up with me again.... look, I swear to you that if he comes back I will tell you. As long as you swear to me you won't go running over there and..snap his neck or whatever it is you Rangers do," I said, squeezing Jax's arm slightly.

Jax gritted his teeth slightly, his gray eyes full of rage. He looked away from me, before reaching over and touching my hand. I felt a quick, brief flutter in my stomach at his touch. "Okay," he said, before letting go. I moved my hand away, placing it back on my lap.

"For the record, Rangers don't just snap necks... we snap everything," he said, a hint of a smile on his face.

I raised an eyebrow at him slightly. "Yeah, I know. You leave one heck of a mess for us MPs to clean up..."

Jax shrugged. "I know, it must be a strain to take a break from issuing parking tickets,"

I slapped him playfully on the arm, and he began to laugh. "That's not all we do, Mr. Jackson McGrath... keep in mind, we went to the same Airborne School,"

He leaned in closer, arching his brow slightly. "That's *Captain* Jackson McGrath to you, *Lieutenant*..." he teased. I blushed slightly at the feel of him being so close to me, before turning away.

"Jerk.." I muttered, with a fake pout.

"You'll get over it," Jax played, before he resumed eating his mashed potatoes.

Not a few moments later, Katie returned with the two guys who were carrying a few loaves of bread. They sat down, and I heard Adam going on a ramble about something to do with testing for new soldiers going on down the hallway and that they were doing some sort of combative training and how Damian was in there now, supervising. I detested the idea of Damian supervising their training, he was only going to poison their minds with his ideals of how a soldier should do their work.

After we devoured our dinner, we all agreed to meet up in the morning to go for our usual morning run. Katie kept whispering jokes to me as we left the chow hall about Jax walking me home after a meal and about how romantic is was. I just let her talk, but completely tuned her out. I was beginning to think that even my tiger was getting annoyed.

Katie gave us a small wave, before scurrying towards the gym with Adam and Andrew. Normally I would have joined her, but after the day I had I was too exhausted to even begin to care about working out. Jax had been surprisingly quiet for the rest of dinner and through the walk back. I wasn't sure if he was just being resilient or if he really was angry with me for not telling him about what was going on with Damian.

Once we got to my door, I opened my mouth to speak, but Jax beat me to it.

"So you know that we have the next forty-eight off, and then we are on for the next forty-eight, right?" he questioned, seeming somewhat off.

I couldn't help but smile slightly. "Yes, Jax. We've always maintained the same schedule for the past five years.." I said, raising my eyebrow at him in question. I watched as Jax fought a smirk.

"Right, I just wanted to remind you.." he said, somewhat awkwardly.

I folded my arms across my chest. "Jax, is everything alright? You seem extremely off today..." I said, tilting my head slightly. Jax looked as though he wanted to say something, possibly something with a heavy heart, but the moment passed and he shook his head.

"Are you still mad about the whole Damian thing?" I asked, biting my lip in worry.

Jax smiled, before nodding his head. "Of course everything is alright. I just had to make sure the *princess*," he paused, mocking what Georgia called me earlier that day "Arrived back at her room safely,"

I reached over and punched him in the arm, hard. "Stop that," I teased, laughing. Jax faked a pout, before smiling widely down at me. I took a moment to just stare at him. He looked *damn* good when he smiled. Before he could ponder on my stare spell for too long, I reached and grabbed my door handle.

"I'll see you tomorrow, we still good for that run we talked about at dinner?" I asked, my heart suddenly in my throat.

Jax nodded. "Sounds good,"

I opened my door as Jax began his way down the hall.

"Hey MacKenzie?" I heard Jax questioned. My heart skipped a beat as I stuck my head back through the doorframe, looking at him.

His serious expression broke out into a smile. "Shall I send a carriage for you, your highness?" he asked, mocking a bow. I laughed, before shutting my door. I could hear Jax laughing down the hall, before I heard the sound of the door shutting.

I walked over to my shower, before stripping away the layers. I highly enjoyed my days off, most of the time I spent with Jax, Katie, Amanda and Matt. As I stepped into the shower, I couldn't help but think about what Katie kept saying about me and Jax. My answer for everything and anything she said concerning the two of us was always me saying 'he's married'.

It had been getting weird though. Normally he would at least mention his wife's name to me at least once a day, and twice a week he would get letters from her saying what was going on in Florida. She had to be very discreet though.

Not having a stable government meant not having stable rules, so letters could be intercepted at any time.

Once my shower was complete, I reached over and wrapped the towel tightly around my figure. I stepped out, enjoying the feel of the cool breeze against my skin rushing through the window. The moon was full tonight, my favorite lunar cycle was the full moon.

I smirked slightly, letting the towel fall. After making sure my door was locked, I turned off the lights to the room. The last thing I needed was someone seeing me standing there naked in the middle of my room, along with what was about to happen. I closed my eyes, before squatting down towards the floor. I bowed my head and closed my eyes, calling for the beast within me to come free. She answered my call, as I saw her in my mind.

I then felt my back straighten out, as my hands dropped to the floor. My shoulders squared, and I instantly felt warm again. I opened my eyes, to see my reflection in the mirror. The elegant, white Siberian tiger stared back at me. I felt a low growl rumble in my throat as I attempted to let out a sigh. I climbed onto my bed, and it creaked in protest under my feline weight. I laid down, resting my head on my paws as I gazed out the window and out at the moon.

A cool breeze blew over my fur, and I closed my eyes at the feel. I loved nights such as this, where I could just let myself be free. I loved how the moon made me feel so secure, even though I knew I was so alone. At least in the aspect of being a skin-walker, as we were called throughout the years. It was the term I preferred at least, over the various other names my kind had been given over the years. During the establishment of the sectors, they began to call us 'Anomics', because were were different than the norm of society.

For the longest time, I hated the change. I hated the fact that I was different from everyone else growing up, and that I had to hide who I really was. We could only marry within our culture, so I had to marry another male Anomic. How quickly that all changed when the war broke out. A shiver traveled up my spine, as I recalled my parents death.

I laid down on my side, my bed protesting as I did so once again. I titled my head back slightly to once again look in my full-length mirror. I could see my tigers bright blue eyes staring back at me in sadness. I let out a final huff, before I turned my gaze back to the moon. I slowly let my eyelids fall as I began to drift off to sleep.

I pulled the M4 semi-automatic rifle close to my body as my heart began to skip a beat. I had not been this afraid since my first combat tour in Afghanistan. Jax ran up next to me, placing his hand on my shoulder. "MacKenzie, we will find them!" he yelled, over the rapid gunfire in the distance. I nodded sharply, trying to steady my breathing.

I watched as Jax reached into his pocket, pulling out a small brown package. "I'm setting off a flare so that the bird can come to our position.." he said, striking the package. The red flames shot up in the air, engulfing my vision as I heard screams cry out.

***

A harsh knocking on my door caught woke me from my nightmare, as I threw myself forward to sit up. I looked around my bed and into the mirror to see that I must have changed back in my sleep. The knocking continued, and I rolled my eyes. If it was Katie randomly waking me up at an early hour just so we could have a picnic and watch the sun rise again, I was going to scream.

I wrapped one of my fleece blankets around myself, as I threw my legs over my bed and hurried to the door. After peeping through the eyehole, I let out a small gasp of surprise. Jax was standing there with Katie and Adam, all dressed in their running shorts. I glanced at my watch and mentally smacked myself.

"Sorry guys, I will be right there!" I yelled, rushing over to my closet. Since we all worked the same shifts together, we all worked out together as well. Normally I was always the first one ready to go.

After finding suitable clothes to wear for our run, I threw open the door to see my friends all standing there. Katie let the huge grin cross her face. "Good morning Sleeping Beauty. I didn't think that you were ever going to wake up," she said, playfully smacking me on the back.

Adam elbowed her in the side. "Give 'er a break. She was probably throwing back a couple, she needs it!" Adam joked, mocking taking some shots at a bar. I narrowed my eyes at him, before holding up my hands in surrender.

"You're right, you caught me..." I stated.

Adam folded his arms with pride. "I know," he said, shrugging the compliment off. We headed outside, before beginning our usual jog around the sector.

The four of us maintained a column formation, as we all had been used to when we ran together in the military. Various people watched us as we passed them, nodding in acknowledgement. I felt so free when I was running, running to me was my way of escape. Whether as the tiger or in my human form, it was the only place where I felt I could go to escape reality.

We never ran for speed time, we ran for the sole purpose of running. We usually allotted an hour of our time just to run throughout the sector. No one talked about work or co-workers, though we ran as soldiers, we also ran as children at heart.

We made a right turn and began to run along-side one of the electrified fences. I could hear the faint buzzing, and it made me cringe slightly as I remembered my beginning days as an MP when we went through our taser training. Let's just say it was quite the electric ride.

I heard a snapping sound, and I quickly halted. I felt someone run into my back, followed by a groan from Katie, and a heavy 'thud'.

"Next time give me a warning, dude..." she said, rubbing the back of her head. Adam reached down and assisted her to her feet. My eyes began scanning the tree-line, searching for the source of the sound. I reached inside me, attempting to summon my tiger senses. I had trained myself to channel certain parts of my tiger, as necessary, without completely turning into the tiger itself. It took much practice, mostly with my father. He trained me to control many things about the connection between myself and my tiger.

I heard the snapping sound again, and I saw a man and a woman standing in the clearing of the wood-line. Her hair was waist-length and brown, and she wore a long, black cloak. The man standing next to her appeared to be wearing charcoal colored clothes. I stepped so that I was a mere inch away from the fence, the buzzing filling my ears.

For a moment the two of them just continued to stare at all of us.

"They're eighty-sixers.." I heard Katie mutter. I had never really seen them post eighty-sixing, but I had always imagined they still looked like normal people. However, my co-workers would spread rumors about them being deformed and cannibalistic. These two seemed like an average Joe and Jane to me. I couldn't help but feel sorry for them.

I could sense Jax's presence right behind me. I began to subtly sniff the air, seeing if I could pick up on anything about these people. They smelled of mud. That's all that I was getting.

I turned away from them, looking back at my friends.

"Let's just go..." I said, beginning to walk away. A sudden whizzing sound buzzed in my left ear and I turned to see that an arrow had struck the telephone pole a mere two feet away from me. I turned around, my attention back on the two strangers.

30

The male still had the bow raised, and I could see the female making rapid hand movements. It appeared as though she was yelling at him for his actions. When he released a second arrow, this one just barely missing my shoulder, I realized she was yelling at him because he missed me.

I watched as Jax reached into the back seam of his pants, before pulling out a small pistol.

"Hey!" he yelled, before firing a warning shot into the woods. I saw the bark fly off of the tree right next to the female, as they both ducked in response. The female made eye contact with me, and that was when I finally sensed something off with her. The fear from the male was flooding my senses but the female was giving off a scent that I couldn't even describe.

I narrowed my eyes at the two of them, daring them to make another move.

"Dude, really? You brought a gun to go running? Do you have any idea how bad that could wind up?" Adam questioned.

"Like you didn't?" Jax asked, nodding to the bulge on Adam's hip.

Adam shifted uncomfortably. "Apples and Oranges,"

Before I could ponder her scent any further, they both took off for the deeper part of the woods. Katie stepped up next to me, before placing her hand on my shoulder.

"Are you alright?" she asked me, concern in her eyes. I nodded, trying to hide the fact that I was shaking like a leaf.

"I'm fine," I said, forcing a smile. It was the first time I had ever been shot at since the great war, just with a different form of a projectile.

I looked at everyone, before shrugging. "Well, what are we waiting for? Let's get back on our run again," I said, leading the way.

After we had finished our run, we all began to walk towards the gym for the rest of our workout routine. Katie began her tangent about how she hoped her favorite machine would be available so she could work on her 'killer abs' as she called it.

As we made our way towards the town square, we spotted a rather large group of people gathering around, a couple people craning their necks to look at something in front of them. I immediately spotted Amanda and Matt, who had their arms folded and were shaking their heads as if in disbelief.

"What's going on?" I questioned, looking back and forth between the two of them.

"They have Stephen up there right now, there was an incident with him and the Sector Commander....they think...." Amanda said, pausing to swallow. I took note of the fact that her eyes were welling up with tears, and she was desperately trying to hold it all together.

"They think what? Who is they? What was the incident?" I questioned, trying to bring Amanda back down to earth. If I was thinking of the correct Stephen, I knew he was one of our soldiers, who mostly kept to himself and loved to fish. Beyond that, I didn't know him all that well.

"Stephen... Patrol 65...he went in to talk to the Sector Commander, there was a disagreement..." Amanda said, covering her face with her hands.
"A disagreement?" I questioned, fearing what that really meant.
Jax put his hand on her shoulder, and turned to look at Matt.
"What's going on with Stephen?" he questioned.

Matt let out a heavy sigh, shaking his head. "They think that he is an Anomic, and they are going to have him executed,"

4.

At the sound of the word, my head snapped in Matt's direction. "That's impossible!" I said, before I could even think.

Matt turned to face me, raising his eyebrows. "Yes, we know. All the Anomics were either eighty-sixed from the sector or...you know. Why would an Anomic suddenly make an appearance right now?" Matt questioned.

"Well not only that, even if he is an Anomic, Stephen is one of the sweetest people I know. Why do they have to do this?" Amanda questioned, wiping her eyes.

Jax looked over at me, shooting me a look of warning. He without a doubt, trusted Matt and Amanda, but given that there was a huge crowd gathering around, it was best that I be careful with my words.

"Ladies and Gentlemen," the Sector Commander's voice boomed over the gathering crowd. I craned my neck slightly to see the Sector Commander standing there with Damian, and two other soldiers. On the ground was Stephen, looking extremely disheveled and beaten up. His lip was split, blood pouring down his chin, and his one eye was swollen shut. His clothing was now torn under the arms, and all the buttons on his shirt looked as though they had been ripped away.

"Jax," I whispered, looking up at him. "This isn't right, I have to do something..."

"Mac, you can't. They'll catch you and take everything you hold dear away from you," Jax argued.

"Ladies and Gentlemen, thank you very much for all gathering here today. I have a very important message for you all..." the Sector Commander said, stepping up on a small wooden platform that was brought out for him. I peered through the cracks in the crowd and saw Phyllis, Major Chase's neighbor standing there, wiping the beads of sweat off of her forehead with a handkerchief.

"As you may all well be aware, seven years ago, we made a peace treaty with all Anomics that they could either eighty-six themselves from us, or if they were discovered hiding, they would be put down. Here, we have a classic example of a...rogue...Anomic, who refuses to obey those laws, and therefore, must be made an example of," the Sector Commander said, pointing a finger at Stephen.

33

"What's going on?" I heard a voice say, and I looked to see Major Chase standing beside Katie and Adam.

"They're saying Stephen is an Anomic," Katie said, her voice shaking slightly.

"How is that possible?" Major Chase questioned, craning his neck over the crowd.

"It's not...there are no Anomics left in the sector," Amanda said, shaking her head in disbelief. "There haven't been reports for years,"

"For years I have kept our sector safe by eliminating these...beasts from our lives. Yes, they did save our kind all those years ago from the horrible *Relinquished*, but what are they really? They are wild animals! Wild animals can not be trusted, and can turn on you at any moment! So my fellow citizens, what should be Stephen's fate? Eighty-sixed or death?!" the Sector Commander questioned, slowly raising a gun at Stephen's head.

"Traitor!"

"He's a liar! Who else knows what secrets he has been hiding?"

"Kill him!"

"He deserves to die!"

"He had his chance to leave!"

The random voices continued to shout harsh words, all overlapping each other.

"I'm not an Anomic! Wait until these people figure out what you've been doing all this time, what you have been planning to do with *her*," Stephen said, spitting out some blood.

"Kill him!"

"He lies!"

"Deceiver!"

"Shoot him!"

"What is he talking about? Who is *her*?" Adam questioned, looking over at Jax. "Is he married or something?"

"I don't know," Jax replied.

"We have to do something," I said, marching towards the front of the crowd. I felt a hand grab onto my wrist and turned to see Major Chase standing there, his hand on my wrist.

"MacKenzie, don't. You can't. If you try to stop it they are going to accuse you of being his partner in crime and may label you as an Anomic as well. You can't," Major Chase said, his voice stern.

I looked back up front, feeling as though my heart had gone heavy. Stephen, who was just a normal person, was being accused of being one of my kind. I was the one with the gift, not Stephen, it should have been me up there.

The sound of a gunshot echoed through the area, and I covered my ears and squatted towards the ground, guilt instantly flooding me. It should have been me if anyone to die. I heard the soft 'thud' of Stephen's body hitting the ground, followed by a murmur through the crowd.

"Let this be a lesson to you all, any Anomics found hiding in this sector will be instantly eliminated. Anyone associating or assisting in the hiding of an Anomic, will be eighty-sixed," the Sector Commander said, taking the handkerchief from Phyllis and wiping his pistol down.

I felt the fire burning in my chest, and I could almost hear my tiger roaring in anger in my head.

With that, he stepped off his pedestal and trotted on his merry way, Phyllis rushing behind him with the wooden block. The two soldiers that were with Damian and the Sector Commander lifted Stephen's now lifeless body, and moved away from the crowd.

I closed my eyes and slowly exhaled, trying to get my anger under control. An innocent man was murdered, because he was suspecting of being just like me, and I did nothing about it.

"MacKenzie," Jax said, interrupting my thoughts. I turned to face him to see his facial expressions were extremely soft. He leaned in, to whisper into my ear. "There was nothing you could have done," he said, pulling away and nodding at me.

He knew how I must have been feeling. Major Chase gave us a somber farewell, heading home. Katie turned to face me and Jax, wiping a tear away from her eye.

"Let's go inside the gym, I think a workout to get our mind off of things is just what we need..." Katie said.

"You're right...let's go, MacKenzie..." Jax said, putting his arm around my shoulders. He leaned in slightly, to whisper in my ear once more. "I'm sure we can find something for you to punch in here,"

I smirked slightly, still not even close to being over what had just happened. I was a little angered at my friends for being so calm about it. Maybe it was because, aside from Jax, they didn't have all the facts. They didn't know what I really was, and they didn't know that I was, for sure, the only one of my kind left in the sector. They didn't know that an innocent man was just murdered.

When we walked in the room we were surprised to see that all of the machines and equipment had been pushed to the sides, up against the glass windows. I heard a faint mummer of protest from Katie as I scanned the room to see Damian standing in the center of a large gymnastics mat, surrounded by about thirty people. At the sound of the door slamming shut behind us, Damian turned our way. When he set his eyes on us, he allowed the eerie grin to cross his face.

"Well, this is a delicious surprise. Just the people I wanted to see," he stated. It sickened me that he could just stand outside and watch someone shot, and then walk inside the gym and happily instruct a class as if meant absolutely nothing.

He clapped his hands together, his eyes scanning all of us. "I was just about to demonstrate the proper way to fight a hostile enemy. I'm so glad that you four decided to volunteer," Damian said, gleefully.

"If it involves you, Damian, believe me...volunteering is the absolute last thing on our mind," Adam stated, folding his arms across his chest. Damian smirked, before turning back to the class, pointing a finger at Adam.

"This, class, is a classic example of a soldier who thinks he is too good for the rest of us. Am I right, Adam?" Damian sneered.

I rolled my eyes, pushing Adam behind me. I just wanted to get my routine done to help ease my mind, and then get back to my room and curl up with a bottle of something strong.

"Thank you for the lesson, Damian. Now if you'll excuse us, we have a routine to get started," I said, moving to walk away. I felt a hand clamp down on my arm and I turned to see another soldier, whom I did not recognize, gripping my forearm tightly.

"That's a good boy, Brutus. Now bring her over here please," Damian ordered. Out of the corner of my eye, I could see Jax attempt to move forward but I prevented his movement by holding up a hand to stop.

I could not even find the words to pinpoint the look in Jax's eyes. It looked as if he were worried, angry and frustrated all at the same time. Katie and Adam moved closer together, Katie now joining Adam in folding her arms across her chest. I nodded back to them, reassuring them that I was okay, as the soldier brought me closer to Damian.

Once we were about a foot away, Brutus let go of my arm and stepped off to the side. Damian smirked, flipping his greasy blonde bangs out of his face. He showed me a sly wink, before looking back at the other soldiers, who began to shift uneasily.

"Now, recruits, MacKenzie and I will demonstrate a proper method to take down a hostile enemy. Have no fear, I will go easy on her and I will not harm a pretty hair on her head..." Damian said, holding up his hands.

My tiger stirred angrily inside of me, wanting nothing more than to rip his heart from his chest and put an end to his life. Very rarely had I allowed these feelings to cross my mind. I had never killed anyone in my tiger form, but Damian was really testing me.

I heard a few of the soldiers laugh, as Damian allowed the same eerie smirk to cross his face. I felt my tiger stirring, raging to be free. Before I could even think, I drew a fist back, punching Damian across the face. I immediately felt a stinging sensation in my knuckles, as he stumbled backwards.

He looked over at me, grabbing his jaw in shock. I began to shake my wrist out, trying to put off the impression that punching another human across the face was an everyday thing for me.

"We will see who will be going easy on who," I hissed, trying to ignore the stinging sensation that was spreading through my knuckles.

Damian smirked, all traces of shock disappearing from his face. "You've got some fire in you, I like that," he teased, before standing back up again. I looked over at my friends to see if I could read what they were feeling. Katie and Adam looked anxious, Katie lightly rocking from foot to foot. Jax had his arms folded and his jaw squared, as if he were ready to rush in to my aid if I needed assistance.

I turned back to face Damian to see that he began moving in a circular motion, the infamous smirk now gone from his face. I followed him with my eyes, not really in the mood to play this circling game like carnivores closing in on their prey. Damian made to quickly move towards me, swiping his arm in an attempt to grab mine. I quickly rolled forward, avoiding his grasp. Damian chuckled, nodding in approval.

"Very good MacKenzie, I see that you are quick on your feet, but you cannot keep running forever..." Damian said, before lunging forward once more. I blocked his punch with my forearm, before making eye contact with him.

"I'm not running," I said, before palming him in the nose. He shook his head, before bringing an open palm across my face.

I stumbled back slightly, feeling a stinging sensation next to my eye. I reached up and touched the area, feeling a light trickle of blood.

Damian took my moment of distraction as an opportunity, his body colliding with mine as he took us both to the floor. Damian was not the largest opponent that I had faced, but he was slippery enough to avoid my attempts to throw him off of me.

Damian grabbed my throat, before forcing me on my back. He captured my other two hands in his, bringing them into his chest as he scrambled on top of me.

He laughed, before leaning down to whisper in my ear.

"On your back, just how I like you..." he teased, before teasingly grinding his hips against mine. I heard the sound of rushing footsteps, and looked to my left to see Jax ripping Damian off of me, before throwing him to the side like a rag doll. I should have been grateful for Jax assisting me and getting Damian off of me, but I couldn't help but feel angry at the fact that he gave off the impression that I needed his help to beat Damian.

Damian stood up, shooting Jax a glare. He opened his mouth to speak, but I rushed forward and elbowed him in the solar plexus before he even had the chance to speak. I leapt on his back, before locking him into a sleeper hold. Damian began to thrash around, in an attempt to get me off of his back.

"In a choke-hold, just how I like you..." I mocked, tightening my grip. Damian collapsed to his knees, and I heard the class gasp in shock at the sight of the Chief of Security being overpowered by a 107 pound female. Damian then threw all of his weight backwards, my spine slamming against the floor. I winced in pain, and forcefully released my hold on him. Damian nodded to the two large soldiers to his left, and I followed their movement to see them blocking Jax from advancing to me.

Though Jax could probably take out any enemy with his advanced skills, he had his limits. The two soldiers that were with Damian were like two Jax's put together, each on their own.

Damian pressed his knee into my abdomen, before sliding his forearm under my neck. I began to breath heavily, staring at Damian with hateful eyes. Damian allowed a playful smirk to cross his face.

"That was quite lovely, dear one. I must say, you continue to surprise me..." he said, before releasing his hold on me. I was not one to easily accept defeat, but when Damian bowed towards his applauding class, I realized that it wasn't even worth it.

He turned back to face me after I stood up. I began to rub my throat, as it felt extremely sore. I shook my head, before attempting to walk away. A few seconds later, I felt Damian's cold fingers snap around my wrist as he pulled me towards him.

"Don't feel bad, my sweet, I'll drop by later and make it all better..." he said, before pushing me away from him. I watched him as he walked back towards his class, before turning to look at Jax. The two soldiers who were watching him quickly moved away, over towards Damian. Jax put his arm around my shoulders, and steered me away from the group.

Katie had a concerned look on her face and Adam was shaking his head. "What an asshole. You did good MacKenzie, don't let him get to you.." he said.

"I'm ready to go home, you guys go ahead and work out..." I said, suddenly feeling weak in my knees.

Between witnessing an innocent man being murdered and getting tossed around on the mat, I had enough for the day.

Damian's words about stopping by later were also really creeping me out. Katie and Adam exchanged glances, before looking back at me.

"We don't have to stay, we can all just go somewhere after this. Want to maybe go get some chow?" Adam questioned.

I shook my head, my mind made up on just crawling up into my bed and dreaming of the way the world used to be when the NFL was still in existence. That and maybe watching some old DVDs while enjoying the comfort of my 9mm laying next to me on my nightstand.

"No, you guys get your workout in. I sort of want to be alone," I said, forcing a smile.

I could tell by the look on Katie's face that she knew I was uncomfortable, but she knew better than to question it. Adam put his arm around Katie's shoulders, steering her away. "Mac, if you need anything please let us know..." he said.

I nodded, "I will" I responded.

Adam looked over at Jax, seemingly to ask him if he were going to stay and work out with them. Jax simply shook his head, and Adam nodded respectfully. I turned to look at Jax as Adam and Katie walked away.

"Jax, you can stay here with them. Its okay, I'm probably just going to go home and head to bed," I stated.

Jax shook his head. "MacKenzie, I'm staying with you...and I'm not just saying this as your partner or your friend," he said. It took me a second to realize that he was telling me as if he were my commanding officer once again.

I nodded, knowing it was best to not argue with him.

We headed back to the barracks, and when we got to my door, Jax stopped. "I'm going to run to the chow hall and bring something back for you. Go in and get dressed into something more comfortable, I will be back here in seven minutes..." he said, finally letting go of my shoulder. I nodded, before walking into my room.

5.

After I threw the keys onto the dresser, I walked over to my bed and sat down. This was so unlike me, being scared of someone like Damian. I had faced the enemy on deployments, and had even been in gun fights. I didn't understand why was Damian shaking me up as much as he was. Before I knew it, there was a knock on my door. I peeked through the eyehole and saw Jax standing there with two cans of soda and a full pizza.

I opened the door, trying to force my best smile. "How did you manage to get a whole pizza out of the chow hall?" I questioned, watching as Jax set the pizza down on my tiny kitchen table.

He smiled coyly, before opening the box. "Let's just say the third shift cook and I go way back,"

"What, he come to one of your infamous guys nights or something?" I asked, pulling out both of the chairs so that we could sit. Jax looked over at me, before taking a seat.
"Well its good to see you've got your infamous snarky personality back..." Jax said. I rolled my eyes, taking a seat as well.

"And you got me a *Mountain Dew*, you're on a roll tonight..." I said, opening the can and taking a quick sip. The bubbly, acidic taste of the ice cold soda felt so good.
"I know you all too well..." Jax said, before he began to put slices on our plates.

Jax and I began throwing the pizza down our throats immediately, enjoying its sweet, savory taste. It reminded me of my favorite pizza shop which was in King of Prussia, Pennsylvania called *Angelos*. It was a private, small-town pizza establishment but it was a hidden gem. The owner, Tony, made the absolute best pizza bar none. After we finished the pizza, and quite a bit of small talk, Jax surprised me with a question.

"What does it feel like?" Jax asked, making eye contact with me. I grabbed the empty box and soda cans, making to move towards the trash can.
"What does what feel like?" I questioned, curious.
"You know...changing like you do," Jax said, leaning back in his chair. I shoved the box in the trash can, before moving back towards the table.

"Well," I paused to sit down. "It's really hard to explain...but if I had to choose a word to describe it...weird,"

"Does it hurt?" Jax asked, tilting his head in question. I shrugged, before nodding slightly.

"A bit, to be honest. It hurt more when I was a child. You aren't really entrusted with the power until your seventh birthday, you're born with it of course, but you mentally cannot access that part of you until you are seven. Don't ask me why, but that's just how its been..." I stated, leaning back in my chair also.

Jax nodded, seemingly intrigued. "How was your first time changing?" he asked. I bit my lip for a second and shifted slightly, before opening my mouth to answer. "I'm sorry, if you don't want to talk about it...we don't have to..." Jax said, shaking his head.

"No, no...its not that. I just need a minute to think of a reply. I don't normally get asked stuff like this," I said, laughing nervously.

I looked back over at Jax, my answer finally in my head.

"It was like nothing I ever felt before, running through those woods as a free tiger. The autumn leaves crunching under my paws, the air rushing through my fur. My siblings by my side, racing through the trees. I remember first connecting with the tiger inside of me. Changing is not just a thing you can decide on your own, you have to connect with your inner tiger first. That way, you are bonded...after that, its all about understanding your control," I said, running a hand over my hair.

"Connect with your tiger?" Jax questioned.

"Well, your first time changing its like your two separate entities. You know how in legends werewolves don't have complete control over their actions or remember who they are? Its because they never connected with their inner wolf. The wolf spirit inside them didn't pay them the respect of balance. In regards to my people, the tiger spirits in us accepted us as equal. They knew that our intentions were good, that we were strong people, and that we had earned their respect. I respected the beauty in the spirit of my tiger, and I acknowledged her power...and that's how it works," I stated.

"Hmm... so it is possible that some of the tigers in the world out there are people who never fully connected with their tiger or were able to gain control are stuck in their tiger form?" Jax asked, folding his arms across his chest. I shrugged, unsure of how to answer that.

"Possibly, although the person who could for sure answer that would be my father...and unfortunately, he is no longer with us to answer that..." I said, drumming my fingers on the table.

For a second Jax's eyes locked with mine, and I felt something spark inside of me. I never had a deep conversation like this with anyone before, especially about my gift. It felt nice to be able to be so care-free, and to just talk about it. I shook my head, before laughing nervously.

"What time is it?" I questioned, ignoring Jax's lingering stare. I looked over at the clock and saw that it was already 2300 hours. I stood up, and began to stretch. "Well, I hope that Damian isn't planning on attempting to pay a late night visit. I'll be sleeping with my M9 on the nightstand, that's for sure..." I said.

Jax stood up as well, pushing his chair in. "That, and an Army Ranger with his loaded weapon on your floor as well..." Jax stated, looking over at me. I began to shake my head in protest.

"Jax, really its okay, for one thats extremely uncomfortable and its also unnecessary... I think I will be okay," I argued.

Jax leaned forward, putting his hands on the table. "MacKenzie, you promised." he stated.

It took me a minute, but I remembered our conversation from the night prior about if Damian ever tried to bug me again, then I would let Jax intervene. "Okay, but will you at least sleep on the couch? Not the floor..." I said, nodding over towards the large, three sectional couch across from the bed.

Jax hesitated, before agreeing.

"Besides, it does give you a better shooting angle if he does try to come through the door," I said, playing a joke. Jax let out a small chuckle, as I tossed him a spare pillow and blanket.

"I can be at peace with that. However, if I really wanted to kill him, I could do it from any angle..." Jax said, laying down on the couch.

I turned my back to Jax, pulling the sheets down so I could get ready to climb in bed. I bit my lip, trying to conceal my growing smile. Though I had known Jax for years, after my conversation with Katie, I couldn't help but feel like a school girl with a secret crush.

I squeezed my pillow and closed my eyes. "He's married, he's married, he's married..." I whispered, to myself. I felt Jax's gaze land on my tense form.

"MacKenzie, you okay?" he asked. I turned to face him, the dark shadows of the room falling on his form at heavenly angles. Damn him, for looking so much like a Jordy Nelson doppleganger. Why did it take me so long to realize my partner looked like my college girl crush?

"I'm perfect. Just...um...looking forward to the next time we wrestle against Damian when I get to kick his ass for real this time," I said, before climbing into bed. I could tell by Jax's facial expression that he did not completely believe me, but he went along with it anyway.

"Okay," he said, before turning to lay on his back. I could see the silver from his pistol as it was tucked in the side of his pants.

"Jax?" I asked, as I laid down. Jax turned his head so he was looking at me. "Thank you," I said, showing him a small smile. Jax nodded and returned the same smile.
"Till the end, battle..." he said, before we both drifted off to sleep.

6.

My breath quickened as I raced through the alley's of Philadelphia, my head constantly on a swivel. I could hear Jax moving behind me along with Sergeant First Class Rester, Sergeant Spooner and Sergeant Spain.   I kept my rifle at the ready position, as I pressed myself against the next building. I peered around the corner, before sprinting across the street. I could hear the other four following my lead.

Balls of fire filled my peripheral vision as the building two blocks over was hit my an RPG. "

MacKenzie, we must move faster if we want to get to them!" I heard Jax yell. He did not need to tell me twice. With that, I broke into a sprint as I headed towards 38th Street. I would find my parents, if it was the last thing I do.

I heard a whizzing sound fly past my ear, followed by a grunt. I turned to see Sergeant First Class Rester grabbing his thigh. Jax leapt to the ground, before firing rounds into the dark alley. A scream could be heard, as we saw a body fall. With my rifle raised, I ran towards the body, ignoring the smoke that was curling all around me. I turned the body over, and saw the red bandana and the three stripes of white war paint on each cheek as well as the big black letter 'R' tattooed on his neck. Another Relinquished member.

I looked back to see Sergeant First Class Rester being helped by Sergeant Spain and Sergeant Spooner to his feet. I looked at Jax. "They need to get him to the medic. Tell them to hide in the alley, you stay with them... I'm going to go find my parents," I yelled, over all the commotion.

"MacKenzie, I cannot let you go alone like this. I'll call it in on the radio and they can hide in this alley..."

I heard rapid gunfire to our left, followed by a woman's scream. I grabbed Jax by the shoulder, before pulling him closer to me. "Jax, I don't have the time to argue this with you. I'm changing and going in. I will be faster that way and I seriously doubt they have the materials to kill me if they cross me," I said. Jax hesitated, before nodding.

"But you better come right back here. If you're not back in 20 minutes, I'm coming after you..." Jax said.

I nodded, before I handed him my rifle. Our eyes lingered on each other for a second, before I turned and sprinted down the street. I didn't care if anyone saw me change at that point, if anyone even was around to see it. My family's life was in jeopardy, and it was up to me to save them.

"I'm coming," I whispered, before I leapt into the air, embracing the tiger inside of me.

44

A sudden knocking on my door threw me off guard, and I fell to the floor and let out a squeal. I looked over to see Jax already on his feet, his hand on his pistol. He looked over at me and I saw him suppress a laugh.

"Cute, MacKenzie..." he said. I scoffed, before standing on my feet. He would pay for that comment later. I walked over to the door and my eyes widened as Katie stood there, knocking impatiently.

I looked over at Jax, and he furrowed his brow in worry. "Who is it?" he questioned.

"It's just Katie...hang on," I said, opening the door enough to stick my head out.

"Hey," I said, forcing a smile.

"Hey... I tried radioing you earlier, is everything alright?" she asked, raising an eyebrow.

"Yeah, everything is good. I just...wanted to sleep in..." I said, rubbing my eyes.

"Yeah, I can tell. You normally are at my door at 0600, ready to go for a run. Its like 0830..." Katie stated.

"Oh wow, I'm sorry..." I said, apologetically. Katie tilted her head and looked up at my hair.

"Someone woke up on the wrong side of the bed this morning," she said, referring to my messed up hair. I rolled my eyes and laughed nervously.

"Well, you know me. I'm a restless sleeper...sometimes," I said, resting my hand on the doorframe. Katie's eyes darted towards my hand like a cat watching a mouse. I raised an eyebrow at this.

"You, on the other hand, need to chill on the coffee..." I said.

"Coffee? Oh that sounds yummy. How about we make some?" Katie questioned. I hesitated for a second.

"Uh..maybe later. I want to get changed real fast...and run some errands," I lied.

I could tell by her expression that she saw right through that.

"Yeah, okay. Come on, lets have some girl talk and drink some..." she said, pushing the door open. As soon as she stepped in the room, I watched her jaw nearly hit the floor when she saw Jax standing there in gym shorts and his loose t-shirt.

"Katie, what's up?" Jax asked, shooting me a nervous look. Katie's shocked expression turned to a huge grin as she leaned in to whisper to me.

45

"No wonder you slept in so late, what did that handsome man do to you? You know what? Whatever it was, its about time it happened!" she whispered.

I shook my head, trying not to blush. "Jax wanted to make sure that Damian didn't pay me a late night visit....again..." I said, folding my arms across my chest. Katie's grin slowly faded as she folded her arms as well.

"Please tell me he didn't," she said. I shook my head, thankful myself. Jax slid his weapon back in its holster, stepping towards me and Katie.

"Well, you ladies do your thing...I'm going to go get a shower and then go find Matt and head to the gym. Mac, did you still want to get chow later?" Jax asked, looking over at me.

I nodded. "Yeah, that sounds good to me. I'll see you in a little bit,"

Jax nodded, before making to move out the door. I watched as Katie moved to the coffee maker, prepping to make us a batch. I don't know what took over me in that moment, but I felt the overwhelming urge to run after Jax.

"Jax," I called, following him out the door. He turned to face me, raising both of his eyebrows. A part of me felt the longing to hug Jax, to seek comfort in his arms with all that was going on. Jax had always been there to see me through my worst times, and I felt like I hadn't really done much for him in return.

I let out a heavy sigh, knowing that given the circumstances, or rather...his circumstances a hug wouldn't be appropriate. "Thank you...for everything," I said, showing him a small smile. Jax winked, a smirk on his face.

"My pleasure," he said, before disappearing into his room.

I walked back in my room, and saw Katie with a huge smirk on her face. "What was *that* all about?" she questioned, crossing her legs. I shook my head, before pulling out another one of my chairs.

"It wasn't anything. He was just making sure that I was okay and that Damian wasn't about to come in unannounced...like I told you," I said, sitting down.

Katie narrowed her eyes and tilted her head. "I'm still suspicious," she whispered. I rolled my eyes, before looking over at the door.

"Want to go for a walk?" I questioned. Katie raised her eyebrows, before standing up.

"Sure, why not? I mean we only patrol a hundred hours a day!" Katie said, sarcastically.

"You'll survive," I said, grabbing my green and white hoodie. I wanted to go back to the fence where I saw the eighty-sixers. I was curious as to why they had come so close to the borders in the first place, let alone fire an arrow at me.

46

As we made our way to the fence, passing the on duty soldiers, Katie began her rant on Damian's speech in regards to the whole private interview process amongst the soldiers...and the possibility of becoming *eighty-sixed.* I never thought that people who got *eighty-sixed* actually survived on their own out there in the woods... until I saw the two who fired their arrows at me. Maybe they blamed us soldiers for them getting being removed from the sector. There were several times when I had witnessed the actual *eighty-sixing* process.

People were just ripped from their homes and pushed into the woods...their belongings either locked up in storage for the purpose of documentation, passed onto their families or destroyed. Although, I wasn't in uniform and the arrows were only fired at me..and there were four of us there. I had never even done the actual pushing into the woods myself. However, what were the chances that it was pure coincidence that the arrows were fired at me twice, at random?

We approached the area again, and I scanned the wood-line looking for any signs of life.   "Wait, isn't this where we saw those...people?" Katie questioned. When I didn't see anything, I let out a sigh.
"Yes," I responded.

"Yay, let's go back to the creepy spot where MacKenzie was almost killed..." Katie said, mockingly. I ignored her comment, getting as close to the fence as I possibly could without being zapped by the electrical current that was buzzing in my ear.
I inhaled as my eyes scanned the area, searching for a sign of life. A few seconds later, the smell of something sweet flooded my nostrils. I turned my head to the left, narrowing my eyes slightly.
"I know you're out there...." I said, my vision tunneling on a cluster of three large oak trees. Katie stepped up next to me, attempting to follow my gaze.
"MacKenzie, there is nothing out there..." Katie stated.
"Just wait for it," I whispered.

Not a few seconds later, I saw two figures emerge from the woods. The first male I saw, was wearing a red tunic and his skin was that of the purest milk chocolate. Standing no less than six feet, his head was shaven and he looked at me with sad almond eyes. My eyes wandered over his impressive build. He had a few bloody scratches all over his muscular arms, making me wonder what creature would dare mess with such a built man. Okay, maybe Jax would give it a try.

The second man, wearing a black tunic and matching pants, stared at me with his icy blue eyes. I had never seen eyes like that before, and I had met a lot of people in my lifetime. Mostly on my deployments or from my study abroad experience, back when colleges still existed. His dirty blonde hair was cropped tight, perfect military style. His physique rivaled that of his companion, with arms built like a WWE fighter. He was no short of six foot himself.

I heard Katie gasp, and take a few steps back. I maintained my ground, staring out at the two men. The one in the red tunic exchanged some words with his partner, who continued to stare at me with that icy glare. I had been so curious to find these people again, but now that I was faced with them, I had no idea what to say.

The man in the black folded his arms across his chest and looked me over as if he were sizing me up.

"You know, if you take a picture it would last longer...." I called out, my glare challenging his.

He moved to step forward, but the man in the red tunic stepped in front of him, putting a hand on his chest. The man in the black eyed me one final time, before turning and disappearing back into the forest. The man in the red moved to do the same, but Katie beat me to the punch.

"Wait!" she called out.

He turned back to face us, raising his chin slightly. Katie looked over at me nervously, unsure of what to do next. She raised her hand and chuckled nervously.

"Hi," she said, embarrassed.

I shoved her slightly, before stepping in front of her. "Two of your people fired arrows at me just the other day. I would like to know what I ever did to offend you all,"

He brought his gaze to meet mine, walking towards the fence. I tensed up slightly, but refused to let my guard down. Something told me that if he really wanted to hurt me, he would have tried to by now...just like his buddies.

He stopped, his face just inches from the fence on the other side. He gave Katie a quick once over, and then turned to face me. He overlooked my figure, and then began sniffing the air. Clearly living in the wild must have made them loose their domestic manners.

He then stopped, taking two steps backward.

"Forgive me, my lady. But my people would never fire an arrow at you...especially since I know who you are," he said, bowing slightly.

My lip parted in slight shock, completely caught off guard.

"Actually, it was two arrows..." Katie spoke up, holding up two fingers.

"Know who I am?" I questioned, my hands clenching in fists of worry at my sides.

"I know much of you, MacKenzie Waters...daughter of Caesar Waters..." he spoke up again, his almond eyes looking deep into mine. My mouth fell completely open this time, unable to hide my growing fear. I backed away from the fence, my hand moving to my chest. If he knew my father, did that mean he knew who I really was? Did he know about my power?

Before I could question it any further, a high-pitched alarm sounded throughout the sector. The stranger on the other side of the fence didn't even look rattled, as he continued to stare at me with the same expression he had when he first walked over.

"MacKenzie, that's the emergency alert...we have to go," Katie said, grabbing my arm and pulling me with her. I turned back to look at the stranger, who continued to stare at me for a good minute before turning and disappearing back into the trees.

I pulled my arm free from Katie, sprinting with her to the center of the sector. I saw multiple civilians scrambling and screaming, as they darted into their homes and began to shut all the doors. To the civilian population, the alarm meant for them to all get inside their homes until soldiers came and gave the 'all clear' sign. For us soldiers, that meant get to the sector vault, as soon as possible. Obviously, the soldiers in the northern-most part of the sector who patrolled what used to be Southern Connecticut would take longer to get there, needing to jump into Blackhawks to make it.

We arrived at the vault, and I was surprised to see that Amanda and Adam were already there. "Where are Matt, Andrew and Jax?" I questioned, looking for my partner.

"They were all at the gym, I'm sure they will be here soon..." Amanda said, as she finished typing in the code. She threw open the door to the vault and hurried inside, Adam immediately behind her. I looked back towards the barracks, anxious to know how much longer our missing comrades would be.

"Any idea what's going on?" Katie questioned, grabbing a M4 off the rack.

"Yeah, *Code Bullet*..." Adam said, tossing me an M4 as well. I swiped a loaded magazine, an anger suddenly washing over me.

Code Bullet, meant an intruder on the premises. More specifically, a hostile one. I threw each of them a *Police* tactical vest, quickly strapping mine on. Was it possible that while I was distracted with the two strangers, they had snuck one of their own into the sector? That was nearly impossible...wasn't it?

"Where is Damian?" I asked, charging the rifle.

"Who knows, last I saw him he said he was heading to a meeting with the commander," Amanda said, loading her M9 along with her rifle.

I sighed. "Alright, well I guess that means its just us for right now. We stick together and find this intruder. Let's go clear the commander's building first," I said, remembering the protocols that were set in place.

We filed out of the vault, Amanda shutting the door as we did so. I raised my rifle to the ready position, and we moved in a file down the street. I saw the Commander's building loom into view, and we all sprinted for it. We all pressed our backs up to the building and began working our way towards the door. I stopped, before leaning forward and running my hand along the door frame, checking for any wires that would cause an explosion. I looked to Adam, who was the last one in line. I waved him forward, ordering him to come and perform a hard knock on the door.

As he ran forward and began doing his check, I couldn't help but remember clearing buildings on my deployment. A hard knock, or kicking in the door in civilian terms, pretty much meant 'knock knock you assholes, America is here and we are coming in to find you!'. Which Jax actually did yell the one time.

Adam nodded to me, before kicking in the door and spinning out of the way. I charged forward, slamming the door against the wall to ensure no one was hiding behind it, before running along the left wall. Amanda went right, hugging the wall as well. Katie rushed in the center, making sure no one was attempting to hide under the coffee table. Adam came in, and checked our six. "It's clear," he said, looking around the room.

He inhaled, his face curling up in disgust at the smell of dust and whiskey.

"What kind of creature could possibly live in these conditions?" he questioned, through a fit of coughs.

"Amanda and I will go check upstairs, Adam can you and Katie make sure that no one else comes in here?" I asked, hurrying towards the steps before he got a chance to reply. I could hear Amanda moving behind me, muttering something about the filth of the place as she did so. I kept my rifle raised, scanning the upstairs area for any signs of life.

"It looks like he's not even here," Amanda said, kicking over a bunch of boxes and pointing her rifle to make sure no one was hiding behind them. I squatted down on the ground, looking at the dust. I could see faint footprints imprinted in the dust bunnies, no more than a few hours old.

"No he hasn't been here for a bit, must be somewhere with Damian... I hope," I said, standing up.

Amanda and I hurried down the stairs, meeting back up with Adam and Katie.

"Where to now?" Adam asked. He winced slightly at the sound of the alarm sounding once again. The intruder was still not found. I stepped outside, and we saw Jax running towards us with Matt, Andrew and Katie's partner, Jeff.

"Mac, are you guys okay?" Jax asked, putting a hand on my shoulder. I couldn't help but take comfort in his touch.

"Yeah we are good, you're in charge now..." I teased, trying to ignore the ringing in my ears from the alarm.

"Right... Matt and Amanda, you come with us. Katie, Jeff, Adam and Andrew head south. We will rendezvous back here in 20 minutes," Jax said, moving his hands in an orderly manner.

Jax turned to face me again. "MacKenzie, will you lead?" he asked. He always let me lead, knowing it would be easier for me to channel my senses from a frontal position so that I could easily pinpoint our target.

"Sure," I said, moving forward to take the lead.

We began moving through the city at a hurried pace, all of us anxious to capture the intruder not only to keep the city safe, but also to get the alarm to stop. The high pitched sound of the alarm echoing through the bare streets was extremely annoying.

I began to focus, trying to summon my tiger senses to try and locate the intruder. Once we got to what used to be the *Philadelphia Pretzel Factory* I paused, holding up my hand for everyone to halt.

I closed my eyes and began to inhale. Something told me that the intruder was close, but I needed to focus and pinpoint them. Jax leaned forward, and I felt his hot breath on my ear. "MacKenzie, is everything alright?" he asked, sounding concerned.

I continued to focus, and let out a deep exhale. Immediately after I did, I heard a faint rustle to our right. I snapped my eyes open, and quickly raised my rifle.

"Over here!" I yelled, charging across the street. I could hear footsteps moving rapidly in front of me, and I rounded the corner to see a figure in all dark clothing darting across the parking lot of an old strip mall.

I could hear Jax and the rest of the group running behind me, but I focused in on my target. Like my tiger, when something was trying to run away from me, I tunneled in on my target like a lone hunter. I slid my rifle so that it was slung across my back, and I began to pump my arms to a full on sprint. I knew Jax wouldn't be too far behind me as I began to close in on the target. All those years of running really did pay off.

The intruder looked over his shoulder once, and attempted to speed up. I extended my stride, before launching myself forward and latching onto the back of my prey.

Being extremely careful not to let my change occur, I brought the intruder down with me. Jax came up on me, not a few seconds later.

"Get off me, you bitch!" The intruder struggled underneath me, doing everything he possibly could to throw me off. Thankfully, Jax grabbed onto his shoulder and forced him onto his back.

When I saw his face, I jumped back in surprise. The white streaks on the cheeks, the black capital 'R' tattooed on his neck....

"Jax," I said, trying to catch my breath. Jax looked over at me, the same look on his face.

"That's a *Relinquished* member..." I said, my heart dropping.

7

It took me a minute to gather my senses, but when I finally did, the first thing that came to my mind was disbelief. For years, there had been no discussion of the *Relinquished* members and there had been no sightings of them. It was believed that all of them were dead.

"What the hell are you doing here?" Jax asked, pressing down on his shoulder to keep him down on the ground. When the prisoner didn't answer, Jax knelt down with his left knee on the prisoners chest. He let out a loud wail of protest under Jax's crushing weight. "You seem like a Richard, so I think I'm going to call you Richard. I mean it does match that mighty fine tattoo on your neck..."

I looked over at Amanda and Matt, who winced slightly. They must not have been used to seeing Jax interrogate someone before, and for those that hadn't, it could come off as him being pretty cruel.

Richard struggled under the weight of Jax, beginning to wheeze for air. "Go pound sand, Ranger..." Richard hissed.

Out of the corner of my eye, I saw Damian approaching with six soldiers along with the Sector Commander. When he saw Richard squirming under Jax's grip, his eyes widened tremendously.

Jax must have also sensed his presence, forcing the prisoner to his feet. Jax pinned Richard's arm behind his back in a locking position. "Sir, I believe this is the intruder that you were looking for..." Jax stated.

The Sector Commander cleared his throat, and then turned to face Damian. "Right...get this gentleman to my quarters, I will want to question him myself along with you, Damian..." he said, his voice shaking slightly.

"But MacKenzie and Jax caught him, don't you want to get their side of the story?" Matt questioned.

Damian turned to face Matt, their faces inches apart. "That will be the last time you ever question the decisions of your Sector Commander, do you understand?" Damian asked. Matt squared his jaw, and nodded after a moment of hesitation.

Damian turned to face me and Jax next. "As for the two of you, you are not even supposed to be on patrol today. Trying to break the rules and get extra pay are we? I want to see you both in my office first thing tomorrow morning before your shift," Damian hissed, glaring at Jax.

He stormed off after the Sector Commander, the prisoner and the six soldiers that traveled with them. Finally, the alarm stopped blaring. I let out a sigh of relief, happy that the deafening tone was now gone.

Amanda waved farewell, saying that she had to get to base and radio to the approaching Blackhawks that their assistance was no longer needed and to ground their flights or head back to their regular patrols.

After we all returned our M4's, Jax and I joined Katie and Adam in walking back to our quarters. "Well, that certainly was quite eventful. Nice tackle, MacKenzie..." Adam stated, patting me on the shoulder.

"Thanks, but apparently we weren't supposed to be there because we were off duty and now we have to go speak with Damian before shift tomorrow morning..." I said, pushing open the door to the barracks.

"Which doesn't make any sense because all soldiers are supposed to answer that alarm," Jax argued.

"It's probably because it was me and you that were there when he got caught," I said, looking back at Jax.

We all headed for my room, which was seemingly becoming the gathering place for us to all hang out on our nights off.

"He won't...eighty-six you will he?" Katie questioned, shooting a worried look my way.

"I seriously doubt that," Adam said, reassuringly. He looked over at Jax. "Besides, you think he is going to let this guy nab the bad guy, eighty-six him and get the girl in the end?" he said, shoving Jax playfully.

Jax chuckled, rolling his eyes slightly. As I put my key in to unlock the door, I couldn't help but think...getting eighty-sixed with Jax? Maybe that wouldn't be so bad after all. I pushed the door open, bowing my head to conceal my smile. Not bad at all.

We all began our discussions about where this *Relinquished* member could have possibly come from. Was he always randomly in the sectors and now he suddenly made his appearance? Or did he somehow come from the woods?

As we continued this discussion, Katie sat behind me and began to do work on my hair, missing the days that she used to be a hairstylist in civilian life. I loved the feeling of having someone do my hair, it was such a warm and calming touch.

"But how would he get past the fence? Remember what happened with Lenny?" Adam questioned. We all nodded silently.

Lenny was another fellow soldier of ours, who attempted to assassinate the Sector Commander after Damian ordered Lenny's wife be eighty sixed for not paying her taxes. Following this, Lenny then try to scale his building and hop the fence. It didn't end well.

"Regardless of how it happened, lets just hope this was a one time thing.." Katie said, finishing putting my hair up in a fancy half up, half down style. I nodded, my gaze on the floor. The only thing on my mind was the discussion that Jax and I were to have with Damian in the morning and how it could possibly change my fate. I looked up at Jax, who was laughing at a joke that Adam had just told.

If we were eighty-sixed, what would the people in the woods do?

* * *

"Are you ready for this?" Jax asked, as I walked out my door that next morning. I zipped up my jacket, before nodding.

"I mean, as ready as I can be..." I said, with a nervous laugh. Jax smirked, before leading the way outside.

We walked in silence for a few minutes, before Jax spoke up. "You know, if we are eighty sixed...at least I could count on you to do all the hunting for us," he teased. I rolled my eyes.

"Sorry, you're not getting off that easily...I'm not doing all the work for you," I retorted.

"Oh, that's not even the beginning of it. I want ten kids, and they are all going to be trained to be Rangers by the time they are five...and they will all speak German," Jax said, a grin plastered on his face.

"You're completely out of your mind," I replied, before laughing.

"Well if we are surviving in the woods, they have to be like true woodmen..." Jax said. As Jax continued his rant, my mind wandered to thoughts of his wife. What would happen with them if we were eighty-sixed? Jax wouldn't be able to send her any money for support...would she be eighty-sixed from her sector as well? If she were eighty-sixed from her sector, would her and Jax reunite?

I saw him writing a letter to her last night, and it amazed me that even though he hadn't seen her in years, he was still loyal to her and he still loved her. I sincerely hoped that she was the same way with him.

As we approached Sanctum, I couldn't help but notice the growing ivy that was twining its way around the building. Our headquarters was starting to look more and more like a club treehouse rather than our headquarters.

Jax pushed open the door, and we made our way past the long rectangular table and for the door that led to Damian's office.

Jax looked at me and rolled his eyes, before knocking. I smirked, before resting my hand on my M9 for comfort. Putting myself, Jax and Damian in the same room probably wasn't the world's best idea.

"Enter!" Damian called. Jax shook his head and muttered a few swear words, before opening the door. As we filed in to Damian's office, my eyes were drawn immediately to the alligator head that he had sitting on his desk. That, and the smell of cinnamon that randomly filled his office.

Damian rested back in his chair, putting his feet up on his desk. "Well, well, well...if it isn't my two favorite soldiers.." he mocked. He allowed a wicked smirk to cross his face.

"Okay, I lied...I only like one of you to be truthfully honest..." he said, winking in my direction. His eerie smile matched the poster of the Heath Ledger Joker from Batman: The Dark Knight that he had hanging directly behind him. I wondered if that placement was intentional.

"The point, Damian?" Jax questioned, tensing up slightly. I knew that if Damian dared to make one more comment about me, there was nothing to stop Jax from leaping over Damian's desk and strangling him...despite all the clutter of random papers and half-ripped books that were sitting on his desk.

Damian slowly took his feet off his desk, before standing up and walking over to Jax. Jax turned to face him, as Damian stopped inches from Jax's face. "I'll be saying what I want to say, when I feel the need to say it, Jaxsy boy... you may have been a superstar in the military but here...you answer to me," Damian growled, his features turning dark.

It was clear that he was hoping Jax would react, but Jax stood his ground. There were very few things that Jax was actually afraid of. Damian placed his hands on his hips, as if he were waiting for a 'yes sir' or a 'I'll do whatever you say' like many soldiers before Jax would do when Damian would give them such a challenging stare.

I finally had enough, stepping so that they both could see me. "Damian, what duty would you like us to perform today?" I questioned, looking back and forth between the two. Damian finally pulled his stare away from Jax, and turned to face me.

"Be careful with your words, MacKenzie...as there are a few too many ideas that come to mind when you word it like that..." he said, throwing a devious smirk my way. He glared at Jax one last time, before moving back to the other side of his desk.

"I want it to be very clear, despite whether your intentions are good or not, that you will not patrol or participate in any such activities when you are off duty. You're assigned to a patrol for a reason. Not only that, but you're making your fellow soldiers feel as though they can't handle the incidents that are going on during their shift," Damian said, resuming his comfortable place in his chair.

"How do you know that?" Jax questioned.

"It was reported back to me, how else?" Damian asked, his eyes darting to the left. *That's a lie,* I thought to myself as I took notice of his body language. Rather then question it, I let out a sigh.

"Well, pass it on to those soldiers that we are sorry. Now, what would you like us to do today?" I asked, starting to get uncomfortable with being in his presence.

Damian began to turn his chair to the left and right, biting his lip as he did so.

"You're going to patrol the inner city, just so I can keep my eye on the two of you. If I see one toe out of line from either one of you, you both will be brought back here for review..." Damian stated, folding his hands and placing them on his lap.

"Great, looking forward to it..." I said, turning to walk out of the office.

"Ah, ah, ah. I wasn't finished, Ms. Waters..." Damian called, mockingly. I turned back to face him, showing him a hard stare.

"What?" I questioned. At this point, maybe getting eighty-sixed wasn't such a horrible idea if I was going to be under a magnifying glass for the rest of my life.

"Tonight, you both will be guarding my quarters...all night...and then you will patrol the inner city tomorrow," Damian stated.

"Awesome," Jax replied. Jax and I were used to sleep deprivation, so if that was what Damian was going for, then we wouldn't be too phased by it. A smirk appeared on Damian's face, and I knew that there had to be more.

"MacKenzie, you'll be in the room with me...and Jaxsy here will be stationed outside the door," he said.

I saw Jax stand up straight, and his hand began to move towards his M9. "Why in the hell would we agree to that?" Jax asked, infuriated.

"I need to make sure that I have two layers of security. If anything were to get past you, I need to make sure I am protected at...close quarters," Damian said, throwing me an attempted seductive look. I felt a burning sensation in my chest and I closed my eyes and inhaled slightly. I couldn't let my anger take over. I couldn't let the tiger out.

"Besides, my good friend Boris is in charge of the detailed security in your wife's sector...now, if you don't do as I tell you... Boris may just have to do a background check on your wife. If we find one cent short on her taxes or one health code violation.... we may just need to take care of that problem accordingly," Damian said, glaring at Jax.

I saw Jax freeze in his place, unsure of what to say next.

"Well we would hate to disappoint you, so we will do as you say..." I replied, putting my hand on Jax's arm for comfort. "Now, may we get on with our patrols?" I questioned.

Damian nodded, before shooing us away from his desk. "Get, I'll be seeing the two of you tonight."

I turned to walk out the door, pulling a stubborn Jax behind me. We walked out of the building in silence, and headed towards the city square. A couple people would either tip their hats to us or nod respectively, as they headed to their duties for the day.

"What do you say, want to go to the market and grab something to eat?" I questioned, nodding to the woman who was slicing up lunchmeat and cheese. Seeing her cut the meat as she did reminded me of the *Reading Terminal Market* in Philadelphia.

"Sure," Jax muttered, his eyes scanning the crowds of people. I could tell that Damian's words really struck him where it hurt. As we made our way towards the counter, we saw Amanda and Matt sitting at a table, off duty.

"Hey guys," I said, making my way over towards them.

"How's it going today? How did it go with Damian?" Amanda questioned.

I shrugged. "It was a meeting," I said, not wanting to concern them with the details of the task that Jax and I had to perform that night.

"Oh, well the two of you still standing here is a good sign...that means you weren't eighty-sixed as well all feared," Matt replied.

"Mac, you want the usual?" Jax asked, referring to my turkey and cheese with mayo. "Yeah," I said, with a small smile. Jax nodded, before walking up to the counter. I pulled up two chairs next to Matt and Amanda. Jax returned a few minutes later, with both of our sandwiches and two bottles of water.

As he sat down, I noticed his features still looked haunted. I bit my lip, trying to think of a way to distract him. Amanda and Matt looked back and forth between me and Jax, not used to seeing silence between the two of us, even on our bad days.

I tried to distract myself, looking across the way and seeing a group of small boys playing a mock version of soccer with a volleyball. There was this one little boy in a red and white stripped shirt, who would fold his arms and stomp his little feet in frustration every time someone kicked the ball past him. His brown bangs blew in the wind as he looked around the market in bewilderment.

"Did you hear about the prisoner?" Matt asked, stabbing at his salad with his fork.

"Nope, what happened?" I asked, watching the little boy as he wandered over to the fruit stand.

"They released him without trial or without punishment..." Amanda stated, looking back and forth between me and Jax. Jax slowly brought his gaze to meet Amanda's.

"Under whose authority?" Jax questioned.

"The Sector Commander," Amanda responded.

"Where did they release him to?" I asked, finally starting to eat my sandwich.

"I think they escorted him to the gate and sent him back out into the woods. That, or he's roaming around the sector somewhere...which I hope isn't the case. Not only for our safety, but also Jax would probably literally tear him limb from limb," Matt joked.

I looked over at Jax's reaction to see faint traces of a smile tugging at his lip.

"Freakin' Richard..." Jax stated, as he began to spread butter on the top of his roll. "Best of luck to him in the free world...killing people among other stupid crap and being able to get away with it. Meanwhile, those who only ever do good have their presence consistently threatened..."

I looked over at Amanda and Matt, and they shared the same worried expression that I had. I knew Jax was referring to the situation with his wife, but I didn't feel as though it was appropriate to discuss with them, despite how strong our friendship was with them.

"Is that an Italian hoagie?" Matt asked, looking at Jax's lunch.

"That it is,"

"He's not even Italian...." I played. I looked over at Jax, showing him a small smile. "Yet it's his favorite," I said. I finally saw a smirk appear on his face.

"What's that got to do with it?" he questioned.

"I'm just saying, you're as Irish as they get. Shouldn't you be munching on corn beef and cabbage and river dancing in the square?" I played. Jax rolled his eyes, before folding his arms across his chest.

"You know what I think?" Jax questioned, looking over at me.

"What?" I asked.

Across the table, Amanda and Matt exchanged an anxious glance. Jax grinned, before pushing me off of my seat and onto the floor. He, Amanda and Matt let out a wave of thunderous laughter as a look of shock spread across my face.

"You're such a jerk!" I exclaimed, shoving Jax with a laugh. My efforts were meaningless, as Jax barely moved in his place. With that, he wrapped his arm around my neck and held me in a headlock.

"What did you call me?" Jax questioned, laughing.

"You heard what I said," I retorted.

Jax went to make another comment, but a sudden scream caught our attention. My eyes scanned the area, looking for the source of the scream.

When I heard a second one, I saw a woman with light brown hair and a red sun dress frantically attempting to run towards one of the on patrol soldiers. He pushed her back, almost shoving her to the ground.

My brow furrowed in confusion, I wondered what would cause her to randomly charge at the soldier. As I had these thoughts, my mind wandered back to the meeting with Damian and how he would probably come up with a ridiculous rules about intervening with our fellow soldiers work. I didn't even recognize the soldier anyway...he was probably one of Damian's new pawns.

She stood up once more, and charged for the soldier again. I went to make a comment to Jax, but Jax slapped his hand on my shoulder and nodded his head just to the left of the woman. I followed his direction, before my jaw dropped in shock.

I watched as one of our very own, one of our soldiers, seized one of the small boys I saw playing soccer by his collar and lift him off the ground slightly. He began crying out in protest, his small feet kicking back and forth, desperate to find the ground. I narrowed my eyes to see better, and I realized it was the small boy I saw wandering by the fruit stand.

I made the assumption by the sandy brown hair that was falling in his eyes, the woman charging for the soldier was his mother.

This was wrong, this was wrong on all sorts of levels. I stood up from my spot, my fists clenching at my sides. Jax stood up as well, striding over towards the incident.

"What the hell is this all about?" he asked, placing his hand on his M9.

The soldier maintained his grip on the boys collar, laughing as he did so. "You can kick those feet as much as you want boy, you ain't going nowhere!"

As we approached, I could feel the rage building up inside of me. I knew the type of rage that was building up. The feline in me felt the need to protect the young boy, to protect the *cub*. I closed my eyes and tried to steady my breath. I had to maintain control over the raging beast inside of me.

"What are you doing, soldier?" Jax hissed, striding so he was five feet in-front of the rogue soldier. I watched as the soldier lowered the boy to the ground, and fixated his grip on the boys arm.

"The boy stole food for the third time this week, and we finally caught the bloke," the soldier stated. I watched as the boy began to thrash around under the arm hold.

"That doesn't given you the right to treat him as an animal," Jax stated, as he squared his jaw. I fixated my eyes upon the soldier's black leather jacket, where the name *Wesson* was stitched.

60

"Look, the Sector Commander said all those that break the law need to be made an example of. This kid has gotten away twice, which means there needs to be extra punishment. Can't have any little rascals going and becoming *Relinquished* members now can we?" Wesson questioned.

"My family needs it! We have no food," the boy protested, trying to pull free again. I went to speak, but Wesson beat us to it.

"You keep your mouth shut when talking to a soldier," Wesson hissed.

"I think you're the one who needs to keep your mouth shut..." I spoke up, beginning to lose my grip. The fire in my chest was burning, and I could feel my breath becoming heavier as I attempted to maintain control.

Wesson turned to face me. "Why don't you get lost, girly? Cause once I'm done taking care of this kid and then your boyfriend, you'll be next. I follow the Sector Commander's orders, not yours...."

So now he was threatening Jax as well as the young boy. This was starting to go too far. I had no idea what he meant by the Sector Commander giving such orders as to harm people, we were always told to protect and serve the public. Wesson was not only going way out of line but he was also a liar. Even if the Sector Commander ordered a release of the prisoner without just cause, I couldn't see him ordering the punishment of his people...especially kids.

Jax stepped so he was a mere foot away from Wesson. "Let the boy go, and we can talk about this like grown adults. Or is your mind still conformed to that of a child?" Jax questioned.

Wesson made to respond, but at that moment the small boy turned and bit Wesson's hand with all of his might. Wesson groaned in agony, before turning and grabbing the boy once again, before his open palm came across the boys face. That was the straw that broke the camels back.

I could no longer control the rage that built up inside me. I could feel the fire that was building up in my chest explode. I couldn't contain the beast anymore. In over a decade, I had never lost control like this.

I let the war cry that was sitting in my throat erupt, as I found myself leaping towards Jax and Wesson. In that moment, I saw all three of them turn and face me and immediately after they did, Wesson's face twisted in fear.

I felt my spine straighten out, and my hands that were outstretched in-front of me slowly began to change. My body collided with his, and I pinned him underneath of me. His body began to shake uncontrollably, as he struggled to form words. His breathing was rapidly increasing, and I could smell the fear on him. I could feel the vibes of his fear pulsating throughout the air. I saw the reflection of my tiger in his eyes.

With the anger still running through my body, I let out a loud roar directly in his face. His fear intensified, and he began to wiggle underneath me. He began to let out squeals of petrified protest, and my senses were flooded with his fear.

I placed my paw next to his face and continued to growl. I could kill him, I could take his life for what he did to the helpless child with no remorse. With that, I pulled my paw back and extended my claws, preparing to strike.

At that moment, I realized what happened. I stepped back, and looked over at Jax and the boy. The boy was smiling widely, as if he were thinking '*cool!*'

Jax's eyes were widened slightly as if to say *'oh shit'*. Everyone else that was in the area was staring at me, and I could smell the fear in the population. It seemed as though no one wanted to move, they were all just staring at me. Wesson's partner began to slowly move towards him, his hands raised in the air and his weapon on the ground behind him.

The young boy's mother brought her hand to her gaping mouth, her eyes still widening in horror. I looked around, beginning to panic myself. It was all over, my secret was out and this time, there was no one, nothing to hide it. The eerie silence that filled the area was making me even more anxious. I hated that kind of silence.

I heard Wesson stir behind me, as he pulled out his can of OC spray. My lip curled up in a snarl, as I let out another roar. I leapt over his figure, and began to take off down the street. I could hear Wesson screaming on his radio for back-up, as well as Jax calling my name. I continued to sprint down the road, in my tiger form. I knew I could not change, for obvious reasons.

Any shape-shifter will tell you that when you change into your alternate form, your clothes get torn and destroyed, and you transform back naked. I sprinted as fast as my legs would carry me, before I stumbled upon our living quarters.

I scanned the area, before closing my eyes. I centered my focus on thinking of my human form, and shortly after I felt my back straighten upright. I opened my eyes and quickly grabbed the potted plant in-front of me, using it to cover myself up.

My hand was shaking as I grabbed onto the door handle, before I sprinted into the building, dropping the plant in the process. My heart was pounding so loud I could hear it in my own ears.

I made my way down the hallway and threw open the door to my room. After quickly slamming the door shut, I took a minute to catch my breath. What had I just done? Why did I just expose myself?

I pressed my palms to my skull, cursing the tiger inside of me. Cursing her existence and my gift. "Why, why did you do that?" I questioned.

"Because you wanted me to," her voice rang in my head. I paused for a second, before looking at the floor. Did I?

I eyed my closet, and rushed over. Jax would not be far behind, and I had to make sure that I was decent before he showed up. I grabbed onto my black laced bra along with the matching underwear. As I began to dress myself, I began to wonder what would happen to me. Now that I had exposed myself to the public, I could no longer hide. My secret was known to the world.

Would they try to kill me? Unless they had a blade made of pure gold lying around, they wouldn't be able to kill me. But how long would it be until they figured that out? My weakness?

My mind immediately raced to being eighty-sixed. Oh god. Being eighty-sixed and on my own in the woods...with those people I saw at the fence.

As I pulled the black tank top over my head, I heard a knock on my door. I hurriedly grabbed my charcoal running shorts, as I scampered over to the door.

I looked through the eyehole to see Jax standing there, looking around. I sighed in relief, before throwing the door open. Before I could say anything, the next thing I knew Jax had his arms around me in a tight embrace. I was so startled that I let the door shut on its own, as I slowly brought my hands to return the hug. We had only ever embraced like this a few times, the last one being two years ago at the funeral for one of our fallen battle buddies.

"That was incredibly brave," he said, into my hair. After a minute he pulled away, and gazed into my eyes.

"Thanks, but I'm pretty screwed right now. Now the whole public knows. Remember what happened last time someone revealed themselves? They were....gone...the next day," I said, looking to the floor.

Jax used his hand to turn my face so that it was back on him. "I'm not going to let that happen to you," he said, softly. He motioned for me to follow him down the hallway, quickly. We arrived at his room, and he pulled me in quickly.

"Jax, this is the first place they will look for me..." I said, taking in the surroundings of his room. It smelt like a fresh, pinewood forest. Jax turned to face me, about to speak. At that moment, there was a knock on his door.

He held a finger up to me, as he looked through the eyehole. "Its your friend, Katie..." he said, sounding somewhat annoyed. I couldn't help but smile at this. He looked back at me, as if to look for permission to let her in. I nodded, suddenly wondering where Amanda and Matt where.

I sincerely hoped that they hadn't been seized for questioning, especially since they didn't know anything. I slowly sat down in the bed, pushing a bunch of folded t-shirts out of my way. Jax opened the door, and moments later Katie came running in and dove to embrace me in a hug. At this point I was zoning out with thoughts of what could happen that I barely heard what she was whispering in my ear.

I began wondering how long it would be before the Sector Commander found out what was going on with me. Especially after the last one of my kind was revealed to the public. The sector commander made a public announcement for any remaining *'Anomics'* as he called us, to come forward or face a heavier penalty if they were to be discovered. What would that penalty be? Would I be...executed? Publicly? Just like the innocent death we witnessed this morning?

"Mac?!" Katie said, shaking my shoulders. I shook my head, and met her gaze.
"What?" I questioned.
"Why didn't you ever tell me about this? I would have.... I would have..." Katie began, struggling to find words. I knew that she was aware what could happen to me, and she felt helpless for not being able to do anything at the moment.
"Katie, its okay..." I said, trying to reassure myself. Jax bit his lip, and began going on a rant with Katie on how they were going to keep me hidden, or what the next move should be. As I looked back and forth between the two of them, I knew that if I couldn't protect myself, I had to protect them. It would destroy me if something happened to them.
"I have to leave," I stated, weakly. Katie and Jax both stopped their talking, and turned to face me.
"Mac, no... we will work this out...." Jax said, trying to hide whatever he was really feeling.
"No, we can't....I'm not taking you all down with me. Maybe if we give it some time, we can figure out a way to get me back in somehow, I don't know. The point is that I have to go," I said, standing up.
Katie began to wipe silent tears away from her face, and Jax put his hands on his hips. He looked around the room before grabbing one of his gray hoodies from his closet. He handed it to me, muttering for me to put the hoodie on. After I was dressed, with the hood up, we began to head in the direction for the gate. Jax ordered Katie to stay back closer to the barracks, to cause a diversion if need be.

64

She embraced me tight, whispering in my ear promises that she would find a way to get me back into the sector. When I pulled away, I patted her shoulder.

"Just keep an eye on this one for me," I said, inclining my head towards Jax. She nodded again, before turning away to hide the tears that were slowly making their way down her face.

Jax put his arm around my shoulders, steering me to continue moving. Katie was probably my best friend here in this sector, aside from Jax. When we created the sectors, any friends that I had from deployments or from growing up had either passed during the war or they were currently in different sectors. Whether they remained alive or not was hard to say. I bit my lip and tilted my head down so that I could hide my tears. I was really, really going to miss Katie.

The gate came into view, and Jax walked over to the control box. I watched him as he began to fiddle with it, trying to get it working as quickly as possible. Jax had been involved in the actual eighty-sixing before, so I couldn't even imagine how he was feeling right now. I folded my arms to try and keep myself warm from the breeze that was suddenly starting to pick up.

After a few minutes, a mechanical buzzing sound was heard and the metal gate swung open. I walked forward, looking deep into the wooded area. The woods seemed calm, and undisturbed...almost as if they were welcoming me to enter them.

"MacKenzie..." Jax said, coming up behind me. I turned to face him just as a crack of thunder echoed through the area, Jax's face lit up from the illumination of the lightning. Moments later, I could feel the rain hitting the ground. The smell of dew and wet pine flooded my senses, and I folded my arms to keep myself warm. I looked up at Jax, unsure of how this was exactly going to happen.

He placed both his hands on my shoulders, stepping so that he was inches away from me. As I gazed into his eyes, I couldn't help but hate myself. I wasn't strong enough to contain my power in such a common situation. I knew that what Wesson was doing was all sorts of wrong, but I had seen much worse happen before and I was actually able to control it. Now, because I was a fool, I had to leave the only life I had grown to know. Jax tilted my head upwards to look at him, a few raindrops slowly making their way down his face. How long would it be until I got to gaze into those eyes again?

My breath quickened, as he brought his body up against mine. He didn't even have to say a word, but in that moment I was instantly intoxicated by his presence. I didn't care if he was married, my heart was absolutely throbbing in my chest for him.

"I'm sorry," I whispered, my voice starting to break. I could feel the burning sensation in my throat, as I struggled to not completely lose it. I was a strong woman, I refused to break.

"I'll get you back," Jax whispered, in return. My heart skipped a beat as Jax leaned into me, his hot breath rolling on my lips. I closed my eyes, taking a quick moment to enjoy and take comfort in the feel of being so close to him.

"Traitor!" A voice cried out.

Jax pulled back, and we watched as the Sector Commander approached with Damian, a few of Damian's minions, and a good group of about thirty civilians. My eyes scanned the crowd, I didn't even have to use my feline senses to know that they were extremely terrified.

My eyes worked their way back to Damian and the Sector Commander. Damian carried a large bundle of rope in his left hand, and a walkie talkie in the other. When the lightning flashed once more, I could see the wicked smirk on Damian's face.

"Heard you had something to show us, MacKenzie. Though I must say... I am surprised. I knew there was something special about you, but I never suspected you to be an Anomic..." Damian said, as he began to unravel the rope.

"I'm leaving, Damian....so whatever your plan is with the rope, is pointless. I'll save you all the trouble..." I said, eyeing it.

Damian shook his head, before pushing his now soaked bangs out of his face. A wicked grin crossed his face. "This isn't for you, my dear..."

Two soldiers seized me underneath my arms, and forced me to my knees. I began to struggle as I attempted to throw them off of me. In my struggle, I could see a third and fourth coming to assist. One of them shoved my head towards the ground, turning me so that I looked over towards Jax, who was fighting off six soldiers about his size as Damian began to tie the rope into what looked like a noose.

"Jax!" I yelled, using whatever strength I had left to get my attackers off of me. Jax was also forced to his knees, a few feet away from me. I looked up at Damian, full of hate. The Sector Commander nodded to him, and Damian's smirk extended to a grin.

"You know...MacKenzie... if you had just followed the rules the first time, you never would have been there to see that small boy getting punished. I must say, being away from the Army has made you go soft...what happened to the tough girl?" Damian questioned, squatting down next to me. I eyed him, gritting my teeth in anger.

"Just let me go, and let Jax go. I'm leaving on my own accord,"

"Exactly. Leaving is supposed to be punishment for you, not something you embrace or decide that its perfectly fine for you whenever you feel the urge. So before you do go, you must be punished first..."

"That's fine, punish me however your heart desires. Now, let Jax go..." I spat. It wouldn't be the first time that I got beaten for withholding information.

"Oh no, that's part of the punishment my dear. You see, Jaxsy over here is going to be a little bit suspended over there while my boys...have some fun with him," Damian said, nodding over to the pull-up bars that were right near the gate. I never understood why they were there, I always assumed that the gate guards got bored and needed some place to practice do pull-ups to pass the time.

"Damian, you're making a huge mistake...." I said, my anger rising as I watched him walk over to Jax and throw a rope over his neck. Damian rolled his eyes in response, and waved at me dismissively. He took a second to use the downpour, and slick his hair back.

"Take care of it, boys...." Damian said, walking back over to the Sector Commander. I was starting to feel so weak from continuing to fight against the soldiers who were pinning me to the ground, but I couldn't let him do this to Jax. I turned my head as much as I could to look up at the Sector Commander, who was biting his fingernails in boredom.

I heard Jax let out a grunt of pain, and I could see them literally dragging him over to the pull-up bars with the rope around his neck, laughing as they did so. I gritted my teeth, my breathing getting out of control. I looked back and forth between the group of people that were in front of me, all their laughter starting to ring in my ears. Damian continued to laugh, as he walked over to Jax, bringing his fist across his face.

In that moment, something inside me snapped. Red blurred my vision. I was literally seeing red.

*Kill them, kill them all....*my tiger's voice rang in my head.

"Get...off..of...me!" I hissed, summoning the tiger inside of me. Within seconds of my change starting, I could hear the soldiers that were pinning me down fleeing towards the group of civilians. When I finally finished changing, I looked over towards the soldiers who had Jax pinned down. They dropped the rope in shock, raising their hands in surrender.

I hissed, before looking over at the Sector Commander, who was attempting to back away very slowly. My eyes narrowed, and I launched myself towards him. He attempted to run, his feet scuttling on the ground in panic. I was much too fast, my body colliding with his within seconds.

I could feel his body wriggling underneath mine, his buttons from his trench coat scratching against my stomach. "P...Please Ms. Waters, I meant no harm to you!!" he cried, as tears of fear mixed with the rain and began to spill down his face. I hissed, bringing my teeth centimeters from his face.

"You meant no harm? I thought that I was a horrible liar...give me one good reason why I shouldn't kill you all right now,"

I heard the sound of a gunshot, and felt something sharp bounce off my side. The bullet ricochet, striking one of Damian's minion soldiers in the chest. As his body collapsed, I looked for the source of the bullet...and saw Damian standing there with his .45 out. I couldn't help but chuckle as I saw traces of fear in Damian's eyes.

"I don't suppose that this is a good time to tell you that your guns mean nothing on me..." I growled.

Damian looked down at the Sector Commander. "Then how did you have the rest of her kind killed?" he questioned, getting agitated.

"I sent them off to be executed..." he said, breathing heavily under my weight.

"That's right, you slimy bastard. Now this is how this is going to work...or I will literally rip your face off. One, you are going to let me go into the woods on my own accord. Two, you will let Jax go back to the sector where he will continue to be a soldier here. Three, you will not pursue after him or any of my friends in this sector....or Jax's wife," I paused to press one of my paws on his chest, causing him to grunt in agony.

"If you violate any of these rules....I will come back. I will find a way back into the sector..." I paused, to think of the eighty-sixers in the woods. "And I won't come back alone either. You think I'm the only one of my kind left?"

"There are others in the sector?" Damian questioned, lowering his gun. I looked up at him, growling as I did so.

"No, I am alone. I have been for the past three years...after you had Leo killed.." I stated, remembering the day I got the news about Leo. We didn't grow close until after we discovered we were the only two in the sector with the gift. When he got discovered, I went to visit him in prison. He told me not to get caught, because it was my father's dying wish that I survive.

I turned my attention back to the Sector Commander. "Will you honor my wishes? Or would you rather I just end this here....and now?" I questioned, putting more weight on his chest. He began to wheeze uncontrollably as purple filled his face. He nodded, struggling to breathe.

"Good, now why don't you let my friend go?" I questioned, looking over at Jax. I released my hold on the Sector Commander, who put his hand to his chest in pain. His breathing slowed, as he made eye contact with me. I curled my lip up slightly, revealing all of my teeth.

"Let the boy go," he coughed. The soldiers standing around Jax looked each other, and then looked at Damian for approval.

"Do it!" the Sector Commander yelled, wheezing.

The immediately began to untie him, tossing the rope to the side. Jax stood up, looking over at me. I could see the sadness in his eyes, knowing that this could very well be one of the last times that he would ever see me. I bowed my head, before giving the Sector Commander one last growl as I walked past him. The hoodie that Jax gave me laid on the ground, now with a huge rip in the middle. I bent down, picking it up with my mouth.

I could hear Damian and his minions ordering the civilians to head back to their homes, as they were about to instill a curfew for all non-essential personnel. I turned around and glared at the Sector Commander one last time.

"I mean it. You better stick to your word, or you will be the first one I come for..." I said.

He nodded, backing away slowly. "I will...." he muttered, turning around and hurrying towards his building. Soon it was just me and Jax standing there, not wanting to say goodbye.

"You know...you could have threatened them to let you stay...would have been perfectly okay with that option," Jax said, forcing a chuckle. I shook my head.

"I'm more vulnerable in my human form. The second I changed back, they would be on me like white on rice...and then they would have the rest of you executed. I can't risk that. This way, I'm still a threat to them," I stated.

Jax nodded, before approaching me. "Well, I will see you down the road, battle..." he said, hesitating to reach up and pet my head. I purred slightly under his touch.

"This just got a little weird..." Jax chuckled. I smiled in return, before backing away.

"I really should go," I said, picking up the hoodie in my mouth again.

"I know you'll be back," Jax said.

I nodded in return, before turning away and facing the woods. I didn't know what would be waiting for me out there, but all I knew was that I had to survive the isolation, at least for awhile so that I could one day return and get my friends back. Maybe I could even start my own sector one day.

I lunged into the woods, taking off through the trees. I forgot how amazing it felt, the rush of being free. No boundaries, and no rules, free. It wasn't until I turned around at the sound of the gate closing that I realized one thing. All freedom came with a cost. My cost right now, was realizing that I was truly alone.

8.

I had been walking through the woods for what I assumed to be a good two hours before I finally decided to stop and take a break. As I laid down, the many leaves crunching under my body as I did so, I began to slap myself mentally for changing like I did without thinking of the repercussions. I now had no clothes, with the exception of Jax's now torn hoodie. I didn't even have a needle and string to sew it back together, so now it could either serve as a bath robe or as a blanket to keep myself warm at night.

I looked up, at the large green leaves that blocked the sunlight. Would this be one of those situations where I became a 'nature girl' or something and put together an outfit made entirely of leaves and grass?

I sighed, before laying my head down on my paws. I began to replay the incident with the small child in my head. I hated myself for changing in public like I did, it cost me everything that I ever had. All my belongings, all my friends, and all the memories were gone. I knew Jax and Katie would probably salvage as much as they could from my belongings before Damian and his soldiers got them, but I loved going to bed every night and being able to say goodnight to my parents, even if it was just a photo on the wall.

I loved having my favorite stuffed animal from my childhood, Kitty, sitting in the corner of my bed. Kitty had even come with me on my deployments, so Jax knew how important she was to me.

As I had these thoughts, I also remembered the face of the mother who embraced her child after I had saved him from Wesson. Even though she was slightly frightened, I saw her smile before I sprinted off towards my quarters. It was a simple, thankful smile. As a soldier, I always took comfort in doing good and saving others at the end of the day.

I laid on my side, resting against the large oak tree. I supposed I could take comfort in that fact. I saved a young boy from an unpredicted fate. Wesson mentioned that he was going to be 'punished'. What did punishment mean nowadays? I looked around the woods, hearing faint chirps of birds. The large oak trees and scattered leaves all over the ground brought me great comfort, as I slowly began to close my eyes. After the day's activities, all I wanted in that moment was to close my eyes and dream of a better solution to my problems...

***

"Dad, I don't want to...."

"MacKenzie, you have to... you have to practice your change, otherwise you will never fully understand how to control your power..."

71

"Dad, I don't want this power! I don't want to be this stupid tiger, I want to be a wolf. Wolves are much cooler, I don't want to be a stupid cat...." the small girl said, crossing her arms angrily. The man laughed, before putting his hands on her shoulders.

"MacKenzie, did you know that tigers symbolize strength and that in history, we are known as Guardians?" he questioned. The small girl looked up at him, tilting her head slightly.

"Really?" she questioned, suddenly intrigued.

He nodded, kneeling down so that he was at her level. "Tigers are the biggest cats in the world, MacKenzie. That is why we symbolize strength. While many people fear us, it is our duty to protect them..."

"But why am I different than anyone else in the family? How come you and momma are white tigers like me, but no one else is? I don't want to be different....I want to be like everyone else,"

"MacKenzie.... you are still young. One day, your mother and I won't be here anymore. One day, our people are going to need a leader. It will be up to you to lead us, to lead our kind and save us...you are my oldest child. One day you will be the ruler of our people,"

She tilted her head, a small smirk on her face. "Like a Queen?" she asked, swaying from side to side. He laughed, nodding.

"Just like a Queen...but before you become that Queen, you have to learn control. You have to learn how to control your gift. Which means, you are going to have to practice changing..." he said, standing up.

He walked behind her, turning her to face the woods. "Now, there is a river in the woods. I want you to run out, and grab us as many fish as you can. As a leader, you must learn to take care of your people. It is your duty tonight to make sure that your family is fed..."

She shuddered slightly, the shadows of the dark woods scaring her. She had never been on a mission without her father before. "Dad, I'm scared..." she said, looking up at him.

"I know, MacKenzie...but remember what I said? A leader must take care of their people...facing their fears to ensure that their people are safe. You're not alone, MacKenzie. Your tiger spirit will guide you...let her in, but don't let her take full control. I have full confidence in you, MacKenzie..." he said, kissing the top of her head.

"Now, go...." he said, folding his arms.

She inhaled deeply, before sprinting off into the woods. She wanted to make her family proud, she wanted to protect them. As she leapt into the air, her tiger ready for her, she started to understand her purpose.

***

I woke up from my dream to the sound of something crashing to my left, and I abruptly sat up, trying to shake myself out of the fog of waking up. I was surprised to still be in my tiger form as I did so, normally whenever I slept I woke up in my human form. Maybe my tiger thought it unethical for me to wake up in the middle of the woods naked in my human form.

I heard the sound of footsteps and I growled slightly. Whatever was out there, had better come prepared. I was currently beyond the point of caring right now. A few seconds later, a man dressed in black stepped out from behind the trees.

The icy blue eyes, the short cropped hair....he was one of the men that I saw in the woods when I was with Katie. I couldn't forget those eyes if I wanted to. I growled again, remembering that he had also been the one to glare at me and attempt to come at me, aggressively so.

However, this time there was no glare in his eyes. He looked, surprisingly relaxed as he stepped closer to me. Even my tiger spirit seemed relaxed, and slightly intrigued by his presence. He raised his hands in surrender, stopping a few feet away from me.

"MacKenzie...." he started, slowly taking one more step towards me. I stood up on all fours, staring him down.

"How do you know who I am?" I asked, gritting my teeth in anger.

"I would be perfectly happy to explain all this to you in given time. First, I need you to change back to yourself. If you follow me back to our camp like that, you're going to freak a lot of people out..." he said, calmly.

"Yeah. Like I'm going to change in front of some wild-man and expose myself to your eyes. I know that it may have been awhile since you had the pleasure of indulging in a naked girl in front of you. Sorry, not all about that..." I hissed, moving to turn away.

"I have clothes for you..." he said, holding up what looked to be a blue tunic and matching pants. I tilted my head, tempted by the lure of being able to get back into my human form and in civilian clothes. A sudden thought brought me back to reality.

"How did you know to bring clothes with you? Do you just happen to carry a spare set with you at all times in case you run into an Anomic like me?" I questioned.

"No, I've been watching you since you had that little showdown at the gate..."

"Yeah, that's not creepy or anything..."

"Look, you have two options. Come back with me, or sit here and never get the opportunity to have clothes or any form of supply again...since I'm the only distributor out here. I'm good, either way..." he stated, holding the clothes out to me.

I sniffed the air subtly, before considering my options. It would be nice to get changed into regular clothes again. Besides, if he betrayed me I could always threaten to eat him. That usually worked.

I overlooked his figure, surveying him. He wasn't all that bad looking, in fact, he was actually quite attractive and I supposed it would be a good idea to rejoin the human population again...especially if they knew something about me and my family's history.

"Fine, but go stand behind the tree while I change." I snapped.

He smirked, placing the clothes on the large root in front of me that was protruding from the ground. "As you wish," he said, moving so that the tree blocked his path. I waited for a second, before closing my eyes and concentrating and focusing on my human self. I felt myself change, and the second I did, I finally realized how cold it was. I let out a slight whimper, as the cool breeze hit my bare skin.

"What seems to be the problem?" his voice called, from the other side of the tree.

"Nothing, its just cold. Stay behind that tree..." I snapped, grabbing the tunic and pants.

I could hear him laughing. "I wasn't planning on moving, anyway.."

After I finished dressing, I hurriedly ran my fingers through my hair, ensuring that there were no leaves or wild critters in it. "Okay, I'm done..." I said, placing my hands on my hips.

He stepped out, his arms folded across his chest. He smirked, overlooking my figure. "That's much better. I think life out here will suit you well, MacKenzie..." he said.

"What's that supposed to mean?"

"What? I can't say that the whole 'wild girl' look suits you?"

"I swear, I will bite you..." I snapped.

"Ohhh...scary," Ryder said, raising his hands mockingly.

"Well since you claim to know so much about me, can I at least know what your name is? Before I follow you off on the yellow brick road?" I questioned, folding my arms across the chest.

He nodded, his eyes making direct contact with mine. "Ryder. Ryder Whitlock,"

He stepped forward, extending his hand to mine. I looked down at his hand, before extending mine to his as well. His hands were strong, and he maintained a good handshake. My father had always taught me that you could tell a lot about a person by their handshake.

Which suited me well later in life, when I interviewed to work at a veterinary hospital as a teenager. The practice manager complimented my positivity along with my handshake.

Ryder let go, inclining his head for me to follow him into the woods. "Let's go, it's not very far,"

9

I turned around and looked back towards the sector one last time, before following him deeper into the woods. The only thing on my mind was what would happen to my friends while I remained out here in the woods, without any guarantee of seeing them ever again. I knew my threat would not be taken lightly, but at the same time, everything was changing. The sector was changing daily, and even though I was now wandering through the woods with a complete stranger, I made it my goal to return and to fix things. I would find a way back, and I would rescue my friends.

I looked at the back of Ryder's head, for once in my life actually getting uncomfortable with the awkward silence.

"How long have you been out here in the woods? I don't remember ever seeing you in our Sector," I questioned.

"There were a lot of people cast into the woods that day, MacKenzie. When the sectors were first established...but I guess you would know that, right? You were one of the soldiers that guarded the gate for hours on end, making sure that no one tried coming back in..." Ryder stated, not even turning around.

"I had no idea what I was doing. I was just following orders, like a soldier is supposed to do,"

"Well, you may recognize some people out here. I'm going to warn you though...they may not be too fond of a Sector Soldier joining our group. Then again, you wouldn't be the first..." Ryder trailed, pausing to look around the woods.

My heart skipped a beat for a second. There was another Soldier like me that had been eighty-sixed? Did that mean that he or she was with Ryder's group of woodland yelpies right now?

"No, he is no longer with us. He passed on to the next life," Ryder said, as if he could read my mind.

"Oh," I said, somewhat disappointed.

"You know, I actually expected more whining to be truthfully honest. Most civilized women have issues when first introduced into the woodland life," Ryder said, with a small laugh.

"Like a damsel in distress in the movies? Sorry to disappoint you...that's not me," I said, defensively. Ryder chuckled slightly, knocking down some tall weeds that were in our path.

We walked on for what seemed to be about thirty minutes, before I could finally see smoke. My nostrils were instantly filled with the scent of meat cooking. Ryder stopped in his tracks, once we reached a bunch of hanging vines, and he turned to face me. We made eye contact for a split second, and then he pushed the vines aside. I stepped through, and stopped as soon as I did.

There were large, fifteen person tents set up variously throughout the open circle in the woods. I could see a fire pit in the center, with some sort of wild animal on a spick roasting. There were people wearing a different colored tunics and pants, wandering variously. I saw one person instructing a teenage boy how to aim a bow and arrow, an elderly woman using her hands to dig a hole in the ground before throwing a seed in it, and two men stacking wood just to name a few.

I couldn't help but let my jaw drop in shock at how civilized they all appeared to be. It looked as though they were a large group of friends on a camping trip, just hanging out in the woods. I heard laughter and turned to see a younger man, in his twenties perhaps, waving his hands around as if he were telling the group of small children some crazy story.

Ryder stepped up so he was next to me. "You know, you really do make a better door than a window." he muttered.

As soon as Ryder stepped up next to me, everyone turned their gaze towards us. There was a wave of silence that passed through the crowd. The two men who were fighting with wood katanas to our left approached us, slamming their fist to their hearts and bowing their heads in respect.

"Chief Ryder, we are most pleased to see that you returned safely..." the first one said, his hazel eyes glowing with relief.

"Thank you, Joseph. She wasn't too much trouble after all..." Ryder said, putting his hand on my shoulder. Joseph turned to face me, bowing his head slightly.

"My lady," he said, respectfully.

The man Joseph was sparring with was quick on the approach, pointing his katana at me accusingly. "Wait, isn't that girl a Sector Soldier?" he hissed, angrily. After this statement, everyone in the camp's eyes turned to face me. I didn't even have to have my feline senses to instantly feel the wave of hate that they were all feeling.

"I've seen her patrolling along the fence before!"

A few people even stood up, and began walking towards me. I eyed them all, trying to plan my attack if they all decided to attempt to mug me. Joseph took a step back, looking at me as if he were sizing me up.

"She shouldn't be welcome here!" a random voice called from the crowd. I looked around, realizing more people must have come out of their tents while I was occupied on the ones that were already in my personal space.

Before I could think any further, I felt Ryder's strong hand land on my shoulder and I couldn't help but feel relieved.

"I'm going to make one thing very clear right now. While MacKenzie is here, she will be treated with the utmost respect. You will treat her just as you would treat your fellow brother and sisters you have known for all these years. Yes, she was a Sector Soldier..." he paused to look at me, and then look back out at the gathering crowd.

"I have been watching her the past week very closely. She stood up to her own to save a child's life, and she made the sacrifice of giving up her civilized life to spare the life of her partner and her friends. Let this be a lesson to you all, judge not someone by their past...for you do not truly know their story," he stated, staring down the original accuser.

He nodded, backing away with his head down in shame. Joseph looked at me, bowing his head. "Welcome to our family, MacKenzie.."

I cringed slightly at his comment. It had been such a long time since I had even been considered a part of anyone's family after what happened to mine.

"Thank you," I said, somewhat uncomfortable. Ryder nudged me forward, his hand still on my shoulder. As he guided me through the crowd, I could feel almost every person reaching out and touching the top of my head. Normally I would lash out at the touch of people I had just met. Now whether it was the fact that I was surrounded and outnumbered, or the comfort of Ryder's touch, I just let it go.

Ryder directed me towards a small brown tent, turning back to the crowd. "Carry on," he ordered, following me into the tent.

"What was with all the touching?" I asked, expressing how uncomfortable I was now that I was no longer in a public setting.

"It was a blessing, welcoming you to us. You'll come to find out that we aren't just a group of tree-huggers who have nothing better to do with their time other than eat roots and roll around in the dirt," Ryder stated, pulling the curtain down to cover the door.

"I could have just changed in front of them and threatened to eat them all. That seems to consistently help me get people to do what I wish,"

Ryder strode over to me, stopping inches from my face. I found myself having to catch my breath due to the now very narrow gap that separated us.

"I'm going to make one thing extremely clear while you are here, MacKenzie. You will not harm or threaten anyone in this camp. You will not reveal your power to them until I feel as though they are ready to see it. Do we understand each other?" he questioned.

"Are there others like me out here?" I asked, intentionally ignoring his question. He let out a deep sigh, before he began to circle me as if he were sizing me up.

78

As he began to circle me, I could feel the tension rising. My muscles tightened, as I turned my head to face him.

His arms were folded across his chest, his biceps were straining to fit in his black tunic. His icy blue eyes connected with mine, and he pressed his lips together in a tight line. I was beginning to grow rapidly annoyed with him observing me the way he was.

"Are we just going to keep playing this circling game or are you actually going to tell me what you're doing? Or answer my question?" I asked, obviously annoyed.

Ryder stopped in his tracks, directly in front of me. He overlooked my figure once more, before taking a step closer to me so that he was merely a foot away. My immediate reaction was to take a step back. I was not used to, nor was I comfortable with having someone extremely close to me.

He allowed a small smirk to cross his face. "Yes, lets talk about that gift of yours. How long have you possessed this power?" he asked. I narrowed my eyes slightly and scoffed.

"Why should I grant you the liberty of knowing that when you didn't even answer my question?" I questioned.

He continued to stare at me, the same hardened expression on his face. I sighed, not wanting to deal with being stared at for the rest of the day, even if he did look a little like Oliver Queen from *Arrow*, a show I frequently watched on my Netflix during my deployment...thanks to Jax for getting me hooked on it.

"Since I was born, if you knew anything about the history of my kind then you would know we were born this way," I replied.

He ran a hand over his buzz cut. I didn't notice it before, but right then I realized that his haircut was most certainly military style. He had to have been in the service at some point, or have had family members in the service.

"Not quite, MacKenzie, it works the same as those creatures...werewolves or whatever they are called these days. You can change by bite as well. Although, it doesn't happen immediately," he said, tilting his head to the side. I watched as he overlooked my figure. "But that's a different story for another day..." he said.

I narrowed my eyes in anger.

"You know what's about to be different? You're face in about ten seconds if you don't stop looking at me like that," I snapped.

He then allowed a light chuckle to escape his lips, his eyes dancing with laughter. "I had a feeling that you would be a feisty one," he said, folding his arms once more.

I rolled my eyes, before copying his movement. "I'm not in the mood to play games with you, and I don't have to stay here if I don't want to. So you and your yuppie tree climbers have fun, thanks for the blessing, I will be just fine on my own.." I said, turning to walk away from him.

Before I could move any further, he slid in-front of me, blocking me from any further movement. "I wouldn't recommend that. There are far worse things than *eighty-sixers* in these woods. I understand your anger, and that you want to go back. You cannot, at least not at this time..." Ryder said.

I opened my mouth to reply, but he spoke up again. "There will come a day when, yes, we will get back home. We will get *you* back home, MacKenzie. Not this day though," he said, his voice getting somewhat quiet. I tilted my head slightly.

"What do you mean that we will get back home?" I questioned, curious.

"Every system fails," he stated.

"System?" I questioned, confused.

"The Sector System. Its changing," he said, looking down at the ground.

The first question on my mind was how Ryder knew that being that he lived in the woods. However, I thought back to the conversation with Major Chase...and how he mentioned something about the sectors changing. I looked back over at Ryder, wondering if he frequently communicated with people in my old sector.

He stared at me for a few seconds, before he began walking away. "I'll show you to your sleeping quarters," he said, motioning for me to follow. I slowly began to move after him, maintaining my situational awareness.

He pushed open the flap that lead outside and I raised my hand to shield myself from the bright sunlight. I continued to follow him, passing by many people who looked up at us from their spots on the ground, doing whatever they were partaking in. I heard the sound of leaves crunching to my left, and my head immediately snapped in the direction.

Out of habit, I reached for my hip to grab my pistol. After realizing it wasn't there, I came to my senses. I no longer had my pistol with me, it was probably sitting in Damian's office for a forensic investigation.

Ryder stopped in-front of me, turning to face the direction also. I could see the tall weeds parting, as something approached the camp.

I watched as a female with waist length brown hair and clear blue eyes approached, a group of four men behind her.

Based on her figure alone, it was clearly obvious that this woman was a fighter. She wore a brown cloak, along with tan pants and a matching shirt. It was clothing that would make it extremely easy for her to maneuver in the event of a battle.

Ryder smirked at her appearance, his eyes overlooking her as she approached. Her athletic built rivaled my own, and I crossed my arms in slight annoyance. I wasn't in the mood to deal with being isolated and then having the leader or chief or whatever the heck he was sucking face with another female directly in-front of me.

She overlooked me on the approach, appearing to be sizing me up. I continued to stare hard at her, daring her to make some smart comment about me being a Sector Soldier.

"Skyler, what brings news of the patrols?" Ryder asked, as she stopped a few inches away from him.

"Everything is clear on the outside, as far as to our south...they have yet to stir. I do not feel as though we need to worry about our newcomer being followed," Skyler said, quickly glancing over at me.

My eyes flew back to Skyler, trying to process what she had just said. Did she really just call me *newcomer* in that condescending voice?

"Well, that is quite pleasant to hear...see that we have watch posted consistently throughout the night," Ryder ordered.

"Absolutely, I think its crucial to make sure that our newcomer does not pose a threat to us," Skyler said.

There it was again.

"The newcomer's name is MacKenzie," I firmly stated. I hated when people talked about me like I was not there. Skyler turned her head slightly to face me, as if I had just slapped her across the face. "And I'm also standing right here, in case you didn't notice, *Skyler.*"

Skyler bit her lip before looking back at Ryder. He closed his eyes for a second, letting out an exhale.

"You'll have to excuse MacKenzie, she's quite the spitfire..." Ryder said.

Skyler turned to face me, sizing me up once more. "Could be useful if she passes her training, I suppose..." she said. Before I got a chance to comment, Ryder held his arm up to my chest to prevent my attempt at an advancement towards her.

"Thank you, Skyler...carry on," Ryder said, turning to lead me away once again.

As I passed her, our eyes meeting in a challenging stare, I couldn't help but feel a familiar aroma coming off of her. I subtly began to sniff as we continued to pass her. I recognized the scent she was giving off. It was that of a feline. I could recognize the smell of a fellow feline anywhere. I continued to follow Ryder, but watched as her figure walked off into the deeper part of the woods.

She couldn't be one of mine, could she?

I followed Ryder into a tent-like building, and he lifted up the flap so that I could proceed in after him. I couldn't help but roll my eyes at his attempt to be a gentlemen. After I walked into the tent, I spotted two rows of cots lined up against either side of the large tent, each one with a blanket and a pillow. I couldn't help but laugh to myself. I suddenly began to have flashbacks of my time in Afghanistan on the FOB. We called it 'tent city' because of the large, 15 person tents that were set up everywhere. The sleeping quarters were exactly identical to this.

"I didn't know that a row of beds could be so amusing," Ryder commented, stepping in-front of me. He folded his arms once again, his eyes staring at me in slight disbelief. I mocked his movement, folding my arms as well. I was getting a little tired of his attitude.

"I was recalling a time when I was stationed in Afghanistan, that's all..."

Ryder raised an eyebrow slightly, before moving to sit down on one of the cots. "Military, huh? Well, that's good to know. That will make your training here a lot easier," Ryder responded, his eyes not leaving mine.

"Training?" I mocked. "What could I possibly have to train for?"

Ryder let out a heavy sigh, unfolding his arms. "There is evil stirring in the sectors. Something big is about to happen. My people have been monitoring the movement of all the commanders. Some of them have even started having secret meetings,"

"That's impossible, they only meet twice a year. That rule has been in place for many years, and the meetings are always discussing trade and peace, nothing more..." I said, shaking my head.

Ryder shrugged slightly. "I'm sure they still do meet twice a year for those meetings. However, our patrols have spotted a few commanders meeting and talking outside of those... designated dates,"

I looked at the ground for a second, and then turned my gaze to slowly overlook his figure. I wasn't quite sure if I should trust him or not. Yet, it seemed as though I had no other choice. I was stranded in the woods and my only hope for human contact again was a clone of a billionaire playboy from a former favorite TV show. I would continue to play this game with him, as long as Jax and my other friends didn't get hurt.

Ryder stood up, and took a few steps towards me. "I understand that you are confused about what is going on, maybe even a little scared. You don't have to admit it. I remember when I was first isolated from the sectors," Ryder said.

I didn't know whether to feel insulted or to feel safe at that point. "I'm not scared," I protested. Ryder smirked slightly, before tilting his head to the side.

"I sense otherwise," he replied. I rolled my eyes, letting out a slight laugh. Ryder turned to face me, a look of confusion on his face.

"What is it that you sense, Ryder?" I questioned. Ryder narrowed his eyes at me slightly, stepping closer.

"Even though you are desperately trying to conceal it, fear..." Ryder stated.

I was taken back slightly. He was correct, I was afraid. I was afraid of what would happen to my friends back in the sector, what would happen to them while I was gone. I wondered if they would be punished for helping me. I quickly hid these thoughts by forcing a laugh.

"How do you sense that? Do you *smell* it on me? Like a wolf smells fear in its prey?" I questioned.

Ryder simply glared at me, and then eventually allowed an odd smirk cross his face.

"All will be explained to you in good time, spit-fire..." he stated. Before I could come up with a response, he spoke up again. "Follow me, we will get you introduced to everyone and familiar with our boundaries.."

"Our boundaries? I thought that the *eighty-sixers* had control of the whole forest," I said, slightly confused. Ryder led me outside the tent and into the further part of the woods, past the various people who were sitting in small groups along the sides of the trail.

"Until such a time where you stop using the term *eighty-sixers*, I don't believe I need to answer any more of your questions." Ryder snapped, continuing to walk. I scoffed slightly, as I continued to stumble along behind him.

"Well what am I supposed to call you? Its what we've always called you in the sectors," I said, truthfully. Ryder turned to face me, stopping abruptly. I was inches away from running into him.

I couldn't help but feel drawn to his presence in that moment. As his eyes glared into mine, I could see how much he truly cared for his family out here.

83

He took comfort in how protective he was, probably because it reminded me so much of how protective Jax was of me.

"Your family," Ryder stated, firmly. My lip parted in slight surprise, as Ryder continued to stride forward again. We were headed towards a group of five people, the woman dressed similar to Skyler with the exception of their coloring colors. They wore black cloaks with green loose fitted pants and a matching shirt. If I were to guess I would say that it was some sort of ranking system.

The men were wearing charcoal colored shirts, along with black loose fitted pants. When Ryder approached, the talking and laughing stopped. A man with blonde cropped hair and piercing blue eyes stepped forward, nodding to Ryder in respect.

"Sir," he said, and Ryder returned the nod. "Trevor, this is MacKenzie. I am tasking her to you for the remainder of the day until we can have her trained and tested to see where she fits in our ranks. I have some business to attend to, Skyler and I will be taking a small team to scout out the business in the sectors. We need to make sure that MacKenzie wasn't followed out here..." Ryder said.

I felt a sense of relief, silently thanking him for not referring me as *'newcomer'*. He turned to give me one more hard stare. "Respect your family, MacKenzie. It's all you will have out here,"

Ryder turned back to face Trevor. "Keep her occupied until I return, then I will take her to meet Darius,"

Once he left, I turned to face the group. "Task me out, huh? I guess I'm sort of like your minion or something,"

I watched as Trevor smiled slightly. "No, its no problem. Ryder can be a bit...extreme. Anyway, how about we introduce you to the rest of the group here..." Trevor stated, before resting a comforting hand on my shoulder.

"This is Austin, Aaron, Erica and Sarah.." he said, pointing to each one of them. They all nodded as their names were called, showing a small smile.

"Pleasure's all mine...." I said, sitting down as Trevor ushered me to a large rock. Aaron knelt down and began to rub two sticks together to start a fire.

"So what's your story?" Sarah piped up, from her spot next to Erica.
"My story?" I questioned.

Erica and Sarah exchanged glances, and then looked back up at me. "I think she means, how did you wind up coming...to join us?" Erica said, a warm smile on her face.

"Oh...." I said, folding my arms to try and keep warm. I then remembered that Ryder made a comment not to share knowledge of my power with anyone until he deemed it necessary.

"I jumped a fellow Sector Soldier who was trying to harm a young boy and then I threatened our Sector Commander for allowing such a thing to happen," I said, truthfully. It was true, I wasn't lying...I just happened to leave out the details of me changing into a 500 pound feline.

Austin nodded, approvingly. "That's pretty awesome, MacKenzie. Way to have a heart,"

"Have a heart? What did you think she was a tin woman?" Trevor questioned, holding up his hands in question.

"I was just trying to be polite, you jerk..." Austin said, throwing some dirt in Trevor's direction.

"That's a first for you," Aaron said, grinning as small flames began to appear. Once the fire started going, he took a seat in between myself and Trevor, grinning at me as he did so.

"So...what do you guys do out here?" I questioned, looking around the group. I was attempting to not do my usual act of clamming up and getting all defensive. If these people were going to become my new family, as Ryder said, I may as well make myself open book status. There wasn't going to be anyone out here who would use the information against me, with the exception of that Skyler girl perhaps.

"We train, practice fighting scenarios, hunt or learn to hunt if you don't know how..." Trevor trailed on, leaning back to relax a bit more.

"Sometimes we do girl's nights," Sarah stated, a huge smile on her face. I returned the smile. What did these girls nights consist of? Braiding leaves in each others hair and talking about who the next mountain man would be?

"I apologize if this comes out wrong, but how did you all get so...." I paused to incline my heads towards the large tents. "Civilized,"

"Ryder still has some contacts inside the sector. They sneak him stuff through the fence consistently, its good to know that some people care about us..." Austin said, with a shrug.

Sarah elbowed him in the ribs, causing him to yipe. "What? Its not like she's going to rush back and tell them about the hole under the fence...she's one of us now," Austin said, defensively.

"Hole under the fence? I've patrolled that sector for years and I've never seen a hole under the fence...." I said, confused.

"You know that *Rocky Balboa* statue that they moved towards the backside? It was moved there for a reason...." Erica stated.

I paused for a second. James Garrison, our old head of security, ordered that statue to be moved to the backside of the Philly patrol zone saying that the Sector Commander deemed the statue to be too 'motivating' for the people of the sectors to stand up and overtake the sector by force. Which, I at first thought was completely bogus but it all made sense now. I looked around the camp, trying to figure out how to word my next question.

"I know the man who ordered that statue to be moved, we never knew what happened to him. Is he out here?" I questioned.

Austin shook his head. "No, we never knew what happened to him either...one day he just disappeared. He always provided us with many supplies. Our new supplier is apparently very giving as well, except very few people know who he actually is..."

I paused in thought, trying to think of anyone who could possibly be aiding the people in the woods. I always knew Jax felt guilty about when he actually had to eighty-six someone, but I knew he would have told me if he were taking part in aiding those that were forced to live outside the sector and in the woods.

"Miss MacKenzie?" a deep voice said, and I turned to see one of the guards who I first saw entering the camp. Joseph, I believed his name was.

I stood up, squaring my shoulders. His lip curled up in a slight snarl, before he turned away. "Follow me," he ordered.

"I can see I'm going to be so well liked here..." I said with a groan, before taking off after him. His strides were large, and it took about five of my steps to equivocate one of his.

"Where are we going?" I questioned.

"I'm taking you to meet Darius, per Ryder's orders..." Joseph replied, waving to two men who were chopping up a rather large log.

"I thought that Ryder was coming back to take me to meet Darius?" I asked, stumbling over a lone rock.

"Nice feet, and he had other business to attend to..."

"What is meeting Darius going to do for me? I'm already overtaxed with the number of people I've met today..." I said, with a heavy sigh.

"Not my problem," Joseph said, with a sneer. As we walked in silence, maintaining my glare on the back of his head, I began to think on how I couldn't blame him for being angry or for any of them being angry.

Prior to my arrival, I didn't know how they lived outside of the sectors. They may have had all this hospitality now, but what about those people who had been eighty-sixed from the beginning?

During my time in the military, I had to survive on almost nothing when we were in the field. It was never easy. I couldn't imagine doing it for years, like most of the people here probably had to do. As Joseph and I approached a circular blue tent, I began to wonder what Joseph's life was like before living in the woods...what Ryder's life must have been like.

"Darius, she is here for you," Joseph said, glancing over his shoulder at me.

A few moments later, I saw the man named Darius step outside into the sunlight. I instantly recognized the chocolate skin and the soft almond eyes that stared back at me. A smirk began to tug at the corner of his lip, before he turned his gaze to Joseph.

"Thank you, Joseph...you may return to your post now," Darius said, his voice smooth as butter. Joseph pounded his fist to his heart and then bowed his head. Once he had wandered off, I turned back to Darius.

"So what do you need with me now?" I questioned, shifting uneasily. Darius smiled, ushering me to follow him inside of the tent. I sighed, following him with a bit of uncertainty. I had seen my fair share of tents for the day.

As I entered, I was surprised to find that the tent was a mere open circle. The only items that were in the tent were four wooden sticks, and a couple of canteens that were sitting in the corner.

"What is this place?" I questioned, turning to face Darius.

"This is where we train. Ryder wanted me to bring you here for an evaluation. To see where you are at," he responded, moving his feet in circles on the sandy floor.

"Lovely. I don't just attack people out of whim unless I have an ultimatum. You can tell Ryder that I'm not interested," I said, folding my arms.

Darius chuckled, rubbing his hands together as if in thought.

"You are not the first person to show hesitation or restraint, MacKenzie. I understand that combatives are not everyone's cup of tea. Especially for you, from what I understand.." he said, folding his arms.

"You've come to realize that I prefer to shoot first and ask questions later. Have you?" I questioned.

Darius nodded slightly, stepping closer to me. "That, or you prefer your....other methods. I'm no stranger when it comes to the changing," Darius stated.

I scoffed, caught off guard. "Look, I don't how you know so much about me or how you know about my power, but its really freaking me out.."

"Hit me," Darius said, staring at me.
"What?"
"I said...hit me,"

"I'm not just going to hit you, okay? Believe it or not, I don't just go up to people and start punching them. I know I'm from Philadelphia and all but please give us some credit where credit is due. Why does everyone assume that Philadelphians just like to hit people?" I questioned, looking at the ground.

"Statistics. That and its been repeatedly voted one of the most dangerous cities," Darius replied.

I cocked an eyebrow at him, and then tilted my head.

"I read a lot, before the separation of the sectors..." Darius said, defensively.

"Got it," I said, smirking slightly.

"I know this seems petty, but I need you to focus. Think of something to drive you. I heard that your Sector Commander threatened your partner before you decided to seclude yourself and join us. Pretend I'm your Sector Commander. Take me down," Darius said, placing his arms comfortably at his sides.

I stood in front of him, getting a serious case of Deja Vu from when I had sessions like this with my father when he was training me to fight in both forms. It had been so long since I fought purely hand to hand, relying heavily on my firearm or my tiger to finish the fight.

"I'm waiting," he said, nodding towards me.

I narrowed my eyes, trying to picture the Sector Commander standing in front of me. I recalled how he nodded to Damian, giving him permission to torture Jax. Jax, a soldier who a week prior was stationed with me outside his door to protect him from whatever danger he was paranoid about that night.

I gritted my teeth, stepping to throw a punch towards Darius chest. He captured my entire fist in his one hand, pushing it aside so that he could look at me.

"You have great strength, MacKenzie..."

"Yeah? Well something tells me that you catching my punch like it was a baseball proves otherwise..." I snapped.

Darius smirked, twisting my arm so that it was pinned behind my back. "I said you had great strength, I didn't say anything about your speed just yet..." he said, pushing me away from him.

I pushed my angled bangs out of my face, trying to tuck them behind my ear. Now, I was beginning to get agitated.

I charged forward, throwing a right hook at his face. He blocked it, throwing a palm heel at my chest. I was quick on the block, jabbing an uppercut into his ribs. He let out a heavy grunt, grabbing my arm and throwing me to the ground. My back hit the sand with a thunderous thud, and I let out a painful wince.

"You're driven, I'll give you that. We need to find something else to drive you. Clearly your anger isn't working," Darius stated.

"You told me to picture you as the Sector Commander, what the heck kind of emotion did you expect to get out of me?" I asked, my hand on my throbbing tailbone.

"Well, for most people anger is what drives them. In your case, I would say it distracts you more than anything. You can't fight with a distraction on your mind," Darius said, squirting some of the canteen water into his mouth. He looked over at me, handing me a canteen as well.

I scoffed, swiping the canteen from him. "How exactly am I supposed to rid myself of the distraction?" I questioned, somewhat sarcastically.

Darius stepped closer to me, the smell of honey washing over me. "We find you a focus. Something to fight towards,"

"My friends in the sect-"

"No. Because then you will be full of anger and spite. You can deny it, but your mind will drift to your former Sector Commander and how you fear he may torture them and that will get you angry," Darius interrupted, his biceps bulging as he folded his arms.

"Well what do you use as your focus?" I questioned, suddenly curious. If this guy was like the Yoda of training here, it wouldn't hurt to learn his secret. Besides, as far as people in the woods went he was the most friendly towards me.

Darius opened his mouth to speak, but was interrupted at the sound of the tent flap opening. A small female with sandy brown hair stood there, looking rather nervous. "Darius..." she said, respectfully. As she bowed her head, I couldn't help but notice a streak of blue in her hair.

"Devon, what is it?" Darius asked, his voice softening considerably.

"I'm here to escort Ms. MacKenzie to her sleeping quarters..." she said, nervously adjusting her thin black glasses.

Darius nodded, turning back to face me. "I'll see you tomorrow. Until then, try to figure out what your focus is..." he said, turning away from me and disappearing out of the tent.

I looked over at this Devon girl, giving her the once over.

"It's alright, Ms. MacKenzie. I have no intentions of harming you...or threatening you... I'm not really much of a fighter. I do love books though!" she said, somewhat enthusiastically.

"Touching. You mentioned something about sleeping quarters?" I asked.

"Yes. Follow me, please..." she said, slipping out of the tent. I was suddenly becoming rapidly annoyed with the different personalities of people that were out here. Why couldn't they all just be like me, straight forward and to the point? Behind all the smiles and glares out here, I wasn't sure what to think. I had spent years training how to pick out and eliminate an enemy, which was easy overseas, because they all hated us. Here, behind all the false smiles and the overly emphasized glares, I didn't know who my enemy was.

"Where is Ryder? I would have thought I would have seen him one final time before I was assigned a bed time," I inquired.

"Oh, apparently he got held up on his last mission. I'm assuming he's staking out for the night. Apparently your joining us is a bigger deal than any of us thought. Did you anger some people in the sectors?" Devon questioned.

As I followed her, I had a quick flashback of everyones face when I transformed into my tiger.

"I wouldn't exactly say that..." I muttered, gazing off into the woods.

Devon showed me into one of the tents, and I saw Erica and Sarah preparing their cot for bed as well. As my eyes scanned the room, I took notice that only about ten of the cots out of the twenty that were in the tent were taken.

"What happened to all the other females?" I asked, spotting the elderly lady I saw planting a seed earlier kneeling next to her cot in prayer.

"There are only ten of us here," Sarah replied, sitting down and stretching her neck.

"Eleven. Don't forget... Skyler," Devon said, her gaze falling to the ground. Erica and Sarah mumbled worked of agreement, sour expressions on their faces.

"What's the deal with this Skyler character? Is she like the school yard bully or something?" I questioned, my eyes going back and forth between the three of them.

Erica began to chuckle, while Devon's eyes darted to the floor again.

"Devon?" I questioned, narrowing my eyes in concern.

"Skyler, she's just..." Devon began, struggling to find the words to say.

"Different," Erica finished, and Devon showed her a smile of gratitude.

"What's so different about her?" I asked, sitting down on what would now be my new bed.

"She pretty much thinks whenever Ryder isn't here, that she runs the place." Sarah said, looking over at me.

"Okay, so she's like the mean high school cheerleader. What else? Are she and him...like..." I said, trying to figure out how to word the rest of my sentence.

"Together?" Erica asked, grinning at my struggle.

"Yeah, let's go with that..." I said, fighting a smirk.

"No one knows to be honest. Skyler seemingly likes to think so though. Every time a new female comes in and tries to get, you know, friendly with Ryder they go for a training session with Skyler and they come back with absolutely no interest what-so-ever..." Devon said, taking her glasses off and tucking them in her pillowcase.

"Hmm...so she's one of those girls. It also seems like she doesn't treat you girls right, and I'm not okay with that. Looks like Ms. Skyler may have a problem on her hands..." I said, laying down on my cot.

"What's that?" Erica inquired.

I turned my head to look at her, allowing the wicked smile to cross my face. "Because, I love a challenge. Knocking Skyler off her pedestal seems as good as any..." I stated. I had nothing to lose, and I loved a fun project.

Erica smirked in return. "We knew we liked you, MacKenzie..."

10.

"Newcomer, wake up newcomer..."

I cracked my eyes open to see a blurry figure standing before me. After blinking a couple of times, the room finally came into view. Erica and Sarah were folding their blankets neatly, and Devon seemed to just be waking up.

"What's the matter, sleeping beauty? Not satisfied with our sleeping arrangements?"

I turned to see that the figure that woke me up was none other than Skyler. I rolled my eyes, before climbing out of bed. "What's that supposed to mean?" I questioned.

"Sorry we didn't have your standard King Size bed or whatever it is you Sector Soldiers slept on," Skyler spat, folding her arms.

I ignored her, as I began to stretch out. I had dealt with people like Skyler all my life, and I learned that the best way to deal with them was to ignore them.

"What, no comment? No snarky remark?" Skyler asked.

Alright, the whole ignoring thing only worked to a point for me.

"Actually, I prefer a cot. Reminds me of my deployments with my battle buddies, but thank you for your concern..." I said, folding my blankets.

"You were in the military?" Erica questioned, walking over to my cot. I nodded, beginning to braid my hair so that it would drape over my left shoulder. Skyler turned to face Erica and rolled her eyes.

"Training starts in an hour. Make sure that our *hero*," she paused to stare me down. "Is there as well,"

She surveyed the room one last time, and then with a flip of her hair, disappeared out of the tent. I had gotten so wrapped up in annoyance with her presence, that a huge knot had formed where my braid was supposed to be. Erica patted my shoulder, motioning for me to sit.

"Seems like she's got something out for you," Erica stated, combing through my hair with her fingers.

"Of course she's got something out for MacKenzie. She's a badass chick who certainly seems to have caught Ryder's eye," Sarah said, putting her own hair into a tight bun.

"I wouldn't exactly say that. Considering he never came back to find me last night," I replied, wincing slighting as Erica began to tug at my hair to restart my side braid. I then heard her mutter something about how she couldn't believe how long my hair was.

"They must have gotten back late from their patrols. Skyler eventually rolled in pretty late last night, I'm willing to bet he's going to come seek you out today..." Devon said, wiping her glasses clean.

She stood up, and began to brush herself off. "I'm going to head out now to breakfast and grab us all a spot. I'll see you out there," she said, quickly disappearing out of the tent. I cocked an eyebrow at the swinging flap, before looking over at Sarah.

"Is she okay?" I questioned. Sarah bit her lip, as if to hesitate to find the right words to say.

"She was...brought to us when she was very young. Sector Soldiers apparently killed her parents right in front of her, and then they tossed her into the woods. Darius found her and brought her to the camp,"

I nodded, realizing that was why Darius had suddenly gotten so soft with her. I had watched this big, macho man turn into a sweetheart in a matter of five seconds. That's what a sweet girl like Devon does. She takes your stone heart and turns it into something beautiful.

While Erica continued to braid my hair, my mind wandered back to my sector and my friends within it. More specifically, to Jax. Today would be one of our working days. I didn't know what time it was, but I assumed from the bright light peeking through the tunnel that it was the early morning and he would be getting ready for his patrol. Who would be his partner though? We were ordered to patrol in pairs.

I smiled at the thought of Jax getting some new, inquiring kid who asked him way too many questions and annoying the heck out of him. My entertaining thoughts were replaced with thoughts of wonder. What if he got another female partner and she worked her way into his heart and he fell in love with her? Even married men have a tendency to, as my mother used to say, 'look at the menu' sometimes. I had once in awhile seen him giving me that look. Would he look at another female like that?

I began to squeeze my cot out of anger and frustration as it turned into thoughts of Damian and the Sector Commander. What if they didn't keep their promise and they tortured my friends? I had to get back there and find out that they were alright. I had to at least make sure that they were still okay.

"Whoa, did it hurt that bad?" Erica questioned.

93

I snapped back into it, pulling my hand away from the cot. I chucked as I ran my fingers along the slight indents that my hand had left.

"No, I was just having a thought..." I said, standing up. I turned to face her and showed her a small smile. "Thank you," I said. I always enjoyed having someone do my hair, especially since I was never good at doing hair myself.

"Well come on, let's go and get something to eat before we begin our training for the day..." Erica said, motioning for us to head out of the tent.

The sunlight felt warm on my face, and I let out a deep exhale. I would love to change and let my tiger run free through the woods, enjoying the feel of the fresh, crisp wind blowing against my fur.

We walked out towards the center of the camp, where there were a group of four men handing out plates of food. As I continued to approach, I was completely surprised to find food such as eggs, bread and sausage on the plate. My mouth began to water and I desired the savory taste of the food. I hadn't eaten since that lunch with Matt and Amanda, and my stomach was aching.

After receiving our plates, we found Devon sitting with her back up against the tree. She waved us over, a happy smile now on her face. As we all took our places, I couldn't help but continue to stare at the food in shock.

"It's called food," Devon said, fighting a smirk.

"Yeah, I know. I just wasn't expecting....." I said, trying to find the proper words to say.

"You were expecting something like berries and leaves or something?" Erica teased.

"Well not to be a downer but, yes, I was expecting something like that. How do you guys get this stuff?" I asked, poking at the scrambled eggs.

"Cyrus and Milo were chefs before the splitting of the sectors. We grow all our own fruits and vegetables and the eggs are from the chickens we keep. I'm sure that Ryder or someone will give you a full scale tour of the place. Our contact inside the sector also places food in that hole the second and fourth Thursday of the month. So he provides us with the meats since we don't really have the livestock out here. It wouldn't survive with...some people anyway," Sarah said, chomping into a piece of toast.

I looked among the group of girls, who had suddenly gone silent after Sarah's comment.

"Why would't livestock survive out here with some people?" I questioned, curiously. Her comment made me slightly suspicious of what I originally thought back in the sectors, that one of my kind could be lurking out here somewhere. I had learned from my parents that many of our kind back in the day could not contain their natural prey instinct that came along with possessing the gift. My mother had told me stories of how our earlier people used to be farmers, but when they would see livestock, their prey drive to kill would come out.

Because of this, only the strongest of our people who had the will to resist the temptation worked with the animals, while everyone else who worked on the farm would work in the crop fields.

"They just don't value life like we do," Erica responded, shooting Sarah a warning stare. I decided not to question it further, after all I had only been here one day and I was just starting to earn their trust.

"So MacKenzie, did you leave anyone special back in the sector?" Devon asked, pushing her empty plate away.

I looked at the ground, feeling guilty for forgetting about my friends back in the sector.

"Nope, no one like that for me. Just my friends and my partner," I replied.

"Partner? Is he cute?" Sarah asked, perking up slightly. I smiled, and shook my head.

"Not that kind of partner. We have known each other for many years, we were even deployed together to Iraq and Afghanistan. When the sectors were created we were assigned together as patrol partners," I said, drawing my knees close to my chest.

"What's his name?" Erica asked.

I hugged my knees, resting my chin on top. "Jax," I responded, my stomach turning slightly.

"Seems like you really care for him," Devon observed.

I nodded, now staring at an ant scurrying away with a piece of egg. "Yeah, I really do. We've been through a lot together. I know he's been suffering with his wife being in a different sector and all. He has been there for me even more so since my parents were killed,"

In that moment I realize that I cared for Jax more than I originally thought. I had taken seeing him for granted, and now that I couldn't see him anymore, I really was hurting. I needed to see him again.

"Look, its Ryder..." Devon said, nodding behind me.

I turned around and saw him heading towards us. Sarah, Erica and Devon all stood up as he approached. I looked around at them, before sighing and standing up myself. I guess I had to get used to the King of the Forest foo-foo rules that were going on out here.

Ryder nodded to my three friends, before turning and looking at me. A smirk appeared on his face, as he looked me up and down. "Good, you've eaten. I need you to come with me, we are going to do a little tour of the area."

"Was I followed?" I questioned.

"Not that we discovered," he replied, motioning for me to follow him. I looked back to see the three of them waving farewell to me, all with nervous smiles on their faces. It seemed as though Ryder knew exactly how to make an impression on these people without saying anything at all.

"I was expecting you to come fetch me last night," I said, grimacing slightly as my foot sounded off with a sickening 'squish'. I sighed, pulling my foot out of the mud puddle. I was going to miss wearing shoes.

"I got occupied," Ryder replied, pulling back the weeds to walk out the way that he brought me in last night. I looked at him, confused.

"We are exiting the camp," I stated.

"Well observed," Ryder said.

"I thought you were giving me a tour," I protested. Ryder sighed, grabbing my arm and pulling me through the opening with him.

"I had to come up with something to get you away from your new friends. I don't want them knowing why we are really out here," he replied.

I paused for a second, remembering Ryder telling me that he wasn't ready for everyone else to be aware of my power just yet. We continued trekking through the woods until we arrived at what appeared to be a large cave with a round stone blocking the entrance.

I rolled my eyes and crossed my arms. "What? Has someone been in there for three days or something?" I questioned. Ryder raised an eyebrow at me, and I figured he probably didn't understand my catholic school girl reference. I waved my hand, dismissing the joke.

I heard the sound of twigs snapping and I turned to my left to see Darius emerging from his spot in the woods.

"Right, cause that's not at all weird or anything..." I muttered to myself.

"Ryder," Darius said, embracing Ryder in an almost brother-like hug.

"Darius, help me move the boulder," Ryder ordered. I watched as the two men rolled the rock to the side, revealing the entrance to the cave.

I stepped in after them, following Darius down the tunnel. I looked back at Ryder, who was still standing at the mouth of the cave. "Go with Darius, I will be there shortly..." he ordered.

I sighed, hurrying down the hall after Darius. "Is this where you guys execute me or something?" I questioned, looking up at him.

Darius smiled, laughing slightly. "Not even close, MacKenzie..." he said.

"Well what am I supposed to expect? You take me to this random cave in the woods that had a stone blocking the entrance, after lying to my friends about where you are actually taking me? This sounds like a horrible, horrible Agatha Christie novel...." I retorted.

We continued walking until the cave opened up to a large circular room. I looked up to see a hole in the roof, about the size of a basketball. It was just enough for the sunlight to shine through and light up the whole room. To my left I saw holes in the wall that appeared to have been carved to serve as shelves, with various articles of clothing folded up inside each one.

"What is this? Where you have your gladiator fights or something?" I questioned, spotting a couple of red stains on the ground, which was unmistakably blood.

Darius laughed, folding his arms. "Yeah, we drop the lions from the ceiling..."

I raised an eyebrow at him. "You know at this point, I would not be surprised..." I said, looking around the room. At that point, I noticed multiple sketches that were etched into the stone walls. I approached the wall, and was surprised to see sketches of tigers. The sketch that really caught my eye was a sketch of a tiger that was fighting a lion, both cats standing on their hind legs, teeth bared and with their claws extended.

"Darius, what is this place?" I questioned, my fingers running over the traces. When Darius didn't respond, I turned and saw Ryder approaching. The two of them exchanged looks, and then both turned to look at me.

"MacKenzie, I know you have a lot of questions about how we know so much about who you are and about your powers. In time, that will all be explained to you," Darius stated, his gaze considerably soft.

"Okay?" I questioned, biting my lip.

Ryder approached me, stopping a few inches away. I inhaled sharply, feeling almost intoxicated by his presence once again. "You're not alone, MacKenzie..." Ryder said. He closed his eyes, and then opened them a few seconds later. When he did, I notice that his once gray eyes were now an amber brown color. I staggered back, startled. He smirked, turning his back towards me and leaping into the air.

I felt the rush of the wind coming down from the hole in the ceiling as the sunlight passed over Ryder's lunging figure, as I witnessed him change. As if on cue, the breeze stopped and I saw Ryder's tiger turn to face me. His tiger's amber eyes lingered on my figure, as he circled around so that his full body was facing me. I didn't know quite how to react, not being familiar with being so close to another Anomic like myself for quite some time now.

I looked over at Darius, snapping out of my stare spell. "Am I supposed to change now?" I questioned, looking over at him.

"Whenever you're ready. We don't want to force you into doing something you are uncomfortable with...." Darius said, resting back on the wall.

"What about you? Do you change too?" I questioned. Darius nodded.

"Would you be more comfortable if I did so as well?" he questioned. I knew that I should take comfort in the fact that my new 'family' possessed the same powers as me, and that I shouldn't be as nervous as I was.

"No...I'll do it," I said, looking back over at Ryder. I sighed, closing my eyes. I reached out to connect with my tiger, and she finally answered my call. I opened my eyes and exhaled, feeling her ready to be called out. I turned to my left, leaping into the air. I felt the clothes tearing off my body, as my body grew. I saw my hands change in front of me, just in time as I hit the ground. I turned and faced Ryder, to see that Darius must have also changed while I did so. Their orange pelts rustled slightly in the wind, as they both glanced at my majestic figure.

Ryder exchanged glances with Darius, before looking back at me.

"We will continue to come here three days a week, building up the confidence in your tiger to connect and take comfort in your own kind once more. On top of that, Darius will continue to train with you on your warrior skills just like yesterday," Ryder stated. I was slightly taken back. It had been a long time since I communicated with another tiger like this.

"Okay, so what are we doing for the rest of the day?" I questioned. I watched as Darius laid down in his spot, his tail curling around one of his rear feet. Ryder did the same, laying down across from me.

"Just sticking together," Ryder replied, observing me. I held back a chuckle, wondering why the heck we were all just going to sit around in a circle and stare at each other. As if reading my thoughts, Darius responded.

"The goal is to see how you react to your own kind after a period of time, and observe your self control. As you know, tigers are usually lone hunters and they allow their predatory instinct take over and try to fight their own kind for prey or a mate. So we will start here today and then from there we can move to take you on a hunt to see how you act as well," Darius replied.

I nodded, it now making sense. I slowly laid down, my eyes going back and forth between the two of them. Once I did, Darius yawned, stretching his paws out in front of him. I turned my gaze back to Ryder, who maintained his taut pose with his gaze still fixated on me. I sighed, laying my head down on my paws, finally taking comfort in realizing that I was no longer alone.

* * *

"Where have you been? How did the tour go?" Erica asked, looking up from her spot on a tree stump.

I looked back and forth between her and the small boy, realizing that she was showing him how to make and shoot a bow and arrow.

"Oh...it was great. Ryder just showed me around the area, and told me a little bit about what we do out here and such," I said, somewhat truthfully. It was one of the things we discussed during our little gathering. Erica nodded.

"So what are you doing?" I asked, looking at the bow in her hands.

"Oh! I'm showing young Ryan here how to shoot. Would you like to join?" she questioned.

"It's been awhile. I don't remember really how to use one, at least decently..." I said, somewhat embarrassed.

"I can show you!" Ryan piped up from his spot. Erica laughed, handing him the bow. "Okay, you can teach her," she said. Ryan grinned up at her, his cheeks turning a slight shade of pink. I smirked, realizing that the youngster probably had a crush on his mentor.

"First, you gotta place the arrow on the string like this..." he said, placing the arrow on the bow string. "Then you pull it in front of you like this," he flipped his sandy brown bangs out of his eyes so that he could see.

"Miss Erica says to find your focus and then....." he exhaled, closing his little eyes. A few seconds later he opened his eyes, releasing the arrow. It skimmed the tree about seven feet in front of him.

I looked over at him as he bowed his head in disappointment. "Only I stink... I'm sorry Miss Erica," he said, walking to sit back down on the rock.

Erica patted his shoulder, and then took the bow from him. "Are you kidding, that was awesome, Ryan! You just have to focus on your breathing a little bit more and I promise you will get it," she stated.

Erica drew the bowstring back and let out a very long exhale. She slowly inhaled one more time and then paused, releasing the arrow. It struck the tree dead center. Ryan began to clap his hands, a goofy grin on his face.

"That was awesome, I'm going to go tell my friends!" Ryan exclaimed, running off towards the camp.

Erica set her bow down and turned to face me. "My father used to practice archery with me all the time growing up. He told me that even if I was stranded in the wild, it was one weapon I could easily make,"

"What did your father do?" I questioned.

"He was a mechanic, but when he was younger he was a boy scout. Anyway, it keeps Skyler off my back for training. Its the one thing I can do better than her," Erica replied.

"I keep hearing about this whole training thing, aside from survival skills what do you guys have to train for?" I asked, watching Ryder join his group of friends. I turned to face Erica when she didn't respond right away. She bit her lip, as it appeared she was struggling for words.

"I'm not sure I'm the best person to answer that, MacKenzie. I'm confident that Ryder or Darius will make it all clear to you soon," she replied.

"They still have a lot they need to disclose to me. For starters, they somehow knew all this information about me before I even had a conversation with them..." I said, feeling suddenly frustrated as I recalled the first time I saw Darius and Ryder outside the gate that day when Katie and I were on our run.

"Well you were a sector soldier, right? And for a good while if I'm not mistaken. Perhaps they studied the way you lived and worked when they were on their daily patrols?" Erica questioned, slinging the bow on her back.

I shrugged. Maybe it was too soon to disclose that they didn't just know about me, but they knew about my family and who I really was. Ryder did tell me to hide my gift, and from what I gathered anything Ryder told me to do was for a good reason. I overlooked Erica for a second. She appeared to be my friend, but what if the second she found out about who I was that I would be judged? It wouldn't be the first time that happened.

"But I can tell you this, the blue moon is approaching. I can't wait for you to witness it, MacKenzie. Every blue moon, the pack leader, being Ryder in this case, selects a group of individuals he deems suitable for receiving this....gift..." Erica said, her eyes lighting up.

"Gift?" I questioned, raising an eyebrow. Erica nodded, her smirk slowly expanding.

"It truly is an amazing gift. I wish I could tell you more, but...its just so...wow. I don't know if you'd believe me if I told you," Erica said, waving her hand to dismiss the idea.

In that moment I recalled the conversation I had with Ryder when I first arrived there. Ryder told me that you could grant the gift of a tiger by being bit by someone who had possessed the power already. Did this mean that every blue moon Ryder chose who the next Anomic's would be? Did he even have the power to do that? I held back a laugh, trying to imagine tiger Ryder walking around, biting everyone to change them.

"Well, we should head back to camp. I'm sure Darius is looking for you to do some training or something. I would take training with him over Skyler any day of the week," Erica said. She paused to tilt her head and look at me in question. "What day is it today anyway?"

"Uhh.." I paused, trying to recall myself. "Not to be rude, but does it matter out here?"

Erica laughed, patting me on my back. "You're quite the character, MacKenzie..." she said, as we headed back towards the camp.

11

A full week had passed since I had joined the eighty-sixers and with everyday that passed, it seemingly started to get easier. I had spent one more day in the cave with Darius and Ryder, and they told me next time they felt like I was ready to go out on a hunting excursion with them. I also had been continuing my private sessions with Darius, avoiding Skyler as much as physically possible. From what Erica had told me, I was quite pleased that I was not training with her.

"Let's go, maggots. Except for you, princess newcomer. You just stay right here and behave okay? I don't know why Ryder wants you getting your little private lessons with Darius, it's not like you're so special anyway. I guess he wants to spare you the embarrassment," Skyler spat, tossing her hair over her shoulder as she walked out of the tent with her bow.

"Jealous much?" Sarah questioned, winking over at me. Erica smiled as she walked past me, squeezing my shoulder in the process. She paused, to squeeze my shoulder again.

"Dang, I don't know what you and Darius have been doing but whatever it is, its working great!" she stated, showing me a quick smile as she walked out after Skyler.

Once I was left alone in the tent, I flexed and ran my hand along my own muscle. Even though it was only a week, I was noticing an improvement myself. I was getting back into the shape that I once was when I was deployed on active duty. I couldn't deny that I wasn't happy about that.

I stood up, pulling my hair into a tight side braid. I felt a pang of guilt in my stomach as I thought about Jax and Katie. Of course, I still missed them, but I was desperate to find out how they were doing. Maybe I could ask Darius if we could do a pass-by on a training run or something, just so I could see how they were doing.

I walked out of the tent, a cool breeze greeting me. I spotted young Ryan, and he ran up to me in excitement. "Ms. MacKenzie!" he said, hugging me around my waist. I smiled, running my hand over his tussled hair.

"Hi Ryan, what are you up to today?" I questioned.

"I'm helping my daddy out, he's going to show me how to cut wood for a fire! Isn't that so cool!?" he asked, his eyes lighting up.

At the mention of his daddy, my stomach twisted in knots and I tried to conceal my feelings by forcing another smile.

"That's awesome, Ryan. I'll come see you later and see how you are doing," I said, giving him a goodbye hug.

He waved me a farewell, scurrying over towards his dad, who nodded to me respectfully. I bit my lip, walking over towards Darius's tent. Seeing the young children here in the wilderness with their parents reminded me so much of the time I spent with my parents growing up, back when we lived in Jim Thorpe, PA before moving to the city. It was never very crowded during the fall and winter seasons, so that was when we elected to do most of our outdoor training.

Joe stood outside Darius's tent, raising an eyebrow at me as I approached.

"You look like crap," he stated.

I rolled my eyes, as I saw a faint smirk appeared on his face.

"That's just how excited I am to be blessed with your presence," I said, mocking a curtsy at him. Joe laughed, folding his arm across his chest. Through my week here I had noticed that Joe and Devon spent an awful lot of time together, but whenever I questioned Devon on it, she would just blush and turn away claiming they were 'just friends'. I had used that excuse before, back in high school. I knew love when I saw it. I was no stranger to it.

"See you, MacKenzie..." Joe said, walking away.

"Oh, well if you wanted to go and talk to him I don't want to chase you away. I can wait," I said, pointing towards the tent.

"Nope, I'm done. I was just taking a minute to enjoy the breeze..." Joe said, waving to me in farewell.

I shrugged, walking into Darius's tent. He smiled at my approach, nodding in my direction. "You seem rather peppy today, unusual for you..." Darius stated, drying his hands on a small white towel.

"How do I usually seem?" I questioned, curious.

"Most days? You just look angry," Darius replied.

I scoffed, rolling my eyes. "I'm not angry. I just have...permanent resting Italian face," I retorted. Darius laughed, tossing the towel to the side.

"So, what are you here to teach me today?" I questioned, rolling up the pants at the legs so that I would be free from them swaying as we moved around. I learned that lesson after my second session. Excess clothing, not the best thing when you're practicing combatives.

"Remember your first day here when I told you to hit me?" he questioned, removing his tunic to reveal a white wife beater.

103

"How could I forget. One, it was only a week ago and Two, I got my ass handed to me," I played.

I removed my tunic as well, so that I only wore the sports bra on-top. I knew Darius wasn't looking to seduce me with his lessons, so the past three days I had been fighting him in a sports bra and my pants. It was how I used to box back when I took Krav Maga in college, and there was more than just one guy in those classes. I figured I could handle my own. I was fit enough to be comfortable with my appearance.

"I want to revisit that lesson, but first. We need to figure out what drives you," he said, approaching me and folding his arms.

"I haven't exactly figured that out just yet to be honest. In the military I used my anger to drive me. You know, terrorists trying to take away our country's freedom...and our lives. It angered me, so I acted upon it. However, I was hiding behind a gun and we obviously don't have those out here so...." I paused to shrug. "I don't know,"

"MacKenzie you weren't hiding behind your gun. You were just using it to guide you. Does holding a weapon give someone more courage? Perhaps, but that's not the case with you. When most people are afraid, you can see it in their eyes. It consumes them, but not you. You face the fear, you challenge it. Now I need you to summon that strength, and let it drive you..." Darius said, circling me.

I looked down at the ground, trying to think if there was anything other than my anger that I could focus on to be my inspiration to fight. After a few seconds, I was struck with a thought. I turned to face Darius, swinging a right hook in his direction. I caught him off guard, striking him on the side of the face. He stumbled back a bit, shaking off the hit. He looked over at me, a look of surprise on his face. I brought my guard up to ready myself, as I lunged towards him. He blocked a few of my strikes, and them aimed to take a strike to my abdomen. I side stepped, grabbing his wrist and spinning into him, elbowing him in the solar plexus. He grunted, twisting my wrist down and delivering a kick to my stomach.

I stomped on his instep, and then jumped back. I lunged forward with a back-fist, hoping he would block it, which he did. I then leapt up and delivered a pike kick to his chest, catching him completely off guard as he stumbled back. He blinked in surprise, wiping the beads of sweat from his forehead.

I continued to breath heavily, my angled bangs sticking to my skin. I inhaled deeply, dropping my guard as my breath slowed down. "MacKenzie...that was...." Darius began, shaking his head in surprise.

He approached me, probably noticing how I suddenly went from being an aggressive fighter to suddenly resilient. "What were you thinking about?" he questioned, his voice softening.

"I was thinking about my parents. I used to train with my father all the time, he told me that one day I would need to lead our people, and that I needed to be an inspiration. Then, I remembered their murder. How I stumbled upon their bodies, and how it made me feel...how much hate I had. How desperately I longed to find their killer," I stated.

"But we said your anger-"

"It wasn't anger that I was feeling, it was honor. My parents wanted me to be a leader for our people. When I was younger, I was a brat. I didn't care about leading anyone other than my own life. I was selfish, but now that I know I'm not alone....and in spending time with you and Ryder... I'm ready to make them proud. I don't know if their killer is still out there, if he is then he better run. Because we aren't dead. We're very much alive," I stated.

"We?" Darius questioned, folding his arms.

I smirked, "Anomics," I replied.

Darius smiled, taking my hand in his. "MacKenzie, your parents would be very proud of you. I know you want to know how we know so much about you, and we plan to disclose that information to you in given time. We just ask that you be patient with us," Darius said.

"So what drives you?" I asked, changing the subject. I was willing to be patient, but the more he talked about it the more I would start getting annoyed. I considered myself a patient person, but the more it was talked about the more annoyed I would get and that patience would slowly begin to fade away.

Darius averted his gaze for a second. "My wife...and my daughter. My wife was killed during the war, and my daughter I have not seen since the war. I have no way of knowing if she is alive or not. I'm trying to honor their memory, so I fight for them," he replied.

"So we both fight for honor," I replied.

"Just like the knights in the old times. They fight for honor and for their leadership, not out of spite, MacKenzie. That is why when we fight out of anger, we lose." Darius stated.

I couldn't help but feel pity for Darius, realizing that we both had suffered major losses in our life. I reached out and took his hand in mine. It was people like Darius, fierce warriors with a heart of gold, that were always the backbone of the group.

"Then let's find your daughter," I said, confident. Darius eyes lit up slightly, as he turned his gaze back to me.

As Darius made to reply, the flap to the tent swung open and Darius let go of my hand as Ryder entered. His icy eyes lingered on me for a second, before he turned to look at Darius. I could see a brotherly look exchanged between the two of them as Ryder approached. I heard the tent flap open a second time and saw Skyler step in with two other warriors. Lovely, just the last person I wanted to see.

"How is she progressing with her training?" Ryder questioned, looking over at me. I folded my arms, trying to cover myself up. I had just gotten used to being half dressed while training with just Darius. Even when I had my private sessions with Ryder and Darius, being half naked in front of Ryder made me uncomfortable. Every-time I changed back from my tiger, I had to ask them to leave the room so that I could grab some clothes off the shelf and change. I wasn't in the mood to deal with having an audience here either.

"She's progressing extremely well, I think she is ready to take on her duty in the patrols..." Darius replied.

I watched as Skyler showed Darius the deadliest glare that I had ever seen.

"Patrols? She can't patrol with us. She has only been here a week, she doesn't even deserve to be selected for the gift of be-"

"Thank you for your concern, Skyler. I'll take that into account when I decide who is worthy of receiving the gift this upcoming Blue Moon..." Ryder responded, keeping his eyes on me.

Skyler's mouth snapped shut, and she looked down at the ground. Note to self, if I ever want to get Skyler to shut up, find a way to get Ryder to snap at her. Ryder looked over at Darius, and then nodded.

"I trust your word, brother. Now time to see how she does..." he said, and then he pulled his tunic over his head.

As soon as he did, I had to stop my jaw from hitting the floor from how ridiculously in shape he looked. His tan complexion made his body looked even more toned than it already was, and I couldn't help but notice the tattoo he had on his left chest plate. Two crossing arrows with a circle where the two arrows met, and inside the circle was an eye. His abs were perfectly stacked and carved, making me feel slightly lightheaded. I forced my eyes to reconnect with his, refusing to gaze at his body for too long. Usually when Ryder transformed, he did it right from clothed to tiger. When he changed back, he had always turned his back to me.

Ryder smirked slightly, walking closer to me. "Does this make you uncomfortable, MacKenzie?" he questioned.

Yes, I thought, a lump suddenly forming in the back of my throat. I tried breathing more steadily, in an attempt to slow my heart rate down. My tiger began to stir curiously, suddenly extremely attracted to him.

"No, why would it?" I lied, biting my lip. I saw his nose twitch slightly, and his smirk grew even more. *Crap*, he definitely could pick up on feline in me being drawn to him. He began to move in a circular motion, and I continued to move opposite of him.

"Let's see how you fight," he said, lunging towards me. I was caught off guard, taking a hit to the sternum. He laughed in amusement, putting his guard up to ready himself for the next attack.

I narrowed my eyes, charging forward and smacking him across the face. He turned to me and opened his mouth to speak, but I was quick to elbow him in the ribs before he made a comment about me hitting like a girl, or whatever he was about to say. He grunted, swiping to grab me. I jumped back out of his reach, spinning and kicking him hard in the stomach. He stumbled back, and the smile disappeared from his face. His icy eyes glared directly into mine, and he knew I was no longer playing a game.

I launched forward, seizing him around the waist and tackling him to the ground with me. I was slightly distracted by the feeling of his warm skin touching my own. I could feel my tiger purring playfully, wanting to break free and calling his to come out. I refused to satisfy her, releasing him. Ryder took the opportunity to roll forward, grabbing my throat in the process. He forced me onto my back, his body positioned over mine.

I struggled, swinging my legs up so that I kneed him in his sides. He grunted, but maintained his stance on top of me.

"Now you're in trouble," Ryder whispered.

"According to you," I replied, swinging my legs up again and pinching his head. He grunted painfully, releasing his grip on my throat. I squatted, and then threw myself on top of him. He began to wiggle under my weight, and I forcefully pinned his legs under my own. We both paused for a second, and it took me a little bit to realize what an awkward and uncomfortable position we were in. I could feel the heat rushing to my cheeks at the feel of his bare skin against mine.

Ryder seized my moment of distraction, rolling to the side and pinning me under him. He straddled my hips, and his chest crushed mine. He pinned both my arms above my head, holding them down at the wrists so that it was near impossible for me to move. I attempted to move my legs to no success, his powerful muscular ones holding mine in place.

"Never let your guard down, MacKenzie. It will bring about the end of you," Ryder stated, breathing heavily. I could instantly smell a hickory scent on him, even through his sweat. I was too lost in his presence to even pay attention to what he was saying.

I hadn't felt an attraction as strong as this in such a long time, which really irked me, because his personality and attitude was anything but attractive at times.

He leaned down so that he could whisper in my ear. "For the record, I am quite flattered by your...feline instincts,"

If I wasn't blushing before, I sure as hell was now. With that, he pulled away and stood up. I gratefully took his hand, but kept my gaze from meeting his. I looked over to see Darius nodding, impressed.

"I will take her on a practice patrol with me now and through tonight. See how she does," Ryder said, sliding his tunic back over his head.

"She lost," Skyler protested, sounding somewhat angry.

Ryder bit his lip, turning to face Skyler. "If I was not clear before, Skyler, I will certainly make it crystal clear for you now. *I*, not Skyler, will be the one who calls the shots around here. Last I checked, this was my clan, not Skyler's clan. Do we understand each other?" Ryder hissed, shooting Skyler a death stare.

I had to turn away, so that Skyler wouldn't see my growing smirk. I made eye contact with Darius, who winked in my direction.

Skyler scoffed slightly, motioning for the two men behind her to follow her out of the tent. Once she left, Ryder turned to face me.

"Come with me, MacKenzie. I'm going to show you what patrol duty consists of. I suggest you go visit Erica and ask her for a bow, you may need it..." he replied. I looked over at Darius, unsure of what to do.

"He's a big boy. He'll be fine, now go..." Ryder ordered, ushering me to leave. I stepped out of the tent, hurrying over towards the tent that served as the armory. I spotted Erica, sharpening a blade. Erica seemed rather occupied with the ten other people that she had there, so I didn't have much time to converse with her. She passed me a bow similar to the one that I held earlier today and showed me a smirk and a 'good luck'.

I rejoined Ryder, who was adjusting the sling so that his quiver fit nicely on his back. "That was quick," he noted, brushing a stray leaf off of his shoulder.

"Didn't want to keep you waiting," I replied, knowing he probably wouldn't care for a story about how my friend was too busy for me to hold a conversation with her.

"Smart choice, my time is scarce these days. Follow me," he said, walking back towards the vined entrance that we walked through when we first entered the camp.

"So, I've noticed that there are day and night patrols. How often does each one usually...patrol for?" I questioned.

"Just until you're finished your section. It should not take more than two hours. Night patrols are for our more...gifted members, as you would put it. Or those who seek to be gifted members," Ryder replied.

I looked over at him, raising an eyebrow. "So there are more people here that are for sure like me out here?" I questioned.

Ryder glanced at me for a second, and then continued to move forward. I rolled my eyes, getting rather annoyed with him not answering my questions. It's like I asked him for an inch and he took it as me asking for a mile.

"Our more senior members also take the night patrol," he said. We continued on for a little while, until I heard a rather familiar buzzing sound. I tilted my head, stopping in my spot.

"Is that..." I paused, pushing away a stray tree branch. I held back a gasp, stumbling backwards into Ryder's hard chest. He barely shifted, placing his hand on my shoulder to steady me.

"We frequently patrol out here to ensure that there are no hostile forces coming our way, such as the Sector Commanders give the order for their soldiers to come into our territory and eliminating us rather than just eighty six us. That is why when you first arrived many feared you. They thought you were a spy sent out by a Sector Commander to figure out how to destroy us," Ryder said, stepping around me.

"How nice of them to think such thoughts," I replied, sarcastically. I pushed the tree branch down again, looking at the sector. It looked like it usually did, all gray and...blockish.

"Come, there is a statue over in the Eastern corner..." he said, motioning for me to follow him.

I rolled my eyes in annoyance. It bothered me for some reason that Ryder somehow knew so much about the sector, especially since I had been in there the entire time it existed. Then again, I wondered how often he studied the ongoings in the sector from the outside. As we scurried around the perimeter, my eyes kept drifting back towards the sector. I could see the Sector Commanders building in plain view, and I felt an anger wash over me following my last encounter with him. Just the mere thought of him made my blood boil.

After walking around the perimeter for about twenty minutes, we arrived at an opening in the wood-line.

There it was, in plain view. The statue of Rocky that had once stood outside the Philadelphia Museum of Art. The statue had begun to rust, being that no one really had time to clean it or in the case of some people like Damian, they really didn't care to.

My heart hardened suddenly. *Damian.*

"MacKenzie," Ryder stated, interrupting my violent day dream. I shook it off, and then walked towards him. Once we were about three feet away, Ryder whistled twice.

As I opened my mouth to make a smart comment, I saw a familiar face step out from behind the statue.

"Major Chase?" I questioned, my voice breaking slightly. I couldn't even begin to describe the many emotions that passed through me at the sight of a familiar face.

Major Chase turned to face me, a smirk appearing on his face. "MacKenzie, it has been awhile," he replied, trying to sound cheerful despite his exhausted expressions.

"I... I don't understand. Have you been meeting with...Ryder this whole time?" I questioned.

Major Chase exchanged glances with Ryder and then turned back to face me. "I have been, actually. Ryder is the son of my late best friend, and battle from my very first deployment. When his father was killed during the war, I made a promise to look after him. So, I have been keeping up on that promise ever since then."

I looked over at Ryder, not sure whether I should be shocked or angered with him for not telling me he knew someone in the sector such as Major Chase. When I saw Ryder shoot me a side glare, I knew that he felt like I didn't need to know that piece of information.

Major Chase bent down, shifting one of the large rocks that were surrounding the base of the statue, which revealed a hole. Ryder bent down and did the same, moving the large rock on our side of the fence. It took me a couple seconds to get over the shock that was passing through me. All this time, Major Chase had been sneaking around and passing supplies into the woods for the eighty-sixers. I knew he had always felt pity for them, but I always thought it was purely based on his heart. I would never have imagined that he actually was close to someone on the inside.

Major Chase stuffed a medium sized box into the hole, and pushed it towards Ryder. I watched as the beige box slowly appeared on our side.

"Thank you," Ryder said, pulling the box out of the hole and setting it on the ground.

Major Chase nodded, and then turned to face me.

"How is Jax?" I questioned, feeling guilty for not asking that question the second I saw Major Chase.

"I haven't really seen him much. Since you left, they've been pulling longer shifts. I saw him maybe two days ago, and he looked like he was really missing his partner," Major Chase replied.

I looked down at the ground, feeling as though a rock had dropped in my stomach. I missed him too, a lot as a matter of fact.

"I'm glad that you found some of your own kind, MacKenzie. I really am," Major Chase said, his expression softening. I found myself stepping back at his words, in pure and utter shock.

"What do you mean? How do you...When did you?" I questioned, not sure which question to ask first. I knew that Damian and the Sector Commander had probably told everyone in the sector, if those who had seen it publicly hadn't spread the word first.

"I've known for years, MacKenzie. Your father knew something big was going to happen in this country before the war that created the sectors broke out. I don't know exactly how he knew, but he did. He told me about your powers, and he asked me to give me his word, as a father, that I would protect your identity and keep you safe," Major Chase responded, nodding in respect at the mention of my father.

"You certainly kept to your promise, sir...although I don't think my father would be very proud of me now. I'm eighty-sixed in the woods and its not like there are many wrongs to right out here," I said, looking over at Ryder. Ryder let out a deep exhale, looking over at Major Chase.

"Maybe you should try to remember what exactly it was your father would want you to do in your case. There are a lot of bad people out there MacKenzie. You'd be surprised. You're born to be a leader, so lead...." Major Chase ordered. I nodded, showing him a small smile. Somehow Major Chase had the effect of making me feel like a better, stronger person after having a conversation with him.

"Will do, sir..." I replied.

As he turned away, I was hit with a thought again. "Major Chase?" I questioned. He slowly turned around to face me, eyebrows raised. "Please tell Jax....I....I'm thinking of him," I said, looking down at the ground.

Major Chase smirked, and then nodded. "You have my word," he said, nodding towards me in acknowledgement. As he walked away, disappearing in the fog, I felt Ryder tap my shoulder.

"Come on, we must return to camp..." he said, motioning for me to follow him.

***

I could feel my head spinning as I stumbled through the streets of West Philly, my small plastic bag of groceries swinging in my hand as I did so. I couldn't help but laugh, wishing that I had taken the extra shot of Fireball Whisky that the cute guy with the blonde hair at the bar had offered to buy me.

As I approached my parents house, I let out a heavy sigh and then I pushed open the door.

"Parents! I'm home!" I sang, and then burst into a fit of laughter.

I heard the thunderous footsteps approach, as my father stormed down the hallway towards me. "MacKenzie, where the hell have you been?" he demanded. I scoffed, and then tossed him the plastic bag.

"I bought you some bread. It was buy one get one, thought you'd like it, Dad..." I replied, and then sat down on the steps.

I could feel the room spinning, and I pressed my forehead against the stairwell.

"MacKenzie, what is wrong with you? You're supposed to be a leader, not this....embarrassment." he snapped.

I laughed, making eye contact with him. "An embarrassment? I just found out that my ever so dear fiancé slept with someone else while on his deployment on top of two other women back here in the states. I think I deserve one night to be an...as you call it...an embarrassment,"

"Perhaps, or seven in your case. Imagine the image you are setting for our people right now. What kind of leader do you think you are? First the incident at Yellowstone Park and now this?" he questioned.

"I never asked to be a leader, Dad. Hell, I never even wanted to be this thing. Do you know how hard it is trying to find someone who cares about you when you have this....this curse?" I asked, finding the will to stand up.

"A curse?" he asked, his amber eyes darkening with anger. "You think your family, your legacy is cursed? You should give your ancestors more respect than that!" he yelled, pointing a finger at me accusingly.

I could feel a lump in the back of my throat, as salty tears formed in my eyes. "I don't want to lead anyone, I just want to be left alone. I'm not like you, I'm sorry I'm not a pompous, perfect asshole!" I said, walking towards the door.

"Where are you going now?" he questioned, his back to me. I could see his fists clenching at his sides, as if he was about to completely lose it.

"It doesn't matter, anywhere but here..." I muttered, throwing open the door and heading out into the streets.

I hurried down the street, trying to stop the slow tears from coming down my face. I hated the fact that whenever I was upset, it was as though I was being viewed as a weak individual in my fathers eyes.

After running a few blocks, I arrived at Jax's house and began knocking on the door. A minute later Jax stood there, his cell phone in his hand. He overlooked my figure, and his expression softened. I couldn't even begin to imagine how I looked.

I knew my eyeliner and mascara was probably running down my face, but I didn't really care much right now.

"MacKenzie....is everything alright?" he asked, stepping off his doorstep and reaching to caress my face.

"I had a falling out...with my dad. Is it okay if I stay here for a little bit?" I questioned.

"Of course, come right in. You don't have to ask," Jax replied, ushering me in.

My buzz was quickly wearing off, and my heart was growing heavy. "Are you sure Emily won't mind?" I asked, rubbing my arms as I approached the fire place.

"She went to Florida to visit some family members, and even if she were here, I'm sure she wouldn't have a problem with it at all..." he said, shutting the door.

He approached me, placing his hands on either one of my biceps. "MacKenzie, do you want to talk about what happened?" he asked, his voice softening.

"Just another fight with my dad....." I replied. Jax stepped closer, and embraced me gently. I could feel his hand stroking the back of my head, as he hugged me tight.

"It's alright, MacKenzie...I'm here to listen...."

***

"Newcomer, you need to get your act together already. Just because you've finished your third week here doesn't mean you're privileged enough to sit around while the rest of us do the hard labor," Skyler yelled, interrupting my thoughts.

I turned my back to face her, and rolled my eyes. Though I had still been continuing my training sessions with Darius, along with patrolling the afternoons with Ryder, the time had finally come when I had to work with Skyler. For the past week I had felt as though I was constantly under her watch, and anything I did was wrong in her eyes.

I threw a few ears of corn into the tan, woven basket and then moved on to the next row of stalks. I could see Erica, and she simply shook her head in response. Erica, Sarah and Devon had also witnessed and made mention to me on how Skyler was behaving towards me. They suspected it was because I was spending so much time with Ryder.

Ryder and I didn't even spend that much time together to begin with, or if we did it wasn't even intimate so I had no idea as to why Skyler was so pissed off about it. I heard footsteps behind me, and saw that she was right on my tail.

Her hair was pulled back into a tight pony tail, with a few stray bumps throughout. I couldn't help but smirk slightly. I never before this could say that I had frustrated someone to the point that they wanted to pull their hair out. Then again, I worked with mostly males in my career.

"Can I help you, Skyler? Or did I not pluck that husk correctly off the stalk?" I asked, narrowing my eyes at her.

113

She gritted her teeth, stepping closer to me. I think she was expecting me to back up in response, because when I didn't, she drew back slightly.

"You should know that I'm the absolute last person you want to piss off out here. I don't know what it is that Ryder sees in you that is so freaking special but I'm going to make sure, and I promise you that, you never get the honor of receiving the gift...." Skyler hissed, and then walked away.

I chuckled, and then made my way over towards Erica and Sarah. The sun was setting now, and it was about time we made our way back to camp.

"What did she say to you?" Erica questioned, as the encampment loomed into view.

"Nothing I couldn't handle, the same old...I don't know why Ryder sees something in you speech...." I replied, rolling my eyes.

"Can someone say jealous much?" Sarah asked, laughing slightly.

"I don't know what her problem with me is, because Ryder and I don't even communicate on an intimate level. We just...train, he's been a pretty complicated mentor actually..." I stated, remembering how Ryder always seemed to find a way to mask his emotions.

"He's paid more attention to you more than anyone else who has come to join us. In fact, I think the last person he paid this much attention to was Skyler herself," Erica replied, setting her basket of snow peas down in front of the tent where we stored the produce.

I went to make a smart comeback, but I saw Ryder approaching our group, Darius not too far behind. "MacKenzie, we need you to come with us..." Ryder stated, looking around at the three of us.

Erica and Sarah nodded their heads in respect, and then they both turned to face me. I had been dealing with Ryder on my own for the most part, so I still wasn't used to the customs nor the place among these people that he had. I nodded in respect towards him as well, meriting an eyebrow raise from Ryder himself.

He ushered for me to follow him, and Darius joined me at my side as we weaved our way through the people at the camp.

"What's this about?" I asked, looking up at Darius.

"We decided it was finally time to take you on your first official night patrol. Our day patrols thought they saw some spies in the woods just on the edge of our Western border..." he replied, pushing a stray bush out of my path so that I could pass.

"Spies?" I questioned, suddenly confused. Why would someone be spying on the camp? What if they were recently eighty-sixed from the sector and they were too petrified to try and approach the rest of the group?

"MacKenzie, all those stories you have been told through the years about us being a threat has not been the full truth..." Darius replied, his eyes scanning the area. Ryder continued on in front of us, remaining silent.

"What do you mean?" I questioned, looking back and forth between the two.

Ryder stopped, to look at me over his shoulder.

"It means, we aren't alone out here...."

12

We had been continuing on for about three miles and I had still been processing the thought. If we weren't alone out here, who else was out here? Rogue eighty-sixers who decided to start their own clan?

We had reached a line of jagged rocks, and Ryder held his hand up for us to stop. My eyes scanned up and down the column, which disappeared into the night. Something told me that this line of jagged, sharp rocks expanded the length of the forest. It was as if it were to serve as some sort of barrier.

Ryder stood up tall, and moved his head on a swivel as if he were looking for something. I was about to question Darius as to what he was doing, but Ryder suddenly snapped his head to the left and gritted his teeth.

It was then that Ryder pulled his shirt over his head, and Darius followed suit. I looked back and forth, unsure of exactly what was happening.

"Uh...What's going on guys?" I asked, confused.

"MacKenzie, I need you to change and go hide behind that mossy boulder over there and do not come out unless I tell you to. Do you understand?" Ryder questioned.

"Uh...." I began, still unsure of what was happening.

Ryder turned to fully face me, breathing heavy now. "MacKenzie, do it!" he whispered, harshly.

I looked at Darius, and then hurried off towards the boulder. My stomach began to turn, and I wasn't sure if it were in excitement or fear. I could feel the blood and adrenaline pumping through my veins. Whatever it was, it actually felt good. I felt like I was on the battlefield overseas again.

I heard a heavy 'thud' and I assumed that Ryder and Darius had now changed. I surveyed the area, and then I undressed myself. Once I was fully undressed, I closed my eyes and called for my tiger to come forth. I felt my body change, and when I opened my eyes, the night seemed so much more clear to me.

I peeked out from behind the boulder, to see that Darius and Ryder had disappeared. I groaned, sitting down on a bed of leaves. I never had thought about all of the dangers that the eighty-sixers had to have faced when I lived back in the sector. Sure, wildlife was always a concern but I never thought of enemies amongst the people out here. I would have thought that they would have all liked to band together and survive as one element.

I heard heavy footsteps approaching along with some heavy panting.

"Please...please...have mercy...please!" I heard a voice cry out. I perked my ears up, and I peeked out from behind the boulder once more. Two men, wearing very torn white t-shirts and black pants, had their backs to me and their hands raised. The one was on his knees, and the other was still standing.

Ryder growled, revealing all his teeth. "You should have considered the consequences of your actions before you decided to venture into *my* territory. Give me one good reason as to why I shouldn't erase you and your names from this planet,"

The two men looked at each other, and I could smell their fear even though I was a good distance away. I watched Darius and Ryder exchange glances, and then look back at their two detainees.

"MacKenzie!" Ryder called out, keeping his eyes on the two prisoners.

"What's a MacKenzie?" the kneeling one asked, looking up at his partner.

The standing man shook his head, "I don't know you idiot. They're going to kill us either way," he said.

I stepped out from my spot behind the boulder, and I slowly approached the group. I suddenly got this warm feeling on my back and I turned slightly to see that the moon was now free from the clouds, and was shining on me. It was as if it were illuminating me as I walked towards the group.

Darius must have noticed it too, as I spotted him tilting his head upwards slightly to look at it.

The two prisoners turned to face me, and the one that had previously been standing fell to his knees. I raised my head slightly, as I continued towards them, trying to put on the impression that I knew what I was doing.

They must have been no strangers to the fact that the white siberian tiger bloodline meant royalty, and it was clear to me that I was probably the first one that they had ever seen.

I slid in between Darius and Ryder and inhaled the scent of their growing fear.

"That's.....that's....." the first kneeling man said, his hands now shaking in fear.

Ryder looked at me, and then turned back to the two men. "Here's how this is going to work. You're going to return home to your master, and tell him that these spies he is sending into my realm must end. Otherwise, we will invade and destroy all of you. You tell him that Caesar Waters daughter is with us now, and she is ready to fulfill her destiny," Ryder said, followed by a snarl.

I was completely confused by what was going on, but I maintained my tough composure.

117

I refused to let these two see me confused and to foil whatever plan Ryder had up his sleeve, or currently, in his paw.

They finally stood up, and backed over the row of rocks. One of them must have nicked himself as they did so, because I could instantly smell the blood. I suddenly felt drawn to this scent, stepping closer towards them.

Darius stepped in front of me, as if he picked up on my arousal.

"Tell Erik that Ryder and Darius send their best regards," Ryder hissed, as the two of them disappeared in the dark.

I shook of the feeling of arousal, and looked over at Ryder. "Who is Erik?" I questioned. Ryder looked at me, and then continued to walk away.

"Come, we may as well finish up the night patrol while we are out here..." he said, and for the rest of the night we patrolled in silence.

***

Three days had passed and as far as I had known, there were no words of those mysterious men in our borders at all. Clearly the impression that myself, Darius and Ryder had left made quite the impression on whoever this Erik guy was.

I looked over at Darius, throwing my tunic over my head. He had been pretty quiet for the past few training sessions, and I suspected it had to do with this Erik person. The moment that Ryder spoke his name to those two men, I noticed that Darius turned away slightly.

"So are you going to tell me who this Erik character is or am I going to have to find out for myself?" I questioned. Darius set down his katana's, his back facing me. I could see his broad shoulders heave as he let out a heavy sigh. He turned to face me, his expression unreadable.

"When we first came out here, there were three of us that stuck together. Ryder, myself and Erik. We all banded together, setting up the stepping stones that built this encampment. We all were, gifted as you call it, in our own way. Ryder appointed himself leader of the group, once more and more people were eighty-sixed from the sector. That didn't sit to well with Erik. Erik was...always different," Darius said, looking down at the ground.

118

"Enraged and hungry for power, Erik murdered Ryder's fiancé...her name was Molly. She had been with the second group that joined us. Erik knew that she caught Ryder's eye, and when she announced their engagement, Erik got infuriated. He claimed he loved her first. I was the one who discovered Molly...Erik was standing above her in his...form. We fought, and he nearly killed me. He would have if Ryder hadn't heard the commotion and came into the tent," Darius said, pulling up the small stool and sitting on it.

I squatted down, listening to Darius with an intent interest. It seemed as though Ryder had a pretty scarred past too. I wasn't the only one who walked in on someone I loved having been murdered.

"Ryder had Erik exiled from our camp, and he had a Wiccan cast a spell on the borders so that Erik could not return," Darius said, his voice breaking slightly.

"Those rocks? Is that where she cast the spell?" I questioned, recalling the line of jagged rocks.

Darius nodded. "Yes," he said, simply.

"I'm assuming the three of you were close..." I said, taking note of Darius's rather unusual soft side.

"We were like brothers," Darius replied.

"You said he killed her in his form. Was he a tiger also?" I questioned. Darius made eye contact with me and sighed.

"Like I said...Erik was always different,"

I wasn't quite sure what to make of this, but I figured it was best that I let it go. As I made to apologize to Darius to asking such intruding questions, the tent flap swung open and Ryder entered the tent.

"MacKenzie, we must make our way to the border. There is something that you probably will want to see," he stated.

Darius turned away from me, and began cleaning the weapons that he brought in for our practice session. I sighed, and then followed Ryder out of the tent. We had walked in silence until the sector had finally come into view.

"Are we doing another drop off with Major Chase?" I questioned, somewhat excited about the idea of seeing an old familiar face again.

"Not exactly," Ryder responded, motioning for us to move towards the statue.

When we finally arrived there, I was surprised to see that there was no one there waiting for us.

"I'll leave you to be, I'm going to keep a look out to make sure no one comes our way." Ryder stated, as he began to march off.

119

"Why? Its not like those men will be coming back anytime soon, right?" I questioned. He continued to march forward until he disappeared into the thick brush. I sighed, suddenly somewhat panicked. I didn't know what game Ryder was playing, but I wasn't very amused by it.

I was about to take off after him, when I heard footsteps approaching the fence. I could see Major Chase looming into view, another figure with him, hooded. I squinted, trying to see who he had brought with him.

A second later, the figure pulled the hood back and I could feel my heart jump in my chest.

"Jax!" I exclaimed, stepping closer to the fence. The buzzing served as a quick reminder of the electronic fence, and its lethal capabilities.

Jax smiled, his lip tight. I overlooked him to see that he had lost a significant amount of weight, and his face looked pale. It was as if he hadn't seen the light of day for weeks.

"Hey Mac," Jax said, attempting to sound cheerful.

"What not happy to see your old partner?" I questioned, my hands on my hips in a mocking manner.

"Of course, I've missed you, MacKenzie. You look....so strong....and beautiful," Jax said, overlooking my figure. I folded my arms across my chest. I knew Jax long enough to know that something was wrong.

"Jax, what's going on? How is everything in the sectors?" I asked, looking back and forth between the two. They exchanged glances, and Jax looked down at the ground. "The truth, preferably..." I stated.

"Everything is...different since you left, MacKenzie. More and more people are getting executed by the day....." Jax said, avoiding my gaze.

I parted my mouth to let out a faint whimper, as I looked over at Major Chase. "Why?" I asked, my voice cracking. They exchanged glances one more time.

"Tell me," I hissed, stepping as close to the fence as I possibly could. A faint 'zap' told me that I probably burnt off a piece of stray hair.

"They are eliminating everyone that they don't believe to be worthy of living in the sector. No more eighty-sixing, just executions. They are even tracing back into people's backgrounds over the past seven years. Remember how if it wasn't a serious crime they would get three strikes before they got eighty sixed? That's all gone now. People who got violations for noise violations after hours are being executed....and I can't help but think its partially my fault," Jax said, looking down at the ground in shame.

"Why would it be your fault, Jax?" I asked, wishing I could just reach through the fence and embrace him.

"Because I gave those people the violations, MacKenzie. If I hadn't done it in the first place they wouldn't be at risk now. Children would still have both of their parents or at least the only parent they had if it weren't for me," Jax argued, looking back up at me.

"Jax, we all issued out those violations. It wasn't just you, you can't put that weight on your shoulders...." I retorted.

"You know me, MacKenzie. Of course I'm going to..." Jax replied.

"There's more," Major Chase spoke up, putting a comforting hand on Jax's shoulder. "They made everyone in the sector undergo a blood test to see if there were anything...different about them. They were looking for something," he stated.

"Anomics," I replied.

Major Chase nodded. "There were some people could not survive the test. Particularly the older ones. A lot of people died, the sector is playing a whole new game right now, MacKenzie,"

I could feel the tears building up in my eyes. "Well whats the deal with the whole no more eighty-sixing thing? Was I the last one?"

"The rules have changed, MacKenzie. It's a new time now," Jax said, his expression haunted. I knew that look. Every single time Jax dropped a body overseas, he would get that same haunted look on his face. Something told me he was forced to act out and execute people in the sector, and it was haunting his dreams and his mind.

"What can I do?" I asked, panicked. I wanted the old Jax back, I wanted my friends back. I wanted the killings to be stopped.

"For now, keep doing your training out here. I can see its made significant improvements. Your father set you on the path to leadership. When the time comes, you will know, MacKenzie..." Major Chase replied, nodding at me.

I bit my lip, and nodded in acknowledgement. I was disappointed that the most I could do was sit around and wait.

"We must make our way back. If we stray for too long it will be noticed," Major Chase replied, patting Jax on his back.

"Goodbye, MacKenzie..." Major Chase said, a small smile on his face. I nodded farewell, and then turned to face Jax.

"Will I see you again?" I questioned, somewhat pleadingly. Jax let out a small chuckle, and forced a wink.

"You know you will, MacKenzie...I promise," he said, and then turned away to walk off with Major Chase.

I turned to face the woods, eyeing a Monarch butterfly as it floated past my gaze. Its wings fluttered peacefully, as it drifted over towards a group of yellow daisies. I used to love chasing the butterflies when I was younger, but now all I was interested in was chasing down the leadership in the sectors. The butterflies were just going to have to wait.

"You can come out of your hiding spot now," I called into the thicket. A few seconds later Ryder emerged, his expression hard.

"What were you doing? Spying on my conversation?" I questioned.

"Sorry to disappoint you, but your conversations with your boyfriend hold little to no interest to me," Ryder hissed, sounding bitter.

"He's not my boyfriend," I said, defensively.

"He was my partner and my best friend for years and years. Why is everyone under the assumption that a female and a male cannot be just friends?" I questioned, shooting Ryder a glare.

"They cannot be," Ryder stated, moving past me. "Come, we are meeting Darius at the cave," he said, heading off in the direction of the cave.

"Really? If men and women cannot be friends, what do you call us then?" I asked, curious.

"We're animals," Ryder responded, not even bothering to make eye contact with me.

As we continued our movement, I began to wonder what Ryder must have been like before he was eighty-sixed. He never spoke to me about his time in the sectors, nor had he told me the reason as to why he was eighty-sixed in the first place. I got the vibe that once he entered the woods, he became the person that he was today. I'm sure the death of his fiancé played a role in it as well.

I knew for a fact that when the love of my life, or so I thought he was, cheated on me and broke my heart, it eventually led to my change also. Although my way of handling it at first took me down the road of booze and debauchery. It took me quite some time to get used to the mere idea of dating once more.

We finally entered the cave, and we immediately realized that Darius had not yet arrived. Ryder suggested that I sit down and rest, as they apparently had some sort of intense training planned for me that day. Maybe today we would actually do something productive instead of just stare at each other's tigers.

I leaned my head back against the wall, sliding down so that I could sit cross legged on the floor. Ryder removed his tunic, and began to walk around the edges of the cave.

At this point, I was used to seeing men walk around shirtless in my life without even having second thoughts about it.

122

A combination of the military, having male friends, and at one point in my life working as a volunteer EMT and firefighter did that to me. However, every-time Ryder walked around without a shirt on there was something about me that was absolutely intoxicated by his presence.

He was probably the most fit person I had ever seen in my life, with strong, protruded pecs and shaved abs. He just passed Jax if I were to compare the two when it came to fitness. I also had never encountered another male Anomic like myself, aside from my family, so I was sure that my tiger was partially to blame for my attraction to him.

He approached the wall, his eyes scanning the sketches. I noticed that was the first thing that he did every single time he walked into the cave. I was suddenly struck with a thought.

"Molly made them, didn't she?" I questioned. Ryder drew back, his body fully facing mine. The look on his face made it seem like I had just slapped him across the face...with a ruler.

"How do you know about her?" Ryder questioned, sounding somewhat demanding. I raised an eyebrow at him for his sudden change in behavior. If someone were to talk about striking a nerve with Ryder, the topic of Molly was certainly it.

Crap, maybe Darius didn't want me to mention anything about it. Knowing Darius, he was probably trusting in me not to.

"There are well over a hundred people in this camp, you think I would not find out about her?" I asked.

Ryder gritted his teeth, and then turned his back to me once more. I could tell he was breathing heavily, as I watched his broad shoulders rise and fall multiple times. I tilted my head, so that my bangs would fall to the side and I could see him more clearly.

"Well?" I inquired.

"Yes, she did..." Ryder finally responded.

I sighed, bringing my knees into my chest. I struggled to come up with another topic, to break the tension that was currently ongoing between the two of us.

"I know Darius told you," Ryder stated, his back still towards me.

"How?" I questioned, not even bothering to deny it. *Oops.*

"I was outside the tent when I heard him telling you. I knew you would find out eventually, without me even telling you. I'm just happy that Darius was the one to tell you about what happened," Ryder said, turning to fully face me.

My gaze fell to the tattoo on his chest area once more.

I had been meaning to ask him what it meant since I saw it the first time, but now probably wasn't the best time to do so.

"About Molly?" I questioned, brining my eyes to meet his.

"Molly, Erik, everything..."

"Darius told me that the three of you used to be like brothers. Have you run into him since you three got...separated?" I asked, trying to be careful with my words. I began to twirl the ends of my long blonde hair, missing having my friend, Theresa, working on it. She took care of my hair even before the sector system was set in place.

"Only once, and that was a year after he was banished from our land. He was scaling the border, trying to find a way back in to come and kill myself and Darius. Luckily our archers were able to scare him off. Until we saw those men in white, I believed Erik to be dead," Ryder said, pacing around the room.

"Well its not like he was there...it was two guys in white," I protested, trying to figure this Erik guy out.

"Initiates of Erik's. He did it the first year he was exiled from our camp constantly, trying to get people to sneak in and grab intel on us. How our camp was now set up, where Darius and I slept, if we were still alive...so that he could one day move in and kill us, which is what I was suspecting he was trying to do when he was spotting patrolling our borders that one day,"

"Initiates? So you think he has something going on over there like we have here?" I asked.

"More than likely, yes. Erik was always dark, from the days I first knew him until...well...probably still," Ryder said, squatting down against the wall.

I nodded, my eyes scanning the sketches on the walls. "And Molly, was she always afraid of Erik?" I asked, looking back over at him.

"No, Molly was the kindest soul that ever existed. I think Erik mistook her kindness for affection, and that's why he...." Ryder paused to clear his throat and to look down at the ground.

I quickly tried to think of something to change the subject. "So...um...I think you should ask Major Chase for some old board games or something the next time he makes a drop," I said.

Ryder looked back up at me, raising an eyebrow in question. Probably concerning my sanity.

"Board games?" he asked, trying to fight a smirk. Wow, he looked sexy when he smirked.

"Yeah, for the kids...I think it would be a cool bonding night for the people in the camp too, ya know?" I said, struggling to validate my point.

Ryder closed his eyes for a second and then chuckled. "Right," he said, looking away from me.

My eyes went back to the sketches, and I resumed my serious expression. "One question though...whats with the fighting tiger and lion?" I asked, pointing towards the design.

Ryder looked over at it, and opened his mouth to respond.

"I'm glad to see that the two of you have already arrived," Darius said, entering the cave. Darius looked back and forth between the two of us, and then shook his head.

"The two of you look so incredibly happy to be seeing me right now," he said, folding his arms across his chest.

"Just tired," I lied. Darius tilted his head slightly at my response.

"So what is it exactly that we are going to be doing today?" I questioned, moving my feet so I was sitting cross legged.

"We wait for nightfall, which shouldn't be too much longer now. We are doing a full-scaled patrol with your tiger. We will be joined by one other as well," Ryder said, beginning to pace again.

"Oh? Who?" I questioned, hoping that he would not be saying Skyler.

"You'll see when we go out," he replied.

I sighed, realizing that he was going back to his game of being stubborn and hard. Even though Darius was like a brother to him, I got the impression that he did not want anyone to catch him at a weak moment. I mean, who would?

I narrowed my eyes, looking back up at him as he continued his pacing. I would always work to find ways to get the information that I wanted, and in the end, I was usually successful. I realized with Ryder that I couldn't take the sweet girl approach, I had to strike for the kill.

"So what's with Skyler's obsession with you? How long were you two together?" I questioned.

I heard a faint chuckle from Darius, which he tried to disguise with his fist resting against his lips.

Ryder slowly brought his hard stare to meet mine.

"We were *never* together," Ryder said, with heavy emphasis.

I held up my hands innocently, shrugging my shoulders. "Hey, look don't shoot the messenger. I was just asking an innocent question because clearly, she's...overstimulated by your presence," I teased.

Darius couldn't even hold back his laugh, as it began to echo the walls of the cave.

"I'm flattered, but I'm going to pass if you don't mind...." Ryder said, a vein clearly pulsing on his neck. I smirked, there was something about the way that he was getting fired up that I found entertaining. I felt a tingling sensation in the left side of my brain and I knew that my tiger was getting somewhat aroused as well. I shook off the thought, maybe I should stop before it got too out of hand. I never had an incident where my tiger broke free at the arousal of another man, but then again, Ryder was the first Anomic outside my family that I met.

Darius looked at the hole in the ceiling to see that the sun had finally disappeared. "The stars have blanketed us, its time for us to get going..." he said, walking down the hall. A tearing sound followed by a heavy thud gave me the impression that he had just changed.

"Interesting way to say that it is now dark outside...." I said, rolling my eyes.

Ryder looked at me, motioning for me to move forward. "After you," he muttered, avoiding eye contact with me. I smirked, finding it somewhat cute that I had managed to embarrass him. I jogged down the hallway, welcoming my tiger as she broke free. I turned back to see that Ryder had already changed, his tiger looking almost as grumpy as he currently was.

The three of us wandered outside, and I tilted my head upwards as I felt the moons warm light wash over my face. Darius walked ahead of me, his tail swinging as he stared into the woods. I assumed that whoever his other person was, this was where they were coming to meet us.

Moments later, I saw another tiger emerge from the woods, wearing glasses. Darius shook his head, a somewhat smile on his face. I recognized those glasses.

"Devon?" I questioned, not even bothering to hide my surprise.

Devon turned to face me, bowing her head in respect.

"MacKenzie, I knew that you were one of us but I had no idea that you were the almighty one's daughter... the one who is going to s-"

"Devon, you're still wearing your glasses..." Ryder cut in.

"Oh, sorry..." Devon said, throwing her head to the side so that her glasses landed in a thick pile of leaves. Devon nodded, impressed. I looked back over to the pile of leaves and saw a shimmer of the moons light reflecting back at me. I assumed that this wasn't the first time Devon had forgotten to take her glasses off once changing, but prior to this time, they probably wound up breaking.

"Let's move out. Devon, you stay close to Darius and MacKenzie...you're with me. Once we get to the clearing we are going to split up and part ways," Ryder stated, trotting ahead of the group.

I looked over at Devon. "Please don't take this the wrong way, but I was never exactly suspicious of you having....being..." I struggled to find the right words so that I wouldn't offend Devon.

Devon smirked, her yellow eyes dancing with laughter. "It's okay, I knew exactly what you meant..." Devon replied.

"How did you know that I was one of them?" I questioned, expanding my stride to keep up with Darius and Ryder, who were ahead of us.

"I'm very spiritual you see, and I meditate with my tiger spirit frequently. On the eve that you arrived, she told me that someone just like me, someone great would be coming to join us. To save us. Then you arrived that night, and I knew it had to be you. I later confirmed my suspicions with Ryder," Devon stated.

I scoffed, somewhat annoyed. So it was okay for Ryder to decide who to tell and who not to tell about my gift? I couldn't help but feel slightly offended by that, it was my life after all.

"I'm sorry, I hope I didn't just make you angry..." Devon said, probably picking up on my anger.

"No, trust me...I'm not angry with you in the slightest, Devon.." I replied, staring daggers into Ryder's back. He and Darius continued to carry on their conversation, their tails swinging happily.

"So Devon," I paused to lower my voice. "What do you know about this Erik character?" I questioned, looking over at her. Devon bowed her head slightly, eyeing me from her peripherals.

"Not too much, only that he is a very evil person. Where did that come from?"

"Oh, nothing. I was talking to Ryder and Darius about it but they didn't say much other than he killed Ryder's fiancé and he has been banished from the lands...or camp..." I stated.

"Yeah, you've pretty much got the gist of it..." Devon replied, seeming somewhat uncomfortable.

We arrived at a 'V' in the woods, and Ryder turned to face me and Devon. Devon sighed, and then walked forward and continued on with Darius. I stood there, realizing that I would be stuck with Ryder for the next eight hours, and how awkward it was going to be considering how our last conversation ended.

I walked up so that I was next to him, and then looked over to await my marching orders.

"Typically, those of us with the gift will take on the night patrols. As you may well know at this point, a tigers vision is extraordinarily better than a human's. With our heightened vision and other senses, it is fitting that we take on the night patrol. As you may know from your military experience, the best time for an enemy to attack is at night. Frequently, we allow those who are seeking or are in the process of receiving the gift to join us on our night patrols, which a designated leader will bestow upon the selected individuals under the light of the blue moon," Ryder stated, as we began moving along the dirt trail.

"How do you select who gets to receive the gift?" I questioned, curiously.

"You're one of us, MacKenzie. Think of it in terms of....who do you think deserves the gift? Who would use it to their advantage and then who would use it to do good rather than do harm unto others?" Ryder questioned.

I smirked. "Not Skyler," I stated.
I was met with silence.

We continued down the path until we arrived at what appeared to be a medium-sized lake. My eyes widened slightly, as I took in its beauty. Fireflies danced across the surface, occasionally hitting the water and sending ripples across the entire girth of the water. White lilies were scattered around the edges, and I spotted a few pink tulips lurking around. As I approached the water, stepping on the large, surprisingly smooth gray rock, a breeze rippled through my fur.
I closed my eyes, enjoying how cool it felt despite the hot summer day. When I opened them, I saw my tiger staring back at me. Even though I had been used to changing for all these years, I was still fascinated every time I looked at my tigers reflection. Everything was so deceiving about the face of a tiger. When not hunting prey, we look so calm, like a house cat.
I saw Ryder's tiger appear next to mine, as he began to gaze back at his reflection as well.

"You act as though you have never seen a tiger before," Ryder stated, somewhat snarky.
"You know how they say that everyone has a demon inside of them?" I questioned.
"Well, this conversation just escalated quickly..."
"I'm being serious,"
"Yes, I do..."

I looked back at my reflection, and saw it tilted its head along with me. "Do you think that our tigers are our demons?" I questioned.

Ryder sighed, and then turned to face me. "No, not necessarily. We embrace who we are, we embrace our gift and our tiger spirit. People tend to keep their demons hidden. A person's demon is not something they tend to embrace, unless you're a sociopath or something. Everyone knows what demons they are hiding.. If you don't know what yours are....then well, I guess you're just special or something," Ryder said, swiping his paw at our reflections.

I watched as the water began to ripple, and our tigers were nothing more than a blur of orange and white. "Come, we are going to post up here..." Ryder stated, inclining his head for me to follow him.

I looked back to see my tiger's reflection re-forming and I let out a heavy sigh, and then trekked after Ryder. I found him laying in a small dirt circle, surrounded by reeds that were dancing freely in the breeze.

He turned to face me just as the breeze washed over my face again. I caught a whiff of something sweet off of him, and I quickly shook it off. This was not the congo, there was nothing romantic or anything of the sorts happening between Ryder and me, especially not while we were in our tiger form.

I growled in warning, and then laid down next to him. I pulled my gaze off of him and stared ahead, slightly surprised. I could see the camp clearly from where we were laying down. Several of the small fire pits were still going, and I was betting that Erica was sitting with a bunch of kids around one, telling them stories of heroes or the great spirits of the forest. I bet Joe was wandering around somewhere also, making sure that everyone was safe and ready for the night.

"Erica and Joe," I said, struck by a thought.

"What did you say?" Ryder asked, sounding rather exhausted.

"Erica and Joe. If it were up to me to decide who gets the gift next, I say it would be Erica and Joe. I've never seen two people care about our...family as much as they do," I replied, looking over at him.

"This is probably the first time you haven't flinched when you referred to us your family," Ryder stated, sounding surprised.

"Is that all that you got out of that sentence?" I questioned, shooting him an icy stare.

"Well, thank you for your input. By the way, we are going to be mixing up your training just a little bit tomorrow morning. I want you to train with everyone else in the camp tomorrow, with Skyler's class. As you know, tomorrow is the blue moon. So everyone is going to be on eggshells tomorrow while we decide who is getting bestowed the gift, along with who will be the one bestowing the gift itself...." Ryder said, extending his paws in-front of him so that he could stretch.

"You don't do it yourself?" I questioned, surprised.

"I host the ceremony, its nearly impossible for me to perform both. Darius normally does the bestowing, but this year it could be different. I think its starting to take a toll on him, the ceremony I mean. He's done it for the past seven years," Ryder said, turning his gaze to look up at the stars.

I joined him in looking upwards, spotting the little dipper immediately.

"How could it take a toll on a person? Aren't you essentially just biting people?" I asked, trying not to smirk at the idea of biting someone.

"Yes, but Darius has been leading our family beside me since the beginning. He's ready to focus more so on mentoring rather than leading constantly in my place when I am...not readily available. He wants to build warriors and spend more time with them, not just supervise and maintain order..." Ryder replied.

"So sort of like a platoon sergeant as opposed to a platoon leader, gotcha..." I said, resting my head on my paws.

I began to wonder where Devon and Darius were, and if they could see us from wherever they were resting right now.

"So I wonder what Devon and Darius are talking about right now?"

"Probably wondering what we are talking about..."

"Yeah, you're not the biggest people person and I'm the military brat who just wants to punch everyone most days. We get along just great," I stated.

We both turned to face each other at the same time, and I saw the smirk spread across his feline features.

"Get some sleep, I will take first watch..." Ryder stated.

My eyes widened in fear for a second, terrified that I would subconsciously change from my tiger form to my bare human form overnight.

"Don't worry, I promise to be a gentlemen..." Ryder stated, probably picking up on my anxiety.

"You better be..." I said, closing my eyes and letting the darkness take me.

13

"So where were you guys last night?" Erica questioned, sharpening her arrow on a small rock.

"Yeah, you guys missed a pretty good fire. Skyler actually managed to burn some of the ends off of her hair... don't ask how...actually, please do, it was quite funny..." Sarah stated, smirking as if she was recalling the memory.

Devon and I exchanged glances, and then Devon turned to face the two of them.

"We were out searching for those really amazing blue and orange berries that you found the other day...but we kind of got tired and fell asleep out there. That's the last time I sleep near a thorn bush," Devon joked, winking over at me.

"I told you to be cautious of your left side," I replied.

"They were on the right!" Devon retorted.

I stuck my tongue out at her, throwing a dandelion in her direction. A crunching of leaves caught my attention and I turned to see Skyler walking towards us, and I immediately noticed that a good third of her hair was completely uneven from the rest, the ends looking singed. Despite this, she still had her long brown hair brushed, cascading over her left side.

"Well, look who it is. The four muskrats. I'm rather looking forward to all four of you training with me today, on the morning of the blue moon. We are going to be having our sparring matches shortly and Devon, lucky you, you're up against me first..." Skyler stated, a wicked smirk on her face.

I couldn't help but notice that she didn't even acknowledge my presence other than the 'four muskrats' comment. Normally she would make every effort to single me out when I was near her, with either a 'newcomer' comment or a dirty stare. I guess Ryder's last comment to her about me really stuck.

Devon's face fell slightly, and she cast her glance to the ground. I realized in that moment that even though Devon possessed the gift, she only wanted to do good. She didn't want to hurt anyone, all she wanted to do was tend to her flowers and read her books. She enjoyed having the gift purely based on connecting with the spirit of the tiger.

"Oh don't worry, it won't be like last time. I promise not to make you look as pathetic as the last time we did this, but someone's gotta be the worst, and I can only do so much to help you...." Skyler said, sticking her nose up slightly.

Erica stood up, her fist clenching at her side. I realized what she was about to do, so I also stood up and stepped in front of both her and Devon. Skyler's eyes turned to face me, so that I received the full effect of her glare.

"I, on the other hand, Skyler, would be willing to go beyond 'so much' to make sure that you don't exceed anyone's expectations..." I stated, returning the same glare.

"Is that so, newcomer? What are you going to do? Go all *'Philly'* on me? Punch me with your iron fists?" she paused, mocking light punches on my bicep. I kept my eye contact with her, but swiped her fist away with my hand.

"Don't touch me," I snarled.

Skyler scoffed, stepping so that her face was inches from my own. She could get in my face all she wanted, I wasn't going to back down. If my tiger wanted to break free right then and there, I wouldn't even try to stop her.

"Stand aside, newcomer... so that I can escort the loser to the ring to spar against me, the champion..." Skyler hissed.

"Well if thats the case, I'm ready to escort you there myself...." I stated, tilting my head in challenge.

She hesitated for a second, and I could see the hatred she had for me burning in her eyes. "Fine, meet me down in the center of camp in fifteen minutes. I'll be there waiting for you..." she said, walking away.

"Come out and play, everyone. The newcomer and I will be having a little duel shortly!" Skyler called out, as she headed down towards the center of camp. I heard Sarah and Devon stand up, stepping closer to me. I felt Erica's warm hand land on my shoulder as I continued to stare down Skyler's back as she walked down the slope.

"MacKenzie, you don't have to do this for me..." Devon said, adjusting her glasses. "I can fight her, it's okay..."

I turned to face Devon, shaking my head. "No, I do. I know how she treats everyone here. You don't treat family this way," I stated, reaching out and putting my hand on Devon's shoulder.

"Especially.... us," I said, nodding my head. Devon smirked, knowing exactly what I was referring to. I was extremely happy to have gained a family in general, but having my own kind join me once again was exceedingly comforting.

"You're very brave," Erica stated.

I nodded in appreciation, and then turned to face the direction Skyler had disappeared off in.

"Let's go," I ordered, moving forward.

Even though I had been training with Darius for the past few weeks, a part of me was still slightly concerned about this battle. I had learned from my past that if you don't go into something confidently, you would for sure lose your way. Even though Skyler probably had years of hand to hand combat experience, I refused to let her get the best of me.

As we approached the center, I saw Ryder coming out of his tent with Darius right behind him. I was guessing someone had alerted them that the training simulations were about to start, and that Skyler and I would be going head to head. Judging by the amount of people that were rushing towards the heart of camp, everyone had heard about it.

I slowed my pace, watching as Darius and Ryder approached me. "You guys go on ahead, I'll be right behind you..." I said, motioning them to move ahead of me.

Erica nodded, and Sarah and Devon walked away with her.

"What do you think you're doing, MacKenzie?" Ryder questioned, his voice sounding surprisingly harsh.

"I'm standing up when standing seems impossible," I stated, referring to how I planned to knock Skyler off of her pedestal. I was going to strip away that image that she had that caused so many people to fear her.

"I think that she will be fine, Ryder. She has been doing very well in her training. I do not feel as though we need to worry about her in this battle today," Darius said, stepping next to Ryder and folding his arms.

"Yeah, well.... thank you. In case you haven't noticed, I have some business to attend to..." I said, turning away.

I instantly felt Ryder's hand clamp onto my bicep, and he stepped closer to me.

"MacKenzie..." he said, his voice softening. "Don't underestimate your opponent, ever. I know you and Skyler have your differences, but do not let your hatred guide you. Despite how...stiff...Skyler may be, she is probably one of the greatest warriors I have ever seen battle. Her father was a master at three different styles of martial arts, and she trained with Darius just as you have been for a longer period of time,"

I looked over at Ryder, for the first time struggling to retort with a comment that wasn't sarcastic.

"I'll be fine," I replied, pulling my arm free. Since when was Ryder so concerned about my well being and my safety?

I continued to walk down the slope, and I saw a large crowd standing there, staring at me. I never realized how many people were actually here with us, how big my family was.

They all turned their heads and followed me as I passed them, and I could almost smell the anxiety that was pulsating throughout the crowd. Not just anxiety, but there were also faint traces of fear. Not for themselves, but for me.

The crowd opened, and I saw Skyler standing in the open circle, kicking the loose dirt with her feet.

"Well, well, its about time that you got your pampered *sector soldier* ass down here..." she said, mockingly.

"A soldier, yes, I was a soldier...but the title before it, was *American* soldier. Always was, and it was never any different. Now I'm assuming you didn't want me to come down here just to chat with you, Skyler. Now how exactly do you want us to get this started?" I questioned.

She scoffed, folding her arms across her chest in defiance. "I don't think you know who you are messing with,"

Her cockiness was just one of the many factors about her that was beginning to piss me off.

"Do you?" I questioned, tilting my head.

I watched as Skyler approached me, her clear blue eyes full of anger. It was clear to me that she was going to attempt to use this training simulation to throw everything and anything that she possibly could at me. I knew she hated me and she knew I hated her. It was a vicious cycle. Two alpha females who refused to be submissive to the other, like in the animal kingdom.

I cracked my neck, returning the hard stare. I wasn't going down without a fight. I was fully aware of the fact that she was extremely capable of throwing down a hard battle. Even though I spent years studying martial arts, I knew a challenging opponent when I was faced with one. Not only that, but I knew better than to take a warning from Ryder lightly.

Skyler would be not be an easy opponent to defeat.

Skyler then launched herself at me, catching me off guard before I could contemplate what maneuver to use. We hit the dirt and gravel hard, my spine screaming in pain. She began to press her thumb into the soft tissue beneath my collarbone, her eyes filled with satisfaction as I let out a groan.

I took the opportunity to bring my fist across her face, sending her flying off of me. I rolled to me knees before standing up in a squatting position.

I was completely ready to strip her rank away from her, especially after the way I saw her treat my friends...my family. All my military career I was trained on how those that whom we called '*toxic leaders*', could severely impact the attitudes of their soldiers. Under Skyler, it was clear that everyone was either miserable or angry. From what Ryder and Darius had told me, she wasn't even really a leader. She just assumed that she was.

She let out a slight war cry, before launching herself forward and clinging onto my waist. I felt her bite my side, hard. I let out a small cry, before bringing my knee up into her neck twice. She collapsed to her knees, her hands falling to the floor. I seized the opportunity to stand over her figure, wrapping my arms around her neck in a sleeper hold technique. She began to flail like a fish out of water, desperately trying to get me off of her back. She threw herself to the side, so that my back hit the ground hard. I refused to give up, as I tightened my grip around her neck.

"Give it up, Skyler... I've got you now..." I whispered into her ear. She let out a strained laugh, tucking her chin down in an attempt to breathe while in my hold.
"That's what you think, bitch.." she said, before throwing her head backwards. Instant pain rushed to my forehead and nose as I was forced to let her go.

She switched positions, straddling me and seizing both of my hands and pinning them above my head. I began to squirm in my place. She leaned down as if to whisper in my ear. "You'll never take my place, and you will never be with Ryder... I guarantee you of that. He's mine," she hissed.
I smirked slightly at her jealousy. This confirmed my suspicions that for one, she had a thing for Ryder, and also that she believed herself to be the top female in the camp.
"Then why did he take *me* to the lake last night instead of you?" I questioned, before bringing my knees up into her kidneys, repeatedly.

She collapsed to my left in slight pain, and I took the opportunity to stand up, before turning her head so that she faced me. I debated saying something smart, but I decided that a punch would be perfect enough. I brought my fist across her face, knocking her to the ground.
I heard a few scattered claps throughout the crowd, and I rolled my eyes. Skyler continued to pant on the ground, frustrated.

"It's okay Skyler, I'll send you a post card from my new office," I stated, turning to walk away. I saw Ryder, a satisfied smirk on his face. I didn't even know that he had finally walked up to watch the fight.

I returned the smirk, waiting for him to comment.

"Newcomer!" I heard Skyler cry out, full of anger. I stopped in my tracks, and began to chuckle. She really didn't give up did she?

I rolled my eyes, before turning around to face her. "What do you want now?" I questioned. When I finished turning around, I widened my eyes slightly. Skyler's hair was a mess, and blood was pouring out of her mouth. She looked like the picture perfect crazy woman.

She pointed a finger at me accusingly, her hand violently shaking.

"I....warned....you...you BITCH!" she yelled, her voice echoing slightly in the silence.

I looked over at Ryder and Darius, wondering what they were thinking about the situation. Darius leaned in to whisper something to Ryder, and Ryder shifted his gaze to me. I couldn't tell if he was worried, or if he was waiting for me to get a handle on the situation.

Skyler threw her head back, screaming in frustration. Her scream turned into a roar as her clothes began to tear away from her and within seconds, I saw an orange tiger standing in front of me.

I narrowed my eyes slightly, I knew it. My instincts from when I first saw her were right, I could sense the smell of another feline from a mile away. With the exception of Devon, which I had yet to figure out how she managed to hide that from me.

I watched as her tiger's amber eyes stared me down, as she let out a roar of challenge. I saw Erica and Sarah push through the crowd, full of panic.

"That's an unfair advantage, you can't expect her to fight Skyler when she's using her power," Sarah stated, looking over at Ryder. Ryder merely held his hand up to her, telling her to silence her thoughts.

Skyler growled, taking a step towards me. I couldn't help but smirk at this. Everyone, with the exception of Ryder, Devon and Darius, were completely blind to the fact that I contained the same power as Skyler did. This included Skyler herself. I looked over at Ryder, who showed me a challenging smirk.

Devon slid in her spot next to Darius, and they both nodded at me. I saw Devon mouth something to the extent of 'you got this'.

I spread my legs so I they were shoulder-width apart, before I bent forward at the waist. I mocked her, using both my hands to motion for her to come forward.

"Come on," I taunted, whistling as well.

She hissed, showing all of her teeth as she began her advancement towards me. I sprinted towards her, my arms pumping at my side. As she leapt towards me, I rolled forward, her body passing over mine. I heard several 'oohs' as Skyler rounded about and turned to face me again, her tiger showing complete anger and hate.

It was then I decided it was finally time to reveal my secret to everyone. Whether Ryder was ready to allow me to reveal it or not, it was happening.

"Cool tricks, Skyler... would you like to see mine as well?" I questioned.

Skyler turned fully to face me, as she growled through her teeth. With that, I sprinted fully towards her, leaping into the air. I closed my eyes, and my tiger was already there for me. My eyes flickered open, as I felt all my senses expand as my tiger and I became one.

I watched as Skyler's tigers eyes were full of shock, as we collided. We tumbled to the ground, rolling in the dirt. I pressed her hard into the dirt to make my point, and then walked away from her. Skyler stood up, struggling to make her head lift to meet my gaze. When our eyes connected, I saw her eyes trailing over my face as if she were at a loss for words.

"The white tiger...." I heard someone from the crowd say.

"She's real!" someone else commented.

I began to breath heavily as I allowed a large roar to erupt from within me. Out of my peripheral vision, I could see several people backing away in fright. It was clear that they were not too familiar with seeing people change into other beings. That, or I was the last person they all expected to have the gift.

Skyler hissed, snapping out of her daze, as she took a swipe at me with her large paw. I ducked, before bringing my own paw up and smacking her across the face. When she turned to face me again, I could see three streaks where my claws had cut her face.

I watched as blood seeped down her whiskers, which she licked it away seconds later with her tongue. Once she tasted the blood, her eyes flared up with anger again. She lunged for me, claws fully extended.

She collided with me, and I felt her bite my shoulder area. I roared in pain, bringing my paw onto her back. I leaned forward, using her body to allow myself to assume almost a standing position.

Skyler released her bite on my shoulder, before attempting to stand on her hind legs as well. Her face was in-front of mine, as my paws rested on her shoulders and hers under my arms. I saw her mouth open wide as she bent down to bite my neck. I ducked, my teeth scrapping against hers. This was very painful for us both, but I was willing to go through the pain to gain the advantage.

I used my positioning to my advantage, pressing down on her shoulders. I heard a faint whimper from her, before I used my full weight to throw her aside. Once she was on the ground, I positioned myself so I was straddling her figure. When she turned to face me, her eyes blinking weakly, I brought my face extremely close to her face before letting out a deafening roar.

This was going to be my kingdom, and I would not let a toxic leader like Skyler continue to think that she was going to be the one who would lead our family. I watched as Skyler grimaced slightly, as she rolled on her back, revealing her stomach to me. She had surrendered.

I snarled slightly, before stepping off of her. Even though she had surrendered, I didn't trust her. She seemed like the kind of person who would play possum and then launch a surprise attack when my back was turned towards her.

Ryder walked forward, and began patting my head.

Skyler slowly stood up from her spot, looking over at me with a glare. Her legs were shaking slightly, and she was panting quite a bit. The fight had obviously taken a lot out of her, and I couldn't help but be pleased with myself.

Ryder took his hand off my head, muttering for me to stand next to him as he turned to address everyone.

"I'm sure you are all wondering why after a little over a months time, you have never been told that MacKenzie possesses the gift. A decision which I did not want to make known to everyone, because from the minute she came here, I had a greater purpose for her. Not just for the prophecy, but she will be the one bestowing the gift to those whom she believes have merited the right to receive it," Ryder said, looking over at me.

I turned to face him, trying not to act as surprised as I actually was. Prophecy?

"I knew that if you all were to find out that she possessed the gift, you would immediately accept her and try to befriend her solely based on who she was. I've learned that many of you have made me proud, accepting her for who she really is..." Ryder paused to look at Erica, Sarah and Devon

"And some of you have not," Ryder stated, looking over at Skyler. Skyler hissed slightly, and began pawing at the ground.

"MacKenzie, the decision is yours. Which two do you believe are fit to receive the honor of gaining the gift?" Ryder questioned, turning to face me once more.

For a second, I felt my stomach flip. I was anticipating having to make a major decision that would affect the lives of multiple people. I turned to look over at Darius, seeing if he would be willing to give me any guidance. He merely inclined his head in my direction, as if he were telling me that I already knew what to do.

I turned to face the group, my eyes glancing over at Ryder. I remembered what I had said to him the other night, realizing that was why he had probably questioned who I would have chosen. He knew all along that I was going to be the one to grant the gift, he was probably curious to see if he was right in deciding to allow me to do so.

"Erica," I paused, looking over at her. She looked beyond surprised, as she raised her fist to her heart. She weaved her way through the small line that was in front of her and moved so she was in front of me. I shifted my gaze from her to look back at the crowd again. "Joe,"

Out of the corner of my eye I saw Devon bring her hand to her face, and when I looked over at her I saw her smiling. Joe turned to face her, returning a smirk, and then headed up towards me, pounding a fist to his heart.

He approached me and nodded respectfully.

Ryder then took his place next to me once again, and addressed the crowd. "MacKenzie has made her selection, take the rest of the day preparing for the ceremony tonight, no more training. Today is a day of celebration, I encourage you all to do so...Darius...ensure that our distinguished members are prepared for their initiation tonight,"

Darius nodded, and motioned for Erica and Joe to follow him. Everyone else broke into conversation, some moving away and going off to do their own thing, while everyone else continued to stare at me in awe.

"Skyler," Ryder stated, looking over at her. Skyler growled slightly, as her gaze shifted between me and Ryder.

"If there is nothing else you need from me, I'll be in my tent. Don't count on seeing me at the ceremony tonight," Skyler hissed.

"This is not your decision to make, Skyler. You will be at the ceremony, because you will support your family members. They were all there for you when you were received your gift," Ryder replied.

"Not to interrupt anything," I said, looking bath and forth between the two. I knew that if Skyler were to attempt to go after him in her tiger form, Ryder would have no hesitation to change as well and throw her down. "But I would like to get out of this form, and I'm sure Skyler would to,"

"I don't need *you* to speak for me, newcomer. But I guess you're calling the shots now anyway," Skyler stated, stalking off into the wood-line.

I turned to face Ryder, unsure of what to say.

He simply smirked in reply. "Go get dressed, you have a big evening to prepare for..."

"Funny, but I don't know what I'm exactly supposed to do..." I replied, watching him walk away.

"When the ceremony begins, you'll know what to do. I'll walk you through it," Ryder replied. "By the way, nice choker hold..."

I smirked, and then headed towards my tent. There were still a good amount of people around, and they all watched me as I walked past them. I was probably the first white tiger they had seen in many years, if ever. Once I arrived at my tent and realized that no one was there, I closed my eyes and allowed the change to come. Once I felt the cool air hit my bare body, I immediately grabbed my spare clothes from under my bed and began getting dressed.

I knew Ryder told me before that people could only become an Anomic by either getting bit, or by having the gift passed down to them at birth. If I was going to be the one bestowing the gift, did that mean I would have to bite them while changed myself? Not only that but if that was the case, how long was too long? How long wold it take to work?

I had never bitten another human in my tiger form before, so I didn't even know how it would feel. I just couldn't picture myself biting Joe and Erica.

A few moments later the tent flap swung open, and Erica entered the tent with some of the other females. Devon was carrying a bunch of bowls in her hand, full of what appeared to be different colors of body paint.

"What is this for?" I questioned, curiously.

"Paint for the ceremony. It's tradition that the selectees are painted by their family members on their faces, and their necks..." Devon responded.

140

I watched as Erica sat down on the edge of her cot, and Sarah immediately began working on her hair. Erica turned to face me, and a smile crossed her face.

"MacKenzie...thank you...." she said, her smile genuine.

I nodded in return, not sure of what else I could say.

"I wonder where Skyler went," I said, suddenly thinking of how she disappeared into the woods, and then wasn't heard from since.

"Who cares, but you totally kicked her butt today. That was pretty awesome.." Sarah said, twirling Erica's hair into a bun with two braids traveling down her scalp into the base of the bun. Sarah was handling Erica's hair with such delicate hands, acting as if Erica's hair were almost sacred to touch.

"Yeah it was, here come sit down...I have to do your makeup as well," Devon said, patting for me to sit down at the edge of my cot.

I slowly sat down, unsure of what to expect. Devon dipped her fingers in the blue and white paint, and moved to touch my face. I flinched at her touch, the paint unexpectantly cold. Devon muttered a 'sorry' and then continued making small lines on my face. I didn't understand how this was relevant, considering I would be changing forms anyway, but I decided to just go with it.

"So, MacKenzie, what is it like to change? I know you'll probably say that *you'll find out* but...I never really have talked to anyone about this before. I don't know what to expect," Erica said, glancing at me through her peripheral vision, knowing that Sarah would have likely smacked her on top of the head for moving while her hair was getting worked on.

"Well..." I paused, trying to find the words to say. I remembered having this conversation with Jax, and my mind was instantly filled with memories of him. Not that I had forgotten about him, it was just that my mind had recently been occupied on other things. "Thrilling. There is nothing like feeling all your senses strengthen, tigers can see much better than that of a human... you'll see sights you never thought possible, you'll smell scents you've never picked up on before...the feeling of the wind rolling through your fur is exhilarating," I said, recalling my first few experiences with the transformation.

"Well I'm sure it hurts just a little bit... a human and tiger body aren't exactly the same thing..." Erica stated, sounding slightly nervous.

"I wouldn't say it hurts, its just a wee bit uncomfortable at first." I replied.

"In other words, yes, it hurts," Sarah said, laughing.

Devon pulled away, standing up and moving onto Erica. I realized that was her way of telling me that she was done. I found it odd at first that Erica and Sarah didn't ask Devon more about her and transforming into her tiger, but thinking about it further, they probably didn't know. I remember in my conversation with Ryder from the night before that he mentioned that Devon's small frame and quick speed gave us a serious advantage. Maybe she was like the spy for the clan? If no one knew her identity, then she would not be compromised.

"How many others are Anomics?" I questioned, looking around at the three of them.

"I would say maybe ten, the others don't ever transform...unless they are patrolling." Sarah stated.

I stood up, and began stretching my arms, being careful not to let my arms brush against my face and ruin Devon's paint job. I didn't even know what it looked like, but I trusted Devon and her judgement. She wouldn't make me look like a fool. Besides, I was going to be changing into my tiger at some point anyway so if I did look ridiculous no one would see it for too long.

"Well, I'm going to go find Ryder and see what I am doing about this thing tonight. I'll see you girls in a little bit," I said, lifting up the tent flap. As soon as I did, a disheveled Skyler appeared, a scowl on her face.

"Shove it, newcomer..." she hissed, as she began to make her way over to her cot. She knelt down, throwing her trunk on the cot, and it bounced in protest.

I looked over at Erica, who couldn't help but chuckle. Skyler looked as if she were about to make a smart comment, but when she made eye contact with me she simply just maintained the scowl on her face, combing a stray leaf out of her hair

I rolled my eyes, and headed outside the tent. There were people gathering already, standing around the area where the fight had taken place earlier. Children were running around and gathering sticks, throwing them on top of what appeared to be a large pile that would host a bonfire.

I spotted Darius, folding his arms and staring off into the woods. I raised an eyebrow at this, and headed towards him.

"I spy something green," I stated, once I reached my place next to him.

"There is a foul stench in the air tonight," Darius replied, continuing to stare into the wood-line.

"Well, maybe someone forgot to cover their slit trench after they went to the bathroom or something..." I replied, trying to pick up on what he was smelling.

"It smells like death, blood has been spilt this night. Friendly blood, by an enemy..." Darius said, looking over at me.

I paused, unsure of how exactly I was supposed to respond to something like that.

"Well, maybe you should bring it to Ryder's attention...if its friendly blood spilt by an enemy," I said, unsure of what 'enemy' Darius was referring to. Maybe one of Erik's men had somehow snuck into our dominion again and killed one of our own? Then I remembered what Jax had said about the executions in the sector. Was Darius picking up on one of them?

"No, he has the ceremony to think of tonight..." Darius said, running a hand over his smooth, bald head.

"Well we need to make sure none of our people are lost, Darius. If we aren't going to tell Ryder than during the ceremony the two of us have to keep an eye out to make sure everyone is accounted for," I said, feeling a little flustered. It had been a good while since I had dealt with a severe enemy, especially one that would ambush so close to home.

"No, MacKenzie. You need to focus on your role in tonight's ceremony. Let me worry about this...situation, if it even is anything at all. Could just be a hunch, or a nervous tick," Darius said, shrugging his shoulders.

"How often are your hunches wrong?" I questioned, knowing what the likely answer was, judging by Darius's body language.

Instead of replying, Darius sighed. "You should start preparing for the ceremony tonight, you are, after all, the main event..." Darius said, a small smirk on his face.

"I don't even know what I'm supposed to do," I confessed.

"Just listen to Ryder when he talks, he will guide you through it. There is no possible way that you could mess anything up," Darius said, putting a hand on my shoulder. "I have full faith in you,"

"Have you met my anxiety lately?" I joked.

Darius smiled, shaking his head. "The ceremony will be starting in three hours. Why don't you take some time to yourself and meditate with your tiger? You'll need to feel more connected to her tonight more than ever for this ceremony," Darius said, nodding towards the wood line.

I nodded, and walked off into the wood line, heading towards the cave where I had done my many training sessions. I wondered what my father would be thinking right now, if he could see me preparing to bestow the gift onto two warriors.

I suspected he would be proud, but there was always a difficult side to him. He harped on me for years, trying to get me to accept that I would one day be a leader to our people. He was always a complicated person. He never really expressed emotion, and he refused to let anyone be under the influence that they could even remotely guess what he was thinking.

Mother, on the other hand, loved expressing emotions. I could always tell when she was proud of me, or when she let that Irish temper fly and she would unleash hell on my siblings and I. She knew that even though I was meant to take a role of leadership, my destiny could take me anywhere I wanted to go. Anywhere I dreamed of going.

I finally arrived to the cave, and sighed. Too long had I trained in the cave, too long had I refused to accept my gift. I sat down, with my back to the wood line and facing the cave. As I stared into the cave, I realized in that moment, I never had a reason to be ashamed of who I was or what I possessed in the first place.

I was always meant to have a purpose, and tonight, I would bestow the gift onto two warriors that I would feel proud to claim as not only my brother and sister in the clan, but a brother and sister in a shared phenomenon. This ceremony, would just be the beginning.

14.

My breath quickened as I sped through the alleyways, desperate to find my parents. I was now wishing we stayed in Jim Thorpe, none of the houses looked the same and I knew the area. I was new to Philadelphia.

I could feel my paws getting sore and heated, but I didn't care. My priority was to find my family, and nothing could stop me from doing so. As I rounded up on our block, I saw five Relinquished members standing there, firing into an alleyway. I hissed, letting out a roar to make them aware of my presence. The one closest to me immediately dropped his weapon, his hands waving in the air.

"You told me we got the last of them!" he yelled over his shoulder, back to his comrades.

The last of them....?

The one that I assumed to be the leader turned to face me, pointing a finger in my direction. "Kill her, and make their kind extinct..." he yelled, his voice muffled by the black ski mask that covered his face.

The other three turned to face me, charging their weapons as they did so. The leader pushed the one that had dropped his gun to the ground, yelling for him to pick up his weapon.

I growled, having a feeling what they meant by the whole 'last of them' comment. The leader headed down a different alley, leaving his four henchmen behind. I didn't have time to deal with these pests, not while I was searching for my family while the fireballs of war and hell were raining down on us.

I lunged for them, and they all scattered, dropping their weapons and yelling in fear. I swiped my paw, grabbing the one that was closest to me and throwing him to the ground. He was shaking rapidly, wiggling like a fish out of water to try and escape my grip.

"Your leader said 'the last of them', you have exactly fifteen seconds to tell me before I rip your face off you worthless little shit," I hissed, my teeth inches from his face.

"I don't know, I don't know!"

"Ten seconds,"

"Guys come back and help me, shoot her!"

"Five Seconds,"

"I didn't sign up for this crap, when I get out of here I'm going to use your fur for my mantel piece!"

"Your time is up," I hissed, raising my paw and unsheathing my claws. The second he saw the claws, he screeched like a small girl.

"Okay, there were four of them back there.... in the house with the White Lilies in the window garden things. We killed them all," he said, salty tears rushing down his face.

My stomach flipped, but I refused to show any signs of weakness. "Killed....who?" I asked, my anger rising.

Panic was flooding my brain.

"The other ones...the other tigers, please don't kill me. I was just following orders," he whined.

I leapt off of him, and continued down the block. Jax and the others would not be too far behind me, they could deal with him. I refused to believe it, I refused to believe that my family was dead.

My eyes set upon my parents townhouse, and the first thing I saw was that our large bay window had been shattered. Not a good first sign. I swallowed hard, nudging the door open. As soon as I stepped inside, I could feel the glass crushing underneath the weight of my paws, but I didn't care. A few cuts and scrapes were the last thing that I was worried about right now.

That was when I smelt it, blood. I knew the smell all too well.

I followed it into the living room, and my jaw nearly hit the floor in horror. My father and my mother were both laying on the area rug, their throats slit. I began to feel my throat close up, as I panted heavily. I felt myself slowly transform, and I reached for the Green Bay Packers snuggie that was on the couch so that I could cover myself up.

I fell to my knees, covering my face with my hands. I didn't even dare to look yet for my brother and my sister, knowing that they had probably shared a similar fate.

"Mom? Dad?" I questioned, crawling over to my mother's body. Her blue eyes stared back at me, glazed over. "Mom?" I asked, running my hand over her hair. I held back a sloppy sob, as I gently laid her back down and crawled towards my father.

"Dad? Dad?" I asked, slowly shaking him. His eyes remained shut, and his face was cold. "Dad, I'm sorry. I'm so sorry, Daddy!" I said, starting to cry hysterically.

"I'm sorry I disappointed you, I'm sorry I didn't get here in time..." I said, and then collapsed on the floor a few feet away from them.

I closed my eyes and began sobbing hysterically, at the moment, not even caring that my world was potentially ending around me. I couldn't believe that the last time I saw my father in person, we were arguing. I should have came and talked to him in person instead of apologizing to him on the phone.

I heard footsteps approaching me, and I could faintly hear Jax calling my name. I covered my face and began to cry again.

Moments later, I felt Jax seize me under my arms and lift me to my feet, pulling my away from my parents bodies.

"What are you doing? I can't leave them!"

"MacKenzie, they're gone. There is nothing you can do,"

"Then let me lay here and die with them, I need to see them again!"

"I'm not going to let you do that, I'll drag you out here if I have to,"

I let out a final scream of protest as a thunderous 'boom' echoed through all of Philadelphia and Jax and I collapsed to the floor, the last thing I saw was the red flash of the explosion reflect off of my parents faces.

***

"MacKenzie?" I heard a voice say, a warm hand landing on my shoulder.

I looked back to see Devon standing there, small yellow and blue streaks on her face as she peered innocently at me from behind her glasses.

"Sorry, I was just...in a thought," I replied, trying to shake the picture of my parents laying dead on our living room floor from my brain.

"I noticed... you were shaking," Devon replied, pushing her glasses back up the bridge of her nose.

"Yeah, I was just...remembering what it was like when I stumbled upon my parents. We had a fight the night before, my father and I. I was young and immature, I didn't care about carrying on my family lineage or anything. I only cared about making Mackenzie happy. I left and spent the night at Jax's house.... he convinced me to call my father the next day and apologize. My father was very forgiving and told me that I could make it up to him by coming over and cooking my Italian Wedding Soup for him that night. I was headed to their house, the groceries in my hand.... that's when the raids and the shooting started. I should have ran to my house and gotten my family out, but instead I followed my soldierly instincts, and went to the armory to get weapons and fight back...take out the enemy. My family paid the price for it," I said, feeling the tears building up in my eyes. I swallowed hard, trying to get rid of the lump in my throat.

"You can't blame yourself, think of all the lives of the people you probably saved. Your father would have been proud of you, he probably would have been infuriated with you for running to them instead of saving everyone else.... from what I've heard, your father was a great leader," Devon stated, squatting down next to me.

147

"Oh, he would have murdered me for coming back for them and not saving everyone else.... but it doesn't matter, I should have at least tried.... that way I could have seen their faces, alive, one last time..." I said, fiddling with the dandelion that was in front of me.

"You know, when the medics pulled me and Jax out of the house.... they had to do a thorough sweep to make sure there were no other survivors. The medic captain wrote in his report that when they went upstairs...they found the bodies of my little brother and sister. They were completely naked, which means they probably changed and tried fighting those *Relinquished* members as their tigers...but... they could barely tell which one was which...those...assholes...mutilated my little brother and sister," I said, feeling a tear slowly sliding down my face.

Devon reached over and put a comforting hand on my shoulder, and her face fell slightly.

"Even in their tiger form, they were only cubs. How could those...monsters...do that to them? They were just kids..." I said, wiping away the tears that were spilling down my face.

I let out a heavy sigh, and then stood up, looking up at the sun. "That's why I became a sector soldier. It was my first thought when I woke up in the hospital bed that next morning. I made a promise to myself that if those *Relinquished* members ever showed their face to me again....I would handle them myself, not just as me, MacKenzie..." I paused, turning to face Devon fully.

"But as the demon inside me," I stated. I could see that in the reflection of Devon's glasses, my eyes were the brilliant blue of my tiger. Every time I told the story, she somehow wormed her way out. I closed my eyes and shook my head, telling her to back off.

"Why do you call it a demon? I don't believe that's what it is at all. You yourself, said that it was a gift...." Devon stated, somewhat confused.

"It is a gift, but there were moments when I had been tested to the point where I nearly lost the control over her...and I've felt her rage. While it is a gift, it is also a danger. You cannot let your rage combine with hers, because if you do.... its near impossible to stop it. Believe me, I let it happen once already. When I was in the sector, one of my own was abusing a child....it made me angry, it made me think about the innocence of that child. All he was doing, was trying to provide for his family. It flashed me back to the abuse my brother and sister suffered from those rebels. It made me so angry," I stated.

148

"And....your tiger? What about her anger?" Devon questioned.

"Motherly instinct, I suppose. The need to protect the cub..." I replied.

"How did you stop yourself from losing control?" Devon asked, folding her arms.

I thought for a moment, recalling the moment as it happened. The fear in Wesson's eyes, the little boy's face when he saw my tiger.....

"Jax was there," I said, turning to face her. "He has this...aurora that calms me. If he wasn't there, and he didn't say my name to snap me out of it...there would have been a blood bath in the middle of the square," I said, running and hand over my hair.

"This Jax, are you close?" Devon questioned.

"We have known each other for years....we deployed together, patrolled the sector together...I feel bad, his wife is being held in another sector. He still writes to her all the time," I said, trying to remember the last time he mentioned getting a letter from her. I hoped for his sanity that she was still alive.

I turned to look at Devon. "But enough about me, when is this ceremony getting started? So I can finally get this whole...biting thing going and whatnot," I said, brushing my hands together to get the stray dirt off.

"That's why I was coming to get you, it will be starting shortly..." Devon said, motioning for me to follow her back to camp.

I must have been 'meditating' with my tiger and my thoughts for a pretty long time.

As we approached camp, I could see the large bonfire in view and several other people were already transformed into their tiger forms. I turned to face Devon.

"Are you going to be transforming as well?" I questioned.

Devon shook her head. "No, its a tactic of Ryder's. Only three people, including you, know that I can transform. It helps out with the whole 'intel' thing, and I'm sort of like the spy if you will for the camp. I'm the one that no one suspects, so, I make the perfect one..."

"Oh...gotcha," I replied, looking over and seeing Darius throwing a few logs into the pile. People were starting to gather around, forming a half moon on the other side of the large fire. I spotted a large wooden platform, and a red carpet lay in front of it.

"What's with the mini stage over there?" I asked.

"That's where you will be standing during the ceremony," Devon answered, turning to walk away from me. "You should get going, I'm going to go find Erica and Joe and make sure that they are ready for the ceremony,"

I nodded, and walked up to Darius. He sighed, staring into the fire.
"That's a sure fine way to go blind," I said, tilting my head at him.

He faced me, a small smile on his face. "Are you prepared to do what you have to do?" he questioned.
"As best as I can be...I still don't know what I'm doing," I said, honestly. I really had no idea what my role was in this thing, aside from biting two people. Where would I even bite them? On their arm? Their head? Oh god, hopefully no where too...grotesque.

Moments later, Ryder emerged from his tent. He was shirtless, his body paint in blue and red streaks all over his rippled abs and two handprints on his fit chest. His hair was newly cropped, and the reflection of the flames created the perfect shadowing on his built arms and shoulders.
He approached me, and I forced my eyes to meet his. The blue moon, the overwhelming fire, the muscles.... it was all too intoxicating. I needed to focus, I had to focus.
"MacKenzie," he said, his voice sounding even more smooth than it normally did.
"Yeah?" I questioned, biting my lower lip and forcing my eyes to meet his again.

He merely smirked. There was no possible way he could not pick up on my attraction for him right then and there.
"Are you ready for your ceremony to start?" he questioned.
"I'm totally ready," I said, mentally slapping myself for sounding like such a ditzy girl with a big crush.

Ryder nodded over to his left, and I saw three people banging sticks on this hollow log to create something of a marching beat. I saw my fellow tigers slowly take their places behind me, out of the corner of my eye.
"MacKenzie...get up on the step..." the closest one to me whispered.
"Oh, right..." I muttered, standing up on the step.
They shifted, so they formed a line directly behind me.

150

I could immediately recognize the grumpy tiger on the end, Skyler, who seems to be more interested in pawing at the protruding tree root than what was going on in the ceremony.

Ryder moved away from me, standing so that he stood diagonal from the step that I was on. He nodded to me, signaling that it was time for me to change.

I closed my eyes, calling for my tiger to come out. There was something very different about this time, as I felt my body slowly transform to hers. It seemed almost...magical, or as close to magical as it could be.

I opened my eyes and saw Erica and Joe standing side by side, dressed in a carbon black tunic and matching pants. They began to walk towards me, their eyes focused on me. I shifted for a second, so that I stood up on all fours. I still wasn't exactly sure of how I was supposed to behave or what I was supposed to do, but standing up was probably a good starting point.

Once Erica and Joe were right in front of me, the crowd directed their attention forward.

Ryder also stepped forward, earning a nod from both Joe and Erica.

"You are wearing black tonight....because this is where your old selves have come to depart this world, and then you will be reborn..." Ryder stated, turning his gaze to stare over at the fire.

"When you are reborn, you will feel ignited with a fire like never before. You will make your ancestors proud," Ryder said, and then he turned to face Erica and Joe again. Joe looked focused, determined for whatever was about to come his way. Erica, appeared slightly nervous, and I couldn't blame her. Though receiving the gift was very honorable, it was also very overwhelming.

"MacKenzie, will you imprint our new brother and sister...on their left shoulder, above their hearts, symbolizing the bond between human...and tiger," Ryder ordered, nodding to me in acknowledgement.

I turned to face Erica and Joe, still feeling uncomfortable. Although Ryder had given me instruction, I still wasn't completely okay with the idea of just outright biting someone in my form. What if this was like a vampire thing, and I couldn't control myself once I tasted blood and I didn't know when to let go?

Joe stepped forward first, kneeling down directly in front of me. I had always been born with the gift, so I couldn't even warn them as to how this was going to feel, but I imagined that regardless, it would probably hurt.

I stepped forward, lowering my head towards Joe's shoulder. He leaned his head to the side, opening up more room for my large head.

"Sorry, this will probably hurt...." I said, apologetically. I opened my mouth, and then clamped down on his shoulder. At first, I didn't feel any different, making me feel like I was only making Joe uncomfortable. Then, I felt a jolt through my body. I clamped down fully on Joe's shoulder, causing him to groan slightly.

I closed my eyes, feeling this energy leaving me and pouring into Joe. After a few seconds, it stopped and I released my hold on him. I backed away, trying to get a look at his face to see if there were any immediate changes.

After a few moments, Devon ran forward, dressing up his wound with a quick dressing. Once he was complete, he shifted back and motioned for Erica to move forward.

Erica knelt down in front of me, the same nervous expression on her face. I tried showing a slight smirk, feeling more confident with myself in the fact that I didn't kill my first initiate, so the second one would be even easier.

I moved towards her, using my snout to nudge her head to the opposite side so that I would have enough room to make my mark.

As I moved towards her shoulder, I could see her body shaking slightly. I couldn't tell if it was fear, nerves, or excitement but either way, it was making me uncomfortable. I moved quickly, clamping onto her shoulder. This time, the rush felt different, almost more overwhelming. With Joe, it felt like butterflies were fluttering in my stomach, giving me that bit of excitement, and then it spread through my whole body.

With Erica, it felt as though my senses were almost electrocuted, something I would have to discuss with Ryder later. Once the feeling passed, I let her go, and Devon rushed over once more to apply dressings.

"This concludes our ceremony, would Joe and Erica's fellow feline's accompany them to the old encampment so that they may prepare for their first change?" Ryder questioned, turning to face the group of tigers that stood behind me.

They all nodded, walking alongside Erica and Joe as they disappeared into the forest. Ryder turned abruptly, grabbing Skyler by the scruff on her neck. She turned towards him, letting out a slight growl.

"This is your chance at redemption, Skyler. If you ever want to have a leadership role again, I expect no casualties. Make sure it all goes smoothly. MacKenzie and I will be down shortly," Ryder stated.

Skyler hissed at him, pulling herself away. She turned and showed me once final glare, and then she disappeared into the woods herself.

I turned to face Ryder, as the group began breaking into celebration and conversation.

The people playing the log continued working a steady, fast paced beat, and some of the people began dancing with each other.

Ryder walked towards me, a small smirk on his face. "Well done, Ms. MacKenzie..." he said, patting my head.

"Thanks, would you like me to change?" I questioned, eyeing a pile of clothes to my right that I assumed were for me. A light tan tunic and dark brown pants, just like I had seen Skyler wearing when I first arrived at camp.

"Go ahead, I'll be waiting for you over here with Darius..." Ryder said, walking over towards him. Darius nodded over to me, a smile on his face. I guessed either I did well, or he was just a festive person.

I picked up the clothes with my mouth, and hurried off into the woods. I closed my eyes, changing back to my form as fast as I possibly could. Even though all it consisted of was a fire, a log that was being banged to make a beat, and my new woodland family, it was the closest to feeling home that I ever felt. I finally felt as though I had a sense of purpose.

Once I was finally a fully dressed human, I combed my fingers through my hair. It had grown significantly since I had been out in the forest, and remained surprisingly healthy.

I headed back up towards the fire, immediately spotting Devon heading towards me.

"That was awesome, MacKenzie!" she said, embracing me in a tight hug. I laughed, hugging her back.

"Thanks, but all I did was bite people..." I replied, looking around for Ryder and Darius.

"Yeah but you still did really good, you've never done anything like that before, right? Don't they say something in the Army about anytime you do something for the first time and its successful its a win in the books?" she questioned.

"Uh, I guess something like that. I suppose you're right, no one died..."

"There you go," Devon said, following my eye movement. "Looking for someone?"

"Darius and Ryder, I thought I saw them over here earlier....I was just curious as to where they wandered off to," I replied. As if on cue, I saw the two of them talking on the other side of the fire, looking like they were deep in conversation.

"Who cares about them, come dance with us!" Devon stated, pulling me over towards Sarah and a few other people. I was instantly surrounded by a group of people, all of whom were moving their bodies to the beat of the log drummers, who were now working on a much faster pace.

"This is living, Mackenzie," Sarah said, a wide smile on her face. I couldn't remember a time when I saw her happier then she was right at that moment. I took both her and Devon's hands, moving to the music with them. For the first time in a long while, I was laughing and highly enjoying myself.

Sarah was right this *was* living. Although, I couldn't help but feel slightly saddened that Erica wasn't there with us to celebrate as well, but I understood why Ryder wanted them segregated. We couldn't risk the idea of them not being able to control their tiger on the first night, along with the fact that they would probably be exhausted.

I felt a sudden shiver down my spine and I turned to see Ryder, looking directly at me with his arms folded, leaning into Darius slightly as Darius continued on their conversation. I felt slightly entranced by his stare, and I couldn't help but smile as I turned away from him and began to dance and move even faster with my friends.

I was finally in my comfort zone, where I was willing to take risks. I was forever a Soldier, but I now was comfortable enough to let my guard down and enjoy life and let loose.

Devon and Sarah began to laugh, mocking my movement as the large group circled around the three of us and began to dance with more speed. It seemed as though we were the life of the party, as college students would call it.

A few moments later, I saw Devon and Sarah's expression look somewhat wicked, as they stepped back and disappeared into the crowd that continued to dance around me.

"Wha..." I was interrupted by someone placing their hand on the small of my back.

I turned to see Ryder dangerously close to me, his hand slowly sliding around to my hip.

"Mind if I cut in?" he whispered, his eyes reflecting the fire.

I shrugged, refusing to give him the satisfaction that he seemed to be seeking.

"It's a free world," I replied, spinning out from him. He extended his hand to me, and I took it, daringly.

He pulled me closer to him, and we began moving in an almost salsa dancing fashion, other people pairing up in a similar manner. I had never felt so connected to another human being before, so being as close to Ryder as I was felt intoxicating.

We continued our dance, his eyes refusing to leave mine, it was as if he were seeking out my soul, or calling my tiger to his. That's when I saw his eyes slowly change, his clear blue eyes slowly getting an orange glow. I inhaled deeply, trying to catch my breath and hold back. It seemed as though everything else around me faded into the background, and it was just me and Ryder dancing to the quickening music.

"What's the matter MacKenzie, why fear a little risk?" Ryder whispered, teasingly.

I saw his eyes slowly change back to their blue color, and I commended him for the strength in his control. I would not be able to release and grasp control as well. I wasn't exactly sure of what his intentions were, but I kind of liked this playful side to him.

I heard the music stop, and the crowd break into applause. Ryder didn't seem to care, maintaining his hold on me as he continued to gaze deep into my eyes, the same daring expression on his face. I leaned in, so I could whisper in his ear.

"You couldn't handle the risk," I said, releasing his hand and shoulder. I backed away from him for a second, before turning and heading towards Devon and Sarah, who had enormous grins on their faces, and two other girls that I had known to be friends of Skyler's.

"What was that all about?" Sarah questioned.

"A dance, what else would it be?" I asked, looking back and forth between the two of them. I pointed at Devon.

"Stop that," I said, winking at her.

"Looks like he's getting a pep talk from Darius," Devon said, nodding behind me. I turned to see Darius, leaning to whisper in Ryder's ear, his hand grasping his shoulder.

"Someone's got to be the chaperone, especially with Ryder..." one of Skyler's friends replied, playfully mock punching Devon's shoulder.

"What do you mean?" I questioned, looking back and forth between the group. For some reason I suddenly felt real defensive.

"It's nothing," Devon protested, shooting Sarah a look that indicated she was looking for help.

"That doesn't sound like nothing," I replied, trying to not get angry and ruin the good mood that I was now in.

"It's just.... Ryder always takes special interest in the females after the ceremony, I don't know.... I guess its like an alpha male thing. So we have been told by Skyler, every ceremony she used to stick to him like glue and follow him around like a lost puppy," the girl with red hair said, nodding over towards him.

Tanya, I think her name was. Tanya and Mia... I had frequently seen them around with Skyler. I guessed now that she was in the doghouse, they were seeking company elsewhere.

I felt my heart drop. Ryder disclosed to me that he and Skyler never had a relationship, but I guess that didn't include....everything.

"Since when does Skyler speak the truth? She probably only came up with that as an excuse so that the other females would stay away from him and give her a shot at him," I said, getting extremely defensive. I don't know why the idea of Ryder being with other females bothered me so much, it wouldn't exactly be my first rodeo.

"I don't know, its just something she told us every year. She said that the ceremony meant Ryder chose a female to claim as his own on a yearly basis. All I know is, that he's been Skyler's all this time... hope you're a fit replacement, Skyler told us some stories..." Mia said, elbowing Tanya. The two of them walked away, giggling slightly.

I turned to face Sarah and Devon, and judging by the looks on their faces, I probably looked pretty pissed off.

"MacKenzie, you know that's not true. They're just trying to ruin your night, they're friends with Skyler for Christ sake...." Devon said, clearly upset.

"Does Skyler normally follow him around every year? The truth," I said, looking back and forth between the two of them.

They both exchanged glances, and then nodded. "Yeah...she does...but MacKenzie, she always tried to be up his butt, and why would Ryder lie to you?" Devon questioned. I exhaled, trying to let off some steam. It would be two of Skyler's friends who ruined my night.

"I don't know, to get me to trust in him," I said, spewing an idea out there. I heard footsteps approaching me, and I turned to see two teenage boys standing there, looking petrified.

"Miss...MacKenzie," the taller one said, bowing to me. The other followed suit. "Mr. Ryder would like to speak with you, he's in his tent..." he continued, moving his feet back and forth nervously.

I smiled, nodding my thanks to them. "Thank you boys, I will be right there...." I said, dismissing them. They nodded, and headed back to the fire.

I looked over at Devon and Sarah and sighed. "I'm not doing this romantic drama bullshit," I said, shaking my head. "I'll be back in a bit," I said, heading towards his tent.

15

I pushed open the flap to Ryder's tent, taking notice that he still had his shirt off, but the paint was now slowly fading off due to the amount of sweat that was pouring out of his body.

"There you are, I wanted to talk to you about the ceremony..." he said, walking over towards me.

"Oh *the* ceremony? Not your little yearly private ceremony that you do afterwards?" I snapped, getting angry.

Ryder raised both his eyebrows, confusion spreading across his face. "What?" he questioned.

I shook my head, a little surprised by his response. "Never mind, what were you about to talk to me about?" I asked, rubbing my temple. I was starting to sprout a headache.

"Oh, right. The ceremony...any thoughts? Any concerns that you had that you want to talk to me about?" Ryder asked, biting a large carrot stick. I realized then that I hadn't eaten all day, completely ignoring the feast table and going to dance right away the second I got changed.

"Not really, it was just weird. When I had to bite Joe, it felt like butterflies flowing through my whole body. When I bit Erica, it was more of an electrocution. That's weird, right? Or is that normal? I wouldn't know..." I said, folding my arms.

Ryder's forehead creased as if he were slightly concerned, making a 'huh' sound.

"We'll just keep an eye on her. I've never felt that before, but the feeling with Joe...that's normal. That's how it always felt for me. Maybe your tiger picked up on something with Erica, not saying its a bad thing...just something different," Ryder said, pulling up a stool and sitting directly in front of me.

"Right," I said, looking down at the floor. A minute passed where no one said anything, and then I started to feel uncomfortable. "Well, if you don't have anything else to talk to me about, I'm going to head back to my friends..." I said, turning away.

I immediately felt him grab my bicep, as he stood up.

"You're not a very good liar, MacKenzie. What's wrong? Was it the dance that upset you?" he questioned.

I began to laugh, pulling my arm away from him. "No, it wasn't the dance. I liked dancing with you... I guess....but the point is, no it wasn't about the dance,"

"Then what is it? You're mood has changed dramatically in the past twenty minutes," he stated, folding his arms as well.

"Its why you did it that bothers me," I hissed.

He blinked in shock. "Because I-"

"I know about your little yearly 'finding the strong women' thing you do and then you chose her as your own every year at this ceremony, trust me I got the full lowdown from Tanya and Mia and I know it's been Skyler every year, even though back in the cave you told me that you and her were never an item..." I snapped, narrowing my eyes at him.

Ryder raised both his eyebrows, and then began to laugh. I blinked in shock, completely caught off guard by his reaction.

"Is that why she follows me around every year? I thought she was just motivated to one day be a leader. I'm telling you, you women come up with some freaky creepy stuff," Ryder said, still laughing as he ran a hand over his hair.

"But...she followed you to your tent afterwards," I said, coming to a realization that Skyler had some serious pathological issues.

"Yes, she did... to plan for the ceremony next year and give me a report on improving patrols, which she somehow drug out for almost two hours..." Ryder retorted, still seeming somewhat humored.

I couldn't help but feel stupid right then and there.

"Wow, she really does have a problem doesn't she? Starting rumors saying that we.....wow..." Ryder said, now pacing a little bit. I had to admit, I really did like seeing this playful side of Ryder. While I was attracted to the strong leader that he was, I enjoyed seeing the down and playful side of a person every now and then. It must have taken him awhile after Eric killed Molly to let that lighter side be shown.

"Wait," Ryder said, facing me with a somewhat devilish look on his face. "Despite this being a rumor...why does it bother you so much?" he questioned.

I began to stutter, not expecting to be asked that question. He slid his black tunic over his head, covering his upper body. Okay, at least now I would be able to focus a lot more.

"I never said it bothered me," I replied, rolling my eyes. I turned to face away from him, and stared down to see a decent group of people still dancing, their shadows moving quickly on the ground.

As I looked up into the sky, I could feel Ryder's eyes on me as he approached. When he stood next to me, and followed my gaze, he smiled.

"Thats it....a blue moon," he stated, with a small smirk. "You know its funny, most people expect the moon to be a full color of blue. In reality, its just a term made up for the second full moon in a month's time. Which is why they are rare. If you look closely you can see the tints of blue around the edges though,"

I nodded in agreement. "Yeah, you can... its funny. All my life growing up, my favorite animal was the wolf. I remember when I was little, being so angry that my family possessed the ability to turn into tigers instead of wolves. Even still, I studied their habits. I learned about how the moon calls to them, and how they bathe in the light of it. I actually went to Yellowstone just to witness it. Of course, humans weren't allowed to get in close contact with the wolves so I had to use....other methods," I said, looking over at Ryder.

He raised his eyebrows at me, before he let the smile spread across his face. "So that story from like...twelve years ago...that was you?" he asked, folding his arms. His elbow brushed against mine and I felt a shiver at his touch.

I smiled in embarrassment, before looking down at the floor. I forgot that there was a time that the sectors didn't exist, and we weren't all hermits. Anyone could watch the news.

"Yeah, that was me. Believe me, my parents gave me hell for it. There were scientists from all over the world coming to Yellowstone to figure out why there was a white siberian tiger roaming around the park. Especially when we aren't indigenous to the area,"

I turned my gaze back to the moon, a small smirk still on my face. "There was a blue moon that night too. The wolves were all gathered under its warm light, the pups were all running around yapping. It seemed like something you could relate to a campfire scene. It was an amazing sight,"

Ryder leaned against the doorframe. "What about the wolves? Surely they noticed your presence?"

I let out a laugh, nodding my head. "Oh they more than noticed my presence. The alpha female was out on a hunting party with two males. She saw me observing their little gathering. I thought she was going to attack me, but she didn't.... she sort of tilted her head as if to tell me to follow her. I wound up spending the night circled by them. I think they knew I meant them no harm, and I had no intentions of hurting their young. I'm sure they were confused because I smelled like a human,"

I watch as Ryder smiled at me, before I continued. "That next morning, when we all woke up...that was when we saw the jeeps. I remember seeing the scientists reaching for those stupid flip cell phones to take a picture of me.

159

I think the alpha male sensed my fear so they formed a sort of barrier around me and escorted me to the wood-line. We parted ways there. I came back to Philadelphia three days later, and I remember walking to the doorstep of my parents house and the next thing I knew my father was screaming at me demanding I tell him exactly what happened. Thankfully, the newspaper released that the scientists figured that I was just a white wolf or something so they abandoned the idea,"

I turned so that I was fully facing him, my back against the other side of the tent opening. He continued to face me with his arms folded, as he casually leaned against the opposite side. The moonlight reflected off of his features, giving him a shady look that made him even more attractive if that was even physically possible.

"What about you?" I asked, inhaling sharply to take my mind off of how attractive he looked. He smirked slightly, probably sensing my discomfort.

"What about me?" he asked, tilting his head slightly.

"Were you always born with this...gift? I don't think we ever talked about your experiences with it," I questioned, remembering what he had called it when they first met.

"I was, I got it from my father. He was bitten by one of his men back when he was a cop. My father was going through a really hard time, especially with my grandparents divorcing. He felt as though he had nothing to live for, and he confided in one of his partners. His partner told him that if he wanted to feel free, to trust him..." Ryder said, remembering the story his father had told him.

I cocked my eyebrow at him in reply. "You mean by 'free' to have the choice to turn into something you're not?" I asked. His face remained stern, as he fixated his eyes on mine again. "Free to escape. Free to run. Free to, for a few hours, days, or weeks to escape reality..."

I nodded, before looking down at the ground. "It does feel nice to be able to talk to someone about this. I mean, I always could talk to Jax about this but he never understood how I really felt,"

Ryder pressed his lips into a tight line again. "You talk about this Jax a lot," he stated. I raised my eyebrows, unsure of where the statement had come from.

"Well, he was my partner and... I guess you could say my best friend. I've known him for almost half my life..."

I watched as Ryder's eyes lingered on my face for a second, before he spoke again.

160

"Do you love him?" he questioned. His question caught me off guard, and for a second it seemed as though a shockwave passed through my body. No one had ever really asked me that question before. I couldn't deny the fact that while I had been out here, he had crossed my mind just about every day.

Had I thought about the idea of me being in love with him? Maybe. I spent a lot of time thinking about how if Jax weren't married, would he and I ever be together?

Granted, when we first met he was just newly married. He was in that newly wed phase, constantly gushing about his wife and how great marriage was. To be honest, I recall it getting annoying.

I had just come out of a complicated engagement myself, and I can only imagine how much worse that could have gotten if my ex knew about my gift. I remember my first deployment with Jax, and I could hear him skyping with her through the wall that we shared. As the days went by, the skyping occurred less and less. Once we got back from our deployment they were back to their honey moon phase for about six months before we were deployed again. We came back from our deployment a year later and then his wife went to Florida to visit relatives after spending about three months with him again. That was when the war occurred and she was not allowed to come home.

Jax didn't like talking about it much, but whenever he actually did, he still would talk to us as if they were still a happily married couple.

I focused back on Ryder's question. I couldn't deny that in the past few years I had grown a lot closer to Jax, and the thought of 'what if' had crossed my mind a lot more.

I shook my head. "He's married, don't be ridiculous..." I said, with a nervous laugh. Ryder narrowed his eyes slightly, as if pondering whether or not he believed me. I cleared my throat, not comfortable with the awkward silence.

"Why do you ask?" I questioned, inhaling the crisp air deeply.

"I just had to make sure...first," he said, whispering the last word.
I tilted my head slightly, confused by his statement.
"First? First for what?" I asked, with a nervous laugh.

He continued to remain silent, before stepping so that he was inches away from me. I stared into Ryder's icy blue eyes, trying to figure out what he was thinking. My question was answered by his face coming closer to mine. I felt his lips brush up against mine, his warm breath rolling over my lips.

161

I inhaled sharply, caught off guard by his brash movements. I could feel my heart jump up in my throat. I felt his lips pull into a slight smile at this reaction, as we remained inches apart.

"You're not resisting this time," he teased, probably remembering how feisty I was when we first met.

I returned the smile. "I guess I've changed," I said.
"That's too bad, I like the feisty MacKenzie..." he said, pressing his lips against mine.

At the feel of his lips pressed against mine, I felt my body start to shudder. I never thought it was possible to feel so overcome with passion in a single touch. I couldn't deny my attraction for Ryder, I would just be lying to myself. Ryder and I may have had different interests, liked different sports teams and whatnot, but there was one thing he and I could connect on that I never found with anyone else. Our tigers. Our tigers were a huge part of who we were, and it felt so comforting to be in the arms of someone else who understood.

I wrapped my arms around his neck, at the same moment he pulled me closer to him by my hips. His touch, his kiss, his presence, it all was intoxicating and addicting. I couldn't put it into words.

For so long I had resisted any forms of emotion or affection. After what my ex-fiancé had put me through, I refused to allow any man get close to me. I refused any forms of affection, even so much as a hug from a female friend. I don't know what it was, but I felt like any form of affection would allow me to develop feelings that would make me care deeply about said person. I had a track record of people I cared about falling out of my life.

Ryder's hands moved from my hips to my head as he began to run his fingers through my hair. His kisses became more passionate, as he put more weight on me so that I leaned backwards and onto his bed. I pulled away from him, taking note of my surroundings.
I felt the bed sink slightly as Ryder also climbed onto the bed, positioning himself so that his face was above mine. His alluring blue eyes gazed deeply into mine, as if he were trying to read what I was feeling.
"What's wrong?" I questioned, suddenly confused to his change of behavior.
Ryder shook his head, his eyes slowly moving down my figure.

"Can I be perfectly frank with you?" he questioned, his normally rough voice softening considerably.

"Well I would hope you wouldn't be anything else," I stated, raising an eyebrow at him.

"After Molly... I turned my back to the idea of...*caring deeply* for anyone else," Ryder paused, bringing his eyes back to mine again. I noticed that he probably didn't want to use the word 'love' for fear of jeopardizing anything, which I was quite familiar with. That, or he hadn't reach the point of loving me yet.

"You're unique, MacKenzie Waters. I can connect with you in a way that I never could connect with her. You set me free," Ryder stated, bringing his face inches from mine again. I felt his lips brush against mine, and then along my jawline towards my neck.

"You know, I kind of like seeing this side to you..." I stated, truthfully.

"Is that so?" Ryder questioned, an authentic laugh escaping his lips.

"Although, the whole 'I'm the chief' thing is pretty sexy too. Not going to lie,"

"So I'm sexy now, am I?" Ryder questioned, his voice sounding playful as he began to give my neck fluttery kisses.

A soft sigh escaped my lips, at his exhilarating touch. I didn't understand why his simple touch was making me react in the way that it was, but based off of his body language, he was rather enjoying it.

"If you're going to be twisting my words like that, sure, we can go with that..." I teased, closing my eyes as his kisses moved towards my collarbone. Ryder paused to sit up, sliding his black tunic off of his body, causing my heart to skip a beat. Or three.

His eyes reconnected with mine, dancing with amusement. He leaned down to whisper in my ear, and I could feel my body tighten in excitement at the feeling of his bare, extremely muscular torso over mine.

"How about now?" he purred.

I couldn't help it but allow a small whimper to sneak out, and I quickly closed my eyes in embarrassment. I could hear him chuckle slightly, as his hand slowly worked his way to my cheek. He began to stroke it gently, encouraging me to reopen my eyes. When I did, his face was a few inches away from mine, a sincere look in his eyes.

"MacKenzie...if you don't want this, I'll stop. Just tell me," he said, his voice softening again.

For a few seconds I just stared at him, and then slowly allowed the smile to cross my face. Based on the fiery burning feeling in my chest, I knew that I wasn't the only one who wanted this moment to happen, but my tiger did also. She was ready to seek a partner as well.

"Just shut the hell up and kiss me already....chief," I teased, wrapping my arms around his neck as our lips met in a passionate, sparking kiss.

16

I stumbled slightly in the silver, high-heeled shoes, grabbing onto the nearby park bench for support. I could hear Jax laughing, as his hand made contact with my shoulder blade. I shot a glare back at him, over my shoulder.

"What are you laughing at, you asshole?" I questioned, before standing up straight again. I ran my hands over the midnight-black dress, smoothing it out. When he didn't answer at first, I flipped my long blonde waves over my shoulder so that he could get the full effect of my glare. "I'm waiting," I stated, firmly.

"I just can't believe how big of a klutz you are outside of your combat boots, MacKenzie..." Jax said, shaking his head. I shot him a glare once again, striding ahead of him this time.

"You know, I didn't have to agree to be your date. I could have very well came as myself and worn my Dress Blues..." I snapped, suddenly regretting the urge to come as a date instead of a soldier. However, Jax's wife had backed out in order to head to Florida to visit her relatives and he had ordered a plate for a date. I was, as usual, lazy in my response to the Army ball and instead of paying for myself as a solider, I took the place of Jax's wife.

"Oh come on, I know how you women feel about wearing these stupid things. Always complaining that you ladies look like flight attendants," Jax said, butting me with his shoulder. I scrunched my nose up slightly in defiance, slapping him playfully.

"Let's just go," I said, walking up to the door. "Hang on," Jax said, stepping next to me on my right side. He stuck his arm out so that I could lace mine through his. I felt a slight heat rise to my cheeks, as I obliged and accepted his gesture.

"I may sound like an asshole, but I can still pull off the appearance of the gentleman," Jax said, a small smirk on his face.

"Alright, Jay Cutler..." I said, rolling my eyes.

Jax laughed, and then pushed open the door. We saw hundreds of our fellow soldiers walking around the grand hall, everyone seemingly engaged in pleasant conversation, and with a glass of wine in their hand. City Hall, Philadelphia did have its benefits. It was rarely used for such occasions, but there was some major meeting in Washington D.C so they decided to move the ball to the country's former capitol.

The orchestrated music began to flood my ears as Jax and I were immediately basked in the bright orange and yellow lights. I subconsciously pulled myself closer to Jax, uncomfortable with how exposed I felt in my tight halter dress. I wasn't expecting there to be as many people as there were present tonight.

Before Jax could say anything to me, I turned to see Colonel Charton standing there. He and I had never formally been introduced before, but I recognized him from one of the photos that Jax had showed me from his Ranger Battalion photos from when he graduated Ranger School.

"Captain Richards," Colonel Charton said, extending his hand towards Jax. Jax looked at me, before returning the handshake.

"Sir, it is good to see you again..." Jax stated. I watched as several different emotions passed through Jax's face. I could not tell if he was too fond of the Senior Officer or not.

Colonel Charton turned his gaze to me, his green eyes staring hard into mine. "You must be his wife, Emily. I'm Colonel Charton," Colonel Charton stated, bowing his head towards me.

"Actually this is First Lieutenant MacKenzie Waters, sir...my wife was unable to attend this evening. She had a family emergency in Florida that she needed to take care of..." Jax spoke up, before I could even get the chance.

I watched as Colonel Charton's expression changed to that of slight surprise, before he respectfully nodded. I hated it when people in the military showed no respect or no interest in the lives of people who were not in the military at all. Just because you weren't ever in the military did not mean that you were not a human being. I forgot how hard it was for some service members to realize that.

"Lieutenant, forgive me..." he said. I knew Jax could sense my discomfort, as he let out a nervous chuckle.

"MacKenzie, perhaps we shall get you some water? I know you said you weren't feeling too well earlier..." Jax spoke up.

"Not feeling well? I'm fine," I argued, pouting as Jax pulled me away from the Colonel. Jax flexed his arm, tightening his grip on me as he continued to pull me away.

"Yeah, well I have seen that Philly temper come out when you're angry and we don't need that here. That, or your..." he paused to make eye contact with me. "Your other temper," he whispered, referring to my tiger. I paused for a moment, before nodding in agreement.

The evening continued quite wonderfully, many war stories were shared along with dozens of laughs. The sight of Adam drunk at the bar was quite amusing in and of itself. I felt someone tap on my shoulder, and I turned to see Jax standing there with his hand extended to me. "Could I have this dance?" he questioned, as the band began to play a much softer tune.

I turned to look at Amanda, who desperately tried to hide her growing smirk. She was another one that insisted there was always a 'spark' between me and Jax.

I rolled my eyes at her, before taking Jax's hand and standing up.

"Why not?" I questioned, allowing him to lead me onto the floor. My heart pounded in my chest when Jax placed his one hand on my hip and took my other hand in his. I immediately could smell the scent of the forest on him, hickory flooding my senses. I closed my eyes at the smell, knowing that my tiger was craving to indulge in the smell...and possibly Jax himself.

I shook the thoughts away, trying to calm the beast within me from jumping out over something so silly. As Jax and I began to move to the music, I couldn't help but notice the curious stares that he and I were getting. There were only a select amount of couples dancing, but they were actually couples. People knew who Jax and I were, they knew Jax was married...and they knew he was technically my commanding officer, holding a rank above me. The beast in me loved the sense of danger, however my human conscience strongly disagreed.

Jax followed my gaze, seeing who I was staring at. "They're probably just jealous," he commented, before looking back at me. I rolled my eyes.

"Yeah, well I hate wearing dresses," I retorted.

"Who said I was talking about you? I was talking about me.. who can resist a Ranger?" Jax teased, before spinning me around. I gasped slightly, before shaking my head.

"You certainly are cocky like one," I teased, laughing slightly.

Jax allowed the ridiculous grin to cross his face. "Are you saying that MPs are never cocky? Because if you are, I call bull-crap..." he stated. I shrugged in response, before showing him a wicked smirk.

"At least we can shoot, not just ruck.." I teased.

Jax laughed, before faking getting 'burned' by my comment. "Its funny though, I didn't know that you could dance so well..." I commented. Jax raised his eyebrow at me in slight challenge, before tightening his grip and then dipping me back slightly, his face coming closer to mine.

"I guess I will just have to continue to surprise you, MacKenzie..." he whispered. There was a light murmur of clapping heard amongst the crowd.

Before I could say anything further, I heard the string band play a familiar song. Dance of the Reed Flutes by Pyotr Illyich Tchaikovsky. Jax assisted in standing me up, noticing how quickly my attention was stolen away by the notes flowing off of the stringed instruments.

My father played this song for me often on our record player when I was very young. We would venture out into the woods in our backyard and he would string about seven extension cords connecting it to the house so that we could listen to it while we changed, our young tiger spirits enjoying how it connected them to nature.

I broke away from Jax, and I began spinning, just like I did when I was a little girl. My hands were folded at my stomach, my arms pulled in tight as I began to spin around. I closed my eyes, seeing my tiger spirit, connecting with her, but not allowing her to take over.

The song began to pick up, and I began to spin faster, now moving my arms like a tree in the breeze. As the song escalated, I lifted my leg slightly to slow down my spin. Right then, it was just me and my tiger in our own world. When the music finally stopped, I opened my eyes and saw Jax standing there with several higher brass military ranking members. Crap, talk about awkward.

Major Chase was among them, and he blinked his eyes in shock. "Lt Waters, I never noticed how blue your eyes were until right now..." he commented. I turned to Jax, suddenly panicked. He knew my eyes were forest green, and if they were suddenly blue, he knew exactly what that meant.

"She's wearing colored contacts sir, she felt like it would go along with the dress..." Jax lied, quickly rushing to my side. I laughed uncomfortably, silently scolding my inner tiger for trying to break free.

"Come on MacKenzie, let's get you something to eat..." Jax spoke up, pushing me away from them. As he guided me, I squeezed my eyes shut and began to picture what my true eye color was.

After a minute, I opened my eyes, before looking back at Jax. Jax meant down slightly, checking me. "You're good, but MacKenzie...you have to be more careful..." Jax said, sounding worried.

I nodded. "I know, I know... I tried controlling it but that song..." I said, turning to face the orchestra once more. They had now carried on with a more pleasant tune, unaware of anything else going on in the world. Jax pulled me into a comforting embrace.

"I know... it's okay, I got you covered. Till the end, battle..." Jax whispered in my ear.

***

I woke with a start, breathing heavily. I could feel that beads of sweat had formed on my forehead, and I could see the white wisps of my breath escaping my lips amongst the cool breeze. I drew the sheets up against my bare figure, suddenly feeling cold. Ryder stirred next to me, turning away from me so that his back muscles reflected in the moonlight that was seeping through the slits in the tent. How the heck could a man be so perfectly built?

Suddenly there was the sound of rushing feet outside the tent, and Ryder immediately sat up, grabbing the knife off of the tree stump next to his bed that was supposed to be some version of a night stand. He put his arm in front of me defensively, as a shadow loomed underneath the tent flap.

"Ryder, its Trevor, may I enter?" Trevor questioned, his voice sounding frantic. Ryder looked over at me, smirking slightly at the sight of me attempting to cover up my naked figure with the thin sheet.

"What? You have less to hide!" I whispered, sharply.

"Give me a minute," Ryder called back, leaping from the bed and grabbing his black pants from the floor. I hurried as well, gathering up my clothes and redressing myself as fast as I possibly could.

Ryder remained shirtless, walking towards the tent flap. He faced me, overlooking my now dressed figure, before opening the tent flap.

Trevor stepped inside, his eyes full of horror. When he saw me standing there was well, his expression changed to that of confusion as he looked back and forth between me and Ryder.

"Uh....." he began, unsure of what to do.

"What seems to be the problem?" Ryder questioned, his voice back to its usual stern tone.

Trevor nodded politely to me, and then turned his attention back to Ryder.

"There's....been a problem, with one of the candidates. They're losing control of their tiger, and if they don't get it back soon... you know what happens," Trevor said, shaking nervously.

"Who?" I cut in, stepping closer to the two of them.

Trevor looked over at me, and then back at Ryder.

Ryder nodded. "Tell her," he ordered, his eyes remaining on me.

169

"Erica," Trevor stated, his voice full of sadness. I knew that he cared deeply for her, she had always talked about how they had grown extremely close, almost like a brother and sister.

I looked at Ryder, unfolding my arms. "I have to go see her," I stated. It wasn't a question, and Ryder knew it.

"Okay, let's go..." he said, grabbing his shirt from the bottom of the bed.

17.

As the three of us sprinted through the thicket, I couldn't help but feel somewhat guilty myself. It was all my fault. I should have stayed with her, knowing there was something very off when I delivered her bite. Ryder was right, there probably was something else going on with her receiving her gift. What had I done?

Trevor slowed his run to a quick walk, and I saw two large, wooden cages in front of me. They looked as though they were built from the strongest oak trees, the wood that was meant to serve as bars looking extremely sturdy and thick all around the large box. They were bound together by thick pieces of rope, along with some chains that I assumed were snuck out to them during the supply runs from the sector. They were so large that they were built to hold three or four tigers, as opposed to just one.

I looked to my right and saw one tiger sitting there, its tail curling and uncurling in frustration. I tilted my head, slowly approaching the cage.

"Joe?" I questioned, still somewhat shaken.

The tiger turned to face me, nodding. I felt a wave of relief wash over me, realizing that at least Joe had seized control of his tiger, and was probably just getting used to the change.

"Has he been able to turn back yet?" I asked, looking over at Trevor.

Trevor nodded. "He has, he just changed back just in case....we needed back up," Trevor said, nodding over towards the other cage.

I slowly turned to my left to face the other cage, and I could see yellow eyes staring back at me from the shadowy corner. I bit my lip and swallowed hard, slowly approaching the cage.

The other three men that were there stepped out of my path, their faces full of concern. They must have been three of the tigers that were standing behind me during the ceremony, Trevor the forth.

"Where is Skyler?" I questioned, keeping my eyes connected with the angry yellow ones that stared back at me.

"She was exhausted from the fight today, she took first watch and is sleeping now. So are Jerrod and Oscar," Trevor stated, slowly following me. I could see Ryder out of my peripheral vision, moving alongside next to me.

I stopped once I reached the cage, seeing the orange tiger curled up defensively in the corner.

It's lip curled up slightly, its snout scrunching up as it revealed its razor sharp teeth. The yellow eyes were full of hate, showing the true beast within.

I had to save Erica before she was too far gone. My father had told me stories of calling a person out of their 'first wake' as we called it, which referred to the period of time during a persons first time changing, their human soul rested and let the tiger out to explore the world...then when you, as the alpha in the relationship, deemed necessary, you would call the tiger back and your human soul would take over.

For some people, it was harder than others to have the spirit of the tiger's trust, the tiger fearing that they would never be able to be free again. Rather than running free in the spirit realm, they would be trapped once again in a mortal form...only exploring when their human allowed them.

"Erica," I said, grabbing one of the wooden bars. The tiger roared, leaping out of the shadows and swiping for my hand. I was quick on the draw, pulling my hand away just seconds before Erica's claws raked the beam.

Ryder and Trevor immediately rushed to my side, Ryder's hand on the small of my back. "I'm fine...I'm fine..." I said, reassuringly. I looked over at Ryder and showed him a small smile, and then did the same to Trevor.

I looked down at the hand I almost lost, and then slowly brought my gaze to meet the gaze of the tiger that was in front of me, angrily.

"Open the door for me," I stated, moving towards the latched side of it. The tiger's eyes followed me, as it stood up defensively. It's ears were straight back, almost against its head, the eyes wide, and its lips were curled up, revealing its petrifying incisors. She hissed at me in challenge.

"Are you...are you insane?" Trevor questioned, sounding alarmed.

"I'm not going to be intimidated by a pissed off house cat, you're going to open the door for me," I ordered, keeping my eyes on the tiger.

Out of my peripheral vision I saw Trevor look over at Ryder, as if seeking his approval. In a way, it kind of pissed me off, but I knew deep down that Trevor was just genuinely concerned about me.

Ryder hesitated for a second, before slowly nodding. "Do it," he muttered, moving around the cage towards me.

Once he was directly next to me, he leaned in towards me. "Want to let me in on your little plan here?" he questioned, his hot break on my ear. I felt goosebumps slowly make their way over my bare arm, remembering the events that happened earlier in the night.

"I created this...beast. I'm going to be the one to put it in its place," I replied, watching Trevor and his buddy as they moved to unlatch the gate on both sides.

They both turned to face me, waiting for my signal. Once I nodded, they each squatted down and began pulling the gate upwards. The tiger remained in the back of the cage, a combination between petrified and pissed off.

I slowly began my approach into the large cage, standing up as straight as I possibly could to make myself look bigger. Thankfully, whoever designed the cages was smart enough to leave a decent amount of head room.

"Erica..." I began, raising my hands in a non-threatening manner. I could hear the low growl slowly coming from the tiger, its ears still pulled back.

"Erica, listen to me. You have to re-take control of your tiger. I know you can hear me," I said, remembering a time when I watched my father give a similar speech to one of my cousins during his first change. He was a 'late bloomer', not being able to change until his teenage years, which wasn't uncommon, just a little rare. My father was so cool and confident about it, refusing to show fear. He knew, and trained me, if you showed a beast that you were afraid of it, it would do exactly what God created it to do. Kill.

The tiger slowly stood up, its shoulders squaring as it began to approach me. I tilted my head, trying to get a read on it. I had never dealt with a first time adult changer, but I knew better than to act rationally. Adult tigers had a more developed, more mature mind. This wouldn't be easy.

"Erica, its MacKenzie...." I said, my voice softening. The tiger's eyes flashed with recognition, but only for a few seconds. Suddenly, the tiger's eyes widened, and it let out a deafening roar. I was beyond messing around. Without a second thought, I leapt towards the tiger, calling mine to meet me.

I felt heavy as my body collided with hers, knocking her to the ground. I turned to face Trevor and Ryder, panting heavily.

"Close the gate!" I roared, and then turned my attention back to Erica.

I heard the *'slam'* of the gate behind me, and I zoned my focus in on Erica.

She slowly stood up, her eyes flared with anger. Unlike my fight with Skyler, this was going to be completely different. Skyler was in control of her tiger, knowing exactly what she was doing when we fought. This was just me versus a near wild tiger, and a struggling Erica. I was fighting the true beast.

She lunged for me, attempting to bite at my neck. I hissed, merely swiping my paw with full force and knocking her down again. I leapt towards her, towering over her so that she was pinned under my body. I didn't want to hurt her, regardless of how untamed she was acting.

"Erica, *listen* to me! You HAVE to get control, and you have to get control right now," I roared, staring the tiger down, daring her to make a move.

She revealed all her teeth to me as she hissed, throwing her head so that she was able to get a good bite on my left leg. I felt the pain instantly flare up, as I roared in agony. I stumbled to the side, releasing my hold on the tiger. She stood up and lunged for me, attempting to take me down.

Luckily for me she had a smaller frame, so I braced myself for the hit, only stumbling slightly. I was now angered at the fact that this tiger thought she could take control over my friend.

I turned to face her, biting her by the small scruff on her back and throwing my weight forward so that we both tumbled to the floor, in a white and orange mess. I pulled myself on top of her, hissing in her face. Her eyes now looked slightly worn, as if she were struggling to maintain control.

"I'm the alpha in this relationship, and you *will* let my friend control you. Do you understand?" I growled, bringing my face close to hers.

I could hear Trevor muttering words to Ryder, but they were mere white noise compared to what was going on right now. Erica was my priority.

The tiger let out a low growl, and then slowly let her gaze soften. Her breathing slowed down, and she rolled her eyes shut. Moments later, her eyes opened again, but this time there was no sign of aggression. My heart leapt in hope, but I continued to remain suspicious.

"Erica?" I questioned.

She turned to face me, blinking multiple times in shock. "MacKenzie?" I heard her question.

I instantly let out a warm sigh of relief. "Erica," I stated, turning to face Trevor and Ryder. Ryder had a small smirk on his face, and Trevor's eyes were widened in what appeared to be pure shock.

"Oh MacKenzie, I'm so sorry... I tried to be strong, I really did. She was just so..." Erica paused, her ears flattening against her head in embarrassment.

"Overwhelming," I finished for her.

"Yeah, overwhelming...." Erica said, her yellow eyes darting to the floor.

I slid off of her, sitting down on the opposite side. She slowly sat up as well, taking in all her surroundings. "So this is what it feels like," she said, sounding as if the experience was breath-taking.

"Yes, and you'll learn that the more and more you connect with her over time, the more you will be able heighten those senses," I stated, observing her behavior.

174

I didn't think she was quite ready yet to hear that you could channel some of your tiger senses as a human over time, she was seemingly overwhelmed enough already for the night.

"Cool!" she exclaimed, turning to face me.

"When can I patrol with you guys?" she questioned, her yellow eyes now glowing with enthusiasm.

"I'll talk to Ryder about it, but I think we should bring you back in here one or two more times for observation before we consider any training. Nothing against you, I just don't trust your tiger to not...do what it did this time," I said, trying to not offend her.

"Oh, I completely understand! That is fine with me," Erica replied, a small smile on her face.

"Right," I paused to stand up. "I'm going to tell these guys to give you some privacy and respect, and turn around so you can practice calling your human self back and then calling your tiger, just keep practicing and try to establish that bond," I said, heading towards the gate.

"MacKenzie!" Erica roared, standing up as well. I turned back around to face her, keeping my guard up.

"Thank you...for everything," she said, and then turned to walk to the shadowy part of the cage.

"You're welcome," I said, unsure exactly of why she felt the need to thank me. Dealing with outrageous people and beings had always been part of my job description.

I exited the cage, and turned to face Ryder as it slammed shut behind me. He smirked, nodding in approval.

"I'm very impressed," he said, his smirk growing, showing off those perfectly white teeth.

"It was nothing," I said, turning to face Trevor. "I think she wants to practice changing back and forth...so if you guys don't mind...." I said, inclining my head towards the other cage.

"Oh, right. We will step aside for a bit," Trevor said, his cheeks turning a slight shade of pink. He bowed his head slightly as he scuttled away to go pass the news onto his fellow guards.

I couldn't help but smirk, as I turned to face Ryder again. "So, where exactly where we?" I questioned, uncurling my tail teasingly.

"Let's find you some new clothes first. As precious and as beautiful as you are, I'm not spooning with a tiger," Ryder replied, motioning for me to follow him.

18

"Blueberries! My day has absolutely been made," Devon exclaimed, happily tossing a few in her mouth. Sarah raised an eyebrow at Devon, as she began to pull apart an orange.

"Well at least one of us is easily entertained," Sarah said, laughing shortly after.

"Oh come on! The sun is shining, the breeze is just right and I'm eating my absolute favorite fruit, ever. My day is complete," Devon said, turning to face me.

I smirked, studying the skin of the peach that I was now holding in my hand. It was perfectly soft and plump, just how I always liked them.

"What about you, MacKenzie? Is a peach your favorite fruit?" Devon questioned, downing two more blueberries in the process.

"It is," I said, smiling over at her.

Moments later I spotted Ryder walking across the encampment, talking to Adam and Trevor. I smirked at his appearance, appreciating his presence. Sarah followed my stare, and then nudged Devon in the side.

"It would appear as though our dear MacKenzie is hungry for something else," she said, winking.

"Shush it," I exclaimed, throwing some dirt here way. She brought her orange into her chest, defensively, as she began to laugh.

I didn't know why I was acting like a little school girl when I noticed Ryder's presence. It was perfectly natural what happened between us, why was I as giddy as I was?

"Have you guys seen Skyler this morning?" Devon questioned, resting against the tree trunk that wrapped around her small frame.

"No, I haven't seen her since last night. She's probably trying to avoid doing any sort of walk of shame today, her pride has been destroyed. Thanks to our MacKenzie here," Sarah said, smiling at me.

Before I could reply, a very exhausted Erica made her way over to us. She smiled weakly at us as she slowly sat down on the gray boulder. Her eyes had dark half-moon shadows under them, and she did not seem to have her usual social aurora about her.

"Tired, are we?" Devon questioned.

"Tired doesn't even quite begin to cover it," Erica replied, sounding groggy.

"Did you get any sleep at all last night?" Sarah asked, reaching over and pulling a leaf out of her friends hair.

"No, not really. I kind of struggled a little last night, took me a couple times to get the hang of it. Changing, I mean. Thanks to Mackenzie, if she hadn't come and seen me, I probably wouldn't be here today," Erica said, her eyes moving onto me.

"Thank you, for everything..." she said, with a weak smile.

"I didn't do anything, but you do need to get some real sleep. How about you go and rest today? You're going to need all your strength to change again tonight," I replied.

Erica's eyes widened slightly, in surprise. "But...my duties...my students," she said, referring to the children she taught archery to.

"Don't concern yourself with that. I'm sure Ryder wouldn't want you overtaxing yourself. Please, go get some rest... take some fruit with you too," I said, tossing her a peach.

She caught it, looking up at me in shock. "Are you sure this is okay?" Erica questioned, trying to mask her excitement at the idea of getting a good nap in before a very long night.

"Positive, now go..." I said, showing her a reassuring smile.

She waved us a farewell, and then disappeared in the direction of our tent. Changing while being exhausted could lead to some disastrous results. I knew from experience. After staying up all night as a child watching my favorite episodes of *Stargate Atlantis* until nearly 4am, my training session the next day didn't go so well. I apparently looked like I had just received a tranquilizer from the Zoologist and was stumbling all over the woods when I was supposed to be chasing prey that day.

I turned my head slightly to see Ryder and Darius approaching us, looking as though they had something important to say. I stood up as they approached.

"MacKenzie, we are heading out for a supply run...its that time again," Ryder spoke up, stopping very close to me.

"Okay, I'm ready whenever you are. I told Erica to go and get some rest, I fear without adequate rest, changing tonight will be really difficult for her. I hope that is alright with you," I said, feeling the butterflies in my stomach once more. This was actually starting to get quite embarrassing.

"Of course," he replied, overlooking my figure. This confirmed that my nervous behavior did not go unnoticed.

"She is concerned, however, about her archery students..." I stated, hoping that wouldn't change his mind on the matter.

"Hmm..." he paused to turn to Sarah. "You are very skilled with a bow and arrow, Sarah, would you mind taking over for her students today?" Ryder questioned.

Sarah nodded, standing up. "Of course not, I will go gather them together now," she said, bowing respectfully and then heading off.

Devon stood up as well, stretching out her legs. "I'll go with you guys, is anyone else coming?" she questioned.

"Yes, Joe and Trevor are waiting for us on the outer cordon of the encampment. Joe insisted on coming, he's ready to start getting into more training," Darius replied, finally speaking up.

I watched as Devon adjusted her glasses, excitedly. "Oh, okay. When are we leaving?" she inquired.

"Let's head out now, the sooner we get there, the better..." Ryder said, motioning for her to go ahead.

Devon scurried forward, walking next to Darius, who immediately engaged her in a conversation.

"You seem rather rattled this morning, is everything okay?" Ryder questioned, his eyes full of concern.

"Oh yeah, everything is fine. I'm just...ya know...taking in all of everything that happened last night," I said, trying to hide my smirk. I didn't want him thinking I was suddenly over the moon in love with him, cause that wasn't the case, at least not at the current moment.

"Hmm," he remarked, raising an eyebrow as a small smirk appeared on his face.

"So, anyway, I thought the supply run wasn't for another week...why did it suddenly jump up?" I questioned, trying to change the subject to something more serious to stop myself from smiling.

"Your...friend, Jax, he reached out to one of our morning patrols and said that it had to be moved up this week. Something about heightened security next week because its going to be the eighth anniversary of the sectors being established," Ryder replied.

I felt as though a weight had been dropped in my stomach at the thought of seeing Jax again. After Ryder and I had spent the night together.

Jax and I used to tell each other everything, we had grown so close. Anytime a guy so much as looked at me the wrong way, Jax was quick to my defense. But he would be happy for me, right? Ryder wasn't a bad guy and after-all, Jax was married. So why did I care so much about breaking the news to him about me and Ryder?

I looked over at Ryder as we approached the outer cordon where Joe and Trevor were waiting for us. What exactly were Ryder and I anyway?

"Good morning sunshine," Ryder said, nodding at a yawning Joe. Joe narrowed his eyes at Ryder and muttered a 'hmm' and something about 'maybe for you'. He and Trevor passed the four of us a quiver full of arrows along with a bow.

"Traveling hot for a supply run?" Devon questioned.

"Yes," Ryder replied.

While Joe and Trevor engaged Ryder and Devon in a conversation, I took the opportunity to slide next to Darius.

"Long time, no talk," I said, a small smile on my face.

"It has only been eighteen hours," Darius replied, matter-of-factly.

I couldn't help but laugh at his dead-pan honesty.

"You seem quite pleasant this morning, my lady. From what I hear from Ryder, you were most impressive last night," Darius said, nodding at me.

My heart skipped a beat as I stood there is shock. "Wait, what? Impressive at what?" I questioned, my voice breaking slightly.

Darius merely raised an his eyebrow in response. "With Erica," he replied.

"Oh," I said, relieved. I knew guys would brag about their 'accomplishments', but I hoped that didn't apply to Darius and Ryder. They were too honorable to talk about women like that.

We continued on our journey, making our way to the top of the hill in about twenty minutes. I paused, once I saw the large electric fence come into view. All the memories of my home life started to hit me again. My friends, my community, my past life.

The group stopped, alarmed by my sudden halt in movement.

"MacKenzie?" Ryder questioned, following my gaze. "What's wrong?"

"Nothing, just...taking it all in, that's all..." I said, continuing onward.

We continued to move until the Rocky Balboa statue came into plain view, and Trevor took up his position as our rear security element, leaving nothing to chance on this journey. Ryder walked up next to me, moving his head back and forth as his eyes scanned the area.

"Something's not right," Ryder replied, reaching back and grabbing an arrow to fit on his bow.

"What do you mean?" I asked, drawing an arrow as well, but keeping it in my right hand.

Ryder did not even respond, he just kept on scanning the area. He motioned for us to move closer to the fence, and I could feel my heart skip a good beat or two. It petrified me that Ryder felt as though something were 'not right' at the current moment.

179

I had grown close with Ryder and his group, but that didn't mean I stopped caring about the well-being of my friends from where I came from. They frequented my thoughts.

A few moments later, I saw Major Chase appear with his hands raised up as if in surrender. Ryder and I both lowered our bows, unsure of what exactly was going on. We slowly approached the fence, as Major Chase approached us, keeping his hands raised.

Suddenly, I heard the sound of more footsteps and I turned my head to see Damian appear from behind the statue, a .38 special pointed at Major Chase. He flipped his greasy blonde hair out of his eyes, and smirked wickedly.

"Hello, MacKenzie..." he hissed.

19.

I immediately repositioned myself, my arrow pulled back and ready to fire at the devil that stood in front of me.

"Ah ah ah, let's not get too ahead of ourselves. We wouldn't want dear Major Chase redecorating the sector with his brains now would we?" Damian asked, stepping forward so that the small barrel of the gun pressed against Major Chase's head. Major Chase grunted slightly at the hard shove nudging his head.

I could feel the hate slowly rising from within me, making my blood boil. I had enjoyed the feeling of being away from Damian's clutches, but now I was back in my nightmare, and this time he had a hostage.

I exhaled heavily, gritting my teeth. "What do you want, Damian?" I hissed.

"Well, let me start by saying I am most impressed that you are still alive. It's been what, months? Then again, you've got the whole 'wilderness family of warriors' going on right now. You always were a strong, stubborn, soldier weren't you?" Damian questioned, tilting his head to the side.

"Cut the crap and get to the point. I'm not going to ask again. What do you want?" I snapped, not in the mood to deal with his mind games.

Damian laughed, his laugh echoing back into the wood-line. "You're in a very weak position to be making demands, Ms. Waters. You're forgetting that I have your dear old commander in front of me with a loaded gun to his head,"

Ryder put his hand on my shoulder, pushing me back slightly. He also cared deeply for Major Chase, but he was very good at not letting his anger cloud his judgement. He turned to face Damian, letting out a deep exhale.

"So you're the one MacKenzie has told me so many stories about," Ryder stated, in a seemingly calm voice.

Whatever trick Ryder was trying to play clearly worked, because Damian's smirk slowly disappeared and was replaced with a surprised expression. He was clearly rattled.

"What?" he asked, double blinking.

I saw a small smirk appear on Ryder's face, as he stepped closer to the fence.

"Damian, right? You know, MacKenzie kept saying about how she loves a man in charge. You wouldn't happen to be the...what was it she called you? The strong, dashing, head of the sector soldiers...would you?" Ryder questioned, folding his arms.

Damian narrowed his eyes at me slightly, and then turned his face back to Ryder.

"She said that?" he questioned.

181

If we weren't currently dealing with a mad-man hostage crisis, I really would have considered slapping Ryder right now. I had hardly mentioned Damian to Ryder and if I did, it wasn't very detailed. I assumed Major Chase had mentioned Damian to Ryder a couple of times in between supply runs.

"Oh yeah," Ryder lied, throwing in an eye-roll. "It was actually starting to get quite annoying. However, since you eighty-sixed her, and sent her out into my woods...well, that's a victory to me. I get to look at her, touch her, and be in the grace of her presence as much as I would like. So really, I should be thanking you," Ryder said, his smirk expanding.

I looked over at Darius, raising an eyebrow. "What the heck am I? A piece of meat?" I whispered.

Darius smirked down at me for a second, and then turned his gaze back to Damian.

Damian's dubious expression completely disappeared, as he turned the gun towards Ryder. "Oh really? What's to say I don't shoot you right now and then you'll never get the opportunity to be with her?" Damian said, clearly getting agitated.

Ryder smirked, shrugging. "Who is to say I already haven't?" he asked.

Major Chase took the opportunity to elbow Damian in the face, and grabbing his wrist and continuously kneeing him in the stomach until Damian was forced to drop the weapon. I knew Major Chase could well handle his own, but my heart skipped a couple beats at the sight of him turning and taking control of Damian. Damian stood up, attempting to throw a cross hook at Major Chase's face. Major Chase leaned to the side, capturing Damian's wrist and bending him down towards the ground. I knew he could snap Damian's arm like a chicken wing if he really wanted to, I had seen him do it to people before.

Damian began to laugh, causing Major Chase to raise an eyebrow. "What the hell are you laughing at, snake?"

"You think I was foolish enough to come alone?" Damian questioned, looking up at him.

As if on cue, about ten more sector soldiers rushed forward, all pointing their weapons at Major Chase. Major Chase maintained his firm grip on Damian, refusing to surrender just because he got surrounded by a group of wanna-be soldiers. He was a member of the 82nd Airborne, and they did not give up without a fight.

The Sector Commander also emerged from the shadows, a somewhat victorious smirk on his plump face. He had clearly gained weight since I had last saw him, judging by how his walk had began to turn into a somewhat waddle.

"So our source was right, the good old Major has been sneaking supplies to the eighty-sixers for quite some time now," he said.

I paused, *source?*
Who would possibly rat out Major Chase for delivering supply runs to us?

It was kept hidden from just about everyone in the sector, and I knew Jax would never say anything to jeopardize my safety. I knew him all too well. There were not any other guards in sight when we made the last supply run, so that meant we weren't ever spotted making a deal with him. That had to mean that someone from the woods somehow went and informed the Sector Commander of our exchanges.

The Sector Commander turned to face me, his eyes glowing with malice. He knew how much I cared about the people I was close to, and that hurting them was the quickest and most effective way to get to me.

"Hello MacKenzie. You know, you always were one of the best Sector Soldiers that we had," he stated.

"Shut-up," I snapped, staring him down. I heard Damian grunt, as he continued to struggle under Major Chase's arm bar.

"She's not very friendly, sir..." Damian stated. Major Chase simply put more pressure on his arm, causing Damian to let out a near squeal in pain.

"Did I say you could talk?" Major Chase said, gritting his teeth in frustration. I knew he always disliked Damian, I just didn't know to what extent.

The Sector Commander turned to face Major Chase, laughing. "How about you let my head of security go, and we can talk about the options on actually allowing you to live as opposed to a tormenting death?"

Major Chase shook his head. "No. If you attempt to take me out, he's coming with me. Good luck though,"

I finally had enough, re-drawing my bow and aiming it for the Sector Commanders head, who snapped his head in my direction.

"MacKenzie..." Ryder warned, stepping towards me.

"No, this is my fight. You can stand with me or get out of my way, but you're not going to stop me. I'm done with the nice girl act," I said, looking at him from my peripheral vision.

He backed away and drew up his bow and joined me at my side, along with Darius, Devon and Joe.

We stood in a perfect line, the other four aiming their weapons at the various soldiers while I kept mine on the Sector Commander. I quickly scanned the other soldiers faces to ensure they weren't any of my friends, before prepping to give the command.

"You're not very good at math, are you MacKenzie? There are twelve of us and five of you over there and the good old Major over here. It doesn't matter how much training you have, you don't stand a chance," the Sector Commander stated.

"You're not very good with history, considering you think a couple AR-15's are going to kill us. Sorry to disappoint you, but they won't. You can't kill us with any weapon that you possess here, and you have no means to detain us while we are on the other side of the fence. You, however, and your little toy soldiers back there, could be killed instantly with the strike of one of our arrows," I paused, watching the soldiers behind him look at each other in slight panic.

"So here is what I'm presenting to you. You're going to release Major Chase to us, because I don't trust you to just allow you to let him go back to wandering the sector in peace. You will not make any attempts to send your soldiers into our wood line once that happens, because if you do, we *will* tear them apart limb by limb," I ordered.

I looked down at Damian, who had finally given up on trying to fight Major Chase. "You can have that thing back though," I said, earning a chuckle from Ryder and Darius. I kept my arrow aimed at the Sector Commander's head, as he pondered the deal. He knew that either way, he was facing a losing battle.

"Fine," he finally stated, waving for the soldiers to stand down.

"Let's all move towards the gate together then..." I said, nodding towards the direction of the gate, which was a few hundred feet away.

"She means all of you," Darius said, eyeing up a soldier on the end who was attempting to slide away.

We all moved as one, keeping eyes on each other through the fence. Major Chase finally released his hold on Damian, who immediately grabbed his arm and began rubbing his wrist.

Joe tapped Trevor, signaling for him to get up from his rear security position and follow us as well.

After about five minutes, we finally reached the gate. Damian slowly slid over to type in the access code, keeping his eyes on Major Chase as if he were expecting him to lunge at him and tear his arm off this time.

Once the gate finally opened, I stepped to the edge of the gate, staring down the Sector Commander, who looked infuriated with the decision he just agreed to.

Like me, he did not like to lose. He seized Major Chase by the arm, and began walking him towards me. I was confused by how he thought this would come off as more intimidating or make him look more purposeful.

"You got lucky this time Ms. MacKenzie," he said, shoving Major Chase our way. Major Chase merely stumbled for a second, and then turned back to wind up and throw a punch at him.

Ryder put his hand on Major Chase's shoulder, telling him to stop.

"Next time don't expect things to go your way. If I so much as find out as a whisper of you and your little...woodland bunch coming near *my* sector, I will line all your friends who are still in here up against the fence and you can watch them all get executed up close," the Sector Commander hissed, spitting at my feet.

I narrowed my eyes at him, as he smirked and turned away.

I could feel the spirit of my tiger burning with rage inside my chest, wanting to leap out and physically claw the smirk off of his face.

Instead, I found myself reaching out and seizing him by his arm, pulling him down so that I could whisper in his ear. The sector soldiers immediately drew their weapons up, all looking down their sights at me.

"Stop you fools! You're going to shoot *me*!" the Sector Commander squealed, waving his free hand at them.

Damian drew his .38 special, moving it as he went back and forth pointing it at Darius and Ryder.

"You think, you can just threaten me? I'm capable of things you could only dream about in your absolute worst night mare. I could completely destroy you and rip you to shreds with a mere change. You may want to consider that next time you threaten my friends," I hissed.

He made to reply, but I tightened my grip on his arm, channeling the strength of my tiger to make it near impossible for him to break the grip. At least I would give my tiger the satisfaction of being somewhat involved.

"You can eighty-six me, but you will *never* contain me," I said, through clenched teeth.

I pushed him forward, shoving him back on the other side of the gate. He turned to face me, panting heavily, just as I hoped.

185

"We're done here," I said, nodding at my group. I heard Damian punch the sequence in again, as the gates slowly began to shut. Damian stared at me though the chain links, an evil look on his face. I knew he was dying to say threatening words to me, but when he turned and saw Ryder standing next to me, he knew better.

"Let's go," I heard the Sector Commander say, moving back towards his metal shack. "But sir," Damian spoke up, turning to face him.

"I said, let's go. Don't worry, we will find a way...." he said, turning back to shoot me one last look.

Once they disappeared from our view, I turned to face Major Chase, shaking slightly. My adrenaline had finally stopped pumping through my veins, and the reality of the situation had finally hit me. What had I just done? What if my bold actions had caused the lives of hundreds of people in the sector, including my friends?

As if reading my mind, Major Chase spoke up. "Do not worry, MacKenzie. He's afraid of you. It's going to take him a good while to come up with counter measures to make an impact on the brave actions that you executed here today,"

"Yeah, I guess so.. but now we just have to figure out what our next move is. The people back at camp are not going to be happy to hear the news that we no longer will be able to get supplies from the sector," I said, slightly crestfallen.

"We will cross that bridge when we come to it," Darius said, putting a comforting hand on my shoulder. "You did very well today,"

I looked over at Ryder, who simply smiled and nodded towards the direction of camp.

"Let's head back," he said, walking ahead of us. I looked over at Darius, who shook his head as if telling me not to worry, but I couldn't help it. I hated when people were disappointed, upset, or mad at me. It was one of my many faults that lead people to believe that I had anxiety.

We all trekked back to camp in silence, until we arrived at the vine-covered opening. Ryder turned to Major Chase.

"Darius will help you get situated, sir. Again, I'm sorry to drag you into this mess and take you away from the only life you ever knew," Ryder stated.

"Son, I have been on four deployments and for three of them I spent the majority of my time in a tent in the middle of the desert. Believe me when I say, I've seen much worse," Major Chase replied, a small smile on his face.

Ryder motioned for everyone else to go ahead of him, but grabbed my arm as I went to walk through the vines.

"We need to have a discussion," he said, his voice unreadable. He was very good at hiding his emotions and how he was actually feeling, which unnerved me even more.

"Okay," was all I managed to say.

He led me through the vines, motioning for me to follow him. I turned to see Major Chase getting surrounded by a bunch of our own, reaching up and touching his head as he passed through them, just like they did to me when I first arrived.

He pushed open the flap to his tent, and once it closed, he turned to face me, his eyes full of fire.

"I don't know what compelled you to act in such a manner back there, MacKenzie, and I don't know what kind of relationship you had with that...Damian snake thing and that Sector Commander, but it is no longer your life that you are toying with out here," he stated, firmly.

I felt as though he had dropped a weight on my chest.

"I made a decision, Ryder. They would have killed Major Chase if I hadn't of said what I said. I don't regret any of it either. I understand that you're concerned about the ones here with us that don't possess the gift," I said, pausing to step closer to him. He merely folded his arms in reply.

"But, I would not have said what I did back there without first considering that myself also. Everyone out here is like family to me, I've told you this before. There is not one person here I would not be willing to fight for," I continued, gazing up at him.

Ryder sighed, placing his hands gently on my shoulders.

"It's not just them I am worried about, MacKenzie. It's you also, I know that you are strong, but I still fear that one day I may...." Ryder trailed off, not wanting to finish his sentence.

His eyes connected with mine, and he leaned forward to rest his forehead against my own. I could feel his sigh escape his lips as he softly brought his lips to my own. I still felt the same butterfly sensation as when he kissed me the first time, my heart skipping a couple beats.

He pulled away after a couple seconds, his eyes capturing mine once more.

"Well, you get the rest..." he said, chuckling slightly. I blinked a few times, still stunned by his actions.

I felt the heat rise to my cheeks, as I turned away bashfully. "Yeah, I guess I do..." I said, biting my lip. I was suddenly struck with another thought, as I turned to face him again.

"Speaking of all this danger, danger stuff...where has Skyler been?" I questioned.

"I don't know, I haven't seen her since she joined the escorting party to take Erica and Joe to their cages. Why?" Ryder questioned.

I felt my heart jump in my throat, as I threw open the tent flap and began to look around frantically. I didn't want to jump to any conclusions, but it was just very odd and suspicious that Skyler had not been seen in about twenty four hours. The camp wasn't that big, she couldn't hide forever.

I heard Ryder step out behind me, and he walked so he was standing directly next to me.

"MacKenzie, why are you asking?" he questioned, confused.

"This camp is only so big. Why would she be hiding for this long?" I questioned, my eyes scanning the area.

I finally spotted her, carrying a basket of fresh berries from the forest. I narrowed my eyes, tunneling my vision on her as I hurried to close in on her. Before Ryder could stop me, I forcefully shoved Skyler against the closest tree, causing her to drop the basket that she was carrying.

"Well done newcomer, now I'll have to tell all the kids there won't be any berries for supper tonight because you just spoiled them all," Skyler snapped.

"We live in the freaking woods, Skyler, I think they will survive washing a little bit of dirt off of their berries," I retorted, shoving my forearm against her chest plate with a crushing amount of force.

She inhaled sharply in pain, but continued to stare hard into my eyes.

"Well then kindly explain what the hell you're doing, shoving me into the tree out of the blue like this?" Skyler asked, rolling her eyes.

"Gladly. Where the heck have you been since last night? You weren't around for any of the usual morning activities or anything, you've just been gone. I'd like to know why," I yelled, pulling her face closer to my own.

"MacKenzie," Ryder warned, but keeping his distance. I could tell by his body language that he was slightly curious also, but did not want to get too involved.

Skyler laughed, and then brought her hands to her face as if to mock being flattered. "My, my, I didn't know that you fancied my presence so much. I guess now that I don't have the responsibility of baby sitting these losers anymore, I felt as though I wasn't obligated to be here for all the morning kum bi ya's,"

I could see a few people coming out of their tents and stopping their chores to turn and face Skyler as she threw out her insults.

188

"We've been compromised. Apparently a 'source' revealed that we've been doing supply runs with the sector," I said, shoving her away from me and back against the tree.

She scoffed, bringing her hand to her chest as if she were offended. "You think I'm the one who went and was this 'source'?" she said, using her hands to put quotes around the words.

"I may hate you, but I live in this sector too. You think I would want to jeopardize my health and life by selling out our only source of product and send us back to square one?" Skyler yelled, causing a few people to turn to each other and mutter words about 'no hope' and 'we are doomed'.

"You still haven't told us where you have been the best good couple of hours," Ryder cut in, trying to get Skyler back on point.

Skyler sighed, and then folded her arms across her chest. "I was at the lake,"

"And who the hell am I supposed to get to verify that for me? A duck?" I questioned.

"Well...you could...or you could ask Ryan. He was there with me," Skyler said, pointing over at the small boy who was standing no more than five feet away.

I recognized the boy, he was one of Erica's archery students, in fact he was the one that Erica was instructing when I was still settling in to the camp.

Ryan nodded, and then looked to the ground. "Its true," he said, softly.

I felt a pang of guilt in my chest for assuming that Skyler was the one, but I refused to apologize to Skyler for accusing her, let alone let it show at all.

"I believe you owe me an apology," Skyler stated, folding her arms across her chest.

I merely looked at her, and then looked at the ground. "Continue on with your berry delivery, and then we can talk about apologies," I said, grabbing Ryder by the arm and motioning for him to follow me over to where Darius and Major Chase were talking.

20

Major Chase and Darius both turned their heads at my approach, both looking comfortably relaxed with each other, which I was thankful for.

"I think the four of us need to have a discussion, as much as I hate to admit that Skyler is right, well....she's right. As much as we can pull the whole 'cave man' thing right now, there are some supplies we will be needing in the future to keep us going," Ryder stated.

"That, and even though I think my little message to the Sector Commander freaked him out to a point, it doesn't mean he's not going to start targeting people and not making it known to us," I said.

Darius looked around, and motioned for us to go inside the training tent. At first I was confused, but then when I looked around I could see why. A couple people here and there seemed extremely curious in what our conversation consisted of.

Ryder held the flap open for all of us, winking at me in the process. I couldn't help but smile. I knew he was trying to put me at ease, and I appreciated the thought, but I was too wrapped up in the possibilities of what could possibly be happening to my friends in the next few hours, or possibly right now.

"You keep calling him *Sector Commander*, does he not have a name?" Darius questioned, tilting his head slightly.

"No, we've always been told to refer to them as *Sector Commander* and nothing except that. It's supposed to make them seem less personable and more authoritative," I replied.

"Yeah, because not having a name makes someone seem more personable. How about we call him *the village idiot* instead?" Ryder suggested, folding his arms across his chest.

"If I remember correctly, his name used to be Charles Anderson," Major Chase spoke up.

"Ah, Mr. Anderson...even better," Ryder remarked, running a hand over his still fresh buzz cut. A few seconds later Devon, Trevor, Joe and a now awake Erica appeared, looking around at the group.

"Sorry, we can come back if you would like us to..." Devon spoke up, turning red with embarrassment.

"No, that's alright. You guys should stay, we could use your opinion on this one," Darius stated.

"Erica, this is Major Chase. Major Chase, this is Erica..." I said, realizing they were the only two in the room who hadn't met.

They shook hands, and I noticed that Erica looked quite bashful. I guess she was a little nervous about meeting new people.

"Sooo...what's going on?" Trevor questioned, breaking the awkward silence that followed.

"We are talking about the situation regarding us getting compromised and not being able to get supplies from the sector anymore," Ryder said, with a heavy sigh.

"Wait, didn't your one friend help out with the exchange once before?" Trevor questioned.

"Yeah he did, but its way too risky for anyone to even attempt...even Jax...as brave and as strong as he is," I said, considering what could happen if Jax even tried to complete it.

"She's right, we don't want to risk innocent lives being lost..." Joe pointed out.

"So we need a plan," I spoke up, realizing what we had to do.

"A plan for what?" Trevor questioned.

I looked around the room, making eye contact with everyone. "To take back the sector, of course..where we won't have to worry about how many of each supply we have, or when we are going to run out of everything," I stated.

In those few seconds following my statement, it seemed as though half the types of emotion listed in the English Dictionary passed through all of their faces.

"That's crazy," Joe said, pausing to approach me. "I approve," he finished, with a respectful nod.

"It's never been done before, its near impossible..." Devon spoke up, shaking her head in disbelief.

"It's never been attempted before," Ryder corrected.

"Okay, let's say we take over the sectors...kill or imprison Mr. Anderson or whatever that commanders name is...then what? There are still seven other sectors out there and seven other leaders. I doubt that they would just let....Anomics...run the Northeast sector," Trevor said, rocking back and forth on his heels.

"I'm more than certain we are not the only Anomics out here, I'm willing to bet the other sectors have them too," Erica said.

"She's right, there are more of us out there. If we were to take over the sector, contacting them would be no problem. But we are thinking large scale here...let's just focus on our problem before we attempt to solve the world's issues," Darius spoke up, with a heavy sigh.

I knew he would love to see us all united as one nation again, but he knew the biggest accomplishments started with the smallest steps. If we could reclaim the sector again, it could be the beginning of a new era.

I could have my friends back...

"MacKenzie, where do suggest we start? You and the good Major know that Sector better than anyone else, you're going to be the ones to help us take it back..." Ryder spoke up, placing his hand on the small of my back.

"Well, I don't know how much the patrolling schedule has changed... and I also don't know how many of the new sector soldiers are members of Damian's groupies or whatever you call them. They'll be our biggest complication," I said, looking over at Major Chase.

"Almost one to every pair of patrols, last I checked..." Major Chase replied.

"I should have assumed Damian would be a pain in the ass, and complicate things even more," I said, sighing.

Major Chase walked towards me, his shoulders straight back and a 'this is about to get real' facial expression.

"MacKenzie," he stated, stopping right in front of me. "You toured Afghanistan and Iraq. You shoot a perfect score on your M9 during qualifications. You've faced enemies that some people couldn't dream of,"

He paused, to lean down slightly. "I have no doubt in my mind that you are not capable of leading this charge,"

I swallowed hard, suddenly moved by his mini, motivational speech.

"Right, well let's start with Damian. He may look the part, but he's not stupid. Between the two of them, they are going to be ordering more patrols. Normally, soldiers work a 72 hour on, 48 hour off schedule. Instead, its more like 96 on and eight off. We did something like this once before, when the sectors were first created. We called it 'hell week', because it was so mentally and physically exhausting. It's only used for severe threats and I guarantee you, this will be one of them. So I believe that we should begin our assault on the third day, when the majority of the soldiers are entering their 72nd hour period. They will be extremely mentally and physically exhausted, giving us the best chance..." I said, looking around the group.

"Well, what about the innocents in the sectors? Who is to say that they won't be executed randomly before that 72 hour period?" Darius questioned, stroking his chin in thought.

He had a point. Even though waiting until the 72 hour period would guarantee us a severe advantage to those of us who weren't skin walkers, because our people would be well rested while the soldiers would be weak and vulnerable.

I paused. Maybe it would be better if only those of us who had the gift would conduct the assault instead of involving everyone from our wooded family.

"So, then how about we do this tomorrow night? Instead of doing a full-fledged attack with everyone out here, we limited to just us, or at least those of us with the gift. That way there will be less casualties and by then, they still won't have the resources to beat us...even if they do figure out what our weakness is," I suggested.

"Is that enough time to formulate a plan?" Erica questioned, speaking up.

"If we were the Air Force, I would say no," Major Chase joked, elbowing me slightly.

I couldn't help but smile, I knew he was just trying to ease the tension.

"Sorry," Major Chase said, raising his hands innocently. "One team, one fight,"

"Alright MacKenzie, what's your plan?" Ryder asked, turning to face me.

21.

I approached the large cage, and saw Erica's tiger laying in the corner, pleasantly calm. I sighed, pleased that this encounter was already much better than our last one when she was in the cage. I turned to face the guard and nodded.

"Open it," I stated, ready to go in and converse with her.

He looked at me confused. If I recalled correctly, his name was Colton and he was recently new to the change, only receiving the gift the year before.

"MacKenzie, don't you want to change first?" he asked, a hint of worry in his voice. He was young, probably no more than twenty four years old, and his face expressed sincere concern along with his youth.

"No, there's no need. I don't detect a threat here today," I said, reassuring him with a small smile.

He nodded, and then stepped to the side, unlocking the gate.

I entered, motioning for Erica's tiger to follow me.

"Let's go," I said, trying to sound somewhat cheerful.

All I got in return was a pair of confused eyes staring back at me, and a head tilt.

"Trust me, you're going to be fine..." I reassured, waving my hand once more for her to come towards me.

She stretched her front paws out and arched her back, letting out a long yawn, before completely standing on all fours.

"You trust me to come out into the wild while in this form? I don't think its safe, MacKenzie..." Erica spoke up, tilting her head down. "I'm not strong enough to maintain complete control,"

"Well, you're doing one hell of a job right now. Just keep doing what you're doing," I replied, trying to get her mind off of that negativity bias. It would for sure lead to her tiger taking over again if she maintained that attitude.

I walked by her side, as I led her into the woods.

"What's the point of this?" she questioned, curious.

I looked down at her, as she turned to face me.

"I want you there with us tomorrow night, so consider this your expedited training. We are just doing to take a simple hour-long walk in the woods, just to get you being in control of your tiger while being in an actual environment, not just in a cage..." I replied.

"You want me to walk around a sector full of, and excuse my French, asshole leaders who threatened one of my close friends and my family members?" Erica questioned, her eyes darkening slightly.

194

Before I could reply, she spoke again. "Even you couldn't hold back when you saw a soldier harming an innocent, and you're one of the strongest people I know..."

"It was different for me. I think through all my years of working in the sector, I chose not to see the evil that was inside of it. As a soldier, I just followed orders, whether I agreed with them or not. Military Code. When the sectors were created, I tried doing the same thing. As the years passed, I realized how evil eighty-sixing really was, so I could feel my anger starting to build up. Then when I witnessed that soldier harming that little boy like he was, I finally snapped. I had years of build up, Erica.... I may be strong, but everyone breaks...eventually," I said, looking over at her again.

"But seeing people getting treated horribly infuriated me even before I had this gift, I don't know how I'm going to be able to control it now that I have it," Erica protested.

"Remember how we had that conversation about Skyler when you and I first met? You told me all about how horribly she treated you guys. You never launched out at her, did you?" I questioned

"No," Erica confessed.

"Well good, then you'll be fine. The more you doubt yourself, the less control you will maintain over your tiger. You need to be strong for yourself, so you can be strong for her. Remember, you and her are one element now. Her fate is tied to yours. This gift is not for the weak, Erica. That is why I chose you. You're stronger than you think," I replied.

We stopped walking once the camp came into view, and we spotted various shadows moving around, everyone finishing their final duties for the day and getting ready to head to bed.

"Are we supposed to hug now or something?" Erica joked, breaking the silence.

I laughed, shaking my head. "Maybe later, but for right now, let's get back to patrolling," I said, patting her on the head.

***

The next morning seemingly flew by faster than usual, and it probably didn't help that I had only gotten about four hours of sleep, at most. I was so wrapped up in building up Erica's confidence in her tiger, that I didn't take time to think about my own health. In a few hours, I would be entering the sector once more, but with a heavy agenda this time.

After today, regardless of the end result, nothing was going to be the same. I spent the majority of the morning with Darius, planning out the best strategy for our attack. I had barely gotten the chance to talk to Ryder, he had been off with Major Chase, trying to scout out activity in the sectors.

Something about trying to study the patterns in the patrols and seeing if there were any loopholes that we could work with.

"What are you thinking, MacKenzie?" Darius questioned, leading me towards camp as we returned from one final training session.

"I'm thinking a lot of things, is there one thing in particular that you are referring to?" I questioned, looking over at him. We were on our way to meet a girl named Syd, who was apparently one of the weapons experts in the camp. I had spoke with her briefly in passing, but beyond that, I wasn't too familiar with her.

"Are you ready to reclaim your home?" he questioned.

I sighed, pondering his thought. Of course I would love to be home once more, to read my favorite books, look at all my old photos to regain long lost memories, and to have some laughs with my old friends...but how would they react to seeing me again?

I thought about how Ryder and I had pretty much established a relationship, and it made me wonder what my friends back in the sector would think about it. Would they think it was seemingly predictable? Would they be extremely happy for me?

What would Jax think?

"It should be interesting," I finally said, showing Darius a small smile.

We headed into a dark blue tent, and as soon as we did a rather large brown squirrel ran up to us as if in greeting. It began to twitch its tail, sniffing me and Darius with a great curiosity.

"Portofino, you get back here!" a voice called out, from the furthest corner of the tent. I looked over to see the girl I assumed to be Syd approaching. She couldn't have been more than 5'6, and her dark brown hair was pulled up into a tight pony tail which rested on top of her head. She had a very fit frame, and she was wearing what appeared to be a clip of AK-47 bullets around her like a toga. I could see some scars on her biceps, as if she had seen quite a few decent battles herself.

The squirrel twitched its tail one last time, and then it ran back towards the girl and jumped up so that it perched on her shoulder.

"Syd," Darius said, smiling at her. I had never seen him smile so much in the time that I had known him. Maybe Darius really did have a secret crush, after all.

She returned the smile, along with a wink. "Good to see you, Darius..." she replied.

"You have an AK-47 here?" I questioned, suddenly feeling awkward. I wonder if this was how Darius felt every time Ryder and I had one of our exchanges.

Syd turned to face me, shaking her head. "Nah, I just like the way the ammo belt suits me. I used to work on a range not too far from Fort Dix, New Jersey. I guess you could say that its something to remind me where I came from,"

"Right... I heard you have something to show us to assist with the assault tonight?" I questioned, still looking back and forth between the two of them.

"That, I do..." Syd said, waving for us to follow her towards the back end of the tent to where a large, gray chest stood.

"Most of these I made myself, I like to, ya know...make some fun stuff," Syd said, spinning the combination on the lock before throwing the chest open.

I looked over at Darius and raised an eyebrow. I was surprised that I hadn't been more formally introduced to Syd before right now. We could have been good friends, and had always been interested in creating weapons myself.

"Oh, that's pretty awesome..." I replied, watching her pull out a smaller black case.

"You've made your own before?" Syd questioned, opening the smaller box as well.

"I mean...when I was seven or something I made my own bow and arrow if that counts..." I said, slightly embarrassed.

"Hmm," Syd said, pausing to look over at me, and then turning her attention back to her box.

"I've got a cross bow here for you and about three of your team members. Had I been given more time, I would have loved to make some more but my sister, Christina and I were not given enough notice with this whole....town takeover...thing you got going on," Syd said, pulling it out and thrusting it at me.

I studied the crossbow, realizing it was no bigger than a throw pillow for a couch or a bed. Syd must have noticed the look on my face, and she began to chuckle slightly.

"It may look small, but its powerful. Comparable to a High-powered crossbow," Syd stated, her eyes overlooking the weapon.

"How did you...?" I questioned, awe-struck.

"I told you, I like to make weapons. Your arm candy, Ryder, would ask that Major to sneak me some parts from military armories in the northeast sector, in small bits of course, we didn't want to look too suspicious, and from there on..... the weapons were slowly, but surely, created!" Syd said, giving me a double thumbs up.

"Oh.. I guess that makes sense," I said, still in shock that I was never aware of all these little secrets that were going on inside the sector.

"But," Syd spoke up, capturing my attention once more. "I actually have something else for you," she said, reaching inside the large chest once more.

"For me?" I questioned, making sure that I heard her correctly.

Syd nodded. "Years ago, when we were first established here... your good friend, Major Chase, delivered something of vast importance to Ryder. He told Ryder that the sector soldiers were increasing their patrols, looking for any one who resisted the Sector Commander's demands....and to search the homes of those skin walkers....or Anomics as you guys call them now-a-days. Major Chase couldn't risk the chance. So he went to your parents old home, and retrieved a very special item..." Syd paused, looking up at me.

I tilted my head slightly, curious. I had never realized how connected with my family Major Chase really was. It was actually starting to weird me out a little bit.

Syd then pulled her hands out of the chest, and in her hands was a medium sized, dark red box. She slowly knelt down on one knee, her amber eyes meeting mine in a sincere stare. Before I could question what she was doing, Darius also knelt down on one knee behind me, completely confusing me.

"What's going on?" I asked, suddenly uncomfortable.

When neither one of them answered me, I stepped forward, touching the red box. The smooth feel of the velvet underneath my fingertips soothed me, making me feel a little less tense. I slowly lifted the lid of the box and held back a gasp.

Resting on top of silk, red cloth was a beautiful pair of silver, twin sai's. Black and red leather was crisscrossed together, wrapping around the hilt of the blades. The blade was so clean, that it reflected the afternoon sun that was seeping through the cracks in the tent. I had seen these blades before, in my fathers desk in his office.

I snapped back into reality, taking a step back and bringing a hand to my chest to prevent myself from crying.

"I don't understand," I said, shaking my head.

Both Sydney and Darius stood up, and I felt Darius's hand land on my shoulder in comfort. "The time of the Anomics is coming, MacKenzie. You said it yourself. Its time to take back the sector. We were given this gift for a greater purpose. We're guardians amongst the human race. You're to lead us, its in your blood. These blades symbolize your leadership," Darius said, nodding towards the blades.

I looked over at them, and then back at Darius. "My father kept many secrets. He was training me to be ready to lead...but he never got the chance to actually show me how to lead,"

"You know how to, MacKenzie. Leading others is not something that one can be shown, because everyone has their own leadership style. I do not doubt that after this victory, you will be set on the right path," Sydney spoke up, passing the box to me.

I took the box, feeling a shiver travel down my spine.

"Thank you," I whispered, more to myself. "Thank you, Dad...."

"Oh, and one final thing..." Syd said, snapping her fingers. She disappeared into the dark corner and then returned moments later carrying a large, black garment bag.

"Can't be a hero, without something appropriate to wear...right?" Syd questioned, unzipping the bag.

22

I paused, looking at myself in the full scale mirror that Syd had brought out from the dark corner. I asked Syd how she was able to get a mirror out of the sector, since most of the packages were small, and she told me that she had salvaged it and carried it with her when she was eighty sixed. Something about being able to look into your soul everyday and knowing that you were going to make it through, despite what was going on around you.

Syd's sister, Christina, a strawberry blonde with pure blue eyes and a similar fit built as her sister, stepped out from behind me and ran a hand over her own hair.

"I would say we've got a badass here," Christina commented, as she turned my head to face her so she could finish applying the sea blue eyeshadow on my face.

When she was done, I turned to face my reflection again.

The dark blue, almost underarmour jacket that I wore fit extremely comfortably, on top of the thin, similarly colored dark blue tank top underneath it. The pants were also a similar dark blue, underarmour material, feeling extremely cool on my bare skin. I zipped up the jacket up to my chest, enjoying the feeling of being able to wear something other than a tunic for a change. Christina had pulled my hair into a very tight, mid-section pony tail, with very tiny braids leading into it on both sides of my head. I was surprised to see that despite it resting higher on my head, my hair still passed my shoulder blades. I reached up and pulled my bangs forward, so that they angled across my forehead.

I hadn't worn makeup in so long, and Christina had used a combination of a dark sea blue eyeshadow along with some earthy tones to make my eyes stand out even more. On my hips were two sheaths for the twin sai's, enabling me to carry my fathers prized possessions with me as we took the fight to the sector.

"Total badass is more like it, heck, I'd follow you to war..." Syd spoke up.

I turned so that I could see Syd in my peripheral vision, and then looked back at my reflection in the mirror again. I had done many years of leading people into war, but right now, that phrase didn't sit quite right with me.

"This isn't a war, in war...there is an enemy that is consistently trying to end your life and the only thing you know is to rely on your instinct to survive. We aren't aiming to kill today, but if that happens, so be it. But I'm not walking in a as a killer, I'm walking in as a leader," I stated, trying to think of what my father would think if he saw me right now.

"So if this is not a war, what do we call this?" Darius asked, appearing behind me.

I turned to face him, smirking slightly. "A conflict,"

I picked up my father's blades, studying them for a second. I had only held them once, but my father told me that they were passed down from generation to generation in the family, being created by a very distant relative, who was a blacksmith.

I sheathed both of them, and turned to face Sydney and Christina. "Thank you, both of you. I'm sure once all this is over, I'll be back to learn how to make some weapons with you Syd," I said, with a smile.

Syd winked, giving me a thumbs up. "I'll be looking forward to it darlin'...come by anytime," she said.

"And I would love to do your hair again, if you don't mind!" Christina added, narrowing her eyes slightly as if she were thinking of what project she could possibly do next with my hair.

"Hey, sounds good to me..." I said, motioning for Darius to follow me out of the tent.

The sun was beginning to descend, and I knew that meant it was time for us to prepare to move into position. I looked over towards Ryder's tent, nodding to Darius.

"Gather the others who are taking part in this mission, I will be right there..." I said, showing him a warm smile.

Darius smirked in return. "Take your time," he said, and then headed to go find the rest of our group.

I approached Ryder's tent, seeing him through the cracks of the tent flap as it blew lightly in the wind. I could tell that he had a lot on his mind, as he was pacing quite a bit.

I lifted the flap, sliding into the tent. "Hey," I said, unsure of how to feel.

Ryder turned to face me, and the second he did he froze. I watched as his eyes trailed over my figure, and when his eyes reconnected with mine, a smirk appeared on his face.

"You look beautiful," he stated, walking over towards me.

"Oh...uh....thanks," I said, looking down at the ground. I could feel the heat rising to my cheeks, and my heart started racing again. I didn't know why I kept reacting this way whenever Ryder was present, we had been together for quite some time now.

"Are you ready for this?" Ryder questioned, stopping once he was right in front of me. He used his hand to lift my gaze to meet his, and I let out a long exhale.

"I am. I just hope that our plan works, I mean... its not much of a plan but hey, we have to do something, right?" I questioned, enjoying the feel of his warm hand that has now stroking my cheek.

"Hmm... I know it's going to work, MacKenzie. You need to stop being so damn hard on yourself," Ryder replied, his eyes softening.

"I can't help it. I'm an Irish-Italian-Catholic," I retorted, trying to ease the tension.

"Well, I can't exactly help you there. But I am going to be by your side when we go through with this thing. I'm not going to let them take you down," Ryder said, stepping closer to me.

I closed my eyes and inhaled his scent for a second, and then when I opened my eyes, I felt my heart jump once more.

"I love you," I said, with a full heart.

Ryder paused, his eyes quickly moving back towards mine. In that moment, I felt as though my heart had stopped beating. *Oh no, maybe that was way too soon to say that. I'm so stupid. MacKenzie, you're a freaking idiot.*

Suddenly, Ryder's lips came crashing against mine, as he pulled me into a passionate kiss. I felt as though my chest was suddenly on fire, so full of emotion.

He pulled away slowly, but still held me close. "I am in love with you also, MacKenzie..." Ryder said, a full smile appearing on his lips. I had seen him smirk and show small smiles every now and then, but this was the first time that I had full on seen him smile like he was right now. I could see the life in his eyes.

I cleared my throat, still taken back by the kiss. "Ahem, well we should probably go rally the troops or whatever and get this thing started,"

"Let's do it," Ryder said, placing his hand on the small of my back. "By the way, I'm *really* loving this outfit," he purred, in my ear.

I felt all the blood rush to my face, as I looked away in embarrassment. "Shush you," I said, playfully punching him in the arm.

23

Ryder and I approached the group of our comrades standing in the middle of camp, and I was completely surprised to see that Skyler was also standing there. I looked around to see that our numbers totaled fourteen. A few women and men were coming forward, wishing us all well on our journey. I looked over and saw Darius talking to Syd, one of his hands holding hers as he said his farewell. I smiled, pleased to see that Darius had found happiness.

I felt something swatting my hand and I turned to see Ryan standing there, his hands folded behind his back, swaying from side to side. Just like that little girl Georgia did, back when I was patrolling the sector with Jax.

"Hey buddy," I said, squatting down to come at his level.

He narrowed his little eyes at me, and then folded his arms.

"You better come back," he said, pouting. I couldn't help but laugh, at the boys genuine concern. It was absolutely adorable.

"I promise you I will, Ryan..." I said, reaching up and patting his head. He returned the smile to me, before his eyes drifted over to the rest of our group. The second his eyes landed on the group, his smile quickly faded and his eyes looked almost haunted.

I turned around to follow his gaze, and then I turned back to face him.

"Ryan, what's wrong?" I questioned, taking his small hand in mine.

"I don't want you to die," he stated, tears starting to well up in his eyes. I felt as though a weight had been dropped on my heart, at the sight of tears rolling down his cheeks. I reached up and began to wipe them away with my thumb, resting my hand against his cheek.

"Ryan, I'm not going to die....why would you think I was going to die?" I whispered, scooting closer to him. His watery eyes connected with mine, and he began to sniffle heavily.

"MacKenzie?" Ryder questioned, appearing behind me. I quickly stood up, turning to face him. Ryder overlooked my figure, before he leaned slightly to the right to look behind me. When he saw the small crying boy, his face softened considerably.

"Hey bud, what's wrong?" Ryder questioned, stepping next to me. Ryan looked back and forth between me and Ryder, and then turned to face our group once more. He let out a heavy sigh, looking back up at Ryder. He pointed a finger at me, wiping a tear from his cheek with the other hand.

"She has to stay safe," he stated, finding his voice again.

Ryder looked over at me, confused. I merely responded with a shrug. I had no idea why Ryan was under the impression that I was the one who was in danger. I knew the sector like the back of my hand, and it was my plan. I was more concerned about everyone else. Then again, Ryan was young, he didn't quite understand.

"She will be bud, I promise..." Ryder replied, rubbing his hand on my back. I closed my eyes for a second, enjoying the mini massage that I was getting.

"Okay, good...." Ryan said, bowing his head and then slowly walking away. I watched as he turned to face the group one last time and then hurried off towards the younger couple standing near the food tent, which I assumed to be his parents.

"What was that about?" Ryder questioned, stepping in front of me.

"Not quite sure," I replied, still staring after him.

"MacKenzie, just keep in mind while we are conducting this whole raid thing...we may not have much time. Now that everyone in the camp knows what we are doing, your Sector Commander may now be aware of the attack..." Ryder said.

"Why would he be aware of it?" I asked, looking back at him.

"Well, he found out about our supply run from some...source. How do we know that this same source, whoever it is, did not inform them of our plan as well?" Ryder questioned, lowering his voice slightly.

"That's why we kept the plan in a very small circle and did not reveal it until just moments ago... I thought the same thing when we started coming up with this plan," I said, trying to reassure him.

He paused in thought, looking over at our group of Anomics.

"The only positive thing about this I guess, is that it will for sure narrow our list of suspects. Especially since we have regular patrols going around making sure no one tries to leave the site," Ryder said.

"Agreed. Although, it kills me to think such things...that one of our own Anomics could do such a thing..." I said, looking down at the ground.

"I know, it kills me too...but we can't help but think like that..." Ryder said, leaning in slightly.

"I know, but it still kills me..." I said, making eye contact with him once more.

"Hmmm...Anomics, let's head on out..." Ryder said, calling all of our group to come back to our small little circle. We turned to face the vined entrance to the camp, lined up in pairs. Somehow, I had found my way next to Skyler.

Out of my peripheral, I saw her overlook my figure. "Nice outfit," she commented. I turned to meet her gaze, and for a second I thought I saw a small smirk on her face.

"Thanks... when this is all over, feel free to borrow it..." I replied, turning to face forward again.

"Blue's not really my color, but thanks anyway..." she stated, sounding firm once more.

We all began to slowly move forward, and with each person we passed, they reached out and placed their hands on top of our heads as if giving us a farewell blessing. Once we had passed through the vines and we all were accounted for, we abandoned the little pairing system that we had going on.

I found myself next to Major Chase, surprised that he was actually there. Unless...

"Sir, I'm pleased to see that you are joining us on this journey," I said, looking over at him.

He looked down at me, a small smile on his face. "Why would I not be? I couldn't leave my fellow...Anomics...to march off to battle alone," he stated. I watched as his eyes changed to a shade of royal blue, and I had to hold back a gasp.

It all made sense now. How he knew so much about my family, and why he had always consistently and ironically found a way to be a constant presence in my life. His eyes slowly changed back, and he looked down at one of the sai's that rested on my hip.

"I'm very pleased that Syd delivered those to you. It goes to show that no matter what road we all take, our fate catches up to us in the end..." Major Chase stated.

"What does that mean?" I questioned, confused.

Major Chase let out a long sigh. "Where to start...."

He turned to face me again, slowing down his pace so that we strayed back from the group slightly.

"I had been well acquainted with your family before you even joined the military and came to my unit, your father and I were both in positions of leadership for our chapters. Your father maintained control of the Northeast, I the Southeast. Our two Western comrades were killed during the war. Prior to the bombings and the destruction, I had a conversation with your father. He sensed that your family was in a state of danger. He didn't say why. Made me promise that if anything happened to them, it would be my responsibility to take care of you. He gave me those blades that you possess today, told me that when you were ready, to pass them onto you. Once all the eighty-sixing started, I found friendship with Darius and Ryder, knowing that many of our kind had made it to the woods. I continued to sneak them supplies for years, undetected. I knew it was too risky to reveal my real identity to you at the time, beyond being your former Commander," Major Chase paused, to push a stay pine needle branch out of my way.

I nodded in thanks, extremely intrigued by his story.

"When I noticed how...different...the sectors started becoming, when Damian took over as head of security, I knew that it was only a matter of time before they started to really crack down on security. Damian has always wanted to be in control and enforce his ideals on other people. When he started recruiting those new soldiers, I decided it was the best time to sneak your father's sai's to Ryder... I wanted to talk to you about everything earlier, and I should have. Before I knew it, Jax showed up at my door, told me that you had eighty-sixed yourself. I hadn't seen that boy so broken since our last deployment," Major Chase said, looking down at me.

I felt something jump in my chest. "Jax came to you when I fled to the wood line?" I questioned.

"Immediately after, so it seemed. Never seen anyone down as much whisky as that boy," he replied.

I stared ahead and saw Ryder walking side by side with Darius, each of them armed with one of Syd's crossbows.

"So your plan was to bring me to Ryder eventually?" I questioned, continuing to watch him.

"Yes...eventually. But it seems fitting that you two crossed paths anyway, doesn't it?" Major Chase questioned, smiling down at me.

We continued walking until we reached the rest of the group, who had stopped about a good twenty feet from the fence, more specifically, the gate. Everyone turned inward, and Ryder stepped towards the center of the circle.

"Okay, we all know what to do now. This is game time right now. If any of you no longer wish to partake in this mission, then please, feel free to leave now before we even begin our involvement," Ryder said, looking around at everyone.

When no one said anything or moved, Ryder nodded.

"Right, let's get this thing started..." Ryder said, motioning for everyone to move into place.

"Ryder," I spoke up, moving towards him. He turned to face me, his jaw squared. I could tell that even he was nervous, but I knew he refused to let me see it.

I stopped once I was about a foot away from him, and I gazed up into his eyes for a minute. Yes, it was true. At one point in my life I would have given anything to have been with Jax, wishing that he would leave his wife and he and I would be together, especially after everything we went through on our deployments together. Although right now, the connection I felt with Ryder was stronger than one I had ever felt, he truly understood everything that I had to go through with my gift.

I then launched myself into his arms, pulling him into me so that our lips locked in a passionate kiss. I could tell that I had genuinely caught him off guard, feeling him smile as he lips pressed warmly onto mine. I heard someone scoff, but I didn't even care at that point. People who overly displayed their affection with their significant other used to really irritate me, but in the moment I was in right now... I fully understood why they did it.

I pulled away from him, and continued to stare up at him. He slowly opened his eyes and allowed a smile to cross his face.

"Wow...what was that for?" he questioned, chuckling slightly.

That once tense look that was on his face had now disappeared, and he seemed much more at ease.

"Just because," I replied, with a wink. "Now let's get this thing going!"

Devon moved towards the edge of the tree line, Colton and another Anomic named Brian followed her. I sighed, secretly wishing them well. The plan was for Devon to act as a woman in distress, while Colton and Brian changed to their tiger form and were to pretend to try to hunt her down. Hopefully the soldiers who passed by on their patrol had a heart, and would open the gate and try to help Devon, giving us ample opportunity to enter the sector.

"Here come the soldiers," Darius said, nodding down the way. I turned to get eyes on the people that he was talking about, craning my neck slightly so that I could see over the nearby bushes.

As the figures came more clearly into view, I let out a small gasp. "Wait," I said, running towards the direction that Devon, Brian and Colton disappeared in. I had gotten to them just in time, as both Brian and Colton had removed their tops as if they were getting ready to change.

"Stop, stop. Hold on a second!" I said, waving my hands frantically. The three of them shot me a look of confusion, and then all looked around at each other.

"MacKenzie, this was the plan...." Devon spoke up.

"I know, I know. I'm changing it, just stay here a second..." I said, moving towards the fence. When I stepped out into the clearly, I realized that I was right. I saw the familiar faces of Amanda and Matt.

"Amanda! Matt!" I whispered, harshly.

Amanda turned to face my direction, and her eyes widened in surprise. "MacKenzie!" she exclaimed, hurrying over.

"Shh!" I said, waving my hands, telling her to keep her voice down.

She and Matt both stopped a couple of inches away from the fence, and I heard one of Amanda's stray hairs get zapped by the electric current.

"What are you doing here?" Matt questioned, seeming extremely happy as well.

"You have no idea how insane its gotten. We really miss you," Amanda said, somewhat sadly.

"I know, I've missed you guys too. Listen, I need you to do me a favor and open the gate," I said, pointing towards it.

Both of their faces fell, and they looked at each other.

I felt my stomach flip, hoping that my instinct in going to my friends instead of sticking with the plan wasn't a horrible idea.

Amanda turned to face me, about to speak.

"Look, I know what you're thinking, you're worried about what is going to happen to you if you let us in and whatever plan I have doesn't work and Damian is probably going to blame the two of you and rip the only life you know away from you. But I promise you, I will not let that happen. You have my word," I said, sincerely.

Amanda raised an eyebrow and showed me a small smile. "I was actually going to ask how many of you were there and if I could have a front row seat to your little destruction of Damian, but sure, I'll hold you to that..." she said, walking over to the keypad to type in the code.

I smiled, turning around and motioning for everyone else to come forward. Matt looked around at the group of us, nodding in satisfaction.

"I think I'm going to enjoy this," he said, turning back to face me.

I smirked wickedly. "Trust me, you will..." I replied, walking towards the gate. We heard the buzzing sound of the gate opening, and I bit my lip. I knew that it was only a matter of time before two more soldiers appeared, per protocol whenever the gate was opened.

I motioned for everyone to hurry on inside the sector, Ryder being the last one. He touched my lower back affectionately, and I followed him inside. Once I had counted everyone up and made sure that we were all there, I nodded for Amanda to close the gate.

I heard Matt's radio immediately go off.

"Patrol 78 this is Patrol 2. We heard gate activity moments ago. We are moving towards your location,"

Amanda quickly swiped the radio, looking over at me.

"Patrol 2 this is Patrol 78. No need. There was a rabid animal in the precinct and we released it into the wood line. We needed to protect the population, we can't afford the sickness,"

I raised my eyebrow at her, not even bothering to fight the smile that was appearing on my face. "A rabid animal?" I questioned.

She shrugged, biting her lip in worry.

We heard the static crack once more.

"How about next time you fools just shoot the damn beast instead of jeopardizing everyone else in the sector. You have guns, don't you? I suggest you use them. Don't disappoint me again," Damian's voice cracked over the radio.

Amanda looked at me, her eyes full of worry.

"Don't worry, he's not going to be a problem much longer..." I said, putting my hand on her shoulder.

I turned to face Ryder, letting out a heavy sigh. "Alright, Damian's headquarters is not too far from here. Amanda and Matt being the patrolling soldiers just solved two of our concerns. Now I need to go find Katie and Jax," I said.

"Katie is actually on duty at Damian's office tonight, he's been doing everything to keep us all apart. Jax is off duty tonight, so he will be in his room..." Amanda said, looking back and forth between me and Ryder.

I looked over at Ryder, and he let out a heavy sigh. "Are you sure, he will be able to handle it?" Ryder questioned, stepping closer to me.

I nodded. "Yes. He's one of the strongest people I know, and we need him.... He's going to be the one most at risk for helping us. If this plan goes South, at least we can guarantee his safety. Damian has no quarrel with Amanda, Matt, Katie or anyone else in the sector. It's always been Jax," I said.

"I know he is your former partner. But I need you to be ready in case this goes very wrong. Only a few people have been able to successfully channel their tiger spirit within minutes of being bestowed the gift. That's why we try to get them all slowly introduced by making them wait a few hours...in isolation...." Ryder said, his gaze softening.

I knew he was only try to look out for my best interest, but I was slightly hurt by his doubt in my decision.

"Trust me," I said, reaching up and touching his chest. Out of the corner of my eye I could see Amanda looking back and forth between me and Ryder, and a big grin appeared on her face.

"Alright, which way to his...quarters?" Ryder questioned.

"Follow me," I said, waving for everyone to follow. I picked up the pace, knowing that since there was a large group of us, it wouldn't be too long before we were discovered. We didn't have much time.

I heard Ryder and Darius join me at my side, narrowing their stride so that they could keep pace with my smaller steps. I had to admit, the adrenaline rush that I was feeling right now was pretty amazing. It was nothing near close to that same rush I felt when in a fire fight overseas, but it was nonetheless exhilarating.

After all this time of living in a world where I hated the way people were treated, it felt amazing to finally being doing something right.

I saw the troop headquarters come into view, and I motioned for the group to halt, kneeling down on one knee.

"Alright. Amanda and Matt, I'm going to send Colton and Brian with you. Keep an eye on things...you're all my eyes and ears. If you notice anything suspicious, or a threat to our presence, we will rendezvous at the Rocky Statue. Trevor I need you, Skyler, Devon and Ryder to secure this building while I go inside. Everyone else, go to your designated points. Do not leave your partner...." I ordered, moving my hands in various directions.

Everyone nodded, taking off in their various positions. Erica slid up to me, tilting her head. "Where do you want me to go?" she questioned.

"I need you and Darius to go scope out the Sector Commander's building. If he leaves, come back and let me know..." I said, putting a comforting hand on her shoulder.

"Darius will take good care of you, he won't let anything happen to you...." I said, trying to build up her confidence.

Darius nodded to her, showing her a warm smile. She shyly returned the smile, and then jogged off with him in the direction of the Commander's building. I turned to look at my group, motioning for them to head forward towards the troop building.

I could feel my heart begin to race and the butterflies fluttering in my stomach at the thought of me seeing Jax again. Even though my heart belonged to Ryder, Jax and I would always have something special. He would always be my 'what if' person. Jax was a strong individual, and I knew he would be perfectly suited to be bestowed the gift.

Ryder and I did have a shared concern that telling him to try and transform almost immediately after being bitten could be disastrous, but I had a strong faith in Jax and in his inner strength.

We finally reached the building, and I motioned for Skyler and Devon to remain on the outer doors. I smiled at Devon, tapping her on the shoulder and then I turned to face Skyler. I leaned in to whisper to her, so I wouldn't rattle anyone else.

"You will not leave her side for any reason, otherwise I will hunt you down and it will not be pretty..." I whispered, harshly.

Skyler rolled her eyes, and turned to fully face me.

"What? After our little fashion moment back there you still don't trust me?" she asked, somewhat mockingly.

I narrowed my eyes slightly, shaking my head. "No,"

I nodded to Ryder, and he, Trevor and myself slowly slid into the building. I inhaled the familiar scent of sweat, lavender, and something that smelt like burnt macaroni and cheese. This was once home.

I turned to face Ryder. "Right, you stay here with Trevor. If I'm not back in 10 minutes with Jax, come and get me. His is the eighth room on the left," I said, gazing up at him.

"Okay, but be careful...." he replied, nodding to me.

"I'll be okay, its just Jax. You can trust me when I say to trust him..." I said, smiling slightly. Ryder nodded in return, turning to face Trevor.

I began walking down the hallway, the butterflies returning once more.

24

I rushed up to Jax's door and began knocking on it in the similar pattern that I had always used for when we went to Major Chase's house. I paused for a second, hearing movement on the other side of the door.

It was late in the evening; he had probably just recently gotten home from the gym and was preparing to either get a beer from the Soldier's Club or was getting ready for bed. I didn't even know what day of the week it was anymore.

Moments later, the door flew open, and I saw Jax with a face full of anger.

When he saw it was me, his expression softened considerably.

"MacKenzie?" he questioned. I looked down the hallway and nodded to Trevor and Ryder, before pushing Jax on his chest and back into his room. I knew Ryder would be counting down the minutes to rush in and check on me.

"Hi Jax, look I know its been awhile but we don't have a lot of-"

I was cut off by Jax pulling me into a tight embrace, securing me in his arms. I couldn't help but smile slightly. Though I had grown very tight bond and even begun a relationship with Ryder, being with Jax once again was comforting. Jax and I would always maintain a special relationship. I pulled away just enough so I could look at him.

"Jax, its really really great to see you too but listen, I need to talk to-"

I was interrupted once again by Jax, but this time it was by him taking my face in his hands as he laid a soft, warm kiss on my lips. I felt my legs start to tremble, as if they were about to melt. I once again felt extremely overwhelmed, like everything in the world had stopped just for that moment. Jax pulled away after a few seconds, but he continued to hold my face in his hands.

Confusion flooded my brain above all else, and for that period of time I completely forgot what I wanted to talk to him about.

"I....I don't...I don't...." I stuttered, too taken back to even form a single thought. Jax merely narrowed his eyes in confusion at my startled reaction, as if he were expecting me to have seen this coming.

"Your wife..." I finally managed to get out. I watched as Jax let out a heavy sigh, as he moved to rest his hands on my shoulders.

"About three months ago, I received a letter from her. She had told me that, being as we were in separate sections, the Section Commander granted her a divorce and allowed her to remarry without my consent. I guess that's how the law is nowadays. It just...blew me away. To think that I had this...strong, beautiful, gifted battle buddy and partner by my side for these past seven years. Even longer if you count our deployments...but not once did I ever act on her because my marriage was so important to me," he paused to grip my shoulders slightly.

"Yet, my wife goes and finds herself another lad. She gets pregnant with his child and they marry. I was willing to wait for her, willing to see if they would one day undo this sector bullshit. I stayed loyal to her, even though the feelings I was growing for my partner, for you, were getting stronger by the day. I had to push that aside...." he continued, his voice starting to shake.

I closed my eyes and exhaled, before opening them again. I was finally able to focus on the reason as to why I came here in the first place. This wasn't the time or the place to be having a heart to heart moment.

"Jax..." I said, making eye contact with him.
"I love you, MacKenzie..." Jax said, his eyes locked with mine. I instantly froze, like a deer in headlights. I could feel my heart beating in my ears and in my thighs. Everything else was suddenly blurred out, except for Jax's lips, which muttered the same four words again.
I blinked, before shaking my head so that I could focus again.

"I need to bite you," I said, rather quickly.
Jax opened his mouth slightly, before letting out a nervous chuckle. "Okay, not at all what I was expecting to hear from you...but..."

"No, no, listen. The reason I came here was to find you. We have a plan to take back the sectors, and its a really good one. But in the event that it goes South, I need to give you the same gift that I have...the sectors have no means to defeat us. I needed to find you so that I can start your changing process so that you can fight these guys with us..." I said, trying to make sense in the short time I had.

"Who is us?" Jax questioned, suspiciously.

"Just more...people who can also change into tigers. When I was eighty-sixed into the woods, I met people...a lot of people...that are just like me. They took good care of me," I said, desperately trying to get this over with.

Jax's expression remained confused, as he raised an eyebrow at me.

"I need to bite you, I need to give you the gift of being... of being someone like me, an Anomic..." I said, moving my hands to try and explain it to him.

Jax removed his hands from my shoulders, standing up straight.

"Right... I tell my partner that I'm in love with her, and her response is that she needs to turn into a furry and bite me...pretty ordinary day I guess,"

I couldn't help but notice the disappointment in his voice.

I sighed empathetically. "Jax, I want to discuss those feelings with you. I really do. You are one of the most important people in my life. But right here, right now, I need to get you and everyone we care about out of here. Then, I promise we can talk..." I said, reaching to take his hand in mine.

Jax's eyes began to search mine for answers, before he nodded in response. I felt guilty, knowing that I had just confessed my love for Ryder, so I wouldn't be able to give Jax what he was looking for. It was too late.

"Okay," he said, his hands squeezing mine. "But you promise we will talk? Because I don't know if you're aware of this but...its not easy for Rangers to admit stuff like that," he said, throwing a subtle joke in there.

I smiled in response, returning the squeeze. "I promise," I whispered, feeling guilty once more.

I heard movement in the hallway, and the next thing I knew the door was being forced open. Ryder stood there with Trevor, a concerned look on his face. At the sign of his entrance, I immediately released Jax's hands, and out of the corner of my eye I could tell that the connection between Ryder coming in the room and me letting go of Jax's hands did not go unnoticed.

"Ryder," I began, licking my lips in slight discomfort.

"This...this is Jax," I said, looking nervously between the two of them.

Ryder strode over towards the two of us, while Trevor remained stationed at the door, peeking down the hall for security reasons. I watched as gray and blue eyes met, and I could instantly sense the tension in the room. As Ryder positioned himself behind me defensively, it was obvious that Ryder was trying to send Jax a message. This was a different side of Ryder that I had not seen.

"Jax," Ryder stated, in a firm tone.

"Pleasure," Jax responded, his tone similar. This was a completely different side to Jax than I was used to seeing as well. Oh god, this wasn't going to be like some dramatic love triangle was it?

Hell no, I thought. *You're so much more mature than that, MacKenzie.*

As the two continued to stare each other down, I cleared my throat.

"Right, now that you two are...acquainted...I was about to complete the change. Ryder, I can guarantee you that Jax will be an excellent fighter. He has never failed me during our deployments, nor in our time here. I trust him," I said, tilting my head slightly.

Ryder nodded. "Of course, my love...our pack is in need of some strong warriors," Ryder said, putting his hand on my shoulder affectionately.

I looked over to see Jax watching the placement of Ryder's hand, before he made eye contact with me again.

"I'm much looking forward to spending time with you both..." Jax responded. He looked down at me, shrugging slightly.

"So how does this...biting work?" Jax questioned. I looked back at Ryder in response.

"It works exactly how you think it works, she changes and bites you," Ryder stated, raising an eyebrow at Jax.

I cleared my throat, getting extremely uncomfortable with the amount of tension between the two.

Ryder turned to face me, folding his arms. I got the impression that he was hoping Jax was some ordinary Joe, who didn't have an incredible physique that rivaled Ryder's own.

"Right..." I said, unzipping the jacket that I was wearing. I threw the jacket to Ryder, and then moved to take off the pants as well. I wasn't about to desecrate such a beautiful outfit.

Jax held his hands up defensively.

"Whoa, whoa, whoa....as much as I would love to see where this is going...MacKenzie, what the heck are you doing?" Jax asked, doing his best to keep his eyes on my face.

"You'll see in a second," I said, tossing the pants to Ryder as well. I pulled the bottom of the tank top down slightly to cover the small black panties that Syd referred to as her 'sexy lil devils', which I didn't even want to know what that meant.

I closed my eyes, calling for my tiger to come to me. I couldn't help but notice the vibe that passed over me as I felt myself begin to change, as if she were extremely humored by our current situation. I opened my eyes, and turned my gaze to look up at Jax.

He slowly sat down on the edge of his bed, looking almost awestruck. It had been quite a long time since he had seen me in my tiger form, and this had been the first time that he ever saw the change occur in person.

I sighed, stepping closer to him.

"After you receive your bite, you're going to feel almost a rushing sensation. Embrace it, but don't give into it. Close your eyes and see the tiger inside, call him to you. He's going to try and give every lasting effort to take over the entirety of your consciousness. Don't let him. Demand control from him," I said, motioning for him to lower himself towards me.

"And if...it...he...takes over?" Jax questioned, sounding concerned.

"That's why were are all here," Ryder cut in, folding his arms and staring hard at Jax.

"But we aren't going to let that happen," I replied, keeping my gaze on Jax. We were running out of time and I knew Jax normally liked this plan laid out from A to Z, but he was just going to have to deal with it this time.

Jax nodded in approval, and leaned forward towards me. I stepped so my head was just above his shoulder.

"This may hurt a bit," I apologized, before lightly biting into the meaty part of his shoulder area.

I heard Jax grunt in slight pain, but he was quick to silence anything he was feeling. Once again, he was refusing to show any sign of weakness. He really hadn't changed since I left.

I felt an exhilarating rush for a moment, and then I pulled away from Jax, feeling slightly light headed. Out of the corner of my eye I could see Ryder and Trevor moving to steady me, but I shook my head.

"I'm fine," I promised, quickly turning my attention back to Jax.

"How are you feeling?" I questioned, overlooking him.

"Well, it stings just a bit. Other than that, not very different..." Jax replied, reaching up and touching the bite mark.

"Okay, I need you to close your eyes and call the tiger to come forward. Literally. Focus on reaching deep inside you and calling him out," I ordered, growing more and more anxious by the minute. Time was of the essence and maybe Ryder was right, maybe this was a bad idea.

Jax closed his eyes and inhaled deeply, trying to find his center. A couple of seconds later he began laughing, and I looked at Ryder, confused.

"MacKenzie....there's nothing.....ARGHHHH!!!" Jax let out a loud cry of pain, throwing his head back slightly.

"Jax, focus!" I yelled, hoping that he could still hear me over the change that was now occurring. Ryder stepped forward, putting a firm hand on Jax's shoulder to steady him.

Jax's eyes connected with mine once more, and that's when I noticed they were now a royal shade of blue. Ryder bent down to look at Jax's face, and then stepped back in surprise.

I stepped back, slightly confused. Those royal blue eyes meant that Jax was going to turn into....

Jax's clothing stripped away and in place of Jax stood the large, white, Siberian tiger. Jax's tiger looked extremely built, and he stood slightly taller than mine. I could feel my heart beating faster and faster by the minute, and I could feel the pulsating in my ears. I tried to stand tall, and proud, fearing that if Jax's tiger were to try and turn on him, I would probably be facing the hardest battle of my life.

"Jax?" I questioned, stepping closer to him.

The large tiger turned his attention back to me, letting out a low growl.

"Jax," I stated, this time with more confidence. "Jax, its MacKenzie,"

Jax's tiger continued to stare at me, and then it let out a large yawn. I let out a sigh of relief, all my fear gone.

"How ridiculous do I look right now?" Jax questioned, turning to face the mirror on the back of his door.

"How is this possible?" Ryder questioned, watching Jax as he wandered over to the mirror to look at himself.

"You guys are the experts, you tell me. It was like MacKenzie told me. I focused on maintaining my consciousness and refused to let him take over. It worked really well. Although to be honest, he...or it...or whatever, didn't seem to put up much of a fight." Jax replied, looking at his reflection in the mirror with interest.

"I meant how are you a White Siberian Tiger. There has never been a recorded instance where a receiver of the gift gained the spirit of the White Siberian," Ryder stated, continuing to stare at Jax with this almost accusatory stare.

I shook my head, not having time for this drama.

"Whatever it is, we can figure it out later. Right now, we need to finish what we started. Take Jax out of here and get him changed back and we will head to Damian's quarters and deal with him first," I stated, picking up my blue outfit in my mouth and hurrying towards the bathroom.

I quickly shut the door and turned back to myself, and began changing back into the outfit as fast as I could. I cursed myself silently for not removing my tank top as well, because now the underarmour material felt cool against my bare skin. I zipped up the jacket, and slid into the pants as well.

I began to pull my hair back into a tight pony tail once more, eyeing my reflection. I realized that the girl who left the sector was not the one who had returned. Sure, I had gotten a lot more tan and built from all the running around like Jane from *Tarzan*, but before my eighty-sixing, I would let people guilt me into absolutely everything. Every time the Sector Commander or Damian asked me to do a task, I would immediately jump up and do whatever they said because they would constantly harp on the excuse of 'you're supposed to be a soldier,'

But this time I wasn't just a soldier, I was a warrior. There would be no guilting this time. As long as we got the mission done without involving any innocent children, which had always been my weak point, I did not doubt that our mission would succeed. We had a lot of strong people with us on this one.

218

The MacKenzie that was eighty-sixed was stubborn, weak-minded, and unsure of what she was really looking for. The MacKenzie that I was now was strong-willed, and I finally understood my purpose. I had come to terms with my fate, and I accepted the responsibility of leading.

I exited the bathroom to see Jax standing there in black shorts and a dark gray shirt, his arms folded as he held a conversation with Ryder. It appeared to be a civil conversation, but knowing both of their alpha personalities, it probably wouldn't last too long.

"Hey, you guys ready to head out?" I questioned, not even waiting for an answer. I threw open the door to head out into the hallway, and I could hear the three of them falling in right behind me.

As we turned outside, Devon and Skyler both turned to face us at almost the exact same time.

"Well, I see he survived..." Skyler said, overlooking Jax's figure. "I'm Skyler," she said, smiling at him wickedly. I would not let Jax get roped into Skyler's web, but I knew deep down he was smarter than that.

"Really? You're going to do this right now?" I hissed, shooting her a glare. She scoffed and rolled her eyes, muttering something about how she was 'just saying hi to the new guy'.

"Damian's quarters are a little under a quarter mile away. Let's get moving," I said, continuing to move forward.

The further we moved into this plan, the more angered I felt myself becoming. I wasn't sure if I was just steadily getting more and more irritated with the way my friends and comrades were acting, or if it was because I was about to face both Damian and the Sector Commander once more after the last time we had seen them.

I heard someone running up to my side, and I turned my head to see Jax standing there.

"MacKenzie, mind telling me exactly what the plan is here?" Jax questioned, looking down at me.

"We're taking back the sectors. The only two people who will stand in our way will be Damian and the Sector Commander," I replied, looking to see the rest of the group not too far behind.

"Well them and the rest of Damian's minion soldiers that he has got running around. I'm more than willing to bet that after we pay Damian a visit they will close in on us. The Sector Commander may look like an idiot, but lately he's doubled the amount of patrols that Damian's new soldiers have been doing in the sector. Since that apparent confrontation with you guys at the gate," Jax argued.

"Good, I'm counting on it. We can rid them all at once," I retorted, swatting at a stray wasp that began buzzing right next to my left ear.

"Hey," Jax said, reaching over and grabbing my arm. We stopped our movement and I turned to fully face him. He still had that concerned look on my face that he had when he was with me right before he let me hurry off into the woods.

"What did Damian and the Commander say to you? I've never seen you so hell bent on taking someone down....well... aside from overseas," Jax questioned, his eyes searching mine for an answer.

"I will line all your friends who are still in here up against the fence and you can watch them all get executed up close,"

I shook my head, snapping back into reality.

"It doesn't matter. What matters is, they are not good people, Jax. I know that is something we can both agree on, but now it's time to take the sector back.... and give everyone in it the freedom they deserve," I stated.

Jax smirked, nodding in agreement.

"Alright, let's do this then.." he replied.

25

Once we reached Damian's quarters, I signaled for everyone to halt. Ryder strode over to me, an enraged look on his face.

"Alright, I call first dibs on being able to shoot this guy..." Ryder stated, raising his crossbow up slightly.

"Whoa, I was going to do it first. That bastard has been like an evil cockroach in this sector for far too long," Jax spoke up.

Ryder looked him up and down, raising an eyebrow.

"You don't have a weapon," Ryder argued, pointedly.

"Well first of all, I'm a Ranger. I don't need one. Second of all, you all essentially just turned me into more of a walking weapon than I already was. I think I'm pretty set," Jax said, clapping his hands together.

Ryder considered it for a second, and then nodded. "Alright how about this, we both shift and rip this guy apart together?"

"Sounds like a plan," Jax said, reaching for the door handle.

"Hey!" I cut in, slapping his wrist. He drew back slightly, raising an eyebrow at me in slight challenge.

"As much as I am loving this whole... 'did we just become best friends' moment the two of you are having, I'm going to have to stop you both right there. I'm going to go in first, and the two of you are going to follow me. Your priority is extracting Katie, okay? Nothing more. Let me handle Damian, if I cannot handle Damian alone... I will call for you guys to come help me," I stated, looking back and forth between the two of them.

Skyler sighed, stepping into my peripheral vision. "I'm guessing you want me, the bookworm and Trevor to stand out here?" she questioned.

"You read my mind, I'm glad we can finally agree of something..." I retorted, throwing open the door and hurrying up the steps.

Once we had reached the top of the stairwell, I heard the familiar sound of the M4 being switched from 'safe to semi'. I froze in place, holding up my hand for Jax and Ryder to halt.

"Whoever you are, state your business...I have a rifle," I heard Katie's familiar voice speak up.

I let out a heavy sigh, nodding to Jax and Ryder.

"Katie, Katie...its MacKenzie. I'm going to come around the corner now, okay? I bring two friends with me. One of them is Jax," I stated.

There was a pause, and I heard her footsteps approaching slowly.

"Impossible, MacKenzie is dead. The Sector Commander and Damian said they saw her body on the edge of the woods, killed by some wild animal..." Katie said, her voice shaking.

I began to chuckle, earning a strange look from both Jax and Ryder.

"Killed by a wild animal? Well that's funny, considering I've got the spirit of one inside of me. I'm going to come around the corner now," I said, stepping around the edge.

"Don't!" I heard Katie screech, firing her weapon.

The next thing I knew I felt as though I had been hit by a semi truck in my left shoulder, the pain instantly flooding my body. I slammed against the back wall, my spine singing a note that would fly off the scales. I held in a scream, biting down on my tongue so that Damian would not hear the scream behind the metal door that led to his apartment.

I could instantly taste the blood in my mouth, and I was quick to spit it out against the wall. I felt two pairs of hands grabbing me to help me stand up. I turned my gaze upwards, looking to see Katie's horrified expression as she slowly lowered her rifle towards the ground.

"MacKenzie?" she questioned, her face turning almost white.

"What's wrong, kid? You look as though you have seen a ghost?" I asked, laughing as I stood up.

"Well, yeah. I mean... how are you still alive?" she questioned, shaking.

"I was never dead. I survived living as your roommate for awhile, you think I couldn't survive in the wild?" I joked, trying to put her at ease.

"The Sector Commander and Damian... they gathered all the soldiers in the room. Told us you were dead...and if anyone had any plans on avenging you or building a resistance with you, not to even bother....you had been slain..." Katie said, walking up to me.

"By what? A lion? A bear?" I questioned, pressing my hand against my wound to stop the blood that was seeping out.

Her eyes fell on the fresh wound on my shoulder and she choked back a sob.

"Oh my god, you're alive and I shot you. Now you won't be alive, because I shot you. I... I shot *you*," Katie said, her hand covering her mouth.

"Hey, its fine. It's merely a flesh wound. Besides, these bullets won't kill me. Long story. I need you to go outside with Jax and Ryder, okay? I will be right behind you guys..." I said, showing her a small smile.

She reached out and embraced me, hugging me tight. I returned the embrace, hugging her tight as well to reassure her that everything was going to be okay.

"You're not going to kill him, are you? I mean he's a bad person... don't get me wrong, but... you're not like him, MacKenzie..." Katie said, wiping a stray tear off of her cheek.

"Katie, I really need you to go outside with Jax and Ryder. This could get very ugly situationally dependent and I don't want you to get caught in the middle of it," I said, motioning for them to head down the stairs.

Katie closed her mouth and nodded in acknowledgement, and then headed down the stairs with Jax right behind her.

"Hey," Ryder said, grabbing my arm. I turned towards him.

"You got this, if you need me... I'll be right at the bottom of the steps," he said, gently caressing my cheek.

I smiled, enjoying his sweet touch. "I will..." I said, as I began to move towards Damian's door.

Once I heard Ryder disappear, I clenched my teeth together and let out a heavy hiss, grasping my now injured shoulder more firmly. Sure, it wouldn't kill me. But damn, did it still freaking hurt like hell. I squeezed my eyes shut as I fought back tears. Once all this was over, my priority was finding someone to remove the damn bullet. The girl sure did know how to leave a killer flesh wound.

I inhaled sharply, trying to block out the pain and focus on the task at hand.

I stepped up to see that the door was slightly cracked, and I tilted my head, wandering if this was all a trap. I placed my hand on the hilt of one of my sai's as I gently nudged the door open with my foot.

That was when I saw Damian sitting on the edge of his bed, looking extremely disheveled. His blonde hair, which was normally very slick was all over the place, looking as though he had just survived a tornado. His white wife beater was covered in all sorts of drainage, ranging from what appeared to be sweat, dirt, ketchup and judging by the smell of the room, some kind of alcohol.

He brought his gaze to meet mine, his eyes bloodshot from the excessive drinking and the dark circles under his eyes suggested that he had gotten little sleep in the past few days.

The radio on his night stand let off a feedback of what appeared to be some static, and he slowly reached over and shut it off, keeping his eyes on my the whole time.

"Well, well, well...if it isn't the wild woman herself, Miss MacKenzie..." Damian spoke up, his voice sounding extremely hoarse.

He had his black boots on his feet, but they were completely loose and untied. His dark pants also had some spills on him. I almost couldn't help but feel sympathetic towards Damian. Compared to the Damian that I had grown used to seeing, this was just completely and utterly sad.

"What the hell happened to you?" I questioned, narrowing my eyes at him. He began to laugh, reaching over to his bookcase and taking a swig of whatever brown drink that was now in his hand.

"Why does it matter? I'm assuming you came here to kill me anyway, am I correct?" he asked, nodding to my hand which was resting on my right sai.

I looked down at my sai and then back at him, taking my hand off of it.

He watched me for a second, and then began to chuckle.

"Well, I figured it was only a matter of time before you showed up at my door. You know, after the whole 'you can eighty-six me but can't contain me speech' that you gave the Sector Commander. I knew that you would eventually come and kick in my door, and tear me to shreds. So, I figured I may as well be drunk for it," Damian said, bringing his glass to eye level to look at it.

"Didn't they used to dump vodka on the wounds of soldiers in the battlefield back in the day? So this should make it hurt less, right?" he questioned.

"I'm not here to kill you, Damian, but the fact that you suspect I would have 'torn you to pieces', suggests that you know you've done something wrong," I stated, doing my best to breathe in as little as possible to avoid the acrid smell.

Damian laughed. "You mean aside from almost killing your former Commander and threatening your partner?"

Before I could reply, Damian spoke up again.

"Would you believe, MacKenzie, that I used to be a good man?" he questioned.

I merely raised my eyebrows in response. *Here we go.*

"Oh yeah, had a wife and a daughter and everything. My daughter, Zoey, she loved all the animals of the world. Every last one of them. A very specific type in fact," Damian said, nodding towards me.

"Tigers," I said.

"She had loads of tigers all over her room. So before I was head of security here, I was a mere soldier in Sector Five. When the sectors were being established, a bunch of my comrades came to my house. They claimed to be searching for Anomics. My wife had been killed during the war. She was a nurse, you see. She tried to help people, but... the people weren't too interested in helping her when she went down. She was trampled to death when they tried to evacuate the local hospital," Damian said, his voice breaking slightly.

I couldn't help but feel sorry for Damian. This entire time I had him under the impression that he was some almost comic book villain. Which reminded me that even people who appeared as 'bad people' were potential to having a back story behind them.

"So they stumbled upon Zoey's room, she was only seven years old. They didn't seem to care about me being one of their own. They took my little Zoey away and began interrogating her about all the tigers in the room. She told them that her...spirit animal...was a tiger. The next thing I know, little Zoey is taken from me. I get a call from the Sector Commander telling me that if I want to come and pick up the body of my daughter, I would be able to do so...." Damian said, reaching into his nightstand drawer.

He pulled out a small picture and held it up to me. I stepped closer, making sure to not let my guard down. The small girl was wearing a pink dress, her long brown hair down to her waist and she was cuddling a small tiger stuffed animal. Her smile went from ear to ear, and I couldn't deny that she was truly adorable.

I backed away, making eye contact with Damian.

"So how did that bring you here, as the Chief of Security?" I questioned, resting my hand on one of my sai's.

Damian watched my hand and began laughing again.

"Always the soldier, maintaining your guard. You know the fact that they accused my little Zoey of being one of you is why I have always *hated* your kind..." Damian said, lifting his glass up to take another sip.

I had enough, ready to move on with our plan and head for the Sector Commanders quarters. Despite what the original plan was, which was to tie Damian up and render him useless. I may have been a soldier, but I had a heart.

I seized Damian by his arm and lifted him up, causing him to drop his glass on the floor, which shattered on impact.

"I've had enough of these shenanigans, let's go..." I said, forcing him out of the door.

He stumbled slightly, and continued on out the door, with his hands raised. I narrowed my eyes at the back of his head, daring him to say a word.

Once we reached the bottom of the stairs, I reached forward and pushed open the door for him. Once we were outside, I saw Jax forcefully shove Damian against the side of the building, his forearm pressed against Damian's throat.

"Hey, hey..." I said, stepping forward and pressing my hand down on Jax's shoulder. Jax turned to face me and that's where I saw that his eyes had changed to the royal shade of blue.

A few seconds later, they changed back to their normal color, and Jax let out a heavy sigh. I couldn't help but feel slightly impressed at how well he was at maintaining control.

"I thought we were tying this clown up and leaving him here," Ryder said, stepping forward and looking Damian up and down.

"We were..." I said, turning to face Damian.

I looked over at Damian, and he looked at me with an empathetic expression that I had never seen Damian wear before.

"But I think we need to reunite this one with the big man, should be much more entertaining for the one to watch the other one crack...and squeal..." I said, narrowing my eyes at Damian. I didn't feel it was appropriate to discuss how Damian's tragic backstory made me change my mind about his involvement in our plan.

"For the record, I am a fan of that..." Trevor spoke up, with a wicked smirk.

I watched as Skyler and Devon came around the corner, and Skyler's eyes widened in shock.

Her mouth opened and closed a few times, as if in shock. "I....I thought you were...just tying him up and leaving him here...." she said, her voice squeaking towards the end.

Devon turned to face her, raising an eyebrow at her. "Why are you suddenly so nervous? Please don't tell me that you think this guy is hot or something, like you do with every new guy you see...."

226

Skyler scoffed and rolled her eyes. "Please," she snapped. "I'm just not in the mood to get caught because we decided to bring the Chief of Security along with us,"

"Yeah, well he's not going to be able to speak up because he's going to be just a wee bit tied up. Jax, do you still have your cuffs on you? Even though you've....changed outfits?" I questioned, looking over at him.

"I never leave home without them," Jax said, reaching into his pocket and turning back at stare at Damian.

"Turn around, or get put down..." Jax stated.

Damian sighed, turning his back to Jax so Jax could cuff him.

"Okay, time to go get the big one and end this," I said, nodding towards the direction of the Sector Commander's headquarters.

26

We arrived at the steel building, and I let out a heavy sigh. The last time that I was in this building was the night that I was on patrol duty with Jax, when we were stationed inside his quarters for a security detail. Katie had finally gotten the color back in her face, and was standing with Skyler and Devon, gripping her rifle tightly. She had never been the worlds greatest at meeting new people.

I looked over my shoulder to see Darius and Erica hurrying up to join us. She tapped me on the shoulder, in greeting.

"Hey, any movement?" I questioned, extremely anxious to get this over with already.

"Well, he's in there. No other soldiers. Are we sure that this is not a trap?" Erica questioned, rocking back and forth on her feet.

I turned to face her, letting out a sigh. At this point, it didn't even matter whether or not it was a trap. We were prepared for anything, and I highly doubt that they had discovered the means to actually defeat us right now.

"Okay, Joe and Colton stay out here and if you see anything suspicious or if one of Damian's...minions...comes along, you know what to do," I said, nodding to them.

"I have minions now?" Damian questioned, looking over at Jax.

"Alright, let's go..." I said, grabbing onto the door handle. I let out a deep exhale, reaching for the door handle.

The second my hand made contact with the door handle, three bullets struck the door just inches from my hand. I turned to face the direction the bullets came from, filled with anger. I knew it, it was only a matter of time before we were compromised.

There were at least twenty soldiers all hurrying to line up, their weapons raised threateningly.

My eyes focused in on the soldier in the center, who wore a wicked grin on his face.

"Wesson," I said, turning fully from the building and walking towards him. Out of the corner of my eye I could see my fellow Anomics lining up beside me.

He stepped forward, lowering his rifle slightly. "Well, well... I see you survived the woods, MacKenzie. I'll be honest with you, you gave me quite the shakes back there in that square..."

"Please, I would love to introduce you to them again..." I said, narrowing my eyes at him.

"You really thought you could just waltz on into the Sector and take out the Sector Commander and reclaim it as yours? Please...we saw that coming," Wesson said.

"I'm reclaiming it from traitors and liars like yourselves. So yes, I do believe I can just *waltz* in here and take it back from all of you. No more games. No more executions. I'm giving these people their freedom back," I said, resting my hands on the hilt of both of my sai's.

"It's funny how you talk about traitors and liars, considering your still standing amongst one of them. How else do you think that we knew you were coming?" Wesson questioned.

I turned to face Ryder, who began to shake his head in disbelief.

Neither one of us wanted to believe it, but we knew what that meant. Once of our Anomics was a traitor, and was the source.

I stepped forward to look down the line of the Anomics that stood with me. They all had sincere looks on their face; none of them looked rattled.

I turned my attention back to Wesson, walking up to him so that I was mere feet away from him.

"I've got bigger problems to deal with at the current moment aside from your lies," I said, trying to shake him.

"Yes, you do..." Wesson said, taking his rifle and striking me across the face with the butt of it, sending me to the ground.

With that, everyone sprung into motion, the other soldiers firing their weapons at my friends behind me. I saw Darius and Ryder immediately firing their crossbows at the soldiers, sending two to their deaths. Joe and Colton immediately sprung into action, changing into their tigers and colliding into two soldiers at a time. Wesson seized my moment of distraction and stomped on the small of my back, his steel tipped boots sending painful jolts up my spine.

"Say hello to your parents, MacKenzie..." I heard him say, charging his rifle.

I reached for my one sai, and thrusted it backwards, immediately causing him to release his hold on me. I turned to see that it landed in his upper thigh, and it began to gush blood. Amongst the rapid gunfire I could still hear his painful scream.

229

I leapt up, charging for him and taking him to the ground with me. As we began our mini wrestling match on the ground, I could see Ryder, Darius and Trevor firing their crossbows at the random soldiers, some of which were trying to take cover behind the park benches and rocks. Colton and Joe were swiping at the random soldiers, taking them out with one paw swipe. I could smell the blood everywhere, as the cement was quickly being covered with it.

I rolled off of Wesson, standing up to face him once more. He turned to face me, his nose now bloody from the fall he took. Probably broken.

I charged for him again, not even giving him the opportunity to speak. I delivered a quick jab to his face, and then pulled my sai from his thigh. He screamed once, and then delivered a kick to my abdomen. I stumbled back, trying not to double over in pain. Wesson continued forward, throwing his rifle to the side.

"If this is how you want it, I'll physically tear you limb from limb myself...with my bare hands and introduce you to your true fate!" He yelled, punching me in the ribs. I let out a cry of pain, bringing an uppercut to his chin, causing his teeth to clack together.

He reached forward and swiped for me, but I was too quick. I quickly put him into a headlock, spinning him around so that his stomach faced the sky, and pulled his head down so that it was lined up with my hip.

"You want to talk about fate? Let me grant you yours..." I said, rolling my palm outward and snapping his neck.

His lifeless body fell to the ground, and I let out a heavy sigh. The fight had taken more out of me than I was willing to admit.

I heard a weapon charging and I turned to see another soldier pointing his weapon at me, shaking violently.

Before he even got the chance to comment, I saw an orange figure collide with him and take him to the ground.

I instantly recognized the small tiger, Devon. She turned to face me, pinning the soldier to the ground. I showed her a grateful smile, and then turned to look around. The majority of the soldiers were lifeless, their haunted eyes gazing up at the skies. About six remained, sitting with their backs together in front of Joe and Colton.

"MacKenzie, you go.... we got this..." Devon said, growling down at her prisoner.

"Okay...just please be careful..." I said, nodding to her. She smirked, and nodded in return. As I walked towards the rest of the group, I couldn't help but take note of how much blood was sprayed everywhere. I overlooked all of my friends and was thankful that it was none of theirs. This was not at all how I imagined our mission going, but I had to be thankful for what I still had. We all survived. Even though only three of us had changed.

Ryder placed his hand on my shoulder, breathing heavily as well. His shirt was torn in several places, but aside from that he appeared to be okay. I looked over to see Katie now had a huge gash on her cheek, but she still somehow had a small smile plastered to her face.

"MacKenzie, are you alright?" Ryder asked, overlooking my figure.

"Yeah, I'm fine..." I said, pressing my hand to my bullet wound once more. It had started to seep blood again, sending a few lines of blood pouring down my outfit.

"Good," he said, reaching up and touching my cheek. I quickly glanced over at Jax, who merely cast his eyes to the ground. I knew he probably figured out what was going on by now, but was quickly trying to mask his emotions.

"We have to finish the mission...is every body up?" I questioned, looking around at my friends.

Everyone nodded, but Jax continued to stare at the ground.

"Jax?" I asked, softening my voice.

He turned to face me, and for a second I thought I saw that his eyes looked glossy, but he was quick to blink it away.

"Yeah, let's go get this guy already..." he said, forcing a laugh.

I reached for the door handle again, my heart skipping a beat. After a moment's pause and realizing that no one else was going to attack us in that moment, I threw open the door to the building.

Darius grabbed onto my arm, motioning for me to allow him to go first. I hesitated for a second, not wanting anyone else to put themselves as a high risk by being the first person in the door, and in the line of fire.

When he held up his crossbow, I understood. He wanted to quickly eliminate any possible threats so that I could get to my final mission, the Sector Commander. The Sector Commander was *my* battle.

I allowed him to continue on with Ryder following him. I could almost feel my heart pounding in my throat as we slowly began our ascension to his upstairs quarters. I couldn't help but feel a slight bit of deja vu.

Last time I had seen the Sector Commander, I had threatened his life. Now, I may have been in the position where I would be forced to take it.

We reached the top of the stairs, and I joined Darius and Ryder in the small, narrow hallway. Even months later, the room still had the same damp, musty smell, despite the fact that the ceiling fan was spinning on high.

The two cots in the hallway had been folded up, a sign that no one had been pulling security there for awhile, or at least overnight. I turned back to face Jax, who was directly behind me, a look of concern on his face. Judging by the way his gaze softened, I didn't have to say a word. Jax could read me like a book, and he knew that even if I didn't want to admit it, I was terrified. I talked up day dreams and fairy tales of one day knocking the Sector Commander out of his seat, but now that the moment was here, they seemed like just mere stories.

Even though I had what some people would consider a super power, I was still human. I still was very afraid of many things in life. My future, was one of them.

"You got this," he whispered, putting his hand on my shoulder for comfort. I looked past him to see Major Chase also nodding towards me in encouragement, standing next to Trevor. I had assumed Erica, Skyler and Katie were waiting on the stairwell, so all our positions were covered.

Damian merely rolled his eyes, probably refraining from saying something incredibly smart. A simple shove from Major Chase captured his attention once more, and he went back to being the mopey drunk again.

I turned and looked up at Ryder, who smirked down at me, bringing his hand up to my cheek affectionately. I closed my eyes for a second, enjoying the warm feel. In less than a minute, the wooden door would be kicked down and the possibility of hell on Earth could be upon us. Well, at least hell in the sector.

I pulled away and faced the door, placing my hand on the right sai in comfort. I shifted my eyes over to Darius, and nodded once, and then turned my attention back to the door. Darius turned to face the door as well, and then kicked it with all of his might.

The door flew open, not even splitting like I expected it to. Darius and Ryder flew into the room, their crossbows raised. I slowly slid in the room after them, surprised to see that the large, leather chair had its back to us. The moonlight shone through the window in the ceiling, creating an almost glare off of the chair.

"You know, the door *was* unlocked...you didn't have to waste your time kicking it in. Remember what I always told you, MacKenzie? I have always believed in an....." he paused, to slowly spin the chair around. He wore a black suit-coat, and a blood red tie. How cute, always so formal.

"Open door policy," he hissed, folding his hands and placing them on the desk in front of him.

"I'm sorry, I don't believe the words of a psychopath and a liar...." I stated, narrowing my eyes at him.

He smirked, his eyes falling behind me on Damian. He rolled his eyes, and leaned back to rest in his chair.

"Now why am I not surprised to see this? My head of security...in the hands of you. You always did have a soft spot for women, Damian..." the Sector Commander said, tilting his head.

Damian squared his jaw, staring him down. The Sector Commander scoffed slightly, and turned to face me once more. He pointed towards Damian.

"You know, this guy....over here, was never a fan of my plan from the beginning. However thanks to you, MacKenzie, it looks like I may have no choice but to start all over again. Bravo to you," he said, clapping his hands mockingly.

"What plan are you talking about?" I questioned.

"MacKenzie, he's just trying to stall... don't pay him any mind..." Jax spoke up, staring him down.

The Sector Commander turned to face him, a smirk appearing on his face. He slowly slid his eyes back over to me, leaning to rest on his elbows once more. He bit his lip for a second, and then continued.

"Damian here... wasn't a fan of the whole eighty-sixing thing from the beginning. You know, we are the only sector that does eighty-six. Everyone else goes on their merry little way, running all over the other commanders. I had a vision, you see. Which is why I have been meeting with the other Sector Commanders in secret. Our country has not been the same any more, not since the war. There are still...rebellions. Eighty-sixing was just the beginning stages of our grand plan. My... outside authoritative superior... has great plans for this country,"

"Outside Authoritative Superior? Like someone from another country?" I questioned.

"Oh, no. They're here alright. In fact, you, MacKenzie, have become the center of their attention. As far as I've been told, you have been on their mind for many...many years now. You're the inspiration behind the plan!"

233

"You knew... who I was....the entire time didn't you?" I questioned, panic rising in my chest.

He inclined his head to me, a wicked grin spreading across his face. It was so creepy that I couldn't help but cringe.

"You're very perceptive, MacKenzie. Yes, I did. I have known for quite some time now. It was our intent to let you continuously wander the sector, until we reached a time where all of us Sector Commanders reached an agreement to begin our little...anarchy," the Sector Commander said, reaching into his desk drawer.

Darius and Ryder both raised their crossbows, both of them aimed for his head. He raised his eye brows, whistling slightly.

"Wow, can't a man even enjoy a simple cigar?" he questioned.

"No," both Ryder and Darius said in unison.

I could have sworn that I heard Major Chase chuckle in the background, but I kept my gaze on the Sector Commander.

"Anarchy?" I questioned.

"The goal was...is....to rid all the sectors of those that we don't believe to be...idealistic towards our future. We will build up the sectors with a supreme line of Soldiers. With a very distinct purpose. To rebuild our nation, and given time... eventually become the World's greatest Army. Where no one would stand in our way. Our nation of super Soldiers would instill fear in the rest of the world, and rid them of that disbelief that our country is weak,"

"So in other words, you wanted to start a World War Three?" Jax questioned, speaking up.

"Someone give that man a cookie. I would offer you a cigar but your friends here have such poor manners that we can't even do that...." he said, looking over at Ryder and Darius. I could feel the spirit of my tiger growing restless.

"So what was the whole point of everything? You wanted to keep me alive yet you eighty-sixed me from the sector. Your plan makes no sense," I stated.

"Well, plans change, my darling. Once you eighty-sixed yourself and I informed my superior, we had planned to continue on with our mission...and he would come and find you himself later. You weren't too far away from him after all...out there...in your little wooden huts," he said, leaning back in his chair.

"So you build up your freaky super soldiers, you take over the world, and you feel all awesome about it. I'm still trying to figure out what my role is in all of this," I said, growing frustrated.

"You're not very patient, my dear. I was getting to that. You see, he wants you to see your face...while your world burns around you. Because he so very much wants to see you suffer, before he kills you himself..." he said, his face growing dark.

I felt a shiver travel up my spine, but I refused to let my true emotions show. I knew he was trying to shake me. Who could he have possibly been referring to? Was it someone from one of my deployments that was angered that I killed enemies overseas? Another Anomic's relative who was angered at something my father had done to theirs in the past and since he was no longer alive, they were going to try and pin the blame on me?

"I know, a master mind of a plan right, MacKenzie? He is quite brilliant. I mean after all... he is the one who orchestrated the fall of this nation anyway..." he said, a smug look now on his face. "If one man can cause a single nation to fall apart, imagine what he could do to an entire world, when you give him an Army..."

I felt as though a weight had dropped on my chest.
"What did you say?" I questioned, gritting my teeth in anger, and in realization.

He smirked, licking his lips in pleasure. "You heard me, MacKenzie. Together, he and I planned out the fall of this country, and we made it happened. I'm sure you are familiar with the group called.... *The Relinquished*, yes?" he questioned.
I heard Jax gasp slightly, stepping back, appalled.

"He and I sensed this country growing weak for years...so we planned this whole thing out. The destruction of the country. He knew where you and your family lived, so he put me in charge of this sector because he knew I would keep tabs on you. Making sure you stayed alive, so that he could be the one to...take your life. As I said before. Would you like to know....the last thing your father said before he died, MacKenzie?" the Sector Commander questioned, leaning forward.
I brought my gaze to meet his, my mind burning with a realization.

"You were there....when they died...." I said, staring at him hard.
His smile only grew.
"Oh no, MacKenzie.... I killed them all myself,"

27

I felt as though my entire world was suddenly in slow motion, as everything else in the room blurred together and my vision was solely focused on the Sector Commander, and the smug look that he had on his face.

"You....killed....my family?" I questioned, breathing angrily in between each word.

"I did. With pleasure, MacKenzie. You see...you were the one *he* wanted to save for himself...when the time came," the Sector Commander said.

I couldn't even get past the confession that he had just told me, I was beyond infuriated. The man who had been the one who killed my family...was right there in front of me all along. I had always known he had been an asshole, I just never knew how evil he truly was.

"So that rogue *Relinquished* member that you were supposed to interrogate after we caught him?" Jax questioned, looking back and forth between me and the Sector Commander.

"Yes, him. He was fleeing from a meeting with myself and was not supposed to leave until night fall. The bloke wouldn't listen, I wonder if he's even still alive after I released him back to our Master,"

"I knew we shouldn't have trusted you," Jax said, stepping towards the edge of the desk.

I drew out one of my sai's, using it to command Jax to halt, but keeping my eyes on the Sector Commander.

He chuckled, quickly pulling an item out from under the pile of scattered, disorganized papers that he had on his desk.

When I saw it, my eyes widened and focused in on the item in his hand. It was unmistakable. A eight inch, pure, golden knife. The exact weapon that could bring about the death of my kind.

"See this MacKenzie? I used this on all the other Anomics that we discovered in the Sector right when we first formed as a Sector. I also used this on your family. The thing about gold, pure gold, is that it is so light....and easy to maneuver... all you need to do..." he paused, slowly standing up.

He brought his gaze to meet mine, his eyes cold.

"Is know how to use it..." he whispered.

Before I could stop what was happening, he flicked his wrist and the knife sailed towards me, spinning in perfect circles. I knew that I had to move, or I would surely die. The next thing I saw was a body jumping front of mine, and I stumbled back slightly. When the body collided with the ground, I saw the face of Trevor, his eyes slowly blinking as blood immediately began to seep out of his chest wound where the hilt of the knife stood out.

I could hear my pulse in my ears as I turned my gaze upwards towards the Sector Commander, whose smirk slowly grew to a wicked smile.

I could feel my tiger raging inside of me, reading to burst out of me. It wasn't her time, as angry as we both were, this one was mine.

I lunged for him, stepping up on his desk and running a second step across it, both of my Sai's now drawn. My feet connected with his chest, a perfect pike kick, and he fell back into his chair, and it slowly rolled back.

My movement didn't stop there, as both of my sai's went sailing into his chest. One of which planted directly into his heart. He let out a long moan, his lungs croaking for air.

I could feel his blood splattered on my face, and probably in my hair. I didn't care. It had been so long since I had killed someone, but this was beyond justified. The man had killed our nation, my family, and now my friend...who had grown to be like my family.

I drew the sai's out and stabbed him once more, in the center of his chest, breaking through his sternum.

"Go dance with the devils in hell...." I hissed, my entire body shaking with rage.
He let out one last gasp, as he croaked for another breath.

"He is merely the first of your friends that you will watch die, MacKenzie. I'm just a pawn...in a much...bigger....game...." he said, gasping for breath as he spat out the last few words. His eyes looked into mine once more, before they rolled into the back of his head, his eyes purely white.

I pulled out my sai's and kicked the chair away from me, his bloody body now completely limp as he sat there, dead.

I turned around to see both Ryder and Jax holding Trevor up to a sitting position. I looked to my left and grabbed a stray button up shirt from the Sector Commander's couch, gripping the hilt of the blade that stuck out of Trevor's chest. Trevor's hand flew up, grabbing onto my wrist.

"No, let it go...MacKenzie...its okay... I've reached my time," Trevor said, his eyes getting heavier and heavier.

"No, no... there has to be a cure somewhere. We can find it." I said, feeling my throat swell up as tears began to build up in my eyes. I heard Ryder clear his throat as well, Trevor was just like another brother to Ryder. Trevor had shown such kindness to me, especially my first week with the eighty-sixers. He had such a pure soul.

"There isn't. MacKenzie if you could just...stop for a second. I really need to tell you something..." he said, fighting unconsciousness.

"What is it?" I questioned, wiping away a stray tear.

"Fight. Fight whoever this guy is, and rebuild us....not just Anomics. This country," he said, putting his hand over his heart.

"I dreamed of the nation becoming one again, please...you need to make it happen..." he wheezed, beginning to cough.

I saw blood appear on his lip and I knew he was gone. Ryder reached up and moved both of Trevor's eyes shut. We all just sat there in silence for a second, and then Damian cleared his throat.

"If I may...he told me these things were toxic to your touch..." Damian said, moving to pull the knife out of Trevor's chest.

Ryder stared Damian down, daring him to do something more.

"It's alright Ryder..." I said, nodding to Damian.

Damian nodded in thanks, and then slowly pulled the knife out, and then slid it across the floor to the other side of the room.

We all continued to sit in silence for a second, and then Darius slowly stood up.

"It's all over..." Ryder said, reaching over and squeezing my shoulder affectionately.

"So, MacKenzie...what do we do now?" he questioned.

I wiped the tears away from my eyes with the sleeve of my jacket and let out a slow exhale, bringing my gaze to meet his.

"We bring everyone home," I stated.

28.

I sat on top of the roof of the Sector Commander's building, staring out into the woods. The sun was now rising up, and it was the beginning of not only a new day, but a new era. At least for this Sector. I had Katie and Amanda get the old local radio station working again, broadcasting a message that the Sector Commander had been removed from office, and there was a new leadership that had come in. We told everyone to prepare for a change, a better change.

I heard footsteps approaching me and I turned to see Erica moving to sit next to me.

"Hey you," she said, pleasantly happy.

I turned to face her, smiling. "You seem very chipper this morning," I said.
"Well aside from the whole victory thing, your friend Katie re-introduced me to coffee. I forgot how good it tasted," she said, smiling over at me.
"Oh God, not another one of you...." I joked.
"We're going to be great friends. I'm really excited for us all to be...civilized once more. I mean, I do love the wild, don't get me wrong. But I missed many things in here. I think we all did," Erica said, staring out into the sunset with me.
I nodded in agreement. "Especially showers," I said, smiling.

"Agreed, as much fun as bathing in the lake was..." Erica replied.

"So I take it everyone else will be back here shortly?" I questioned.
"Yes, Skyler, Devon, Joe and Colton went to go spread the word to everyone else. Major Chase, Darius and your friend Jax are....figuring out what to do with Damian and how to prepare for everyone who is coming," Erica stated.
"Well, there aren't that many of us out there in the woods.... shouldn't be too bad," I retorted, rolling my eyes slightly.
"Not just our family out there, MacKenzie...but the people who will be coming form further parts of the sector to see you. You did what most people couldn't do, MacKenzie...and people admire that," Erica said, turning to face me.
I looked over at her, blushing slightly. Before I could speak, I heard another familiar voice.

"I hope I'm not interrupting anything, ladies..." I heard Ryder's voice say.

I heard Erica giggle. "And on that note, I will leave you two love birds to be..."

She stood up and headed towards the window, where she had climbed up from.

"Oh no, you don't have to..."

"No thats okay, I was just leaving. Going to get some more of that coffee stuff!"

"Dear Lord,"

I chucked slightly at their conversation, and then out of the corner of my eye I saw Ryder sitting next to me. I smiled over at him, and he slid his arm around my shoulders. I began to blush, resting my head on his shoulder.

"We did it, MacKenzie... just like you said we would,"

"What, you doubted me?"

"No, I never said that...."

"You're just jealous because I thought of it first,"

"Sure, we will go with that..."

We both turned to face each other and started laughing, and then we turned back to face the sunset.

"So, how long until the crew meets up with us here?" I questioned.

"Tomorrow, I figure. Give everyone time to gather up the stuff and make their way here. But in the mean time, I hear there is a bar conveniently located somewhere around here, and boy have I missed the taste of tequila," Ryder stated, looking down at me.

"There is still one thing we have yet to figure out though," I said, staring out into the woods.

"What's that?" Ryder questioned.

"The... source...we need to figure out who it is. Especially if we have this new enemy out there. If he's as powerful as he sounds, having a traitor, especially now, will be extremely dangerous..." I said.

"Yes, we will have to get to work on that....but tonight... focus on celebrating this victory. Finding the source is tomorrow's problem. We did good here today MacKenzie. You did good. Now, let us go celebrate," Ryder said, nudging me with his shoulder.

I smiled up at him, rolling my eyes as I did so. "Sure, we can do that...but one thing first," I said, my eyes falling to his lips.

"What's that?" he questioned, his lips meeting mine for a sweet kiss. I once again felt completely intoxicated by his kiss, everything else merely stopping all around me.

When he pulled away, I looked up at him with a smile.

"Let's go grab our friends, this is a family celebration," I stated.
"I couldn't agree with you more, my love..." Ryder agreed.

I turned to stare into the sunset one last time, inhaling the cool breeze. It was done. I was no longer a scared girl, afraid of showing the world who I was. A warrior. A Soldier. An Anomic.

29

The woman continued to trek into the woods, holding the lantern in front of her face. She had no idea how far she needed to travel, but she could tell that she was approaching the border and fast. The smell of blood and carnage instantly flooded her senses. She knew that she was getting closer to them. She was limited on time, as her friends would soon be looking for her.

She heard the sound of wood crunching to her left and she stopped, before raising the lantern up so that she could see who was there.

The large, golden, female lion stood there, growling slightly. The woman watched as the lion nodded to her, before turning her head slightly and walking away, signaling to follow her. She obeyed the order, walking deeper into the woods. As she continued walking, she saw several other lions starting to appear, coming out of hiding. They were curious as to who their visitor was, or maybe it was because of the specific scent they picked up on her as she walked into their camp.

The female lion finally stopped in front of a rather large cave, before letting out a roar.

After a few moments, a large, black African lion emerged from the cave. His eyes focused on her, before he let out a low roar of pleasure. He tilted his head downward, as he began to change. When he was finished, he stood there as a man in front of her. His tan skin glowed under the light of her lantern, his muscles clearly defined, causing shadows to cast over the more forbidden parts of his now bare body.

He smiled, his pearly white teeth gleaming back at her. He reached down and picked up what appeared to be a leather material with some string from the nearby plant. As he continued to approach her, he tied the string around his waist so that the leather material formed a somewhat modification of pants to cover himself up.

He stared at her dangerously through his black hair that was now cascading over his now brown eyes. Once he finished tying his string, he ran his hand over his shoulder-length, black hair.

"To what do I owe the please of Skyler Layorn coming to visit me?" he questioned, stopping a few inches away from her. She smirked, a playful look on her face.

242

"What? I can't stop in for a social call as I please?" she asked, tilting her head upwards to look at him. He leaned down, his lips brushing against hers.

"Of course you may, love. However, I sense you come here with a greater purpose other than to accompany me in my quarters tonight.." he whispered, his hot breath rolling off of her lips. She closed her eyes, enjoying the feel.

When she opened her eyes again, she saw that he had pulled away enough to look at her.

"Ryder and...his clan have taken back the sector. Its only a matter of time before they figure out our plan and discover....*it*," Skyler said, choosing her words carefully.

He smirked at her, before pulling her closer to him by his hips. "Well my love, we must make sure that never happens. You've done well. Spying on Ryder all this time for me,"

"I did what I could. However, now he has the almighty's daughter with him on his side. She was too powerful for me alone...but if we can find her weakness, we can destroy her.. and Ryder will follow along with her. I'm sorry I failed, my love..." Skyler said, looking away.

He shook his head, raising her chin with a few fingers so that she looked at him. "Nay, dear one. This is perfect, now that they are in the seat of power...it will be that much simpler to strip it away from them and then immediately take it,"

Skyler smirked wickedly at the idea of MacKenzie and Ryder begging for their lives at the strike of her claws. She hated them both, especially MacKenzie. MacKenzie should have been dead from day one, when she had snuck clothing from Ryder's clan and gave it to Erik's clan.

When MacKenzie had been on that run with three of her friends that day, Erik's clan members dressed as though they were in Ryder's clan when the assassination attempt by arrow was made. It was a safety net so that if and when MacKenzie found Ryder's clan, she would not trust Ryder after recognizing the clothing as those that attempted to kill her. A clever trick made by Skyler herself.

Skyler looked back up at Erik, raising an eyebrow at him. "What if she realizes her true strength and overcomes us all?" she questioned. Erik caught her off guard by pulling her body against his, his lips crashing onto hers in a hot, passionate kiss that made Skyler's knees tremble. When he pulled away, his lips continued to brush hers, his steaming breath dancing on her lips. Skyler found herself at a loss for words.

"Lions, dear one, have always been known as Kings..." he said, before his one hand began to run through her hair.

His eyes locked with hers, and she could feel the smile forming on his lips.

"No one can overcome the King of the Jungle, and the *Relinquished* shall rise again...." Erik stated.

AUTHOR BIO:

Julia Valenti lives in Philadelphia, PA and has always had a passion for writing. She graduated from King's College with a B.A in Communications, and is also a Soldier in the United States Military. In her free time, she enjoys writing, hiking, cosplaying and training her German Shepherd, Soot.